By Reason of Insanity

By
Reason of
Insanity

James Neal Harvey

St. Martin's Press | New York

This novel is a work of fiction. All of the events, characters, names and places depicted in this novel are entirely fictitious or are used fictitiously. No representation that any statement made in this novel is true or that any incident depicted in this novel actually occurred is intended or should be inferred by the reader.

Library of Congress Cataloging-in-Publication Data

Harvey, James Neal.
    By reason of insanity / James Neal Harvey.
        p.   cm.
    "A Thomas Dunne Book"
    ISBN 0-312-04295-7
    I. Title.
PS3558.A7183B9   1990
813'.54—dc20   89-78089
                                                    CIP

10 9 8 7 6 5 4 3 2

This book is for Uschi,
with all my love.

I wish to thank the many members of the New York City Police Department who so generously gave me their help, particularly the detectives of the Sixth, Seventeenth, and Twentieth Precincts. I am especially indebted to Lieutenant Richard Marcus, the detective who was in charge of the Manhattan Sex Crimes unit when this book was written; retired Inspector William Knapp; and Howard Steinhaus, M.D., Ph.D., a psychiatrist who has long studied and treated homicidal psychopaths. My special thanks also to Chief James Tilbe of the Hamilton, New York, Police Department.

—J.N.H.

By Reason of Insanity

1

THE blonde was heavier than she looked. He eased her into a sitting position against the wall and propped her up with the half-dozen white pillows he'd bought when he planned the shoot. The pillows were thick and fluffy and he put one behind her neck to rest her head against. He placed another under her right arm, letting the hand dangle. Her naked flesh was pale under the lights.

The legs were next. He spread them a little and raised them by bending them at the knees. Her pubic hair was a dark patch, but it would not be visible when he was ready to begin shooting. He stepped back and cocked his head, studying the composition. It was starting to come together, and he could feel his excitement building as he looked at her. Now for the key prop, the touch of genius. He left the studio and went into the kitchen.

The lollipop was in the freezer. It was grape flavored, a purple disk three inches across. He'd left it on a sheet of aluminum foil so that it wouldn't stick to the rack. He got it out and carried it back to the set. He was enthusiastic about his work, and the anger he had felt earlier had completely disappeared.

But he was still sweating heavily. His white polo shirt was soggy and there were damp patches on his gray cotton pants. He picked up a rag from the counter and wiped his face with it. As he tossed the rag aside he was aware that his hands were trembling.

He knelt beside the girl and placed the lollipop in her left hand, closing her fingers around the stick and moving the candy so that she was holding it over her crotch. She was almost ready. But he was a perfectionist, and that meant it had to be exactly right. He stood up and then walked slowly back and forth in front of the setup, looking at it from different angles.

The girl really was quite pretty. Her hair was long and straight and hung to her shoulders in shimmering strands. She had blue eyes, large and almond shaped, like a cat's. The nose was a little fleshy across the bridge, but the attitude of her head and the way he was lighting her would take care of that. Best of all was her expression. Her lips were parted and between them the tip of her tongue was showing, and that together with the vacant stare in the blue eyes was highly erotic to him.

Her body was good too, slender and well proportioned. Her breasts were on the small side but that was an advantage. Tits beyond a 34-B had a tendency to sag. Even as physically drained as he was, he felt himself stir when he looked at her.

But a model? Jesus, the arrogance. Exactly like every other conceited little bitch who thinks she's something special, something far above the ordinary, just waiting to be discovered. You'd see it in the way she walked, the way she carried her head, with her nose up in the air. Look at me, she'd seem to say. I could be on the cover of *Vogue*, or *Cosmopolitan*, if the right photographer came along. Well, for this one the right photographer *had* come along, and she'd been discovered, all right. He'd shoot her with an expertise that would lift her to a plane higher than she ever could have imagined. And in the end it would be his talent, his extraordinary skills, that would create not merely a photograph, but a work of art.

The camera he was using was his favorite, the Hasselblad. It was mounted on a tripod and he set it in place carefully, about eight feet from his subject. He bent over the viewfinder and rolled the focusing ring until the image was sharp. The magazine was loaded with Ektachrome to give him the effect he wanted. He checked the lights and the reflectors. After that he went to a drawer and got out a meter, then took readings on the girl's face and belly. He stuffed the meter into his pocket and adjusted the camera's diaphragm and shutter speed.

There was a tape deck on the counter. He picked a Bruce Springsteen cassette out of a rack and put it into the machine, switching on the power and turning up the volume until his ears buzzed and he could feel the beat jarring the soles of his feet. Everything was ready now. He returned to the camera and again squinted into the viewfinder.

It was beautiful. Just as he'd seen it in his mind when he conceived the shoot, except that now it was real and it was even better than he had envisioned. Exultantly he pressed the trigger and there was a brilliant explosion of light as the strobes boomed. His voice was taut with excitement. "Yeah, baby. Great. I love it. Looking good. That's fantastic."

The camera was fitted with a motor drive, so that he could shoot rapidly. He fired off frame after frame, pausing now and then just long enough to reset the f-stop and the shutter speed, bracketing the exposures. The pictures would be wonderful. He couldn't wait to finish shooting and begin processing the film in his darkroom.

And besides, he wanted to get the girl out of here. Before rigor mortis set in.

2

THE construction site was on West Thirteenth Street. It was under excavation, the hole in the ground shielded by a high, green wooden fence. The buildings flanking it were ivy-covered brick town houses built in the mid-nineteenth century, four stories tall, with slate roofs and white window frames and shutters. Only a few ramshackle houses remained in this area, and those were quickly razed whenever a developer could lay hands on one. Real estate values here would never go anywhere but up. Apartments in a new, modern building would circumvent rent controls and could be leased for astronomical amounts, and selling them as condos could triple a speculator's investment. Either way, there were fortunes to be made in Greenwich Village.

When Lieutenant Ben Tolliver pulled up in his battered gray Ford sedan, cops had already blocked off the street with wooden barricades painted blue and POLICE LINE DO NOT CROSS lettered in white. A patrolman from the Sixth Precinct recognized him and moved one of the sawhorses aside so he could pass through. Up ahead he saw two patrol cars and a Dodge hatchback that belonged to Frank Petrusky, one of the detectives in his squad. All of the vehicles were in front of the green fence. Tolliver parked the Ford behind them and got out.

The lieutenant was a tall man, rangy and lean, with a shag of black hair flecked with gray. A thick mustache covered his upper lip. He looked more like a construction worker himself than a detective, wearing worn corduroys and a faded blue oxford-cloth shirt, rolled-up sleeves revealing the thick muscles of his forearms. His skin was

4

deeply tanned from spending as much time as possible outdoors, and his eyes were the same washed-out color as his shirt. He had been on the Job for fourteen years, and as far as he knew he had never been made as a cop.

His watch showed a few minutes after eight. A gaggle of pedestrians had gathered on the sidewalk across from the site, people who lived on the block, some of them on their way to work. They stood gawking at the police and their vehicles, and a cop waved a hand and told them to move on. Two more uniformed officers were in front of the green fence, one of them a young guy, the other a sergeant Tolliver recognized, a red-faced veteran named Weber. The sergeant was keeping the log, recording the times of arrival and departure of anyone working there.

Ben said good morning as he approached and inclined his head toward the fence. "Who's in there?"

"Petrusky and two guys who run the equipment," Weber said. "They found it when they showed up for work this morning."

Ben nodded. He had come directly from his apartment on Bank Street, rolled out of bed by the telephone call from the Sixth. He reached into his hip pocket and took out the leather folder, clipping it onto his shirt so that the shield would show. Wearing it was a strict rule at a crime scene; it was the only way you could identify the plain-clothes cops. As the detective in charge he outranked all other officers there, no matter who they were. Technically, that would include even the PC himself. Not that the commissioner was likely to show up, but if he did he would be obliged to take orders from Tolliver.

Ben glanced across the street to where another knot of spectators had begun to gather. "Keep the civilians away from here."

"Will do," Weber said.

A pair of ragged boys about eight years old inched close

to where Ben stood talking with the cops. One of them spoke to Weber. "Hey, Officer. What's in there?"

The sergeant looked down. "A monster."

The boy's eyes grew wide. "A monster?"

"Yeah," Weber said. "It eats kids. Now you little shits get outta here."

The boys scurried away, and the younger cop crossed the street to break up the gathering of curious bystanders. Ben turned and stepped through a door in the center of the fence.

Just inside was a steep incline, running down to a level about ten feet below that of the street. Lying on the rubble-strewn earth at the base of the slope was a bundle perhaps five and a half feet long, wrapped in black plastic. A dozen paces beyond it were two pieces of yellow-painted construction equipment, a power shovel and a dump truck. The words DINARDO CONSTRUCTION CO., BROOKLYN, N.Y. were lettered on the sides of the machines. Frank Petrusky stood near the truck, talking with two men in yellow hard hats who were leaning against the vehicle's front fender, smoking and drinking coffee out of paper cups.

Tolliver scrambled down the slope to where the bundle lay. Some of the black plastic had been torn away at one end, revealing an indistinct, whitish object inside. He stood beside the bundle as Petrusky approached. The hard hats stayed where they were.

"'Morning, Lieutenant." Petrusky was broad and slope-shouldered, and his head was bald except for a few wispy brown hairs above his ears. He wore a baggy gray suit and a garish green-and-white tie. His shield was clipped to his jacket.

"Hya, Frank. What've we got?"

"Another one, looks like."

Tolliver grunted. He had seen bundles like this twice before in the last few months, both times in other parts of

6

Greenwich Village. One had been lying in an alley, the other had been crammed into a trash barrel. He knelt beside this one. The plastic was thin vinyl sheeting, a large garbage bag tied with twine. He pulled back the torn flap, revealing the face of a dead woman. Her blue eyes stared at nothing, and between her lips her tongue was showing. An odor rose from the bag, faint but sickening, the beginning of putrefaction.

The face was young and unusually pretty. Or had been, anyway. It was framed by lank strands of bleached-blond hair, and there were mottled bruises under her jaw. Her skin was very pale, except for the bruises and spots where deep blue shadows of cyanosis had formed around her eyes and near her mouth. A fly lit on her upper lip and crawled down onto one of her front teeth. Ben shooed it away.

Over the years he had dealt with more dead bodies than he could count, but none of them made the impact on him that one of these did. As he studied the lifeless features, they seemed to change, until he felt he was looking at the face of another girl, from a time in his life before he ever thought of becoming a cop. The sight was like ripping the scab off a wound.

Petrusky brushed a hand over his bald head. "I think her neck's broken."

"Uh-huh."

"Just like the other two."

"Could be, Frank. ME on his way?"

"Yeah. Should be here any minute."

"Okay." Tolliver stood up, his gaze moving to the pair of hard hats. "What about the boys?"

"They drove over together from Brooklyn," Petrusky said. "Like every day. When they came in they saw the bag. They opened it and went down the street there to the deli and called 911." He pulled a small, spiral-bound notebook out of his hip pocket. "I got everything on them."

Tolliver stepped over to the truck, Petrusky following. "'Morning."

The men nodded. They were rugged and unshaven, burned dark by the sun.

"This here is Lieutenant Tolliver," Petrusky said.

The taller of the two flicked away his cigarette and put out his hand. "Sal Ricci."

The hand felt like a piece of cracked leather. Tolliver shook it and turned to the other.

"Tony DiNardo."

Ben gripped this one's hand also and looked at the lettering on the door of the truck. "This your company?"

"My uncle's."

Tolliver motioned with his head toward the green fence. "Gate locked when you got here?"

"Yeah," DiNardo said. "Chain with a padlock. I opened it and put the chain in the truck." He thrust out his chin, indicating the black plastic bag. "We didn't pay much attention, at first."

Ricci shifted his feet. "Lots of times people throw garbage over the fence at night. We figured that's what it was. Except it was so big, you know?"

"So I pulled it open a little," DiNardo said. He rolled his eyes. "And oh, shit."

"You guys usually work alone?" Tolliver asked.

"Most of the time," DiNardo replied. "Foreman comes by around eleven. My cousin Freddy." He waved a hand. "We thought we'd finish this up today."

Tolliver glanced over at the black garbage bag. "Not now, you won't."

Petrusky looked up toward the gate. "Here come the troops."

Two detectives from the Crime Scene Unit were descending the slope, both wearing suits and ties and carrying equipment cases. A uniformed cop was following them,

8

and behind him were two men in hospital whites, the ambulance crew. Ben recognized the leader of the CSU detectives, an older man named McGuire he had worked with before.

Tolliver raised a hand. "Hello, Mac."

"How you doing, Ben?"

"Okay, for a Monday morning."

McGuire introduced his partner, a guy named Walsh who was taking a 35-mm camera out of a case. McGuire stepped over to the black bag. He studied it for a minute or two before returning to Tolliver. "Looks familiar."

"You recognize her?"

"No. I meant it's like the other two. The garbage bag and all."

"Yeah."

"We looking for anything special?"

"Not that I can think of," Ben said. "She had to be killed someplace else and then dumped here. Check the top of that fence, and go over the sidewalk and the street. She must've landed just inside and then rolled down the bank."

McGuire nodded, looking at the garbage bag again and then at the slope.

"Give me a grid with measurements on everything," Ben said. "Position, how far she rolled, and so on."

"Right." McGuire moved away.

Another man came through the gate and made his way down the bank. This was the deputy medical examiner. He was thin and angular, carrying a satchel and wearing a shirt and tie but no jacket. With his jerky movements he looked like an oversized bird. He grinned when he saw Tolliver. "Ah, my favorite detective."

Ben hooked his thumbs into the belt loops of his pants. "Doctor Feldman, I presume."

The ME looked at the black bundle. "What've we got here, a surprise package?" He crouched beside the bag and tore a large piece of it away from the girl's body, revealing her upper torso.

"Go easy," Tolliver cautioned him. "We might get some prints off that."

Feldman put his satchel down on the ground. He peered at the girl and then up at Tolliver, still grinning. Even his head resembled a bird's, with its prominent beak and shock of reddish hair. "What would you say, Lieutenant—an eight, maybe an eight and a half?"

Ben didn't bother to answer. He found undertaker jokes boring.

"Of course, she's not at her best this morning," Feldman went on. "No makeup, and she hasn't had breakfast." He stood up and waved to the two men of the ambulance crew. "Let's have the bag over here."

The medics opened a rubberized body bag and laid it flat beside the corpse. The CSU detective with the camera was snapping pictures. At Feldman's instruction, the medics picked up the body and placed it gently on the spread-out bag, then untied the twine and eased the black vinyl away from the still form. McGuire took the twine and the plastic bag, carefully depositing them in a sack that he labeled with a string tag. The girl lay on her back, the clean whiteness of her nude body contrasting sharply with the dirt and the broken bits of brick and concrete surrounding her.

Tolliver noticed the hard hats moving in for a closer look. "You guys can go get yourselves some more coffee," he said to them. "Check back here in a couple hours. You might be able to get back to work then." The men clambered up the bank and out the gate.

Ben redirected his attention to the girl's body. She was slim and well proportioned, with long, shapely legs. He noted that the hairs on her pubis were black. Her natural

10

hair color must have been quite dark, before she bleached it. More bruises were visible now, on her neck and shoulders.

Tolliver turned to Feldman. "So what do you think?"

The ME shrugged. "Can't say, until I do the autopsy."

"Yeah, but say anyhow."

Feldman smiled. "You know I'm not supposed to make an examination here. Regulations."

"Fuck regulations," Ben said. "Take a look and tell me what you can."

Feldman shook his head, clucking his tongue. But he squatted beside the body. He went over the flesh on the undersides of the girl's forearms and on the insides of her thighs. "No bad habits so far." He poked at her mouth and her nostrils with a long forefinger. "Daddy's little cream puff." He raised her breasts, feeling underneath each. Then he took her head between his hands and lifted it, turning it from side to side. He eased the head back down and signaled to one of the medics, and together they turned the girl over onto her belly.

Whereas the front of the body had been almost unblemished, except for the bruises, this side was a mess. The flesh of her buttocks was full of bite marks, deep imprints in the shape of human teeth. The impressions were purple, and blood had seeped from them and dried in crusty smears. There were ragged tears in the skin at the edges of the bites.

Tolliver beckoned to the CSU detective with the camera. "Hey, you'll want this." Feldman stood up and got out of the way while the guy took more pictures.

The ME looked at Tolliver. "Déjà vu, eh Lieutenant? We've heard this song before."

"How long?" Ben asked him.

Feldman folded his arms. "She's still a little stiff, but rigor

11

mortis is almost gone. I would say Friday, probably. I can pin it down better for you when I open her up. But for right now, Friday night would be a good bet."

Yes it would, Ben thought. That would mean she was here over the weekend, when no work was going on. Which would explain why she hadn't been discovered until this morning. "What else?"

The ME pursed his lips. "Looks to me like we're picking up after the same guy that knocked off the other two. The bites tell you that. I think what happened was, he grabbed her by the neck and shoulders and held her while she gave him a blowjob. After he came he pulled his cock out of her mouth and took hold of her head and twisted it. Bang. Broken neck. She died almost instantly. Then when she fell on her face, he got down there and bit her ass. Biggest difference I see now is that he bit this one more times than the others. Really chewed the shit out of her. Maybe she tasted better, huh?"

Tolliver stared at the bites. Her buttocks looked as if she had been attacked by a wild animal. There were tears at the corners of the wounds, as if the biter had pulled his head back while his jaws were still clamped onto her flesh.

"I'll want to know what's in her mouth," Ben said. "Whether you find semen, and if it matches what was in the others."

Feldman's head bobbed. "Sure, may get saliva in the bites, too. I think we'll find both and they'll check out." He pointed to the wounds. "You don't often get that good a signature."

"Okay, Doc. Thanks."

"A pleasure, Lieutenant."

Tolliver turned to Petrusky. "I'm going to the precinct house, Frank. You stay here and work with these guys. Soon as they're gone, start a house-to-house in the neighborhood. Maybe somebody saw her get dumped. I'll send somebody over to help you."

Petrusky looked up at the gate. "Here comes Carlos, Ben. He'll give me a hand."

Carlos Rodriguez was another member of Tolliver's squad, a slim Puerto Rican with dreamy eyes and a headful of tight black curls. He trotted down the bank and approached the other detectives, his walk an insolent swagger that went with his maroon sports shirt and fawn-colored slacks. The shield attached to his belt looked out of place on him. He raised a hand in greeting, staring at the corpse lying on the open body bag. "Good morning, everyone."

"Hya, Carlos," Ben said. "You stick with Frank, here. I want a thorough canvass of all these houses."

Carlos nodded, still looking at the girl's body. "Sure thing, Lou."

Ben turned to Feldman. "When are you going to work on her? I want to be there."

The ME grinned. "Great. I love an audience. It'll be tomorrow morning."

Ben walked to where the incline began and stopped, turning to study the scene. The cops were taking measurements. The ambulance guys had unfolded a portable gurney and were trussing up the body bag, and the ME was writing in a notebook. Everything in hand, everybody going about his task with the cool efficiency of the professional. All of it in accord with NYPD procedures, under the watchful eye of a seasoned detective lieutenant. And it didn't mean shit. If they solved this case, it would be a miracle.

For one thing, maybe the most important thing, the animal who had killed this girl was smart. He was the same guy who had murdered the other two, there was little question about that. The MO was identical in all three homicides. Naked female, broken neck, semen in the mouth, a chewed ass. Wrapped in a black plastic garbage bag and dumped. And if this one was like the others, there would be no fingerprints, no fibers, no clues. And no connection among any of the victims. The hundreds of police man-hours spent so far on the first two hadn't produced a single decent lead.

And what were the odds on their turning up something this time? Lousy. There were fifteen hundred homicides a year in New York, and half of them were never solved. Of those that were, 90 percent were nailed shut in the first twenty-four hours. If the investigation went much beyond that, you could forget it.

The remainder, the ones that stayed open forever, had been committed by people with intelligence. A few months earlier, cops from the Sixth had pulled a floater out of the river. Twenty minutes later Ben had been on the wharf, looking at the body. That corpse, too, had been naked. It was a male, about forty years old. All the teeth had been smashed out of the head, and the hands had been chopped off. The guy's pecker had been cut off as well, but that was incidental. Ben knew from the first glance they'd probably never even learn who he was, let alone who killed him. The work had been done by experts.

Contrast that with the ones that did get solved. One evening last February a sculptor on West Fourth Street had hacked his girlfriend to pieces with an ax. Afterward he went into a bar on Hudson Street and got loaded. He told the bartender and two of the patrons what he'd done, and when the cops arrived he was still slobbering into his Old Crow and giving graphic descriptions to anyone who'd listen.

So that was the trouble here, clearly enough: the killer had brains. He might be a brute, but at the same time he was coldly calculating and clever and he did not intend to get caught. If they got him, it would not be because of ingenious detective work, brilliant deductions drawn from a maze of clues—that was TV bullshit. It would be because somebody ratted, or because that was how the dice came up. A stroke of good luck for the cops, a stroke of bad for the killer. Ben knew that as well as anybody else who'd put in years on the Job. And he also knew it was a pretty good bet they'd never get him at all.

Meantime you ground it out, hoping that by following the exhausting procedures you might stumble onto something. And while you were doing that you made sure the detectives under your direction never doubted for a moment you had everything under control. Even though frustration was burning a hole in your belly and you were wondering why you stayed in this fucking business. He turned and clambered up the bank.

Outside the green fence a few more of the curious had gathered, and cops were moving them away. The Crime Scene Unit station wagon was parked there now, along with the ambulance and the ME's car. Ben was about to get into his Ford when a woman suddenly stepped into his path on the sidewalk. Her dark blond hair was tied back and she was wearing a pin-striped suit. He recognized her at once as a reporter from WPIC-TV. Just behind her was a guy with a hand-held camera. The lens was pointed at him, and a red light on top told him it was taking.

The woman shoved a mike into his face. "Lieutenant Tolliver?"

"Yes?"

"We understand you're in charge of this investigation."

How the hell did they get into it so fast? A couple of hours ago he himself hadn't known anything about this homicide, and now here was this reporter sticking her nose in. That was bad enough, but what really pissed him off was knowing his face would be on TV all over New York. "That's correct."

Her eyes were a deep green, and they seemed to bore into his as she spoke. "Is it true the nude body of a girl wrapped in a garbage bag has been found here?"

Reluctantly he muttered that it was.

"Lieutenant, does this appear to be another of the Greenwich Village murders?"

Would you listen to this shit? Now they had a name, like they were a novel by Agatha Christie. He took a deep breath before replying. "The deceased is an unidentified white female in her early twenties."

The reporter pushed the mike toward him. "What killed her?"

"We haven't completed out initial investigation, and we don't have a report from the medical examiner."

"Does it look as if she was murdered by the same assailant? The one who killed the two girls whose bodies were found earlier this year?"

"There's nothing more I can say until we get the results of the autopsy."

"Do you have any idea who the girl might be?"

"Not at this time. Now if you'll excuse me—" Ben brushed past her and strode to his car.

As he climbed into the vehicle he heard the woman say, "This is Sarah Weston, reporting to you from West Thirteenth Street, where there appears to be another—"

He slammed the door and started the engine, revving it loudly before pulling away from the curb. Jesus, as if this case wasn't tough enough. He looked back at the reporter and thought about how it would be to take that mike and stick it up her pin-striped ass.

3

THE station house of the NYPD's Sixth Precinct was a sprawl of gray brick between West Tenth and Charles streets, with entrances on both. There was a parking lot beside the building, but when Tolliver got there it was jammed with police vehicles: patrol cars, three-wheeled traffic scooters, a van. More blue-and-whites were parked on Tenth Street, along with personal cars belonging to members of the Sixth's detective squad. The lieutenant was lucky to find a space on the street for the Ford. He got out of the car and walked to the entrance of the station house. The sidewalk in front of the metal doors had been worn down by the footsteps of cops, thieves, drunks, lawyers, vagrants, whores, addicts, murderers. As he passed through the doors he thought it was a shame to go inside on a day as nice as this.

The eight-to-four tour had gone out over an hour ago, and at this time of the morning the Sixth wasn't so busy. Nothing like two or three A.M., when the action reached its peak and it could be dangerous to set foot in the place. Knifings, clubbings, shootings, anything was possible. The cops would frisk a guy and bring him in and he would be docile enough; then maybe a shiv would come out of no-where, or a gun even, and there would be war. Last week a PR on junk had got hold of a patrolman's pistol, pulling it out of his holster and shooting the cop in the balls before others wrestled the piece away from him and then beat his head in with their nightsticks. The cop was still in St. Vincent's, minus one nut. The Rican was dead.

When Ben walked in, a couple of drug collars were being booked. It was hard to say who was what; both the cops and the perpetrators wore flashy clothes and gold chains around their necks. One guy was a tall, skinny jig, dressed in a silver-gray suit. A pearl gleamed from his left earlobe. His name was Mayberry and he was a detective second grade. Another black man was standing to the left of the desk, holding off two cops who were trying to coax him into the drunk tank, calling them jive motherfuckers. The guy looked as if he were ready to fall down and the officers were being patient, reasoning with him.

Across the way a hooker wearing red shorts and three-inch heels was sitting on a bench, peering into a compact mirror and applying lipstick. She had on a blond wig and about a pound of makeup, but she was still a very good-looking girl. Her legs were long and slim and she had crossed them for the benefit of the cops on the desk, who kept glancing over at her admiringly. A fat man in a rumpled suit was standing beside her, arguing with a plain-clothes vice cop. The fat guy was holding a briefcase and there were sweat stains in the armpits of the suit. Ben assumed he was the girl's lawyer.

The hooker looked up and caught sight of Tolliver. She smiled and gave him a little wave with the fingers of the hand holding the compact and he grinned back at her as he made his way to the stairs leading up to the second floor. What a crazy fucking world. Cops busted whores while other cops depended on them for street information.

The detective squad room was standard issue: a large, open space containing a half-dozen battered gray metal desks with typewriters on them, and a scattering of straight-backed chairs. A holding cage stood in the far corner. The walls were pale green cinder block, with bulletin boards displaying wanted posters. Mounted high up on the wall at one end of the room was a cardboard sign listing frequently called telephone numbers: other precincts, head-quarters departments, the DA's office, the morgue.

Of the sixteen men in Ben's squad, only Detective Sergeant Ed Flynn and a rookie investigator were there when he arrived. A young black man was sitting in a chair beside Flynn's desk. Flynn slouched in his seat, looking bored. The rookie was standing, his arms folded, wearing a sleeveless athletic shirt. The black man's hair was cut short, with a narrow swath tweezed out of the left side to look like a part. His shirt and pants were of blue cotton, and he had on a pair of brand-new, red-and-white-striped Adidas running shoes. Ben wanted to talk to the sergeant; he stopped and listened.

Flynn was the only man in the room wearing a tie. The jacket of his tan tropical worsted suit hung on the back of his chair. A tall Irishman with dark, wavy hair, he was vain about his appearance. He had been divorced a year ago, and claimed to get more ass than any other man on the squad. A leather purse lay on the desk in front of him. He pointed to it, looking at the youth. "So how come you were carrying this thing, Leroy? You a swish?"

Leroy was offended. "Hey, man. I find a lady's purse, I try to locate somebody to return it to."

"You thought maybe you'd locate her in an elevator?"

The black man shook his head patiently. "No. See, I find the purse *in* the elevator. It be just layin' there when I got in. So I figure I'll look for whoever lost it." His eyes brightened. "You know, like maybe there's a reward."

The detective's face was expressionless. "Lady on the third floor of the building says somebody grabbed her purse in the hall and punched her in the mouth. Knocked out a couple of her teeth. Then the guy took off, jumped in the elevator."

Leroy slapped his thigh. "See? That must be the one dropped her purse. 'Fore I found it."

1 9

Flynn's gaze traveled down the length of the man's body and back up to his face. "Lady says the guy who punched her was black and had on red-and-white sneakers."

Leroy looked at his feet. "That right? Well you know, lot of guys want kicks like these."

"Tell me something," Flynn said. "When the elevator got to the ground floor, why'd you start running, after the officer here told you to stop?"

A look of astonishment crossed Leroy's features. "Man, how I suppose to know he a cop? I thought maybe he be a mugger. This fuckin' neighborhood is *dangerous*, man."

Flynn nodded. "You do have a point there, Leroy. But if you don't mind, we'll give the lady a look at you." He lifted his gaze to the investigator. "Book him on suspicion. Robbery, aggravated assault." He handed the purse to the cop. "Be sure you get a voucher."

The investigator and the suspect moved off, Leroy shaking his head at police stupidity.

Ben sat on the edge of the desk. "You heard?"

"Yeah," Flynn said. "Petrusky told me. He was catching when the call came in. What've we got?"

"A dead blonde in a garbage bag."

"Same MO?"

"Down the line. Except there were more bites this time."

"And no ID?"

"No. She was stripped, just like the others."

Flynn tapped his fingers on his desk. "The media are gonna be all over us."

"They already were," Ben said. "The body was dumped in a lot where a construction crew is working. The minute I walked out of there, this Weston from WPIC had a mike and a camera on me."

Flynn grinned. "Hey, don't complain, Ben. That's a good-looking broad. Maybe next time you get to interview her."

Tolliver looked at him. "What is it, you're a TV fan now?"

"No, but what the hell, a little publicity couldn't hurt. At least it shows we're right there, you know?"

"I know I don't want my face all over the tube. There won't be a stool left in New York who'll talk to me."

"Anything worthwhile show up?"

"Not while I was there. And if anything does, I'll be surprised. The CSU were still going over it when I left, but this one was just like the others."

"When, any idea?"

"Friday night, the ME says. So there won't be tire tracks, and I don't think they'll find anything in the excavation, either. But they're combing it, anyway."

"Good. You never know."

"Yeah. I got Petrusky and Carlos checking the neighborhood for witnesses."

"Sure. I'll get over there myself, soon as I can."

"Do these things," Ben ordered. "Notify the DA's office. Then call Missing Persons, make a report. Give her age as about twenty-three, roughly five-five, hundred fifteen. See if there's a match with anything they've got."

"Will do."

"Set up a hot line with a number here for any information somebody might have. When we get prints and pictures, put out a flyer on her. Should have her dental impressions on it, too."

"Okay."

"Where's Kurwitz?"

"Talking to the store owner in the Liebold case."

"Uh-huh." Kurwitz was a detective third grade. Fran Liebold had been a clerk in a boutique on Christopher Street. A week earlier she had gone into the store one morning and apparently surprised a burglar, who fractured her skull with a blunt object. She had been in a coma ever since. Thus far the best lead the cops had was on a junkie who hung around Washington Square. They were looking for the guy now. "When he gets back, tell him to see me," Tolliver said.

"Sure thing, Lieutenant."

"Any reporters show up, give 'em the girl's description and the number for the hot line, and then get rid of 'em."

"Right."

Ben wanted to be alone, to think. He went into his office, shutting the door behind him. The room was a small cubicle containing a metal desk and a swivel chair, three straight-backed chairs, a steel filing cabinet and a table. The walls in here were painted the same bilious shade of green. The surfaces of the desk, table and filing cabinets held stacks of papers and file folders. Light came from overhead fluorescent bars and through a single window with panes of frosted glass.

He sat down at his desk and looked at the folders. It had been almost five months since the first body in this case had turned up, the one in the alley off Broome Street. It had been winter then, the weather snowy and raw, and the girl's naked corpse had been frozen. The second had been found in late March, stuffed into a trash barrel on Prince Street, along with old newspapers and empty beer cans and rotting scraps of garbage. That body had begun to decompose, and it stank. Now it was May and they had another. And after all the months of work, after the hundreds of interviews and the lab work and the chasing of a thousand possible leads, they had nothing to show for it but these fucking piles of paper. These women might as well have been struck by lightning.

There was a card file of telephone numbers on the desk. He flipped through the cards until he found the number for Dr. Albert Brody, an odontologist on staff at the NYPD lab who had worked on the earlier murders. An expert in forensic dentistry, he was considered one of the country's foremost authorities on human bites. Ben called him and told him about the discovery of another mutilated body, asking him to attend the autopsy scheduled for the following morning. Brody said he'd have to cancel some appointments, but he'd be there.

Next Ben called the NYPD's Manhattan Sex Crimes Unit, which was housed in the Twentieth Precinct Headquarters on West Eighty-second Street. The unit was commanded by a young detective sergeant named Dick Farber. Ben got Farber on the line and filled him in.

Farber listened quietly until Ben finished. "So it's the same creep?"

"I'd bet on it. You got anything new?"

"No. Some rapes, aggravated assault. The usual shit."

"Arrests?"

"Oh, yeah. But nothing like what you're after. Couple a these guys, you already ran 'em down. You want, I'll send you the reports."

"Okay. You get anything, call me."

"Sure."

Ben hung up, frustration hanging on his neck like a lead weight. Over the past twenty weeks, he and his squad must have talked to every weirdo in New York—the rapists and the child-molesters, the woman-beaters and fetishists, every kind of sexual deviant he'd ever heard of and a number he hadn't.

A couple of these characters had even confessed to the murders of the two girls, despite the fact that there was no way they could have been involved. It had been like fishing in the sewers. What the cops had come up with was revolting, but it wasn't what they were after. He pulled the case folders toward him and opened the one on the first victim, going through it for what had to be the hundredth time.

The girl had been eighteen years old, a secretary with a

stock brokerage firm on Fifty-second Street. Name, Helen Malik. Lived with her family in the Bay Ridge section of Brooklyn. Father was a machine shop foreman. Mother worked part-time as a bookkeeper for a fur-storage and cleaning company. Two younger sisters, both in high school. She had a boyfriend and they had been talking about moving in together. Young man was a bank teller in the financial district. Name, John Corrigan. He shared a two-room apartment on West Twenty-second Street with another guy, and he and Helen used to make it there when they could get the place to themselves. Once they had managed to sneak away for a weekend in Atlantic City. Corrigan was clean; he had been visiting his mother in Albany when Helen Malik disappeared. The girl did not drink, and the only dope she touched was the occasional joint she smoked with John. She hated living with her family, under her father's thumb, but she was never any trouble. One night she simply had not arrived home after leaving her office at five o'clock.

The file contained a thick stack of reports: interviews with Corrigan and Helen's family and her friends and her fellow workers in the brokerage firm and her priest and her high-school teachers and her neighbors and everybody else the police could find who had had any contact with her. Ben spent another couple of hours on the file now, finding nothing he hadn't known or thought about.

There was a knock on the door and Joe Kurwitz stuck his head into the office. "Hey, Ben. You looking for me?"

"Yeah, Joe. Come on in."

"Listen, we got some pizza here. You want some?"

Tolliver suddenly realized he had eaten nothing from the time he had got up. Now it was past noon and he was hungry as hell. "Sure, if you've got enough."

"We got plenty," Kurwitz said. He ducked out, returning

a minute later carrying a pepperoni pizza in a greasy card-board carton, and two cans of Budweiser. Ben closed the folder, pushing it aside to make room, and Kurwitz set the pizza and the beer down on the desk.

Tolliver picked up a stringy slice and bit off half of it. As he chewed he asked Kurwitz what was happening. The detective sat opposite Ben, stuffing his mouth with pizza. He was in his forties, sloppy and twenty pounds over-weight, his thin black hair combed over the top of his skull in an unsuccessful attempt to cover a bald spot. Tolliver considered him unimaginative and knew he had a booze problem, but for all that Kurwitz was somehow depend-able.

"We got a tip on where this guy Weizel might show," Kurwitz said. Weizel was a suspect in the Liebold case.

"Which is?"

"Sometimes he visits a broad on East Fourth Street. She's a junkie, too. I'm going over there and sit on the place."

"Okay." Tolliver drank some of the beer. It was ice-cold and tasted wonderful. "You know we got another garbage bag?"

"Yeah, Ed was just telling me. You rather have me work on that?"

"No. Stay on the Liebold thing. Any luck and we can clean that up."

"I hope so."

"So do I. But the shit'll hit the fan on this one."

The telephone rang. It had been ringing all morning but Tolliver had ignored it; Flynn was catching in the squad room. This time the sergeant buzzed him. Ben picked up the phone. "Yeah?"

"Ben, it's that reporter from WPIC, Sarah Weston."

"Tell her I'm out."

"Okay. This is the second time she called."

"So keep telling her."

"We're getting calls from all kinds of reporters. Four of them already been up here."

"Give 'em the description and the number and then brush 'em off, I told you."

"Will do. Also the lab says they got pictures for us. They're sending 'em right up."

"Good."

"And Brennan's on his way."

"Yeah." Ben put the phone down and looked at Kurwitz. "Captain Brennan is paying us a visit." Brennan was the zone commander in charge of the detective squads of the Sixth, Ninth, and Tenth Precincts.

Kurwitz belched and licked grease from his fingers. "Just like you said, Ben. Here comes the shit, looking for the fan."

4

WHEN Kurwitz left his office, Tolliver swept the empty beer cans and the pizza carton into his wastebasket and opened the file on the second victim. The girl's name was Donna Cunningham. Age twenty-two. Production assistant in a sales-promotion company on Fifty-eighth Street. Lived on West Eightieth with a roommate, a girl named Janice Mead who was a clerk at Saks Fifth Avenue. Cunningham's hometown was Mobile, Alabama. She'd come to New York two years earlier. Parents divorced. Donna had been raised by her mother and hadn't seen her father since she was five years old.

This one had been a party girl. She liked booze and grass and coke—whatever was available. She had a lot of boy-friends and slept with all of them. Had an affair with her boss that ended when his wife became suspicious. As a candidate for murder she had been a much higher risk than Malik. The stack of reports in this file was even thicker, but the investigation had been no more productive. One night Cunningham hadn't come home, which her room-mate had paid no attention to, and then a week later some kids knocked over the trash barrel on Prince Street, and a stray dog tore open the garbage bag to get at the decaying meat inside.

There had been no worthwhile leads; not one of the string of men in Cunningham's life had turned out to be a legitimate suspect. And there had been no connection between the two victims. Nothing suggested they might have known each other, and their backgrounds could not have been more disparate. The only things they had in common were that they had been young and pretty and had turned up dead in Greenwich Village.

The door opened and Captain Michael Brennan walked into the office. Tolliver got to his feet and shook the zone commander's hand. "Afternoon, Captain."

"Hello, Ben."

Whenever he saw him, Tolliver was struck by the physical presence of this man. Nearly as wide as he was tall, Brennan might have been an old heavyweight fighter who was retired now but stayed in good shape. His chest was a barrel, and he had no neck; his massive shoulders simply flowed into the base of his skull. His gray hair was cropped to a half inch, and his nose was a blob of cartilage in the middle of his face. Brennan was wearing a shapeless blue suit, but that was no more deceptive than his shoulders or his nose. Dressed in swim trunks or a tuxedo, there was no way you would make him as anything but a cop.

Brennan eased his bulk onto one of the straight-backed chairs opposite Tolliver's desk.

"How about some coffee, Cap?"

"No thanks."

"Lemonade?"

There was no change in the big Irishman's expression. "Yeah, that I could take."

Ben smiled and sat down, reaching into his lower desk drawer for a bottle of Popov and two paper cups. He filled the cups and handed one to Brennan, returning the bottle to the drawer. He raised his drink. *"Salut."*

"Good luck." The captain drained his cup.

Ben drank his vodka in a gulp, the liquor seeming much stronger than when it was cold. "I could use some luck. Good luck, anyhow. So far it's been all bad."

"Seems that way, don't it? I hear we got a new one."

"Correct."

"Tell me about it."

Ben gave him a rundown on what he had seen at the construction site on Thirteenth Street.

Brennan listened intently, asking an occasional question and issuing a grunt now and then, until Tolliver finished. Then he extended his cup for a refill.

Ben poured him one and topped off his own.

"There'll be a lot of heat on this," Brennan said. "Couple reporters were in the squad room when I got here, working on Flynn."

"Yeah. A TV reporter was on me at the scene. Didn't take long for them to smell it."

"Uh-huh."

"They've even got a name for the case. The Greenwich Village Murders. Can you believe it?"

Brennan tossed off his vodka. "Sure. TV news ain't reporting anyhow, it's show biz. And they love homicides. Guy gets bombed on a Saturday night and bats his old lady around, she sticks a bread knife in his gut. TV covers it like it's the story of the year. But that's nothing, compared to this."

"No, it's not."

"A sex maniac raping and killing beautiful girls and dumping their nude bodies in garbage bags. Two of 'em was bad enough, but now three? And no leads? You wait and see, they'll turn this into a carnival. His Honor'll get into it, that asshole. And that'll stir up the PC. Things will get very hot."

Ben downed his drink. The vodka went down easier this time. He held up the bottle but the captain shook his head.

"So what have you got going?" Brennan asked.

Ben told him they were canvassing the neighborhood around the construction site, that they were in touch with Missing Persons, that they'd get out a flyer as soon as possible, that he'd have the bite expert at the autopsy. "I'm also going to talk to Stein again."

"Who's Stein?"

"He's a psychiatrist, gave me some help before."

Brennan's eyes narrowed. "A shrink? What's he going to tell you?"

Too late, Ben realized he should have kept his mouth shut about it. "Maybe something. Maybe nothing."

"You mean positively nothing. One thing I learned a long time ago about head doctors is they're full of shit. All of them."

"Uh-huh." He wanted to get off the subject.

But the captain warmed to it. He rested heavy forearms on the desk. "You think I'm wrong? You watch when they get into a trial. Defense attorney brings one in and he testifies the accused is not capable of committing murder. So the prosecutor comes back with two more who swear the guy's a werewolf. Regular medical doctors are bad enough, but at least they can tell you when your leg is cut off. The thing about shrinks is, nobody can prove what they say. Which is fine with them. The more mystery the better. They deal in an area so complicated, only they can understand it. So they must be geniuses."

Ben should have left it alone, but he didn't. Maybe it was the vodka. "Stein's different. He was on the staff at Fairlawn for eight years."

"What's Fairlawn?"

"Hospital in Virginia for the criminally insane. I think he can tell us things."

"Like what?"

"Like what kind of a mind we're dealing with."

Brennan snorted. "What kind of a mind? I'll tell you what kind. This character gets his rocks off killing young ladies. For him, a little head isn't enough. He wants a bigger experience. The ultimate thrill. So after he drops his load, he gets an extra kick knocking the girl off. Then when she's used up, he dumps her. Even putting her in a garbage bag tells you a lot about him."

"Stein says it's more complicated. A special form of obsession."

One corner of the captain's mouth twisted into a familiar expression. "Sure it is, Ben. They're all special. Like the guys who push broads off subway platforms. Or that dickhead who poured acid down his kid's throat. Or the one in Bed-Stuy who cut off the girl's tit. You ever hear about him? Did it with a straight razor, while she was still alive. When we got him we found tits from five other girls in his room, and you know what? We never found the rest of those girls or learned who they were. He was a special case, too."

This time Ben made no reply.

Brennan ran a hand through the gray stubble on his head. His voice was a rasp. "Listen to me, Lieutenant. You know what solves these things, same as I do. Hard, ass-busting work. Not screwing around with some witch doctor. Our job is to find the perpetrator and deliver him to the DA with as good a case as we can put together. Just don't get caught up with his obsession, as the shrink calls it— that's no good for your own head. It's bad enough that eighty percent of the shitballs get away with a plea bargain, without cops worrying about what kind of emotional problems somebody's got. So you find out the guy was mistreated when he was little. So who gives a fuck? Does that give him the right to do something like this?"

"Okay, Cap. I hear you."

"Yeah. And one other thing. Remember you're supposed to be running a precinct squad. You got guys to do the street work. What you do is administrate. The rest of the action around here isn't going to quit just because you got a case you find fascinating."

31

Tolliver felt his anger rise, but he said nothing.

The captain still held the empty paper cup in his fist. He set it down on the desk and got to his feet. "Keep me closely informed. Soon as you got an ID, I'll assign you extra detectives from other squads."

Tolliver stood up. "Yes sir, Captain."

"Thanks for the lemonade." Brennan went out of the office, shutting the door behind him.

Ben picked up both paper cups and fired them into his wastebasket. There were times when the zone commander's Stone Age ideas were more than he could take. Impulsively he kicked the bottom drawer of his desk, sending the vodka bottle rolling around inside it. *My job is to administrate. Jesus Christ.*

He sat down again, looking at the stacks of paper in front of him, forcing himself to cool off. From the folders he got out photographs of both murdered girls, before and after. He selected a photo of each young woman that had been made while she was alive and placed them side by side. They had been taken by portrait photographers, and were the kind of pictures a girl had made to give to her family and friends. Both were close head shots, the girls posed with wide smiles and the photos printed in colors that looked artificial. Malik had been a dark-eyed brunette, Cunningham a strawberry blonde. Even their appearances suggested no connection. Except that they had been un-usually pretty, there was no resemblance in the features.

As he had so many times, Ben thought about the man who had killed them. What was *he* like? Intelligent, yes. But what else? Was he a New Yorker? Or maybe he fit the pattern of a serial murderer—a drifter who stayed in one part of the country for a time and then wandered some-where else, leaving a trail of bodies behind him, committing murders with no apparent motive, except to inflict pain, to cause death.

Idly, the lieutenant picked up another photograph from the pile. This was also a shot of Helen Malik, but it was very different from the portrait of a girl in what she obviously had considered a glamorous pose. This one showed her lying face down, arms by her sides, the hands curled and clawlike. The left side of her face was visible, the mouth partly open, the eye an opaque disc. Unlike the rosy tone it had in the portrait, her skin here was bluish white.

Tolliver studied the photograph for a long time. Try as he might, he couldn't keep from seeing another face, the same one he had been unable to blot out when he'd looked at the dead blonde at the construction site. He thought again about his conversation with Brennan. Could the shrink really help? Maybe, maybe not. But the killer was crazy, wasn't he? The guy could be murdering another woman right now.

Ben put the photograph down and flipped through his file until he found the card on Dr. Stein. Then picked up the telephone and called the number.

5

MARGOT Dennis awakened slowly, drawn reluctantly from sleep by a dull, droning noise. She opened her eyes and looked at the ceiling, trying to remember where she was. Her gaze moved to heavy, gold-brocaded drapes that covered the windows, and then to a French Provincial table and a pair of chairs across the room from the bed. There was an open bottle of Scotch on the table, two empty glasses, and an ice bowl containing a pool of stale water. A blouse lay across the back of one of the chairs. The light in the room was dim, but she could make out that the blouse was of green silk. It was hers. She was in the Helmsley Palace and it was Monday morning.

She rolled onto her side, burrowing deeper under the covers in an unsuccessful attempt to shut out the droning noise. There was a foul taste in her mouth. For several minutes she tried to go back to sleep, but it was hopeless. Images of the previous evening drifted through her mind: cocktails in the bar at Elaine's, dinner at Laurent with more drinks and two bottles of wine, still more drinks here in the hotel between bouts of lovemaking. No wonder her mouth tasted so bad.

The droning noise stopped abruptly. Margot poked her head out of the covers, curious. It had been the shower, she realized. The water had been turned on full blast. Without the noise the room seemed oddly quiet, the only sound a faint rumble of traffic from the Manhattan streets far below.

The bathroom door opened, and Jeff Parker emerged in a cloud of steam. His skin was pale, except for his sun-tanned face and hands. He had wrapped a towel around his middle, and his black hair had been brushed back, wet. He was smiling as he approached the bed and looked down at her. "'Morning, honey."

Margot stretched sleepily and returned his smile. "Got a kiss?"

"Sure." He sat on the edge of the bed and bent over, his lips brushing hers lightly. "How'd you sleep?"

"Great, when you finally let me."

He chuckled, obviously pleased by this reference to his virility. But he made no move to get back into bed with her, which wasn't like him. When they spent a night together, Jeff always wanted one more before leaving in the morning. His disinterest now made Margot wonder.

He waved toward the living room of the suite. "I ordered some breakfast. There's eggs and coffee and stuff in there if you want it. I already ate."

"Why didn't you wake me?"

"You were in a deep sleep. I didn't have the heart."

"Big day today?"

He stood up. "Yeah. Meeting with the banks, then lunch with some guys from Piedmont. That's an investment company that specializes in oil leases. If I can make the deal with them, it'll be a real big day."

"How does it look?"

"Good, but there's no telling. The business is crazy right now. West Texas crude is at eighteen dollars a barrel, but all that mess in the Persian Gulf could drive the price up fast. Maybe to twenty, twenty-one." As he spoke he dropped the towel to the floor and went to a dresser, opening a drawer and getting out socks and underwear.

Watching him, Margot was reminded of how proud he was of his body, how he worked at keeping himself trim, the one-time star fullback at Baylor. "Wish you luck."

"Thanks, honey." He went on dressing.

35

"When are you going back to Houston?"

"Flight's at three-fifteen."

"Jeff?"

"Mm-m?"

She hated to ask, but she couldn't help herself. "When are you going to tell her?"

His back was turned to her. He was studying his image in a mirror as he buttoned his shirt. "Soon as I can. Not the best time right now. The kids have got some problems—Cindy's been sick, the doctor thinks she may have mono. And Bobby's on academic pro. Could lose his eligibility. Those things have to get sorted out first."

Her resentment rose, but she controlled it. "Will you be back soon?"

"Depends on how I make out today. I'll let you know, whenever I get a clear picture of what's gonna happen with the deal."

"You'll call me?"

"Sure. Should be in just a couple days." He knotted a red-and-white-striped tie and stepped into the pants of his suit, a dark gray sharkskin. Then he put on a pair of black loafers. His jacket came last. He turned to her. "How about you, honey—you working today?"

Her pride wouldn't let her tell him the truth, that she hadn't had a booking for two weeks. "Yes. Later on."

"Good photographer?"

"One of the best."

He went about getting his things together, packing his suitcase, putting his wallet and his address book and other odds and ends into his pockets. "What kind of thing is it?"

She realized he wasn't really interested. He was only making conversation, staying away from the subject she wanted to talk about. "Oh, just some fashion shots."

"Uh-huh. For a magazine?"

"Yes. For a magazine. Jeff?"

"Yeah?"

"Nothing. Be sure to call me soon, will you?"

"Sure, honey." He came back to the bed and again bent down to her. This time his lips barely touched hers. He picked up his bag and his attaché case and went to the door. "Bye, Margot." He nodded toward the dresser top. "There's a little something there for you." He left the room.

For a moment she didn't know whether to curse or cry. But she certainly had no illusions as to what was happening to the relationship. She had seen the signs before at other times and with other people, and she had seen them from both sides. Giving and receiving. Damn Jeff to hell, anyway.

But she also knew better than to indulge herself in a lot of self-pity. That could be even more damaging than the problems themselves. She got out of bed and stretched. The drapes were still drawn, so she had no idea what the weather was like outside. May could be tricky. She went over to the dresser, curious to see what he had left for her.

Under a glass ashtray, neatly folded, were some bills. She picked them up and looked at them, half disbelieving what she was seeing. There were five of them, all hundreds. Jesus. If he had kicked her, it wouldn't have hurt as much. For a moment she thought about tearing them into pieces and flushing them down the toilet, but then she put the money down and went into the bathroom.

The bastard. The lousy bastard. Kissing her off with a few hundred bucks, just as he would some whore he'd spent the night with. Here you go, baby—now get lost. She bit her lip, struggling to hold the tears back, and at the same time wishing she could kill him. It took awhile to get herself together, but finally she resolved not to think about him. Later on, when she could reason more clearly, she'd try to deal with it.

She looked at herself in the mirror and grimaced. Mornings were when you saw the truth. When you saw the lines

3 7

and the pores and the blemishes and you came face to face with what it was to be thirty-three years old in a business that worshiped youth. God. At least her body was in good shape, thanks to almost daily workouts at her health club and a routine that usually avoided nights like the one she'd just spent.

A quick shower made her feel a little better, physically at least. There would be plenty of time for a bath when she got home. She was conscious of a slight hangover, but that would pass as soon as she had something to eat. She got dressed, and when she opened the drapes sunlight poured into the suite.

After a second cup of coffee she telephoned her agency, knowing intuitively there would be nothing doing. She was right, there wasn't. Next she checked her answering service. One call the previous evening, from Jean Sandoval, her business manager. She returned the call, aware that it was still early, and that the older woman liked to sleep late.

The voice that answered, however, was cheerful. "Darling. Sorry I missed you last night."

"I had a date."

"That's nice. Where did you have dinner?"

"Laurent."

"Uh-huh. Not many places open on Sunday nights."

"No."

"You don't sound too happy, Margot. Everything okay?"

"Oh, sure."

"Shooting today?"

She stiffened. Dear Jean knew exactly where to insert the knife. "No, not today."

Jean's tone became even brighter. "Say, why don't we have lunch? My treat. There's something I want to talk to you about."

"What is it?"

"Tell you all about it when I see you. Let's say Le Cygne at one. I'll make the reservation."

"All right. See you then." Margot hung up and collected her things. When she had everything together she picked up the hundred-dollar bills from the dresser top and looked at them again. She felt another surge of anger, but she stuffed the bills into her bag before she left the suite.

Walking through the lobby on her way to get a taxi, she was aware of a mixture of fragrances: fresh flowers, lemon oil, French perfume. The smell of money. It had a character all its own. Even the other guests she passed seemed different from ordinary people. They were beautifully groomed, and their clothes often had an unmistakably European cut. As always in a public place, several men stared at her.

The cab drove up Madison Avenue and turned east, and in less than ten minutes she was home. The doorman tipped his cap and said good morning as he held the door for her. She returned his greeting with a smile and went on up to her apartment.

She took her time getting ready for lunch, luxuriating in a tub topped with Chanel-scented suds and razoring under her arms. She washed her hair and then blew it dry, styling it to look casual. Thick and healthy, with its deep auburn color, it was one of her best features. She put on a favorite dress, a pale yellow silk, and as she checked her reflection in a mirror she wondered what Jean had in mind. She'd find out soon enough. When Jean Sandoval took you to lunch, you could be sure she wanted something.

6

Lᴇ Cygne was crowded. The small but elegant restaurant seemed especially pleasant to Margot this afternoon, its silver and crystal polished and shining, bouquets of spring flowers everywhere.

When the maître d' led her to Jean Sandoval's table, the older woman leaned forward to exchange the customary kiss. She shook her head admiringly as Margot sat down. "Darling, you look simply wonderful."

"Thanks, so do you." Margot meant it. Jean had to be in her early sixties, but you'd never know it. Her glossy black hair was cut stylishly short, and her dark eyes were luminous under slim, carefully shaped eyebrows. Her skin was tan and firm, with no trace of wrinkles. She was wearing a handsome beige Dior suit.

They ordered Bloody Marys and then lobster salads while they made small talk, much of it to do with Jean's efforts to get her place in Southampton ready for the summer.

Margot feigned interest as long as she could, finally putting her fork down. "What was it you wanted to talk to me about?"

Jean's expression grew serious. "Margot, I'm going to be very blunt. We've known each other for too long not to say exactly what we mean, don't you think?"

"Of course."

"What's more, we have a professional relationship. As your business manager, I have to give you the best advice I can, always."

"Also true."

"Then let's take an objective look at how you're doing."

"If you mean my career, at the moment it stinks. But you know what the business is like. Things will change."

"Will they? Just remember that I manage other girls, as well as you, and I've been managing models for a long time. Have you any idea how many I've worked with, over the years?"

"Lots, I guess."

"More than I could count. Some of them were not too bright. Just fell apart, for one reason or another. Drinking or drugs or the wrong man."

"I don't think you have to worry about those things with me."

"Oh, I know I don't. You're much too smart for that. But darling, let's face it. When it comes to money, you've been just plain irresponsible. I've tried to get you to save something, to get you into investments, but you paid no attention. I've also told you over and over again to cut back on your spending, and you've ignored that, too. The fact is, you're damn near broke."

"So what are you telling me now?"

"Simply this. You have to find a new direction, for your own good."

Margot froze. She hadn't expected this. "Are you saying I'm over-the-hill?"

"Certainly not. I've never seen you look lovelier. But right now what everybody wants to hire is kids. The younger the better. The hottest models are teenagers, right?"

"I guess so. But that's the way it's always been."

"Margot, without a star contract, like the deal Christie Brinkley has with Cover Girl, or Paulina with Estee Lauder, you have nothing to fall back on."

She had to admit that what she was hearing was the truth. She'd known girls herself who'd hung on until they couldn't

41

get even the crappiest catalog work. "So what are you suggesting—I should marry some jerk and go to seed in Larchmont or someplace?"

"Nothing of the kind. I'm only pointing out that while you're still one of the best-looking girls in New York, you ought to make the most of it. And I can help you do it."

"How?"

"Again, I'm going to be completely frank. You have affairs, which is normal enough, but somehow none of them have become the kind of relationship you'd like them to be. For instance, I know from what you've told me that your current love—what's his name?"

"Jeff Parker."

"That's it. From Texas, isn't he?"

"Yes."

"And it's not turning out too well. Forgive me, but that's so, isn't it?"

"Yes. That's so."

"Okay. And what happens in these things is typical. You give a man everything, and what does he give you in return? Some happy times, sure. But also a lot of heartache. And now and then some insignificant little present. A piece of jewelry, or whatever."

A picture of the hundred-dollar bills Jeff had left her that morning came into Margot's mind. She winced.

Jean caught it. "I'm right, aren't I?"

"What are you getting at?"

"Just this. I can introduce you to people who would make your evenings worthwhile. You'd meet fascinating men who'd take you to the best places in New York. You'd have a wonderful time, capped off by making love. Just the same as you're doing now. The only difference would be that instead of a lot of misery and a silly gift from time to time, you'd be seeing something of real value. Money. And plenty of it."

42

Margot was stunned. "Are you serious?"

"Of course I am."

"In other words, at this point in my life, I'm fit to be nothing but a hooker."

The older woman's tone took on an edge. "Look, sweetie, let's not confuse the issue. What I'm saying is that in the end, money is the only thing that counts. You'd better get as much of it as you can, while you can."

Before Margot could reply, a waiter arrived with coffee. As he set the cups and saucers in front of them and poured from a silver pot, a string of thoughts ran through her mind. For as long as she could remember, men had dominated her, used her. Was it so terrible to consider that maybe she ought to be getting more in return than a cheap little slap in the face like the one Jeff had given her? And for that matter, wasn't part of her anger with Jeff not just that it had been money, but that it had been so *little* money? And then there was her career. As much as she hated to admit it, what Jean had said about that was undeniable. The business had an insatiable appetite for fresh talent, and Margot was getting on. Maybe the idea wasn't so outrageous at that. *Money is the only thing that counts.*

After the waiter left, Jean lit a cigarette. "Think about it, Margot. That's all I want you to do. Ask yourself whether it's going to matter a few years from now, how many times your picture was in *Vogue*. Or if it might be better for your souvenirs to be blue-chip stock certificates."

Margot sat back. "All right, I'll think about it. But I want some time."

"So who's rushing you? Just remember, there are some interesting people I'd like you to meet. Not just semi-rich, but rich-rich."

"Okay, but I'm not ready to give up. I keep thinking something good is about to happen."

"Did I say anything about giving up your modeling? I understand how you feel about that."

"I'm sure you do."

"Might be a good idea to consider changing agencies, though. Seems to me Farrelli hasn't been getting you much work lately."

"No, he hasn't. Could be time for a lot of changes, for that matter. Maybe there's some hot new photographer who'll do wonderful things with me. You never know."

Jean Sandoval's eyes were cool and steady. "That's true. You never know."

7

D R. Stein's office was on East Tenth Street. It was twilight when Tolliver got there. The streetlights were coming on, and a light breeze rustled the leaves of the trees. Kids were playing stickball in the narrow roadway between the rows of parked cars, shouting a mixture of curses and encouragement. The vehicles were jammed together parallel to the curbs, the only open space in front of a fire hydrant. Ben pulled the Ford into the opening and reached behind the sun visor for a police identification plate, dropping it onto the dashboard before getting out of the car. He carried with him a thick manila envelope.

The kids' ball bounced off the hood of the Ford with a loud *thunk*. A dirty-faced boy stood glaring at him. "Hey, ya not suppose to park there."

Up yours, kid. Ben went up the steps to the front door and pressed the buzzer. These were row houses, narrow structures with stone and plaster facades, three and four stories high, the only noticeable difference among them the colors they were painted. A metallic voice asked who was there and Ben gave his name. A moment later the door swung open and Alan Stein told him to come in.

The shrink was about fifty, Ben would guess. His hair was a spray of gray wool, and his eyes were magnified by heavy, horn-rimmed glasses that made him look like an owl. He was wearing a short-sleeved shirt and khaki pants and his gut hung out over his belt. Stein had been on retainer from the NYPD for the past year, but without many takers; most cops had the same distrust of psychia-

trists Captain Brennan had. For that matter Ben himself
had his doubts about learning anything of value from one
of these guys, even one who'd spent years working with
the criminally insane. The zone commander could be
right—so much of what they had to say was nothing but
psychobabble, a lot of bullshit terminology designed to confuse the suckers.

Nevertheless you could never tell, could you? Dr. Freud
just might give you something you could use. Ben followed
him down a hallway to his study at the rear of the house.

Stein turned to him. "You want a drink?"

"Yeah, great. Vodka, if you got it."

"Sure. Have a seat." Stein shuffled over to a cabinet and
got out a bottle and glasses and an ice bucket.

Ben sat down in an armchair and looked around. Each
time he came into this cramped room he wondered how
anybody could work in it. There were no windows, the only
light coming from a couple of dingy lamps, and every inch
of wall space was covered with jam-packed bookcases. More
books were heaped on the floor, along with still more in
cardboard cartons. Piles of paper were everywhere. The
only sign of order was an IBM PC that stood on a desk.
The musty air made him think of an attic that hadn't been
opened for a long time.

Stein handed him his drink and wished him luck. The
vodka tasted clean and cold but did nothing to relax him.

"You brought pictures?" Stein gestured toward the envelope.

Ben passed it to him. "Yeah. I got them from the lab
just before I came over."

The doctor sat down at the desk and pushed some of
the mess out of the way. He swallowed half his drink and
put the glass aside, then pulled a set of eight-by-ten-inch
glossies out of the envelope, spreading them out on the
surface of the desk. The photographs were of the body

46

discovered that morning in the construction site. There were a half dozen of them, front and rear shots, including close-ups of the girl's face and her mangled buttocks.

Stein hunched over the photos, studying them intently for several minutes. Then he opened a drawer and got out photographs of the corpses of Malik and Cunningham that Ben had given him earlier. He lined these up beside the new set and spent a few more minutes poring over all of them. Finally he sat back and peered at Ben with his owl's eyes. "So now he's telling us a few things."

"Like what?"

"Like whatever emotional pressure he's under, it's become more intense."

"How do you figure?"

Stein flicked a hand over the photos. "For one thing, the bites. You saw how much worse these were than the others?"

"Yeah, I saw. What else?"

"The intervals between killings. Shorter this time, because the pressure keeps building. And now it's building faster. When it gets so he can't stand it, he rapes a girl and kills her."

Ben didn't need a psychiatrist to tell him this. He felt his frustration working again. "Okay, so he's under pressure. You told me that last time we talked. What I want to know is, what kind of pressure? What's it coming from? I realize that's a tall order, but if you had to guess, what would you say?"

Stein pursed his lips. "From his family, maybe. If he has one. Or maybe his job, his career. But whatever it is, it most likely has to do with the social environment he's living in. You understand I'm hypothesizing, but there's a pattern. It suggests to me he's subject to manic-depressive mood swings. That's paranoia, of course. And he's very likely schizophrenic."

47

Here it comes, Ben thought. Double-talk time. "Look, Doc. No offense, but I hear that description damn near every day. We got bums living in Grand Central the social workers say are paranoid schizophrenics. But they hardly ever seem to hurt anybody."

Stein smiled. "All right, let me give it to you in plain English. What we're talking about here is somebody who has a mental illness that often prevents him from distinguishing between reality and illusion. He thinks he's making perfect sense, that what he's doing is entirely rational."

"Even killing these girls?"

"Sure. Oh, he knows it's wrong, at least by the rules of our society. But that doesn't mean anything to him. It's just a complication—something he has to deal with. When the pressure gets to the boiling point, for whatever reason, he hallucinates, and acts out the hallucination. In other words, he takes orders from his own sick mind."

That rang a bell. "Like the nut who says, God told me to do it?"

"Exactly."

"What about the bites?"

"There may be symbolism involved, but that's a remote possibility. Usually when one human being bites another, it's because he's berserk with anger. So he brings man's oldest and most primitive weapons into play. His teeth. I believe your murderer is expressing rage."

Ben thought of Brennan again. "Let me ask you, Doc. Is it true that all of this goes back to something that happened when he was a kid?"

Stein sat back in his chair and drank more of his vodka. "Yes, almost invariably. A little boy is abused by an adult. Probably raped, or sodomized. Maybe beaten, as well. His ideas of what sex is all about become twisted. Same thing happens with girls, but they're more passive. They might become lesbians later on. Or prostitutes. But they almost never turn into killers. With a boy it's different. A boy who's been abused grows up believing sex is a weapon."

"Okay, but even though it's violent, you couldn't call it a very active sex life, what this guy's doing. Once every couple of months?"

The owl eyes gleamed. "Ah, but you don't know what else there may be."

"You mean the rest of it could be normal, except when he goes off the deep end?"

"No, that's very unlikely. He might have what *seems* like a normal relationship with a woman. Might even be married, although I doubt it. But while he's having intercourse, he fantasizes about the last murder he committed. Or maybe he doesn't have other women at all. Maybe he masturbates, thinking about what he did to his victim. How she reacted, the expression on her face—how it felt to him, seeing her die."

Ben tried to picture it: some weird bastard with his cock in his hand.

"That's why the rape murderer often steals personal items from a victim. You've run into that in other cases, probably."

"Yeah," Ben said. "I have. He'd take a glove, or her bra, or whatever."

"Okay, why?"

"Souvenirs, we thought. But you're telling me there was more to it than that."

"Right. What your rapist most likely did was get that stuff out and look at it and touch it while he masturbated. He might rub his penis with it. Or he might put it on."

"Ah."

"What is it?"

"I just thought of what somebody was telling me today, about a guy who cut off girls' tits with a razor. Afterward he kept them, but the cops didn't know why."

49

"Uh-huh. And now you do know. That could be the answer in this case, too. All three bodies were nude, weren't they?"

It was an angle Ben hadn't thought of. "We figured it was because he didn't want to leave anything we could trace."

"And you were probably correct," Stein said. "I'm just pointing out there could have been another reason, as well."

"Yeah, I see." The shrink had given him a number of useful insights after all—things he never would have come up with on his own. "Is there anything else you've thought about?"

Stein settled back in his chair. "I think I told you last time you were here, he's probably young."

"Uh-huh. Dentist who's working with us confirmed that. Said the condition of his teeth was excellent."

"Yes. Rape murderers are usually young men."

"But not always. We've seen them at different ages."

"True enough. We had a patient at Fairlawn who'd raped an eleven-year-old and then cut her heart out with a carving knife. He was past sixty when he did it. But that's rare. Usually these things take place when the killer is at the height of his sexual activity. Which is when he's young, of course."

"Yeah. It also looks as if he could be fairly bright. You agree with that?"

"Yes, I do. In fact, he probably considers himself superior to other people. And except for these outbursts, he could be leading what is otherwise a relatively conventional life."

Ben was silent for a moment. He finished his drink and set the glass down, waving Stein away when the doctor reached for it. "No thanks, Doc. I've got work to do. But I appreciate your help."

"Anytime, Lieutenant. I know this is no ordinary case for you."

Ben looked at him. "Meaning?"

"I wouldn't say you're obsessed by it, exactly, but then again . . . Let me ask you something. Was there another case, or perhaps something in your own life, that might relate to what's happened here?"

He flushed. "Maybe."

"Someone close to you?"

"Yeah," Ben said. "Someone close to me."

"Want to talk about it?"

"What am I, a patient now?"

Stein made no reply, the owl eyes staring through thick lenses.

"Maybe some other time, Doc." Ben got to his feet.

There was an awkward moment, and then Stein stood up and led him back to the front door.

Outside it had grown dark, but the kids were still playing stickball under the streetlights. He got into the Ford and sat there for a few minutes, thinking back over the discussion. What he was looking for was an intelligent young man with a nice smile. Somebody who thought he was better than other people. A guy who was leading a perfectly normal life, except that he enjoyed raping and murdering young women and then mutilating their bodies.

And did all of this relate to anything in Ben's own life? You bet your fat ass it did, Dr. Stein. It related so much that it was hard for him even to think about it, let alone discuss it with anybody. It related in a way that made him want desperately to find this crazy fucker he was after— find him and then put him through all the terror and the agony he'd caused those girls. All of it, that is, except dying. That was something that wouldn't be rushed. Death would be an escape for him that Ben would hold off as long as possible.

51

He looked at his watch. There was still a lot of work he had to get done. But hadn't this been some bitch of a day? As he started the Ford's engine and pulled out into the street he thought once more about the guy he was looking for. What kind of a day had *he* had?

8

THE ocean was cool and blue-green and its surface shimmered with golden reflections of the sun's rays. Breakers cascaded onto the beach and exploded in a frenzy of white froth, filling the air with salt tang. He stepped to the water's edge and watched his mother come out of the surf.

She was beautiful. Her wet hair hung to her shoulders in thick strands and her eyes were a shade of violet so deep they made him think of the beginning of the night sky. Her hips swung as she walked and her one-piece bathing suit clung to her body. He could see every line of her breasts, large and deep with the nipples protruding, bobbing with each step as if beckoning him to kiss them. Water ran from her hair and her shoulders and down her legs in tiny rivulets, and she laughed with wonderful abandon, throwing her head back and raising her hands.

He wanted to run to her and hug her and laugh with her. But he couldn't. As hard as he tried, as much as he strained every muscle, he could move no closer. As he watched, a man wearing swim trunks bounded down to where she stood knee-deep in the tumbling waves and drew her to him. He grasped her wrists and she gave in to him, pressing herself against his body. The man was tall and powerfully built and he gripped her buttocks in his hands and kissed her mouth, thrusting against her as her arms encircled his neck and her pelvis began to move in phase with his. She freed one hand, bringing it down between her body and the man's, reaching into his swim trunks.

He couldn't watch any longer. But neither could he look away. Now suddenly they were not in the sunshine but in a dark place and they were not wearing the swimsuits. The man was lying on top of her and his buttocks contracted as he drove into her and sounds were coming from her throat that seemed to express pleasure and pain at the same time.

Freda was there. Her dark, yellow-flecked eyes were narrow and knowing and her lips were stretched back in a cynical leer. She had been watching him from a secret place, just as he had been watching his mother and the man. Freda was so close he could see the tiny hairs that sprouted beside her mouth, could smell her foul breath. He wanted to shove her away, to run from her, but again he could not move. She bent over him, and her face was devil-like, the pink tip of her tongue showing as she mocked him. To his surprise, he had an iron-hard erection.

Freda began sucking him. Her mouth was incredibly warm and wet as it moved slowly up and down, even the rhythm conveying how well she knew him. He was begging her to stop, to leave him alone, to go away, but he knew he didn't mean it. His orgasm erupted and there were sparks now in the devil eyes, and drops of milky fluid on the thick lips.

"Filthy boy!"

Her open hand struck his face with stunning force, again and again. He struggled to escape, to scramble away from the blows. His stomach heaved scalding vomit that burned his throat and his mouth, choking him. The puke hung from his jaw in strings and her foot was on the back of his head, forcing his face down into the stinking puddle.

"You are nothing," she hissed. "Not fit to live with decent people. A rotten, hideous little animal."

He sat up in bed, trembling. His pajamas were drenched with sweat and semen and he saw vomit on the sheets. For Christ's sake, he actually *had* thrown up. His throat was constricted and it hurt him to swallow. He got out of bed on unsteady legs and made his way into the bathroom, stripping off the pajamas as he went.

His urine was almost brown, which was hardly surprising. He had drunk a whole bottle of wine with his dinner, on top of the Scotch he'd consumed before. And later there had been brandy. He stared at his reflection in the mirror over the sink and grimaced. You look lousy, he thought. Cut down on the booze and be more careful of what you eat. He rinsed out his mouth with tap water in an effort to expunge the awful taste, then scrubbed vigorously with his toothbrush. The minty foam and the brushing helped, but his throat continued to burn. He'd have to get moving, if he hoped to work out and still get to his office early. This would be a big day—one of the most important of his career.

But ah, the pictures. The pictures were fabulous. All he had hoped for, and then some. The colors, the composition, and most of all the pose of that little fool, sitting there against the pillows and holding the lollipop between her legs. It was like Tom Kelly's famous calendar shot of Monroe, in some ways. But much more sophisticated. More like a painting by one of the great modernists—Picasso, or Modigliani.

He put down his toothbrush and walked from the bathroom into his studio. He had intended to look at the pictures later, but he couldn't wait to see them again, even though he had worked with them all weekend. There was a long, white table at one end of the room. His work was laid out on its surface, the contact sheets and dozens of prints. He picked up an eight-by-ten of the shot he had selected to use. Seeing it elated him. The photograph had such *impact*.

And it had something else, as well. The girl seemed so sexy, looking out at him through those glazed eyes, her lips parted just enough to reveal her tongue, as if once again she was teasing him, daring him to stick his cock into her mouth. Oddly, he experienced none of the anger now, could hardly even recall what it had been like. He put the print down and left the studio.

From there he went into the small, windowless room he used as a gym. There was a mat on the floor and a rack held a set of weights. An exercise bike stood in a corner, and a speed bag hung from a platform. There were full-length mirrors on three of the walls. He loosened up by stretching and touching his toes a few times, and then began to work with the weights.

On most days he went through a full routine, hitting the bag, pedaling several miles on the stationary bike, jumping rope, all before he started lifting. But this morning his hangover had leeched his enthusiasm for the workout, and he didn't have much time, so he confined his efforts to the weights. That was the most satisfying part of it anyway, not only because it did the most to build his strength, but also because it gave him intense pleasure to see the reflection of his naked body in the mirrors.

He began by lying on his back and doing pull-overs with a forty-pound barbell in each hand, and then he stood up for a series of curls, all the while watching the multiple images as his skin grew slick and his face became flushed from the exertion. After a time he put the lighter weights aside and locked 150 pounds onto a bar. He did squats first, and then pressed the weights relentlessly, until his arms and his shoulders and his back burned with the strain. It was only when he absolutely could not heave the iron overhead one more time that he quit. He dropped the weights to the floor and stood looking at himself in the mirrors, glancing from one to the other, his chest heaving, sweatdrops falling from his nose and his chin.

For a slim guy he had a wonderful body, if he did say so himself. He was tall and lithe and his muscles were clearly defined—especially the pectorals and lattisimus dorsi. And when he tensed his gut, his midsection was like a grid. The sight was more than merely sensuous to him; seeing himself like this was sexually exciting. Which was strange, because he had never been conscious of any homosexual desire. It was only the sight of his own body that was arousing to him. He raised his arms and flexed his biceps, reveling in this display of his strength. Slim, yes. But powerful? Like Adonis, and just as beautiful. He grinned at the thought, and with one last glance at his reflection, left the room.

After a few minutes in the shower, he felt great. It was a lovely spring day and he had done superb work and he was strong and refreshed and hungry. He was looking forward to going to his office with growing excitement. He'd get the word today, he was almost sure of it.

After shaving he put on a terry robe and went into the kitchen, where he made himself a breakfast of fresh orange juice, coffee, and a croissant. There was a small Sony TV on the table. He turned it on and watched the news as he ate.

It was a steady stream of the usual crap. The secretary of state, with his baggy eyes and his perpetual look of astonishment, was departing for Europe and another round of bullshit with our alleged European allies. Automobile workers in Detroit were mystified that they were out of work. How could their Japanese counterparts be willing to labor longer for less money and still turn out a better product? It was baffling. It was unAmerican. It was comical. The consumer price index was down in the latest report, after having been up for the last two months. Down up, up down.

The commercials were more interesting. Pepsi-Cola had a new one, showing girls playing tennis. They were long-legged golden athletes who moved with wonderful grace, and much of the footage had been shot at high speed to portray the action in slow motion. Burger King also had one he hadn't seen before. A lush brunette shoved a revolting hamburger at the camera lens and babbled that you could have it any way you wanted it. Her mouth was wide and red-lipped and as he looked at her he knew how *he* wanted it.

But there was nothing about a mysterious black plastic bundle turning up on West Thirteenth Street. Good. No one would have been working at the construction site over the weekend, which was one of the reasons he had chosen it. The evening news would have the story. And by then the photograph would have arrived. The timing would be perfect. This would be a day of not just one triumph, but two.

He turned off the set and put his dishes into the sink. The bedroom still smelled when he walked into it, a mixture of sweat and puke and semen. He opened the skylight and then stripped the bed of its rank linen, rolling it into a ball and adding his pajamas to it. Back in the kitchen he stuffed the whole mess into the automatic washer, threw in some detergent and turned on the machine.

Even though he was in a hurry, he went into the living room for a quick look at the huge black-and-white blowups that decorated the walls. God, but she was beautiful. Despite all the thousands of times he'd seen these old photographs, they never failed to move him. The high cheekbones, the large, wide-set eyes, the soft dark sweep of hair, were timeless.

And as well as he knew them, he almost always found something in the photographs he hadn't noticed before. There'd be some detail, some clue to her personality he hadn't been aware of. He often sat staring at them for hours, mesmerized by the images. Sometimes it was like a game, searching for nuances he'd somehow overlooked. And at other times it was unbearably sad, as if by finding something new he was drawing closer to her, only to realize he could never reach her. But even then, it was gratifying to look at them.

This was his favorite room. With the vaulted ceilings and the sleek modern furniture, and especially the photographs, it was always soothing to him. For that matter, he loved everything about the old loft building that had been such a wreck before he bought and restored it. His was the only apartment in it, and the thick walls made it seem like a fortress.

But he had to get going. He returned to the bedroom, thinking about what he would wear. After poking among the suits in his closet he chose one of his newest and best, a Bertilli that had cost him twelve hundred dollars, and put it on. The suit was extremely light in weight, and its lines draped perfectly. It was tan with just a hint of ochre, and with a yellow-and-blue Sulka tie it looked marvelous.

He surveyed himself in the full-length mirror beside the door of his closet, grinning exuberantly. His appearance now was that of a well-bred young man on his way up, the type you'd see moving into the higher management echelons of a blue-chip company, or a newly elected partner in one of the big law firms. He was very good-looking, in a careless, offhand way, with his clean-cut features and his mop of curly brown hair that appeared never to have had a comb drawn through it. And his smile. His smile was so damned friendly, with his strong, even white teeth, that you knew from the first moment you saw him you were going to like him.

He spent several minutes in front of the mirror, admiring his reflection. Today of all days it was important that he look his best. He went into his studio and put the envelope containing the photograph into his attaché case. Then he left the apartment, carrying the case, taking care to lock and double-lock the heavy steel door behind him.

9

THE Whitechapel Drug Company building was on Park Avenue at Fortieth Street. A monolith of matte-black metal and smoked glass, it had an air of strength and determination the young man admired. It was an assertion of the company's power, and of its ability to make vast sums of money. Waist-high stone flower boxes in front of the building contained rows of tulips whose scarlet blossoms were as bright as flames in the morning sunlight. It was only a little past eight when he walked by them on his way in, but already people were arriving, eager to get started on the first day of the new week. Whitechapel was that kind of company; if you hoped to get anywhere, you worked as long and as hard as you possibly could.

His office was on the forty-third floor, on the Park Avenue side of the building. When he stepped off the elevator he noticed that the lights were on in more than half the other offices. He hung his jacket on the back of the door and set his case down behind his desk. The room was unostentatious, with a pair of straight-backed chairs and a glass-fronted cabinet. His Dufy prints hung on one wall; the one opposite held a map of the United States marked off by marketing areas. From the single window he could see the UN headquarters to his left, and across the East River the grimy buildings of Brooklyn and Queens. He sat down and started at once on the work he had left behind on Friday afternoon when he had gone to meet that stupid blonde.

There was a flash Nielsen report from Whitechapel's research department. It showed that Tynex sales were up sharply. He'd known they would be; factory orders had been consistently strong. But Nielsen measured retail movement, which made it official that the product was moving off the shelves of drugstores, supermarkets, and mass merchandisers at a steadily increasing rate. Even a conservative projection would put sales above $200 million for the year. Seeing the Nielsen figures now was deeply gratifying to him. It was just one more confirmation of something else he knew: he was a man of extraordinary intellect, of outstanding ability.

As manager of the Tynex brand, he was on record as the chief proponent of the new strategy, which was to attack aspirin directly, rather than try to take a share of market away from the other acetaminophen brands in the category. If the plan hadn't worked, it would have been disastrous. Rick Torrey, the vice president for marketing, had let him know from the beginning that a failure would weigh heavily against him. He knew the company well enough to understand what that meant. They wouldn't fire him, but a freeze would set in. He'd be reassigned to some nothing brand, such as one of the old stomach remedies that was dying an inch at a time. And if that didn't send him a clear message, Torrey would have a quiet talk with him, suggesting that it might be in their mutual best interests if he were to look for another job. The pressure was incredible.

But nothing like that would happen now. Tynex was up, and it was going to keep right on going. The strategy was working, and the advertising was working. And no matter how many of the company's resident marketing geniuses tried to take credit, the corner office had to know it was Peter Barrows who had brought off a brilliant stroke.

Which meant the next rung was a sure thing. The rumor on Friday was that Bob Carpenter, the group product manager and therefore his immediate boss, had been canned. Carpenter was a nice guy but weak, and he was having trouble at home. His wife was screwing around, and there had been scenes, some of them public, including a screaming match during a Saturday night dance at the Plainfield Country Club. That alone was enough to cast a cloud over you at Whitechapel, but to top it off Carpenter had begun drinking heavily. Most of the time he came back from lunch bombed, and once in a while he didn't come back at all. With Carpenter out, Peter had it made.

There were a number of things that needed his attention this morning: a proposed new safety cap that would add a quarter of a cent a unit to package costs; approval of a stack of invoices from the agency; a change in label copy that the company's legal department believed would help keep the FDA off their backs. He remained deeply immersed in his work, and was surprised when his secretary put his coffee down in front of him. That meant it was nine o'clock, her regular arrival time. He looked up. "Good morning, Evelyn. How are you?"

She wrinkled her nose. "Okay, I guess. But God, I hate Mondays. 'Specially when it's nice out."

"I know exactly what you mean." She was such a klutz —slow-moving and bovine, with a blemished face that betrayed her craving for sweets. He would have preferred a more attractive secretary, but Evelyn got the work out.

"Mr. Torrey wants to see you. He's in his office." She turned and lumbered back to her desk.

Peter tensed. This was it—he was sure of it. Especially because the marketing vp would have seen the Nielsen figures when the report came out on Friday. A lot of the peckerheads around here had probably been astounded. And envious. As he put his jacket on, he was aware that his palms were suddenly moist and his pulse was racing. He walked quickly down the carpeted hallway and knocked on Torrey's door before opening it and poking his head inside.

"Hey, Peter. Come on in." Torrey had been leafing

62

through *The Wall Street Journal*. He was balding and flabby, although Peter knew he was only in his early forties. He put the newspaper down on his desk and indicated a chair.

Peter sank into the comfortable seat. "How was your weekend, Rick—hit a few?"

"No, damn it. My wife had me roped into a family thing. I'd much rather have been playing. God knows I need the practice."

Peter smiled. He knew Torrey took pride in his prowess as a golfer and was flattered when anyone referred to his game.

Torrey leaned forward and put his elbows on his desk. His face took on an expression of great seriousness, and his tone dropped a couple of notches, as if they were discussing a cataclysmic event. "Saw the early Nielsens. Terrific."

"Yeah, they looked pretty good." He'd already thought about how he'd play this, and had decided on sincere but modest. "Hope it's more than just a temporary bump."

"Oh, I'm sure it is. Up four share points, on top of three last time? Fantastic. You deserve a lot of credit."

You're damned right I do. Aloud he said, "I'm just glad the brand's moving."

"It's going great, Peter. And I want you to know I'm proud of you." Torrey sat back in his chair. His tone was warm now, his manner expansive. "I'm predicting big things for you here. Whitechapel's future will be riding on ability like yours."

"Thanks, Rick. I really appreciate that."

Torrey cleared his throat and leaned forward again. "There are some changes in the wind. They'll be officially announced this morning."

Peter waited.

"First of all, Bob Carpenter's leaving us."

His eyebrows arched. "Oh? I'm sorry to hear it."

"We all are. But it's no secret that he's been having some, ah, personal problems. We felt it would be best for Bob and for the company if he were to find a spot somewhere else."

"Damn, that's too bad. I really hate to see things like that."

"Everyone does, Peter. But the company is like a ship's crew. We have to pull together, if we're going to get where we want to go."

A ship's crew. Torrey wouldn't know a ship's crew if they shoved an anchor up his ass. "When does this happen?"

"It already has. Bob left Friday afternoon."

That was another Whitechapel technique Peter was familiar with. Get yourself into trouble and they cut you out of here like a cancer. Tough shit for Carpenter, but that meant the door to the group job was wide open. He looked at Torrey expectantly.

The vice president cleared his throat. "So we're assigning a new group product manager."

He felt his gut muscles tighten.

"As of this morning, Marilyn Farnsworth is taking over Carpenter's responsibilities."

Peter was staggered. It was as if Torrey had suddenly slugged him. *Marilyn Farnsworth?* The bubbleheaded bitch who ran the personal products group? It couldn't be true. Jesus Christ—*it couldn't be.*

Torrey was watching him closely. "She's done a super job with her brands. Moderne is way up. I don't know whether you've noticed, but it's gaining share points even faster than Tynex."

Sure it was. In a lousy category not one-twentieth the size of analgesics, where Tynex competed. Moderne. A feminine deodorant. A goddamn pussy perfume. He was all but overwhelmed by disappointment and anger, but he kept his features carefully composed.

64

"You'll be reporting to her, of course. And I know we can count on you to give her all the support she needs."

He took a deep breath. "Of course you can, Rick. I'll do my best to bring her up to speed on this category."

The jab went right past Torrey, who stood up and smiled broadly. "Good, Peter, good. I knew you'd come through. There'll be a memo going around a little later."

He went back to his own office, his belly churning, and sat down at his desk. He noticed his hands were shaking and picked up a SAMI deck, just to keep them occupied. The tables were a meaningless jumble to him, but he stared at them intently.

Son of a bitch. So this was the reward he'd earned? This was the thanks Whitechapel had for him after he'd turned a brand around against damn near impossible odds? He'd made the fucking company millions of dollars and this was what they thought of him?

Marilyn Farnsworth—good God. Of all the developments he had tried to anticipate, the possibility of Farnsworth taking over the analgesics group was one that had never occurred to him. As far as he could see, she was just another dipshit female, put in charge of personal products only because the brands were used by women—an assortment of junk designed to overcome the stink of armpits or crotch or to relieve menstrual cramps. So how had she brought this off? Did she and Torrey have something going? Were they meeting in a hotel at lunchtime, or before Torrey caught the 7:06 for Westport?

An antique dagger lay on Peter's desk. He'd bought it years ago in a shop on Second Avenue to use as a letter opener. He picked it up now and gently touched the point with his forefinger. His anger was no longer hot, but colder than ice—a frozen mass deep inside him. So Farnsworth had been moving behind his back? How stupid of her to think she could outmaneuver him. To his surprise, a drop of blood appeared on his finger. But he felt no pain. He put the dagger down and left his office.

Whitechapel was in full swing now. The area was filled with energetic, determined people, members of one of the best marketing organizations in the proprietary drug industry. Peter walked quickly and purposefully, nodding to many of them as he moved along. At the south end of the floor he turned right, hearing the rapid soft clicking of the computer keyboards and the hum of the laser printers, sensing the pace and the tension of the company.

Halfway along the corridor he came to her office. The door was open. He knocked once and walked in, a pleasant smile on his face. "Hi, Marilyn."

10

FARNSWORTH wasn't ugly, exactly. In fact, she was far from it. Her face was a little horsey, but most people would probably find it reasonably attractive, nevertheless. She dressed well, her taste running to skirts and blouses that were on the severe side, most likely to help her project an image of competence in a man's business world. And her body was trim, albeit without much in the way of curves. But to Peter Barrows, with her tightly wound brown hair and her harsh mouth and her dark eyes that held no hint of feminine warmth, she was repulsive.

She looked up. "Oh, good morning, Peter."

"I hear congratulations are in order."

"Thanks. I didn't realize you—"

"Rick spoke to me about it. Wanted to know what I thought. I said it was a damned smart move. Women do the actual purchasing of over sixty percent of all the Tynex sold."

"Yes, I saw that in the reading I did over the weekend."

"So it'll be good to have your point of view."

"Well, I'm delighted, of course. And I think you've done a fine job. Those Nielsens look great."

"Uh-huh. If there's anything I can help you with, just ask."

She folded her hands. "When's the next meeting with the agency?"

"This morning, as a matter of fact. Eleven o'clock."

"Good. They coming here?"

"Yes."

"What's the subject?"

"Why, ah, we'll be going over some new commercials before we start production."

"Okay. I'll look forward to it."

He wanted to ask why she didn't keep her fucking nose out of things until she had some idea of what was going on, but he didn't. Instead he went back to his own office, his resentment even deeper than it had been earlier. He kept busy with the pile on his desk until Evelyn told him the people from Jarvis & Cullen had arrived, and then he went into the conference room.

The account supervisor from J&C was Jock McLean, a senior vp. He was what Peter considered a standard agency type, well-dressed and smooth. With him was the creative director, an intense, bushy-haired character named Marty Krakaur, and the account executive on Tynex, Bill Phillips. Phillips was young and agreeable, a Wharton MBA. Peter usually treated him as a servant.

When they were all assembled, he was startled to hear McLean launch into a congratulatory speech to Farnsworth. Peter had been about to announce the news of her promotion himself, and it galled him that the agency knew all about it. That had to be the result of McLean keeping his nose up Rick Torrey's ass at all times.

"We think it's wonderful," McLean said. "Especially with your track record on the personal products brands, Marilyn. This should be the start of a whole new thrust for Tynex, and we're very excited about it. So from all of us at J&C, our best wishes."

A whole new thrust for Tynex? With the brand taking off, thanks to Peter's management, they were now going to have a whole new thrust? He ought to thrust the conference table down this shitwit's throat.

McLean then asked Krakaur to review the proposed set of commercials. The creative director got to his feet and held up the storyboards one at a time, explaining the action and reading the copy. The situation in each was a slice of life, involving dialogue between two people, the headache sufferer and the sympathetic friend who recommended Tynex. There were four commercials, and Peter knew the production costs would be close to a half million dollars.

He was surprised that Krakaur seemed nervous, the jerk. They'd gone over the damned boards a dozen times, making revisions in the copy, changing one of the principal roles from a storekeeper to a truck driver on advice from research, adjusting countless details. So what was there to be uptight about? He looked around the table, his gaze fixing on Marilyn Farnsworth. That's what it was. First meeting with the new lady honcho.

Krakaur stumbled along, interrupted from time to time by questions from Farnsworth, many of which were fielded by McLean or Phillips. Peter remained quiet with some effort. Goddamn it, they were playing entirely to her, as if he weren't even there. As the discussion continued, he found it difficult to concentrate on what was being said. His anger was like a swarm of hornets, not knowing which one of these fools to sting. Farnsworth, the arrogant slut? McLean and his pussy-lickers?

"What do you think, Marilyn?" McLean asked, when Krakaur had finished.

The agency men leaned forward, so as not to miss a word.

She frowned. "To tell you the truth, I'm concerned. For one thing, I don't think there's much originality in this stuff. It's workmanlike, but there must be a million slice commercials on the air these days."

Peter couldn't believe it. She was damning work that had taken weeks to prepare.

There was a moment's silence. McLean broke it, his tone unctuous. "Frankly, Marilyn, we've had some of the same reservations ourselves." He glanced at Barrows. "That's not to take anything away from the help Peter has given us.

69

But Marty and our creative people have felt somewhat restricted in all this. They've had to force-fit everything into what they consider a cliché format."

Peter's eyes widened. *Cliché format?* The miserable bastard. Last week McLean had been falling all over himself with enthusiasm for the new advertising, praising Barrows for his direction. Now suddenly the stuff was no good. And the crap about the creative people being *restricted* and having to *force-fit* their ideas left no doubt as to where the responsibility lay. McLean had reversed direction so fast he was running up his own asshole.

Farnsworth nodded. "I'm glad you recognize the problem. Any new Tynex advertising has to be nothing less than outstanding."

There was a chorus of agreement from the agency men.

She addressed the creative director. "Don't you feel we could do better?"

Krakaur was no fool. "Sure. A unique creative idea would give us more punch."

Farnsworth zeroed in. "Then how about taking another shot at it?"

"No problem at all," Krakaur said. "We'd welcome the opportunity."

"Wonderful." She turned to Peter. "And there'd be no problem on our end, would there?"

"What? No, no problem." He looked down at the table. The others went on talking, but Peter didn't hear. The agency would go along with whatever she wanted, no matter what. It was infuriating. But after all, how could you blame them? They were desperately anxious to protect their miserable little jobs, eager to do anything that would please this monstrous whore who now controlled them. She was the one who had done this to him. By destroying his work, she'd stripped him naked before the others, made him out to be an ineffectual fool. Christ, how they'd be laughing at him.

He glanced up. Farnsworth was gone. In her place Freda was sitting, the familiar narrow eyes mocking, the thin lips twisted in a sneer. Looking at her, he could feel a current of hatred passing between them, as palpable as a river of blue sparks. And with that came an equally familiar sensation, one of fear. The room grew cold, and he shuddered. He wanted to get out, to run away from here and find a place to hide.

"Peter?" It was McLean.

"Yes?"

"I said we'll get back with new boards in just a few days."

"Fine. That'll be fine." He blinked, looking around the table. Freda was gone, Farnsworth was back in place. Suddenly his face felt hot.

McLean smiled. "Terrific. I think we'll do some great work."

Peter nodded. "Of course you will. And there's something I want all of you to know."

They looked at him expectantly.

"You can be sure I'll do my part."

THE reception room of the Farrelli Model Agency was full of women. They sprawled in the chairs, their black vinyl portfolio cases nearby, waiting to see Matthew Farrelli or one of his assistants. They were dressed in jeans and sweaters or windbreakers and most of them had tied up their hair in scarves or wore slouch hats. But despite their sloppiness it was obvious that they were young and slim and pretty. All of them had long legs.

When she walked into the reception room, Margot Dennis was dressed casually herself, but her idea of casual was different from the others. She was wearing a light skirt and a box-cut jacket of crushed linen with the sleeves pushed up.

The receptionist smiled as she approached the desk. "Hi, Margot. Matt's busy at the moment."

"Hello, Beryl. Somebody with him?"

"No, but he's on the—"

Margot didn't wait to hear more. She walked through the door into the office area, where a half dozen more women were working at desks piled high with photographs and brochures and head sheets. All of them were talking on telephones, booking models, juggling shoots, answering queries from photographers and art directors. The Farrelli Agency was not one of the larger ones in New York, but it represented a number of the better-known people, including a select few top models, and it was always busy. Margot stepped through the cluttered space to Matthew Farrelli's office and entered, shutting the door behind her.

Farrelli was also on the telephone. His office was even

messier than the outer work area, with portfolios and stacks of photographs on the black leather sofa and the chairs as well as covering the surface of his desk. His jacket had been tossed over the back of the sofa, and he was working in an elegant pale blue shirt. Heavy gold links gleamed from the cuffs. He would have been well suited to working in front of a camera himself. His features were strongly masculine under a mass of thick black hair, and his teeth had been expertly capped. From his end of the conversation he seemed to be involved in solving a problem for somebody who was trying to arrange a shoot in Majorca. But at the same time he was holding a sheet of 35-mm transparencies up to the light and squinting at them. When he caught sight of Margot he dropped the transparencies onto the pile in front of him and indicated the nearest chair, smiling and silently mouthing a hello.

Margot picked up the junk off the seat and added it to the heap on his desk, then sat down. She had known him for a long time, since the days when he had first started his agency by pirating a couple of girls from another model house.

He put the phone down. "Hey, Margot. How are you, babe?"

"I'm all right, Matt. How are you?"

"Fine." He leaned over and kissed her mouth lightly. "You look terrific. Jeez, it's great to see you."

"If seeing me makes you so happy, why haven't you returned my phone calls?"

He waved at the heap on his desk. "I tried a couple times, but then I've been so goddamn busy you wouldn't believe it."

"Oh, I believe it. At least I believe you haven't had time for me."

"I always got time for you, Margot. Tell you what." he gripped both her wrists. "I'll lock the door, tell Beryl no

73

phone calls, and we'll do a couple lines of coke. Then we'll go over on the couch and screw. Okay?"

Margot laughed in spite of herself. "You're too much, Matthew."

"What more could I do, babe? I mean, how much more of me could I give?"

"You can save yourself for the kids outside. What I want from you is work."

He frowned. "You know it's not up to me, Margot. Hell, I talk you up every chance I get. But I can't force somebody to book you. Either they think you're right for something or they don't."

"So maybe I should change my image."

"Yeah. Maybe you should."

"Are you serious?"

He rubbed his jaw. "Margot, it wouldn't be such a bad idea. You know I don't bullshit you, don't you?"

"Not too often, Matthew. What are you getting at?"

"What I'm getting at is, you have to go where the opportunities are. What everybody wants now is not your type. They want kids. Teenagers."

God. This was the same speech she'd heard from Jean Sandoval. "It's a little late for plastic surgery."

"Who said anything about that? I'm just suggesting maybe you should try a different approach."

"Such as?"

He chewed his lip for a moment. "I get a lot of calls from agencies wanting housewives. All-American dames who look like they could have a couple kids and live in a little house in the suburbs. You know what I'm saying? They're not glamorous, they're real. The models who do that stuff get detergent commercials and oven-cleaner commercials and products like that. Why? Because the broads at home looking at TV say to themselves, yeah—she knows what

7 4

it's like to wash all that goddamn laundry and scrub the oven. I believe her."

Margot held up a hand. "Hold it right there, Matthew. An actress I'm not. The only commercials I've ever done, I just had to look pretty."

"How the hell do you know you couldn't do it, if you never tried?"

"I don't know. But it would be like starting over again."

"What's wrong with that? Maybe we put you into a whole new market, okay?"

"At this point I'll take any market I can get. I was saying to a friend of mine it could be good for me to work with a new photographer, too. Somebody with different ideas."

"Sure, maybe work up a book along those lines. Meantime, I'll give it some more thought, too." The phone rang and he answered it.

Her visit was over. Margot waved as she left, but he didn't notice.

Back out on the street she hailed a taxi. When she'd given the driver her address she sat back on the seat and thought over what Farrelli had said. A housewife? That was a laugh. But then Jean Sandoval's proposition came back into her mind and she felt a faint twinge of disgust. Maybe the agent's idea wasn't so crazy, at that. But what a set of choices. A housewife . . . or a hooker.

12

THE suspect stank of urine and vomit and rancid sweat. He was about twenty-five years old, but he looked sixty. His face was gaunt, his body emaciated. He sat slumped in the chair beside Joe Kurwitz's desk, with his nose dripping and his eyes rolling back in his head. The sleeves of his shirt had been pushed up, revealing the punctured and scabbed flesh of his forearms. Kurwitz and a detective named O'Brien sat watching him, looking bored, while Ed Flynn hovered in the background.

Kurwitz tapped a forefinger on his desk. "Listen, Harry. Why don't you tell us about it, and I'll help you out. You give us a statement, I'll give you a fix. It's as simple as that. Why should you have to go on suffering, feeling bad? All we want is a couple words and you got it, see?"

The man in the chair made no response.

Kurwitz went on: "Hey. You know you hit that woman, and we know it, too. Maybe you didn't mean to, huh? She came in the store, you got excited, made a mistake. Why don't you tell us about it?"

The suspect shook his head and drops of moisture flew from his nose and his chin. "No. Can't do that."

Joe was patient. "Sure you can. You will, sooner or later, so why not make it easy on yourself? You give us a little speech, I give you some of the best shit you ever had." He reached into a drawer of the desk and took out a small glassine bag filled with white powder, holding it up for Harry to see. He placed the bag in the center of the desk. "Come on now, Harry, what do you say?"

Ben stood leaning against the doorway of his office,

watching the scene as he would a rat caught in a trap, waiting for the creature to be put out of its misery. The junkie was the guy they'd been hunting in the Liebold case. Kurwitz and O'Brien had brought him in a couple of hours earlier, just after Ben had returned from his visit to Dr. Stein. When they read him *Miranda* the guy kept nodding off, but the cops couldn't have cared less. It wouldn't be long now. The suspect was staring at the bag, his face twitching, his hands clasping, the drops falling from his chin.

"Hey man," O'Brien said to him, "Why don't you get smart?" The detective was wiry and thin-faced, a tough Irishman who liked to lean on people. "You don't start talking pretty soon, we put you in the cage for tonight, forget all about you. That what you want?"

Ben yawned and headed down the hall for the bunk-room, where the coffee urn was. The phone had quieted down a little by now. The media had made a lot of noise about the discovery of the latest body, and two men in his squad had been catching on the hot line all day. They were still getting calls, but nowhere near the volume they'd had earlier. Most of the calls had been well-intentioned but worthless. Some of the others had been from pranksters, a few had been from people who thought they saw an opportunity to stick it to a neighbor they had it in for, and a few more had been from straight-out nutballs. Maybe 10 percent would merit a rundown, and Ben had his doubts about the value of those. But you couldn't afford to over-look anything. Tedium went with the Job.

As he poured himself a cup he wondered how many he'd drunk since this morning. One of these days the stuff would eat its way through his gut and he'd squirt coffee like a rusted-out radiator. Christ, what a habit.

He sat down at the table and turned on the small TV, intending to catch the ten o'clock news on WPIC. He was curious as to how they'd handle the story, and hoping that somehow they wouldn't use the shot of him being questioned by the reporter. As an independent station, WPIC couldn't compete with the networks for coverage of the world news. For that they bought footage from the news services and more or less highlighted the day's top stories. The local action was where they did their digging, and the more bizarre the subjects the better. To them, this case was a bonanza.

When the story came on, the anchorman announced that they had a sensational exclusive on the latest Greenwich Village Murder, as well as a stunning new development. Cut to Sarah Weston standing in front of the green fence on Thirteenth Street, looking beautiful but businesslike with her honey-colored hair and her green eyes and her pin-striped suit. Not ten seconds into it, she was interviewing Tolliver in a tight close-up. Ben had to admit he came off like a first-class asshole.

After that was a shot of the body being loaded into the ambulance, and then they cut away to Weston live in the studio. She had changed suits—something gray, this time—but her delivery was the same, as if she was taking you inside the most important event since Hiroshima.

Weston: "As yet the latest homicide victim remains unidentified, but she appeared to have been in her early twenties, with blond hair and blue eyes. She was five feet five inches tall, and weighed one hundred fifteen pounds. Like the others, she had been sexually attacked and died of a broken neck. And now, here is that stunning new development we promised you. Today this reporter received a photograph of the victim that is sure to have an important bearing on the case. At the very least, it may help us to learn who she was. And it also may provide a direct link to the killer."

Ben was pop-eyed. What the fuck was this?

Weston: "The photograph is very unusual. But there is no doubt that the young woman is the same pretty blonde whose dead body was found this morning on Thirteenth Street, wrapped only in a black plastic garbage bag. We're going to show it to you, in the hope that someone may recognize her, or may know who took the photograph. But I must warn you that she is nude, which some viewers may find offensive."

Offensive? Jesus, Ben thought, deliver us. Every voyeur in New York would be breaking his balls for a look at it. Along with everybody who passed for normal in this whacked-out city.

Weston milked it: "Those of you with young children may not want them to see this photo. You may wish to send them out of the room while it's being shown."

Will you show the goddamn picture?

Weston: "But because of its great significance, we feel it is our duty to show it to you."

At that point they cut to a full-screen close-up of the photograph. And the sight of it rocked him. Ben moved in until he was only a couple of inches away, trying to peer into the fuzzy, half-focused image to get a better look. But unclear or not, he could see it well enough to be blown away.

The thing was so goddamn *weird*. There was the whiteness of it—from the girl's skin to the background, as if she were some ghostlike creature floating in white, even her hair nearly the same pale shade. And the lollipop. An obscene splash of purple, dangling between her legs. Her face was even stranger. The eyes were glazed, as if she were on something—crack, maybe. And the tip of her tongue was showing, just as it had been when—Oh, Christ, *it couldn't be*. And yet—

Weston was speaking over the shot. "We have no idea who sent this to me, or who took it. But we can draw some

79

conclusions and make some conjectures. For one, it's obvious that the photographer has a powerful creative talent. No matter how you may feel about it, there's no question that this is a brilliantly conceived photograph. In fact, you can be sure that many critics would call it a masterful piece of work."

Cut back to Weston on camera: "What's more, if the photographer is indeed the Greenwich Village murderer, it's equally obvious that he is a man of considerable intelligence. Which may offer some insight into why he hasn't been apprehended. If anything, he's probably someone who right now is laughing at the clumsy efforts of the police. This is Sarah Weston, reporting to you from the WPIC newsroom in New York. You have just seen our exclusive report on the latest developments in one of the most bizarre murder cases in modern times."

As soon as it was over, Ben ran back to his office and grabbed a telephone. It took him several minutes to get the station's switchboard to answer, and several more to get through to the newsroom. Then he had to dodge some crap about how Miss Weston was busy and would call him back. When he finally got her on the line, he told her to stay put—he'd be there to talk to her as soon as he could get uptown.

Back in the squad room the suspect had begun to cry. His shoulders shook, and his face contorted as tears mingled with the sweat and the snot. Kurwitz and O'Brien and Flynn were watching, their expressions indifferent. O'Brien was smoking a cigarette. He blew a smoke ring toward the junkie. Ben turned the corner and bounded down the stairs.

13

THE ten o'clock news was near the windup each night at WPIC. After that the station ran a movie that was usually both ancient and shitty, and when that ended it went dead until 6:00 A.M. By the time Ben walked into the newsroom, it was empty except for a few stragglers on their way out, leaving behind them desktops littered with papers and Styrofoam coffee containers. Sarah Weston was sitting at one of the desks, working on a word processor.

She looked up as he approached, green eyes appraising him. She smiled. "Good evening, Lieutenant."

"Hello, Miss Weston. There someplace we can talk?"

"How about right here?"

"Where's your producer?"

"Gone for the night."

"And the head of the news department?"

"Also left."

Sure, Ben thought, as soon as they heard I was coming. He pulled over a chair from a neighboring desk and sat down. "That picture you showed on the air tonight. Where did you get it?"

"As I said, it was sent to me."

"Who by?"

"As I also said, I don't know."

"How did you know it was the girl whose body was found this morning?"

She hesitated. "I got a look at her before the ambulance took her away."

His first reaction was to ask how the hell she had pulled

that off, but he bit his tongue. It wasn't the major issue, by a long shot. "How was the photo sent?"

"I have no idea. It was in an envelope on my desk when I got back from editing this afternoon."

He made a mental note to check the station's mailroom, see if anybody might know who had made the delivery. "You have the envelope?"

"Yes." She picked up an 8½-by-11-inch gray envelope off a pile of papers and handed it to him. Her name was on the front in block capital letters, crudely printed in black marker. Under that was the word PERSONAL. And nothing more.

Ben looked it over, holding it by one corner on the unlikely chance the lab might find a worthwhile fingerprint. Other than those of Sarah Weston and God only knew how many other people here who could have handled it.

He put the envelope down. "Where's the photograph?"

She opened a manila folder and withdrew an eight-by-ten, passing it over without a word.

Christ. The thing was even stranger than when he'd seen it on the tube. And the suspicion he'd had then was confirmed now. Looking at her face in the picture, he was sure, as sure as he'd been that morning when he crouched over the garbage bag and saw those blue eyes for the first time. The girl in the photo was *dead*. Iced. Off. Gone. She hadn't said cheese and she hadn't looked at the birdie. When the shutter had clicked, she was already out of it. Forever.

With conviction came another realization. Except for the bodies themselves—and the bites on them—this was the first time in all these months he'd had anything like a piece of hard evidence the cops might follow. The guy who shot this was almost surely the killer. Unless this was part of some mad ritual—the work of a pack like the one Manson had sent to carve up Sharon Tate and her friends. That was a possibility, of course. But Ben doubted it. Cop's instinct, experience, or whatever, it just didn't fit. No. This had been done by one guy. Somebody who was a highly skilled photographer. And somebody who was probably very much like the creep Stein had described. In fact, a lot of what the shrink had conjectured could fit this. Find him, Ben thought, and you've got your boy.

He looked up to see the reporter watching him closely. "You have any idea who she might be?"

"No."

"Ever seen her before—in person or in a photograph?"

She shook her head. "No, never."

He wondered if she suspected what the girl's condition had been when the photo was shot. "Her expression look odd to you?"

Weston shrugged. "Maybe on drugs, or drunk."

"Uh-huh. Any other ideas?"

"Like what?"

"Like the picture itself. Does it make you think of anything?"

She looked at it again. "A lot of things, actually. It's sort of . . . sexy, in a way. But mostly it's like some kind of peculiar dream."

He tried another tack. "Does it remind you of anybody's work—some photographer whose stuff you might have seen?"

"No. I've never seen anything like this."

"I'll want to take the picture with me, and the envelope."

"All right."

He asked for a folder to put them in and she handed him one. Ben put the envelope and the photograph into the folder and then a thought occurred to him. "This the original?"

Again she hesitated. But this time she made no reply.

"So it isn't. Where is it?"

"I have it."

"Yeah. And I need it." He withdrew the print from the folder and put it back on her desk. "We'll trade. You can keep this one."

She put her hand on his arm. "Lieutenant, be reasonable. The photograph is my property. It was sent to me. I have no objection to giving you a copy—I even had this one made for you. Anticipating you'd want it. But the original belongs to me."

He kept his patience. "And what you have to realize is that this photograph is evidence, material to a murder investigation. Which I'm in charge of. Now hand it over."

"I do realize that, Ben. Believe me, I do. Is it okay if I call you Ben?"

"Sure." He noticed she still had hold of his arm. Her hand was warm, and so was the tone of her voice.

She leaned closer. "But I want you to understand my position, as well. This case is the hottest news story in New York. And not just because it's so lurid, either, I mean with the sex part of it and all. The big thing is that women are scared out of their wits. You know, this city is dangerous enough as it is, somebody always getting raped or mugged, but here you have a real monster attacking women and killing them. So people are not just fascinated, they're also terrified."

She was telling him this? "Yeah, I'm aware."

The expression in the green eyes was very sincere. "I try hard to be a good reporter. I feel I have a great responsibility to the public to do that. And for some reason, the guy picked me to send this picture to. So of course I feel a deep personal involvement. And a commitment, too. You can understand that, can't you?"

"Yes, I can." What he understood was that she saw herself right in the middle of it now, part of the action. Of all the TV news hustlers, *she* was the one who'd been chosen to receive the photo. *She* was the one who'd had the exclusive, showing it on the air. And so now she was seeing this case as her Big Break. The direct route from newshen on a local station to a network shot if she played it right. The next Diane Sawyer. But stay cool, he reminded himself. Experience had taught him a long time ago that the media could not only be obstructive, they could also cause you more trouble than you could lift. Everybody from the PC on down to a rookie patrolman knew that. Just as they knew that if the press said shit, His Honor himself would go into a deep squat.

He spoke gently. "Look. I want to have the original analyzed. I want to know if the lab has an angle on tracing it to whoever shot it. Paper, chemicals, whatever. Just might be some latents on it, too."

"I see."

"You realize I could get a court order signed in less than an hour, forcing you to turn it over." He couldn't; it would take all goddamn day tomorrow. But she wouldn't know that.

Weston thought about it. "Okay, but listen. Why don't we try to help each other? Of course I'll give you the original. But let's cooperate, okay?"

"What do you have in mind?"

"If I get anything else, I'll contact you right away. Anything you need that I can help you with, you've got it."

So there's the quid, he thought. Now let's get to the pro quo. "And in return?"

"You could give me stuff. Not attributed, of course. Just let me know what's going on."

"Uh-huh."

"And when you find out who she is, I get an exclusive interview."

"You know I can't promise that. NYPD regulations. Has to be given out to everybody at the same time."

"That's not what I was talking about. I meant with you."

"Oh, Jesus."

"Well?"

"Maybe not right then, but I'll see what I can do."

She opened a drawer and took out another print of the photograph, handing it to him.

He knew at a glance this was it; the colors were sharper and it had better definition. Otherwise it was identical to the copy. He studied it for a few seconds, then slid it into the folder and got to his feet. "Okay, Sarah, thanks. And remember, anything else at all, you call me first."

She also stood up, moving close enough for her breasts to brush against him. The green eyes held him in a steady gaze. "And you'll remember to call me too, okay?"

"Yeah. Good night, Sarah."

"Good night, Ben."

He turned and headed for the door. He'd been around determined females before, women who got their way no matter what it took. But he had a feeling Sarah Weston was something else again.

14

HE was higher than he'd ever been, higher than he'd ever hoped to be. From abject misery he'd gone to the top of the universe in one dizzying rocket ride. His anger was still there, blackened and charred raw from the humiliation Torrey and Farnsworth and the others had caused him, but somehow it was suspended, as if encased in Lucite. Whatever it was, he couldn't feel it, because there was no room in his nervous system now for anything but euphoria. His photograph—his brilliant, beautiful, bittersweet work of art—had been held up for countless people to see and admire. How much better that was than having it in a museum, or in a showing at some gallery.

Television had *presented* it. To all those people. With a commentary! For the first time, the public had come to know the talent he possessed, the spark that set him aside from ordinary human beings. They'd seen it with their own eyes. They'd seen it in the composition, the use of contrasting color, the ethereal setting. And most of all, in the *concept*. With its sly humor, and its insight into what that agglomeration of female cells was really all about, captured as only he could.

The photographer has a powerful creative talent, the commentator had said. *The photograph was brilliantly conceived. Critics would call it a masterful piece of work. By someone who was laughing at the clumsy efforts of the police.*

Marvelous!

And now this triumph belonged to him forever. Sitting in front of the television set in his bedroom, he punched the rewind on the VCR. He had no idea how many times he'd seen the tape, but each time he had experienced sexual pleasure almost as intense as on the night he'd made the photograph. Maybe even *more* intense, only different.

He hit the play button, and although he'd thought he was drained, he felt the excitement begin again. There was the anchorman and then Sarah Weston and then that simpleton of a detective who looked like a cowboy and then *there it was*. He stopped the frame. His hand closed around his penis, and he was up, up, and away.

15

BELLEVUE was a fifteen-minute trip from the Sixth Precinct station house. Ben cut across Fourteenth Street to the East Side and then drove north on First Avenue. He had a slight hangover and he was bleary-eyed from lack of sleep, but he knew he could forget about living a normal life until they broke this case.

Not that there was anything very normal about the way he lived anyway. Life was the Job. The rare good times consisted of getting loaded, usually with other cops. His relationships with women rarely went beyond one-night stands, and when they did, they never lasted more than a week or two. As the saying went, love was a four-letter word.

But hung over or not, he was feeling pretty good this morning. At least he had something to go on, something concrete for the first time since the first of the bodies had turned up all those months ago. He'd raised enough hell with the lab to get copies of the photograph rushed through, and he had a stack of them with him now. He'd also spoken to Stein, telling him he'd send one of the copies right away. The shrink had said that taking the photograph fit the profile, as Ben had expected him to. He'd promised to call after he'd had a chance to study the shot. Meantime Ben would see to it that his men got started on running down every photographer in New York. And every model agency and everyone else who just might have information on the girl or the photographer or both.

He glanced at his watch. He was late, damn it. He put his foot down and made himself concentrate on his driving.

A truck cut in front of him, and Ben hit his horn. The driver gave him the finger.

Bellevue Hospital was in the huge complex of medical buildings that ran from Twenty-third Street to Thirty-fourth, bordering the East River. The Veterans Administration Hospital was to the south, the NYU Medical Center to the north, Bellevue in the center. He pulled through the gate into an area reserved for official vehicles and parked the Ford, taking one of the photographs with him.

The morgue was in the hospital basement. He went down the steps and into the refrigerated air, walking along corridors formed by rows of stainless steel boxes, his footsteps echoing from the tiled floors. Bodies not yet consigned to metal containers lay face up on trays, tags hanging from big toes. Some of the corpses were covered with sheets, but many were not. They were of all ages and colors, male and female, some unmarked, some with massive wounds. To Ben they looked less like people than like store dummies. One of them was a young man whose heavy muscles seemed merely at rest, his hands crossed comfortably over his belly, his features unblemished except for a small blue hole in the center of his forehead. The cold air carried an odor of antiseptic chemicals and dampness and decay.

A uniformed patrolman stood outside the double doors of the autopsy room. Ben showed the cop his shield and went inside. There was a row of tables in the room, equipped with sinks and hoses. The body of the blonde lay on one of the tables, split open from throat to crotch. Her face had been peeled down and lay inside-out over her jaw, revealing her bare skull. A two-man team in white coats was working on her, and there were two onlookers. Ben recognized one of them as Dr. Brody, the forensic odontologist who was an authority on human bites. The other guy was a cop. Ed Feldman looked up and waved a scalpel in greeting as Ben approached. "Welcome to the party, Lieutenant."

"How's it going, Ed?"

"It's beautiful. One of my best performances. I'm only sorry you missed some of it."

Ben would just as soon have missed all of it. He hated this bizarre place, where what had once been human beings were now pieces of meat in a butcher shop. He nodded to the cop and shook hands with Brody. "Thanks for coming, Doc."

The dentist was gray-haired but vigorous, his eyes bright behind metal-rimmed glasses. He wore a conservative brown suit. "Glad to be of assistance, Lieutenant. Call me anytime."

Ben watched in silence as Feldman resumed his work. The blonde seemed even more vulnerable now than when he had first seen her. Her ribs had been clamped open, and stood away from her body. As Feldman removed each organ from the yawning abdominal cavity he weighed it on a scale, and then examined it on the table, recording his findings by speaking into a microphone that hung from overhead. His assistant brought a circular saw to the top of her skull and made an incision, the blade whining as it cut into the bone.

The medical examiner turned to Ben and grinned. "I was right, you know."

"About what?"

"Their little love affair. She sucked him off and then he broke her neck. Maybe she did a lousy job. Cause of death, upper cervical transverse necrotizing myelopathy, resulting in cardiac arrest. Afterward he bit her in the ass, as a further expression of his dissatisfaction. We got residue of his semen and saliva both. One from her mouth, the other from her tush. My hunch is the blood type'll be A, just like the others. And we'll also have his DNA. But you'll get all that in the lab report. Soon as we take out some of her brain we'll flip her over, so the doc here can look at the bites."

"Get anything else?" Ben asked.

"No. There was nothing worthwhile under her fingernails and no fibers on her skin or in her hair."

"And the CSU got no fingerprints off the garbage bag."

"Feldman gestured with his scalpel. "Funny, isn't it?"

"What?"

"The guy could be such a nutcake, go completely berserk, and then be so careful about tidying up."

"Yeah." Ben looked at the gaping hole in her torso. "What was in her stomach?"

"Spaghetti," Feldman said. "With red clam sauce. And a tossed green salad, oil and vinegar. A little garlic bread, a couple glasses of Chianti. Lovely." He brought his fingers close to his mouth and kissed the air, flipping the fingers open. "Makes you hungry just to hear about it, doesn't it?"

"Not quite. She eat anything else?"

Feldman beamed. "Only that little mouthful for dessert, and she never even got to swallow it."

Ben exhaled. He should have known better. "Okay. Time of death?"

"Like I thought, Friday night around midnight."

"And the meal?"

Feldman shrugged. "Couple hours earlier, I would say. With that soft stuff, it's hard to tell." He brightened. "Give me a steak, a good rugged piece of steer meat, and I could really nail it down for you. But earlier that evening, for sure. And anyhow, that figures, doesn't it? Some candlelight, nice music, the wine—no wonder she went down on him."

"How about the bites?"

"Directly after death. Wait a minute and we'll show you."

The ME turned back to the body and sliced into the brain with his scalpel, cutting out a section of the cerebrum.

When Feldman and his assistant had finished their work, they put the girl's ribs back into place and turned the body over. Some of the bites were on the lower back and thighs, but most of them were on her buttocks. Many of them overlapped, leaving a mass of torn flesh. A few, however, had made a clean pattern, with each impression as sharply defined as on a dental chart. There was blood in the wounds, dried and black, and dark smears of it on her skin.

Brody moved in for a closer look. "Different, this time."

"We noticed," Ben said. "There's more of them, and they're worse."

"Not only that, but they were made differently."

That was unexpected. "In what way?"

"He got more of her flesh into his mouth." Brody pointed. "Look here. You can see there were as many as twenty teeth in each bite. Some of them molars."

"Back teeth."

"Right. He literally crammed her flesh into his jaws. And these tears in her skin at the edges of the wounds. They're the result of the biter pulling his head back while his teeth were clamped onto her. To maintain his grip, he had to exert great pressure. Something around a thousand pounds per square inch. From the look of the tears, I'd say he pulled in one direction and then another, and then let go and bit her again."

An image came into Ben's mind of a man crouched over the girl's body, gripping her buttocks in his jaws, his head swinging from side to side. Wolves did that, and bears.

Brody placed a black case on the table. He opened it and took out a jar of plaster powder and calipers and other pieces of equipment.

"No question, is there, Doc?" Ben asked. "That it's the same guy?"

93

"No, I don't think so. I'll make casts and match them with the other impressions, but I think we'll find it was definitely the same man."

As Brody went on with his work, Ben took Feldman aside. "There's one other thing, Ed." He handed him the photograph he'd brought with him.

Feldman looked at it. "This the picture was on TV last night?"

"Yes. Did you see it?"

"No, but I heard about it. She's our sweetheart, all right. Man, this thing is freaky."

"Uh-huh. What else?"

The ME looked at the print again, and then at Tolliver. "She's dead. I mean, she was dead when this was taken."

"I thought so, too. You sure?"

"Yeah, I'm sure. Gravity drained the blood out of her face. That's why she's so pale. Also the eyes. See how the pupils are dilated?"

"Yes."

"So the guy's a photographer."

"Could be."

"He must be some spook. A rape killing, the bites, then a picture. And I thought I'd seen everything. Still no ID, huh?"

"No. But maybe the photo will help."

"Maybe it will." Feldman took one more look before handing back the photograph. "I wonder what the others look like."

"Other what?"

"Pictures. You don't think this is the first one he took, do you?"

"No," Ben said. "I don't."

16

WHEN he got back to the Sixth, Ben found several reporters in the squad room. He ignored their yapping and went into his office, Flynn following. He told the sergeant to promise them a statement later in the day and then get them out. Also to put the area off-limits to anybody not on official police business. As Flynn started to leave, Ben asked him if they'd got a statement from the junkie suspect in the Liebold case.

Flynn looked sheepish. "No."

"No? What the hell do you mean, no?"

"Last night he was, uh—out of it. Then this morning his scumbag lawyer came in screaming we didn't have probable cause. We couldn't hold him."

Ben expelled a stream of air. Before he could say more, Flynn ducked back into the squad room.

Goddamn it, Ben thought. That means we start all over again. The evidence on the suspect had been paper-thin, and there had been no witnesses. Everything had depended on a confession. Now what they had was nothing. And if the woman died, they'd be faced with another unsolved homicide.

He sat down at his desk and saw that somebody had dropped off a copy of that morning's *Daily News*. There was the photo, all over the front page.

MURDERED BLONDE IN TV PIC, the headline read.

There wasn't much question how they'd got it so fast. Little Miss Weston had to be hustling this one for all she was worth. Ben flipped the paper open and there was a shot of her with a three-column story headlined TV RE-

95

PORTER AIRS PHOTO OF LATEST GREENWICH VILLAGE MURDER VICTIM.

He was halfway through the piece when the phone rang. The caller was Captain Michael Brennan, who asked him what the fuck was this picture. Ben told him what had happened with Weston, and when he finished, Brennan sounded as if he was having a shit fit.

"Are you telling me that goddamn picture was the same girl?"

"It appears to be."

"Then the perpetrator took it?"

"That's a pretty good bet, Captain."

"Christ. What are you doing to check it out?"

"We're going after the film labs first."

"And then what?"

"And then any other angle we can come up with."

Brennan said the heat was really on the cops now. He'd had his ass reamed by Chief of Detectives Anthony Galupo, who'd had his reamed by the PC, who'd had his reamed by the mayor.

So now it's my turn, Ben thought. And what's really bothering him the most is the exposure. The NYPD was being made to look like a troop of assholes with TV putting the spotlight on them. More than anything else, that was what was driving the brass batshit. He told Brennan they'd be running down photographers and model agencies and film processors, and Brennan said to call him as soon as they had anything on the girl. Ben said he would and hung up.

Five minutes later Frank Petrusky walked into the office. "Ben, we got a witness."

"Who? Where?"

Petrusky was sweating. He wiped his bald head with a handkerchief and dropped into a chair, flipping open his notebook. "She's an old lady. Name is Koppel, Bessie Koppel. Her house is catty-corner across the street, southeast from the site. She lives alone on the third floor."

"Okay, go."

"She says on Friday night, sometime after midnight, she saw a car stop in front of the fence around the site. She can't sleep too good, she says, on account of her arthritis. So a lot of the time at night she sits up, and if she gets bored or she hasn't got anything to read, she looks out the window."

"Yeah. So?"

Petrusky glanced at his notes. "So the street was quiet, one or two people walking on the sidewalk. She noticed this car park there, a station wagon. The lights went out, but nobody got out. At least, not right away."

"Waiting for the sidewalk to clear."

"I would say so, yeah. And from what she can remember, only a few cars went by. Then after a couple minutes, a guy got out of the driver's seat and went around to the rear of the wagon."

"Description?"

"She couldn't see him too well at that distance. The street lights weren't very bright, and her eyes are getting weak. But he seemed like a young guy because he moved quick. And she thought he had on a windbreaker."

A slight sensation passed through Ben's chest. A young guy, wearing a windbreaker. He could almost see him. "Hair color?"

"Not sure, but she thought it was dark."

"She notice anything else about him?"

"No, that was it."

"Then what?"

"He opened the back of the wagon and pulled out a big bundle. It looked to her like maybe it was a rolled-up rug. He put it over his shoulder and carried it to the fence around the construction. She says it seemed like it was heavy. He heaved it over the fence and then he got back in his car and drove away."

"You check the height of that fence?"

Petrusky again consulted his notes. "Seven feet six inches."

"Okay. And?"

"That's everything she could remember. Says she didn't think much about it at the time."

The fucking public, Ben thought. Always so helpful. "What about when she found out the bundle was the dead body of a girl? She must have noticed all the cops and the commotion around the construction site. And then there was the story on TV and in the papers. And the picture on WPIC. Why didn't she contact us?"

"Says she was afraid."

"And yet when you went to her apartment, she told you all about it."

Petrusky grinned. "It's the way I have with broads, Lou. Even old ones."

"So what did you do then—give her a jump, just to be nice?"

"Not me."

Ben was quiet for a few moments. "How about the station wagon?"

"Nothing much. She don't know anything about makes. She thought it was a dark color. She has no idea of the license plate. Not even what state."

"That's it?"

"Yeah."

So now the guy had taken on some definite form. As Stein had theorized, he was young. And he had a way of moving quickly. And he drove a station wagon. Which could have been stolen, of course. But at least that's what he'd been driving Friday night. Ben looked at Petrusky. "You tell the old lady to stay put?"

"Yes. But she's not going anyplace. Her arthritis is so bad she can hardly walk."

"Okay. Get an artist over there to work with her, do a sketch of the guy."

"Sure. Right away."

The phone rang. Ben picked it up. "Lieutenant Tolliver."

"Kurwitz, Lou."

"Yeah."

"We got an ID on the girl."

"What happened?"

"Her roommate came home from a long weekend. She saw the *Daily News* and flipped out. She called 911 and they called us. I'm with her now. Flynn was out and you were at Bellevue. I got right up here."

"The roommate sure?"

"Says she's positive."

Ben told him to stay where he was, that he'd get there as soon as he could. He took down the address and hung up.

Petrusky again wiped sweat from his head. "ID?"

"Yeah. Kurwitz says from her roommate."

"Looks like things are starting to pop."

Ben stood up. "I sure as hell hope so."

17

THE building was one of the newer ones on the Upper East Side, a glitzy tower with a fountain in front of it, just off Lexington Avenue. The lobby was done in maroon and gold, including the uniform of the doorman. Ben flashed his shield at the guy and stepped into an elevator. When he got to the apartment and buzzed, Kurwitz opened the door.

Joe motioned him into a small foyer, inclining his head toward the room behind him and speaking in low tones. "She says her roommate's name was Danvers. Ellen Danvers. Her name is Carol Patterson. I been talking to her for over an hour, but she's been leading me around in circles. At first I figured she was just kind of hysterical at finding out her roommate was murdered, but now I think it's more than that. She says she don't know anything about Danvers' social life, which has to be bullshit. She's covering something, but I don't know what."

Ben nodded and stepped into the living room. A young woman was sitting on a sofa, dabbing her eyes with a sodden wad of Kleenex. She was wearing a wrinkled, light-blue cotton suit, and her brown hair was in disarray. She would have been fairly attractive, even pretty, but crying hadn't improved her any. He glanced around, taking in the cheap modern furniture: two chairs matching the sofa in tan upholstery and ugliness, a coffee table littered with dirty plates and glasses and an overflowing ashtray, a TV on a mobile cart. Scattered about the floor were an open suitcase filled with women's clothing, and a copy of the *Daily News* with the photograph of the blonde on the front page.

Ben pulled one of the chairs close to the sofa and sat down on it. "I'm Lieutenant Tolliver, Miss Patterson. I'm really sorry to put you through this, but I'd appreciate any help you can give us."

She met his gaze, her expression sullen. "I told him," she gestured toward Kurwitz with her head, "everything I could."

Ben's tone was friendly and understanding. "Sure. But I'd like to hear it from you directly, if you don't mind."

She nodded.

"Your roommate's name was Ellen Danvers, is that right?"

"Yes."

"What happened?"

"I was away for the weekend. When I got back I saw the newspaper and there was her picture. At first I couldn't believe it. But then I took a good look and I was sure it was Ellen." Her shoulders shook and she jammed the Kleenex against her mouth.

Ben picked up the copy of the *News*. "Who took this picture, do you know?"

"I have no idea."

"Was Ellen a model?"

"No."

"She know any photographers?"

"I don't know."

"Ever mention one, or talk about modeling, or photography?"

"She talked about modeling a few times, but just in a general way. She never actually did anything about it."

"When was the last time you saw her?"

"Friday morning, when she left for work."

He wanted to get her talking, to loosen her up. "How long have you roomed together?"

"Two years."

"How did you meet?"

"We worked in the same office."

"Which office?"

"Stellman and Black. Insurance brokers."

He took no notes. Kurwitz would be doing that, picking up anything he hadn't gotten earlier. "Are you with that company now?"

"Yes."

"What's your job?"

"Secretary."

"Was Miss Danvers still there?"

"No."

"Where did she work after she left?"

"She was with an architectural firm."

"Name of the company?"

"Parnell, Rabin and Williams."

"What was her job there?"

"Secretary."

"How about her boyfriends—who were they?"

"I don't know."

Kurwitz was right. Anything they got, they'd have to drag out of her. "Maybe I should check with the doorman, see who her visitors were."

Her eyes flickered. "That isn't necessary. She, uh—had one friend I know of."

"Who is that?"

"He—his name is Howard Hennessey."

"What was his relationship with Miss Danvers?"

"They were just friends."

"Where does Mr. Hennessey work?"

"He's with the Wachtel Company."

"What type of business?"

"Investment banking."

"How good a friend was he of Miss Danvers?"

"I don't know."

"Uh-huh. Where did you go, over this past weekend?"

"Is that important?"

"Everything is important. Or could be. Where were you?"

"At a place in the Poconos."

"Which place?"

"It's called The Pines. It's a resort hotel."

"Did you go with somebody?"

Her mouth tightened. "Look, Lieutenant, what does my personal life have to do with it?"

"I don't know. Maybe nothing. But your roommate was murdered. So I'm going to ask you anything I think might help us. Now who were you with?"

"His name is Barry Kessler."

"And where does he work?"

She hesitated. "He's with—Stellman and Black."

"Your company."

"Yes."

"Is he married?'

Her tone softened. "Yes."

He looked around the room. A luxury apartment in an expensive building, but cheaply furnished. "Nice place you have here."

Her eyes narrowed, accenting the puffiness.

"How much is the rent?"

She made no reply.

He leaned forward a little. "Listen. Everything I ask you I can get the answers to, one way or another. You cooperate, it'll make things easier for everybody, including you. Understand?"

She was motionless for a moment, then her head bobbed once.

"Okay. Now what's the rent?"

"Three thousand a month."

"That's fifteen hundred apiece, and you were both working as secretaries."

A small white rim appeared around her mouth as the muscles contracted.

"So maybe you get some help. Say, from Mr. Kessler?"

The look she gave him could have burned a hole in his face.

"And how about your roommate? Was she getting some help too?"

"I have no idea."

"You ought to give your memory a jog about a few things. I'm going to talk to Kessler, you know. Maybe in his office, or maybe at his home. Where Mrs. Kessler lives."

She looked startled. "Lieutenant, I'll tell you anything I can. But do you have to drag Barry into it? I mean, he hardly knew Ellen, except to say hello to."

"Let me put it this way, Miss Patterson. I can be discreet, or I can be the biggest pain in the ass you ever met. Cooperate, and you get the discreet version."

She dabbed at her eyes. "The other half of the rent was paid by Howard Hennessey. That is, he gave Ellen the money."

"Hennessey is also married, I assume."

"Yes."

"How often did she see him?"

"A couple of times a week."

"Ever on weekends?"

"Maybe once or twice. Mostly it was on weeknights. Weekends he was with his family."

"Same as Kessler, right?"

She didn't reply.

"How'd Kessler cover going off with you this past weekend, by the way? What'd he tell his wife?"

Again she gave him the burning look, but she answered the question. "He told her he was going to a sales meeting."

"At The Pines?"

"Yes."

"Did he call her from there?"

She opened her mouth to protest, then changed her mind. "Yes. Once. On Sunday."

"Okay. Now let's talk about Howard Hennessey. Tell me what you know about him. His job, background, and so on."

As he had intended, she seemed so relieved to get off the subject of Barry Kessler, the words came pouring out of her. "He's about fifty. Vice president at Wachtel. Lives in Connecticut, in Darien. He's got two kids, both in college. He was real nice to Ellen, gave her a lot of presents and stuff."

"What did they do, when they were together?"

She looked at him questioningly.

"I mean, how would they spend a typical evening?"

"Oh. They'd go out to dinner, early. He'd meet her somewhere. Maybe Tre Scalini or Giambelli's, someplace like that. Then they'd come back here."

"Did he stay over?"

"No. Afterward he went home."

And told his wife he'd been working late, Ben thought. Jesus, honey—the workload in that damned company is unbelievable. "What did you do, when they were here?"

"Went out."

"And she did the same thing when you were seeing Kessler?"

"Yes."

"Was she dating anybody else?"

"No. That is, not for a long time. A year, at least."

"But before that?"

"Before that she used to, once in a while. But Howard didn't like it. So she cut it out. From then on she wasn't seeing anybody but him."

"Would you say they had any problems between them?"

She was emphatic. "No. They got along great. He used to talk about leaving his wife to marry her, but she knew that was crap."

"Did it bother her?"

"Yeah. She really cared a lot about Howard."

"Was she having any other problems, that you know about?"

"Like what?"

"Like anything. Any trouble at work, or were there any former boyfriends who didn't like it because she wasn't seeing them anymore?"

She thought about it. "No former boyfriends that she was still in touch with. At least she never mentioned anything like that. She didn't get along with one of her bosses very well, though."

"Who was that?"

"The office manager. Ellen said she was an old maid who gave everybody a bad time."

"Anything else?"

"Not that I know of. Really."

"Where did Miss Danvers come from?"

"Bellwood, Michigan. She used to say nobody ever heard of it, not even the people in Michigan."

"Family?"

"Some. Her father was dead, and her mother was married to somebody else. She had an older brother who was killed in Vietnam. I think she had some cousins somewhere."

"What brought her to New York?"

She shrugged. "I guess she thought it would be exciting to live here. She was kind of naive about things."

"Such as?"

"Men, life, a lot of things. But oh, God—who would want to do that to her? It's just so horrible." She dissolved into a fit of sobbing.

Ben waited for her to get herself back together.

She shook her head. "Ellen was such a nice girl."

"I'm sure she was."

"Much prettier than that awful newspaper picture. I mean beautiful, even. She had long blond hair, and big blue eyes. People used to tell her she ought to be a model. But like I said, she never did anything about it."

"Would you have any idea where that picture might have come from?"

"No. When I saw it I just couldn't believe it."

"You have any other pictures of her?"

"I think so. Wait a minute." She got up and left the room. When Ben saw her walk, he understood why this Kessler character would spring for fifteen hundred a month, just for her half of the rent. There would have been plenty of extras on top of that. Kessler probably figured he had a bargain.

Ben looked over at Kurwitz, who was sitting on a hassock in the far corner of the room, an open notebook on his lap. Joe had a sour look on his face, which Ben understood. He'd be pissed that Patterson had opened up for the lieutenant after he hadn't been able to get anything out of her himself.

She returned a minute later with a couple of cardboard-mounted prints and handed them to Ben. They were cheap color portraits, their subject stiff and unnatural and the hues duller than they should have been. But he could see what Patterson had meant. Alive, Ellen Danvers had been a knockout. He contrasted these images with the bizarre shot he'd first seen on TV. And with the ones he had seen on West Thirteenth Street and in the autopsy room at

Bellevue: a girl whose eyes were glazed and whose skin was bluish white and whose mouth was full of dried come. And in Bellevue her face had been turned inside-out and the top of her skull had been missing.

Ben looked up at Patterson. "May I borrow one of these?"

"Yes, of course."

"You'll get a receipt for it. Do you happen to have Ellen's mother's phone number? We'll want to notify her."

"No, I don't."

"Okay, we'll get it." He stood up. "Thanks for all your help, Miss Patterson. We'll be talking to you again. Don't go anywhere without letting us know your whereabouts. And don't discuss the case with anyone. You may be called as a material witness, when the time comes."

"Is that all?"

"Not quite. Detective Kurwitz here is going to take you down to Bellevue. We want you to make a positive identification."

She grimaced. "Oh, God."

Yeah, Ben thought, I know what you mean. He told Kurwitz he'd see him later and left the apartment.

On the corner near the entrance of the building there was a public telephone with a Manhattan directory chained to the glass and steel enclosure. Ben flipped through the directory until he found a listing for the Wachtel Company. It was on Third Avenue, only a few blocks from where he stood. He went back to where he'd parked the Ford and took out an envelope containing the photo of the girl he now knew had been Ellen Danvers. He slipped the portraits Carol Patterson had given him in along with the photo and headed for Third Avenue.

18

THE receptionist was café au lait, with dark eyes and a wide mouth. She displayed dazzling white teeth and asked Tolliver if she could help him. He told her his name and showed her his shield, saying he wanted to see Mr. Howard Hennessey. The girl picked up a telephone and spoke into it briefly, then hung up. "Mr. Hennessey is in conference. Did you have an appointment?"

"Was that Mr. Hennessey's secretary you spoke to?"

"Yes, it was."

"Call her back and tell her to get Mr. Hennessey out of his conference. This is official police business. Either he comes out, or I go in."

She did as she was told, her eyes never leaving his as she spoke again into the phone. There was a pause, and then she put the phone down. "Miss Kirk will be right out to take you into his office."

Ben thanked her and she flashed her teeth again. He realized something was passing between them, as it sometimes did when a girl sensed cop power. To some of them it had a macho smell all its own. He wondered briefly if he shouldn't ask her out for a drink later, but then he thought better of it. She was probably living with some seven-foot motherfucker who played for the Knicks.

Miss Kirk appeared and asked him to follow her. As he did, Ben decided Hennessey followed the rule of not dipping his pen into the company inkwell. Not this inkwell, anyway; Miss Kirk was at least sixty and looked a lot like George Washington. She opened a door and said to make himself comfortable, Mr. Hennessey would be with him shortly.

The office was spacious, furnished in rosewood and squashy brown leather. Behind the desk was a bookcase that ran the length of the wall under the windows, the upper surface displaying a dozen photographs in silver frames. There were group shots and kid shots, pictures taken on beaches and golf courses and on a wide lawn with a large colonial house in the background. Hennessey's children were big, athletic-looking boys with wide-open faces. There were also photos of an attractive woman who might have been in her forties. Quite the family man, Ben thought. He had a picture of everyone he loved. With the exception of Ellen Danvers.

A voice boomed behind him. "Yes sir, sorry to keep you waiting."

Ben turned to see a tall, ruggedly handsome man with iron gray hair. He seemed to be the hearty sales executive type, maybe a one-time jock. His grip was firm, and he looked you straight in the eye.

"Sit down, Lieutenant. What can I do for you?" Hennessey was in his shirtsleeves, and as he moved behind his desk to take his seat, Ben noticed that his gut was flat. A jogger, probably, as well as a golfer, proud that he was in good shape. All part of the youthful image he had of himself, the virile male who kept a twenty-three-year-old girlfriend.

Ben stayed on his feet, returning Hennessey's steady gaze. Interrogation was a lot like street-fighting; your best chance was to give the guy a hard shot before he could get set. "Last Friday night Ellen Danvers was murdered. What do you know about it?"

He was right. Hennessey looked as if he'd been slugged in the solar plexus. His jaw dropped, and he bent over his desk as the air went out of his lungs. He said nothing for several seconds, and then began sputtering. "Ellen Danvers? Murdered? I don't—Friday night. I don't know anything about it. Are you sure it was, uh—"

"Mr. Hennessey, you had a girlfriend named Ellen Danvers, is that correct?"

His eyes shifted. "I, uh—know an Ellen Danvers, yes."

Ben took the portrait out of the envelope and laid it on the desk. "Is this Ellen Danvers?"

Hennessey's face had turned a pasty color. He looked at the portrait. "Yes. It's Ellen."

Ben took out the photograph that had been sent to WPIC and placed it alongside the portrait. "And this?"

Again the big man's jaw dropped. "Wha—where did this—"

"Well, is it? Is this Ellen Danvers?"

"I think so. It—looks like her."

"You'd know, wouldn't you? After all, you knew Ellen well enough to pay her rent, right?"

Hennessey's expression turned instantly from shock to fear. Ben knew what was going through his mind; the guy figured if the cops had that much, they probably knew everything there was to know about his relationship with the girl. He had gone from man-in-charge to shit-scared in an eye blink. He straightened up. "Lieutenant, I don't know anything about a murder. I was in Connecticut from the middle of Friday afternoon right through until Monday morning. I played golf at my club on Friday and got home around six-thirty. We had some friends in for dinner and they stayed till about one o'clock."

"Where do you live, Mr. Hennessey?"

"Three-ten Dogwood Lane, in Darien."

"And what are your friends' names?"

"Billings. Tom and Jane Billings. But how far does this have to go? I mean, I know you have to question me, but I wouldn't want to have other people get mixed up in it."

111

Ben gave him a hard stare. "You want to prove where you were on Friday night, don't you?"

Hennessey sat back in his chair slowly, his face revealing that a whole new line of thought had come into his mind. "Maybe I should call my lawyer."

"You can do that, if you want to."

He clasped his hands in front of him. "Look, I'm a married man. I'll tell you anything you want to know, if you'll keep this as low-key as possible."

Everybody wants to make a deal, Ben thought. "This is a homicide investigation, Mr. Hennessey. I can't promise you anything."

"Will the newspapers get hold of this?"

"Of your involvement, you mean?"

"I told you, I was not involved."

"You were involved with Ellen Danvers, weren't you? What would you call it?"

"I'm sorry. This is a hell of a shock. I'm sure you can understand that. I meant, would the newspapers get my name?"

"Not from me. But that doesn't mean they might not get it from some other source. When was the last time you saw Danvers?"

"It was, ah—last Wednesday night."

"Tell me about it."

"We had dinner at Scarlatti's. Then we, uh, went back to her apartment. I left about eleven and caught a train to Darien."

"What did you do in her apartment?"

Hennessey swallowed. "We went to bed."

"Which you've been doing for about two years, is that correct?"

"I—yes. Lieutenant, what happened? To Ellen?"

So now he was finally showing some concern about that. "Her body was found in a construction site on West Thirteenth Street on Monday morning. Her neck had been broken."

Hennessey looked as if he'd taken another punch in the belly. "That's horrible."

"Yes."

"Do you have any idea who did it?"

Ben said nothing, continuing to hold Hennessey in an unwavering stare.

The big man licked his lips. "I swear to God I don't know anything about this. She was a nice kid. She didn't have much money, and I agreed to help her with her rent."

"Sure. Was that her suggestion, or yours?"

"Why, it was mine, I guess."

"How serious a relationship was it?"

Hennessey seemed to relax, just a touch. "Oh, not very. I mean, you know." He tried a smile, one guy talking to another about broads. "We were just friends."

Ben kept his expression stony. "Balls. You told her you wanted to marry her."

Hennessey's mouth popped open. "But I didn't mean it. That is—"

"Yeah. You were just stringing her along, is that right?"

Tiny beads of moisture appeared on Hennessey's upper lip.

Ben let him cook in it for a few seconds. He wanted this middle-aged, red-hot lover to be afraid to so much as bend the truth, let alone lie. "Who were her other friends? Other men beside you?"

"Other men?"

"That's right—when you weren't fucking her, who was?"

"Lieutenant, I honestly believe she wasn't seeing anyone but me, and that she hadn't for about a year."

"And before that?"

"There were some others, yes. But I don't know who any of them were."

Ben tried another direction. "What were her interests, what did she like to do?"

"Well, she liked to go out to dinner."

"How about the theatre, or the clubs?"

"Uh, yes. Once in a while."

"But not very often, is that right?"

"No. Not very often."

"Because all you wanted was a few drinks, some food, and a piece of ass. Correct?"

The drops on Hennessey's lip grew larger. He wiped them away with a forefinger.

"What did she do when you weren't around? At night, for example. Or on weekends?"

Hennessey thought about it. "I think she went to the movies pretty often."

"What else?"

"Art galleries. She liked to go to the Museum of Modern Art. And the Guggenheim. And there's a private one on Lex not far from her place. I bought a couple of prints for her there."

"That's nice. You bought her a lot of presents, I suppose. Jewelry, clothes, stuff like that?"

"I gave her a few things, yes."

"And you told her you'd marry her, didn't you?"

"I told her I wanted to, but we never got down to making any definite plans."

"She pressure you? Tell you she'd go to Mrs. Hennessey, if you didn't live up to your promise?"

"No, nothing like that. I told you, I never promised to marry her. We just talked about it."

This guy was a prize, Ben decided. Captain Bullshit. He looked around the office, at the heavy furniture and the drapes and the view south through the windows behind Hennessey. He could see the Pan Am building looming up

114

over Park, and to the left the Chrysler building. "You're a vice president of this company, I understand."

"Yes, I am." There was a twitch in the flesh beside Hennessey's nose. The question had sent his mind down another road, as Ben had wanted it to. He'd be thinking now of his salary and his stock and his profit-sharing trust, and the perks he enjoyed, not to mention a fat expense account. The expense account would have come in handy for writing off all those intimate little dinners in the nice restaurants Ellen Danvers liked so much.

Ben pointed to the photograph of Danvers nude. "Who took this picture?"

"I have no idea. Believe me, I don't. It's—"

"It's what?"

"It's just so unlike her. I mean, to be doing something like that."

"And you can't think of anything she might have said, anything you know about, that might relate to this picture?"

"No. Nothing."

Ben picked up the photograph and the framed portrait and put them back into the envelope. "I want you to think over our discussion. Anything comes into your mind that might help our investigation, I want you to make notes about it. Then call me."

"Yes sir, Lieutenant, I will."

"Tolliver, Sixth Precinct."

"Right, I've got that."

Miss Kirk led him back out to the reception room. The girl at the desk looked even better than she had on the way in. And her smile was a notch wider. He said goodbye and, as he passed her, she handed him a folded piece of paper. He stuck it into his shirt pocket without looking at it and headed out the doors toward the elevator.

There was a bar a couple of blocks down, on the west

side of Third. Ben went in and climbed onto a stool. It was cool and dark inside and there was a TV at one end where a couple of guys were watching the Mets kick the shit out of Cincinnati at Shea. He ordered a draft beer and took a long swallow, thinking about what he had learned.

Howard Hennessey was an asshole. But he almost certainly wasn't a murderer. Ben tried to work out a scenario in which Danvers had put the squeeze on Hennessey to marry her. Hennessey had then hired somebody to kill her and dump the body. But it wouldn't fly.

He finished his beer and ordered another, even though he knew he should be getting back to the Sixth. When the bartender put it in front of him he thought about the receptionist at Wachtel. He pulled out the slip of paper she'd given him and squinted at it in the dim light. Written in a looping hand was *Sandra 643–1761*.

What the hell, he thought. So it shouldn't be a total loss. He shoved the paper back into his pocket. Maybe he'd give her a call sometime, when they got this goddamn case put away.

If they ever did.

19

FARNSWORTH was tapping a pencil on the surface of her desk, a habit Peter found annoying. Her thin lips were tightly compressed, as if thinking took a great deal of physical effort. She was wearing a mannish gray jacket, and with her brown hair wrapped close to her skull, she looked even more like a caricature of a Prussian officer than usual.

She glanced over at him. "You know what the trouble is? The damned agency doesn't study the data. They go through the motions, but they don't really analyze. They don't dig deep enough."

They should, he thought. They should dig a deep pit and heave you into it, you arrogant bitch. But he kept his voice steady. "What is it you want them to do?"

She continued to tap the pencil, as if to emphasize her words. "I told you, I want them to analyze the marketing opportunity. Look—women do most of the actual purchasing of Tynex, right?"

He seemed to remember calling that fact to her attention himself. "That's right."

"So wouldn't it be logical to design the advertising to appeal to women?"

"Yes, but one of the—"

"And yet they keep screwing around with all this male-oriented crap. The commercials are full of men. The store clerk, the coach—all men. That's stupid."

It was a struggle to remain calm. "Perhaps we should tell them to work up some ideas involving women."

"Exactly. Maybe even a woman spokesperson. You know

what research shows. Women are likelier to trust advice from women than they are from men."

He stood up. "I'll get them going on it right away."

"Good. And light a fire, will you? Agencies are very good at spouting bullshit about how eager they are to show you their exciting new ideas, but if you don't raise hell, they take forever."

"Sure. Will do." By the time he got back to his office he could hardly see. His head ached and his heart was pounding. He sat down at his desk and picked up the letter opener, then slammed it down again.

Goddamn it. Taking orders from her was bad enough, but having her treat him like some mailboy was unbearable. It was worse than humiliating, it was infuriating. And her objective was so absolutely clear. She was trying to emasculate him, trying to destroy the best young marketing executive Whitechapel had.

This shit about putting women in Tynex advertising. What an idiotic idea. Sure, women bought the product. But it was men who influenced brand choice. He ought to tell the dumb slut *she* was the one who wasn't thinking it through. But no—that would draw him straight into her trap.

Again he forced himself to settle down. He took deep breaths until he was sure he could control his voice, and then he picked up the phone and called Jock McLean at Jarvis & Cullen.

The account supervisor's tone was warm and friendly, full of his standard phony jocularity. "How you doing, Peter—is there something I can help you with?"

"As a matter of fact there is, Jock. I've been looking over the research, and I think it could be a good idea to put more emphasis on women in the advertising."

"Oh? that's interesting."

"Yes. Maybe even a female spokesperson."

"Uh-huh. What does Marilyn think?"

God. What McLean was really asking was whether he had Marilyn's permission. The prick. But Peter responded smoothly. "She thinks it's a great idea."

"I see. Well, I'm sure we could work up something along those lines."

"Let's get right on it, Jock. I'll want to see boards in a hurry."

"Okay, Peter. Right away."

He hung up and sat back in his chair. Having to deal with this was disgusting. But whoever said life was easy? And besides, *one* part of his life was fantastic. What would Farnsworth and McLean and the rest of these shitbirds think if they knew *everything* about him? That not only was he an outstanding marketing executive, but that his creative brilliance had knocked this city on its ass. Wouldn't *that* stun a few people. He smiled as he imagined the incredulous expressions on their dull faces.

He looked at his watch. Twelve-twenty. A jolt of excitement coursed through him, building as he thought about what he was going to do. He put on his jacket and buzzed Evelyn, telling her he was going out to lunch. Then he picked up his attaché case and hurried out of his office.

Park Avenue was crowded with people enjoying the warm spring sunshine. Peter moved quickly among the throngs, crossing Forty-second Street and cutting through Grand Central and the Pan Am building. He continued north on Park and turned right at Forty-eighth Street, heading for the Inter-Continental Hotel.

There was a men's room in the lobby, just to the right of the main entrance. He went inside and ducked into a stall, locking the door behind him. Placing his case on the toilet seat, he took off his jacket and tie and hung them on the hook on the door. Then he opened the case. Inside were two cameras, a Mamiyaflex and a Nikon F. He took

119

them out and slung both around his neck by their leather straps. There was also a pair of sunglasses in the case, which he put on. Next he took out a wide leather shoulder strap and snapped it onto metal rings on the case. Then he stuffed his jacket and tie into the case and closed it.

On his way out of the men's room he unbuttoned his shirt collar and stopped to check his reflection in the mirror, smiling at what he saw. A man was standing at one of the urinals, and another was washing his hands at a sink. Neither of them so much as glanced at him.

Back outside on the street, a transformation had taken place. The well-tailored young executive who had entered was now a photographer, apparently on his way to or from an assignment. If he'd been carrying just one camera, he might have been a tourist, but the heavy pair of them hanging from his neck, along with the equipment case with the strap over his shoulder, marked him unmistakably as a professional. He walked east on Forty-eighth Street, turning left when he reached Lexington Avenue.

Lex was also crowded, even more than Park had been, partly because its sidewalks were so much narrower. Peter moved along at a steady pace, not hurrying, just taking his time. He paid no attention to the men he passed, nor to the older women. But he carefully gauged each of the girls.

Most of them were dogs. Overweight. Or too skinny. Sloppy. Ugly. Pimples. Flat-chested. Or with tits that sagged like pillows. Jesus, that one looked like a ferret. So many were chewing gum, jaws working, mouths open. Now there was a horror—wearing white lipstick. And look at that one—a chimpanzee in a red dress. It was enough to make you puke, except that at the same time it was so funny, in a bizarre way. Why did all the fat-assed ones wear jeans? They looked like sausages stuffed into too-small casings, waddling along. And the appalling dumbness. You could see it in their eyes, vacant, dull, stupid. It was like a carnival midway he had been to as a kid. Some of the freaks had been up on platforms in front of the tents, but at the time it had seemed to him you could see more of them strolling along in the crowds. Here they were all strolling.

And yet every so often, at intervals of perhaps every fifteenth or twentieth girl he passed, he'd spot something halfway decent. Nothing really great, but better than the rest. Usually it was a matter of her having one or two good features: a pretty face, or nice tits, or beautiful hair, or well-turned legs. It wasn't until he'd walked about ten blocks that he saw one who really had it all together.

She was standing in front of a store window, looking in at a display of shoes. Tall, slim but shapely, with chestnut hair that tumbled to her shoulders. Wearing a gray skirt and a blue sweater over a white blouse. Not bad. Not bad at all. Peter eased in alongside her, pretending to look into the window, taking care not to get too near.

Now that he could examine her at close range, he decided she was a very good candidate. Pretty enough to believe his approach could be for real, which was vital. Homely girls, or girls who were patently nothing out of the ordinary, would never take the bait. Not that he would want them to, or that he would even hold it out to them. No, a girl had to be well above average, somehow special. Not only were those the ones who were worth the effort, but they were also the ones who would take him seriously. They were the ones who would consider it possible. They would believe him because they *wanted* to believe.

He moved closer. "Excuse me."

She glanced up, her eyes narrowing with suspicion while she made an instant appraisal. If there was any city where a girl had to be careful, it was this one. She took in his pleasant smile, his courteous manner, the cameras. "Yes?"

"Are you a model?"

Something registered. There was a flicker in her blue

eyes, and her neutral expression changed almost imperceptibly. But Peter noticed; he'd seen that reaction before. She shook her head. "No, I'm not."

"Oh. Sorry, I thought I recognized you. You look very much like somebody I've worked with."

She glanced at his cameras again. "You're a photographer?"

"Yeah, I've got a shoot just up the street a ways." He shook his head. "Funny, you look so much like this gal. She's with Zoli." It was beautiful. A left-handed pitch that was so subtle it rarely failed. Flattery that didn't seem like flattery at all. And the implication that he was on his way to work, just stopping to chat for a moment, was also disarming.

She relaxed, and smiled. Her teeth were white and even. "Some of my friends think I ought to model, but I've never done any. Always been too busy to look into it."

"Gee, you really should." He was very sincere. "There's always room for somebody new and fresh, and you've got some unusual qualities."

"Do you think so?"

He took off his sunglasses and looked at her face critically, first at her eyes and then deliberately shifting his attention to her mouth and after that to her hair. Finally he brought his gaze back to hers. "Yeah, I do. Great eyes, good bones. And your mouth gives you kind of a distinctive look. That's important, you know. See, the trouble is, too many models are so much alike. So we look for qualities that will work well on film, and also not be so run-of-the-mill."

"I see."

He put the glasses back on. "Well, nice talking to you, but I've got to get moving."

"What are you shooting?" It was apparent that she didn't want the conversation to end.

"It's a publicity thing. But most of my work is studio stuff on fashion. I do a lot of work for designers, here and in Paris."

She smiled again. "That must be nice."

He laughed. "Hey, you can't beat it. As a friend of mine says, imagine getting paid for living like that." He thrust out his hand. "My name's Bill Hewitt."

She shook the proffered hand. "Sue Connery."

He started to move away, and then seemingly as an after-thought reached into a trouser pocket and produced a card, *holding* it out to her. The card bore a printed inscription:

BILL HEWITT
PHOTOGRAPHY
Studio: 115 West 14th Street
New York, N.Y. 10011   Tel: (212) 675–2414

She took the card from him and read it.

"Listen, Sue. If you ever want to do some test shots— you know, put a portfolio together, I'd be glad to shoot them for you."

"Oh, gee. As I said, I've never done any modeling. But that's very nice of you. Do you really think it would be worth doing?"

"Hey, I'm in the business. You never know, of course, but I'd say you've got an awful lot going for you."

"Well, if it wouldn't be too much trouble for you—"

"No trouble at all. I've helped some very good people get started. Tell you what." He dug back into his pocket and pulled out the stub of a pencil, handing it to her. "Write down your name and phone number, and if I get some free time, I'll give you a call."

She carefully printed the information on the back of his card and returned the card to him, along with the pencil. Her smile was radiant.

He waved, and hurried on his way.

Bingo. It was so goddamned easy, when you played it right. And he had played her perfectly. Even getting her to give him back his card, so that she'd have nothing, but he'd have her name and number. She really was very good. Better even than he had thought when he first spotted her. Fine body, lovely hair and eyes, and best of all, a terrific smile. So she wanted to be a model? Wonderful. He would turn her into one, just like that. Because underneath that pretty surface, Sue Connery was no different from any other vain little bitch. Outwardly cool, sophisticated, self-composed and modest, and inwardly convinced that she was one of the world's great beauties, if only somebody would take the time to notice. Well. Peter Barrows had noticed.

He walked several blocks farther north before turning left and then left again. Back on Park, he headed down to the Waldorf. Two flags were flying high above the sidewalk in front of the hotel, one U.S., the other Japanese. The great rectangles of color extended from the building's gilded facade, billowing slowly in the breeze.

As he walked in and went up the stairs to the lobby, he wondered why the Japanese flag was on display. Honoring visitors from that country, he decided. Once again, no one paid any attention to him; photographers were a common sight in the hotel. He crossed the main reception area to a men's room and stepped inside.

Minutes later the same transformation that had occurred earlier had now taken place in reverse. The photographer was gone, and a well-dressed young executive carrying an attaché case skipped lightly down the main staircase and strode out onto Park Avenue, quickly disappearing into the stream of pedestrian traffic.

20

PETER spent most of the afternoon working on sales projections by territory, irritated by the sloppiness of the data the sales department had given him. The lazy bastards were nothing but order takers anyway, coasting along on the consumer demand his work had created for the brand. In the not too distant future the whole damned crowd of them would be replaced by a system in which chain buyers would do all their ordering by computer linkup to headquarters, and as far as he was concerned it couldn't happen soon enough.

By the time he got home it was a little past eight, and he was already itching to see the ten o'clock news. After glancing through his mail, he stripped and went into the shower, the needle-spray washing away the day's grime. When he had toweled dry he put on white cotton trousers and a loose white shirt and poured himself a Scotch on the rocks. He wasn't really hungry, but he got a steak out of the fridge anyway, broiled it, and made a salad and some garlic bread to round out the meal.

As he ate he fiddled with the Sony, flipping from one channel to another, aware that he was just killing time. Waiting made his nerves jump with excitement. This was what actors must feel, he thought, when they were about to see a film they were in. Or better still what a politician would experience, knowing there would be TV coverage of an important event involving him. When he had finished his dinner he put the dishes into the dishwasher and cleaned up the kitchen and then wandered around the apartment.

There was a new issue of *Cosmopolitan* on the coffee table in the living room. Kim Alexis was on the cover. The shot was by Francesco Scavullo, who had been doing all the *Cosmo* covers for years. It was a little harsh, he thought, but that was typical Scavullo. He riffled through the magazine, pausing to look at ads featuring Kelly Emberg and Jane Seymour. The photography wasn't bad, although he would have handled the lighting and the staging differently. Peter often bought women's magazines just to look at the ads and the fashion shots, amused by knowing he could have done better work.

And then at last his watch told him it was time for the news. He went into his bedroom and tuned the set in there to WPIC. He also turned on the VCR, in case the piece might be worth saving.

The opening in WPIC's news format used short clips of upcoming stories to hook viewers into watching the program. As he had hoped, one of the clips tonight featured Sarah Weston. But when she came on, what she had to say jolted him. The mystery blonde found murdered in Greenwich Village, she announced breathlessly, had been identified.

This was electrifying. He hadn't anticipated it, although it had to have been inevitable. What was unfolding was high drama, and he was a vital part of it. He leaned forward, eager to see the report.

But first he had to sit through a parade of idiotic commercials for house paint and dog food and one featuring some greaseball hawking frozen lasagna. After that came a story about new troubles in the Middle East and then one about a drug bust in Harlem and then more commercials. For God's sake—would they get on with it? Finally, there was Weston again.

She was wearing a pink blouse tonight, instead of the usual suit, and it was soft and feminine-looking and it contrasted nicely with her green eyes and her honey-colored hair. When she opened her mouth, his palms were wet.

Weston: "Today the beautiful blonde who was the latest victim of the Greenwich Village murderer was identified as Ellen Danvers, a twenty-three-year-old secretary with the architectural firm of Parnell, Rabin and Williams here in Manhattan."

Cut to a full-screen close-up of Danvers, in one of those awful photographic portraits that made the subject look like a painted dummy. Weston, voice over: "Alive, Ellen Danvers was a warm, vivacious, fun-loving girl, according to her roommate."

Cut to a shot of an ugly apartment building with a ridiculous fountain in front of it. Weston over: "They shared an apartment in this luxury building just off Lexington Avenue, not far from Bloomingdale's."

Cut back to Weston: "As they have been from the beginning, the police were unable to supply any information as to who might have murdered Ellen Danvers. Just as they still have no leads in the two earlier murders in this horrifying series of crimes. Here now is the scene today at the headquarters of the Sixth Precinct, where the investigation is being conducted."

Cut to a bunch of cops and detectives standing outside the precinct house in what appeared to be an impromtu press conference. The police were surrounded by media people poking cameras and yelling questions. Speaking for the cops was a detective who didn't look as if he'd be able to find his fly when he had to take a leak. Weston's voice-over said he was Detective Joseph Kurwitz.

Detective Kurwitz was obviously ill at ease. There were beads of sweat on his fat face, and from time to time he brushed back the few remaining wisps of hair on his head in a nervous gesture. As reporters fired questions he seemed increasingly flustered, responding with platitudes.

127

"Did Ellen have a boyfriend?"

"We are talking to everybody who knew her."

"Was there any connection between her and the other two murder victims?"

"We don't have information on that at this time."

"Who took that picture of her naked?"

"We are investigating that."

Peter grinned. This oaf would make a great character in a police comedy. Joseph Kurwitz and the Keystone Kops. Brought back by popular demand. Not one of the police appeared to own a brain. Peter thought he spotted the guy who'd been interviewed at the construction site, but he wasn't sure. He was hoping Weston would show the photograph again.

She did, but once again it wasn't what he'd expected. Cut to Weston: "So as the police grope and fumble, people everywhere are talking about the eerie photograph of Ellen Danvers that was sent to this reporter. We're going to show it again, with the warning that Miss Danvers is nude. But before we do, I know you'll be interested in hearing about a very disturbing reaction we've had from a number of viewers, some of them members of the medical profession. In their opinion—" Weston slowed her pace for dramatic effect "—when the photograph was made, Ellen Danvers was already . . . *dead*. Now, you be the judge."

Cut to the photograph.

Peter was shocked. Instead of the surge of sexual excitement he had experienced the first time it had been on the air, he felt let down, deflated. The photograph was as beautiful as ever, and every bit as powerful. But somehow Weston's comments had cheapened it. He half-heard her saying something about it having a *strangely surrealistic* quality. And how the image *stayed with you for a long time*.

Then it was gone, and Weston was back on camera. He focused on what she was saying: "So the mystery deepens.

What kind of man took that haunting picture? Is he the creative genius some people think? Is he the monster who raped and then destroyed lovely Ellen Danvers in a brutal attack? Is he both? Was Ellen Danvers indeed dead when the photograph was taken? As you've just seen, the police have no answers to any of these questions. But a lot of frightened citizens are praying that something will be done soon to prevent the occurrence of another of the terrible Greenwich Village murders. I'm Sarah Weston, reporting to you from WPIC-TV in New York."

Goddamn it.

Peter snapped off the set and stood up, trembling with anger and frustration. How dare she say those things? The fickle bitch. Describing him one minute as a creative genius, and the next as a monster. Suddenly much of it seemed tawdry to him, looking back. The TV coverage of the discovery of the body. All that crap about the garbage bag and the girl's broken neck. And now this absurd conjecture. What the hell difference did any of that make? The *photograph* was what was important. Did anyone care what pigments a painter used? Did they argue about where a sculptor's marble had been mined? Of course not. It was the artistry that counted. And nothing else.

He walked into his studio, still angry, but restless now as well—as if he were looking for something but didn't know what it was. On the table a pile of contact sheets and prints lay scattered about, all remnants of the shoot with the blonde. He picked up one of the prints and glanced at it briefly before tossing it down again. It was perhaps the best work he'd ever done—wasn't it? Suddenly, he wasn't so sure.

From there he went into the small room off the studio he used as a gallery and switched on the lights. Tiny spots recessed in the ceiling bathed the framed pictures on the walls in a soft glow. Looking up at the photographs, seeing

129

the faces in them, he again felt a sense of emptiness, of disappointment, as if this work in which he'd always taken such deep pride had suddenly crumbled to dust. He turned off the lights and left the room.

Continuing to wander aimlessly, he went into the living room. This was where he was always drawn sooner or later, the place where he found inspiration and at the same time a kind of peace. He sat down on the sofa and put his feet on the coffee table, letting his gaze drift over the black-and-white blowups on the walls.

She was just so damned *beautiful*. He'd always been disdainful of the girls he'd used as models, the stupid little pretenders whose looks never lived up to their egos, because he knew that in the end it was his talent that made the photographs what they were. Yet whenever he looked at these huge, grainy old photos, he couldn't help wondering what it would be like to have a model like her, to have a face like that to shoot. God, the mere thought of it made his flesh tingle.

But he didn't have her. And he never would. Not now, not tomorrow, not ever. Instead, he had to make do with what was at hand. And was that so terrible? He had his creative gifts, didn't he? Of course he did. And it was up to him to make the most of them.

Suddenly he knew what to do, knew precisely. It would be what any artist would do. He would create something better than anything he'd ever done before. Something so overpowering it would blow people away when they looked at it. He was already planning it, already thinking about the concept. He could actually see the photograph begin to take shape in his mind.

21

"THE product is Tynex," Farrelli said.

Margot frowned. "Like aspirin?"

"That's it."

She wasn't so sure about this, wasn't at all comfortable with the idea. When he'd called and told her to come to his office, that he had her up for something good, she hadn't known what to expect. And now here she was sitting with him and he was telling her that this big deal he'd dredged up was for some patent medicine. "What would I have to do in the commercial—get a headache?"

"Maybe. I don't know what the creative idea is. But what I do know is they're looking for a female spokesperson. And baby, that would be dynamite."

"Why—what's so great about that?"

He looked at her as if she had suddenly sprouted horns. "Are you kidding? Margot, listen to me. These products are all alike. There's the same shit in every brand, a couple cents' worth of chemicals. But the sales volume runs into the hundreds of millions of dollars. The only difference is in the advertising. Now do you get it?"

"What you're trying to tell me is they spend a lot of money."

"Ah, that's my girl. Believe me, they spend more than you could count. And like I said, what they want here is a *spokesperson*. We're not talking about just one commercial, but a whole campaign. And not only that, but the stuff is network. No spot. So if you get it, every time a commercial goes on the air, baboom! The goose shits you a big fat golden egg."

"Uh-huh, so who do I have to blow?"

He grinned. "As the producer said to the starlet, it ain't that easy. What they're doing is screening people on video-tape."

"Oh, God—a cattle call."

"Wrong. When the casting service called me, I told them about you, and then I sent a head sheet. They think you might be just right."

Her eyes narrowed. "What did you tell them?"

"The truth, sweetie. That even though you were very glamorous, you were a terrific actress and could come off absolutely natural."

Margot groaned.

"For Christ's sake, will you do me a favor and pay attention? You think you have to be Meryl Streep to do these things? We're talking about thirty-second commercials. All you have to do is say a couple lines and hold up the fucking bottle or something and that's it. Come on, Margot. Where's your confidence? I thought you wanted me to help you."

"I do want you to help me, Matthew. It's just that I've never done anything like this."

"So what? I keep telling you, playing these parts is where it's at. Remember what I said about the calls I get for housewife types? This could be your big opportunity. Now how about it?"

"Okay, I guess so."

"That's better. Christ, the average broad would bust her brassiere for a shot at one of these."

"I said okay, didn't I? When's the taping and how many girls are they seeing?"

"It's next Tuesday. Doris'll give you the address and all that. And they're only going to see a few people."

"Okay, but I still—"

The telephone rang. He answered it, and listened for a moment. "A cop? What's he want, a contribution? Tell him

132

I'm busy. What? Oh, shit. Okay." He put the phone down. "There's some detective here, wants to ask me questions about a model."

"You want me to leave?"

He brushed a hand through the air. "Nah. Only take a second."

"I hope you're not in trouble, Matthew."

He smiled. "Me too."

22

BEN looked around the reception room at the young women sitting there. All of them had long legs encased in jeans, and all of them looked as if they could use a square meal. As far as he was concerned, the trouble with models was that it was hard to tell the girls from the boys.

The woman who came out to meet him was another story. She was short and squat and she waddled. He followed her through an area filled with more women, all of them jabbering into phones, their desks spilling over with stacks of brochures and photographs, and on to a door with Matthew Farrelli's name on it. She knocked on the door and opened it, and when Ben went in she closed it behind him.

Farrelli got up and came around from behind his desk. He was in shirtsleeves, a fancy blue stripe with a white collar and cuffs and massive gold cufflinks. His tie was red, and so were his suspenders. Despite the outfit, he struck Tolliver as a guy who could take care of himself.

Ben showed him his shield and said he was sorry to interrupt, but he would appreciate any help that could be given him. Farrelli said he'd do whatever he could. He introduced a woman who was sitting in a chair in front of his desk.

Her name was Margot Dennis, and Ben saw at a glance she was something special. She had high cheekbones and wideset eyes like the kids outside, but beyond that there was hardly any similarity. For one thing she was older, maybe in her early thirties. For another, she hadn't tied her hair up in a scarf, the way most of them did. Instead, it hung almost to her shoulders in loose, dark waves. She also had a body; you could see the curves, even with her sitting down. She was wearing a skirt and her legs were crossed, and to him they appeared to be about perfect.

Farrelli seemed very sure of himself. "So how can I help you, Lieutenant?"

Ben got out a copy of the photograph, as he had dozens of times over the past few weeks, and showed it to him. "I'm conducting a homicide investigation. Do you know this girl, or do you know who she is?"

Farrelli looked at the print. "This the one was on TV, right?"

"Yes."

He studied the shot and then shook his head.

Ben wasn't surprised; he'd seen that same reaction often enough. "Her name was Ellen Danvers. The name mean anything?"

"No, but wait a minute." Farrelli picked up a phone from his desk and spoke into it. "Doris, see if you can find a model named Ellen Danvers listed anyplace. And check if maybe she might have applied here. Call me right back." He put the phone down.

Ben assumed Margot Dennis was in the business; he showed her the photograph. "How about you, miss—you know her?"

She also looked at the print and said she didn't recognize Danvers. Her voice was soft and low-pitched, and to Ben it seemed to go with the rest of her.

"And the photograph? Does it look like anybody's work to either of you—make you think of any particular photographer?"

Both of them again gave him negative answers.

Ben then asked Farrelli his opinion of Danvers as a model.

This time the agent screwed down the corners of his mouth. "Not our type. I mean, she's a pretty girl, or was.

But nothing very unusual. She'd never cut it with the kind of clients we deal with. Maybe she could get work on Seventh Avenue or catalog stuff, but beyond that, forget it."

The phone rang and Farrelli answered it. When he hung up he said they could find no record of anybody with the name Ellen Danvers.

Ben thanked them both for their time. He asked them to be sure to call him if they happened to think of anything that could be helpful. He also left copies of the photograph, requesting Farrelli to show them around to models and people the agency worked with in the hope of jogging somebody's memory.

On the way out he didn't even glance at the girls sitting in the reception room. All he could think of was Margot Dennis.

Outside the sky had turned to the color of lead, and there was the crack and rumble of thunder. Rain bounced off the sidewalk and the roofs of the cars in fat gray drops. Ben ducked into the Ford and looked at a notebook where he'd listed places he wanted to cover. It was getting late; businesses would be closing soon.

He was tired and frustrated by the lack of progress he'd made on this goddamn case, sick of hearing the same thing over and over every time he asked anyone if they had known Ellen Danvers or if they had any idea who might have taken the photograph. True to his word, Brennan had assigned extra detectives immediately after Danvers had been identified. Ben now had a total of sixty men working on it. Sometimes it seemed to him he had cops falling all over each other, and at other times it seemed he didn't have enough. They were combing photographers and studios, talking to agents and ad agencies, checking photo labs, interviewing magazine and catalog art directors, looking at every aspect of everything to do with the in-

136

dustry. He even had one team working with the vice guys, on the chance that Danvers might have gotten herself mixed up with some porn house. But all of it had produced the same results. What they had come up with was *nada.* Zip. Doodily shit.

As he started the engine he looked up and there she was, standing in the doorway he'd just come out of. She had no raincoat and no umbrella, and she was squinting up at the sky as the rain became heavier.

He leaned over to the passenger side and rolled down the window, calling out to her, "Give you a lift?"

She smiled, and then ran through the downpour to the car. When she was inside he reached across her to shut the door and roll the window back up, and as he did he caught a wave of her perfume.

"Where to, miss?"

"It's Margot."

"Okay, I'm Ben. Where can I take you?"

"I'm going a few blocks north. I hope that's not out of your way?"

He would have been happy if she wanted to go to Westchester. "No problem. That where you live?"

"Yes. It's just off Park. I'll show you."

It figured. Anybody who looked like that had to be from a world so different from his own, it might as well have been the moon.

"This is really great," she said. "I never would have gotten a cab."

"Glad I could help you."

"Doesn't look like a police car, though."

"It's not. Belongs to me."

"And for that matter, you don't look like a policeman."

He was pleased. "Comes in handy, sometimes."

"How about you, Ben—where do you live?"

Was she just being polite? Grateful for the ride on a rainy spring afternoon? Of course she was. You jerk. "I'm in the Village. Bank Street. Know where that is?"

"Sure. I lived on Bleecker when I first came to New York."

"Where from?"

"Pennsylvania. A little town called Holtzer. Ever heard of it?"

"Nope."

"Not many people have. It's in the southwestern part of the state. Not far from Lancaster. I came from there right to the big city, a real hayseed."

He tried probing a little further. "That when you were poor and struggling?"

"Don't kid yourself. Only my address has changed."

He sneaked a look at her left hand. No rings, but that didn't mean anything; she still could be private property, and probably was. Of some character with a jillion bucks. If she wasn't, he'd be surprised.

The rain was pounding now, and the cars and taxis were crawling bumper-to-bumper. New York traffic was bad enough in dry weather, but let there be any kind of precipitation—rain, snow, sleet, even mist—and bang. Paralysis. Ben could hardly see through the windshield; the steadily ticking wipers did no good at all.

But maybe this deluge was a blessing. He toyed with an idea. "Hope you're not in a hurry."

"No, I'm in no rush."

What the hell, he thought. What have I got to lose? "Maybe we ought to stop for a drink."

"Sounds good to me."

He pulled to the curb in front of a hydrant and dropped the police plate onto the dash.

"Some system," she remarked.

"That comes in handy sometimes, too. Sit tight."

He got out of the car and ran around to her side, opening the door and taking her hand, guiding her to the sidewalk. There was a small restaurant a few doors down and they made a dash for it, still holding hands and laughing like a couple of kids. Once inside they shook raindrops off their clothing and made their way to a booth. When a waiter came by she asked for a Campari and soda and Ben ordered vodka on the rocks.

They exchanged banalities about the rain and spring weather until their drinks came, and when they touched glasses he astonished himself by saying, "Margot, you are the most beautiful woman I have ever seen."

She seemed faintly amused. "Thank you."

He swallowed some of his vodka, feeling a little foolish. But what he had said was the truth. Now that he could get a really good look at her, facing her across the table in the small booth, he was sure he had never been so close to anybody who could have such impact on him. And it wasn't just her features, he realized now, although they were as close to perfection as he would ever hope to see. There was also this directness about her, this lack of pretense, that seemed to reach out to him.

He put his glass down. "You didn't mean what you said, did you—about struggling?"

"As it happens, that's exactly what I meant."

"You're a model, aren't you?"

"Yes."

"So how could you be anything but successful?"

"You flatter me."

"I didn't mean to." Which was a lie.

"The fact is, I'm at that stage where I have to start thinking about what to do next."

"Such as?"

"Oh, maybe a housewife, or—something."

"You're married?"

"No."

"Just thinking about it?"

"Lieutenant, are you grilling me?"

He grinned. "Sure."

She returned the smile. "No. And no candidates. And you?"

"Nope. My hours are too weird."

"This case you're working on. It gives me the creeps."

"Me too."

"Really? I thought cops were too—hardened, I guess. By what you have to deal with."

"Not so. Not with me, anyway. I think a rape murder is as bad as it gets."

She looked at her glass. "So do I."

Something was going through her mind; instinct told him it was more than thinking about the horror of Ellen Danvers' murder. He wondered what it was. "Maybe you could help us."

Her gaze flicked up to meet his. "How?"

"I don't know anybody in your business. It might help if I could ask you questions once in a while. Like how photographers operate, where they get their models besides agencies, things like that. Also inside stuff on how the business works. It could be a big help."

She cocked her head, thinking about it. "Sure. That would be okay. Here, wait a minute." She opened her handbag and got out a scrap of paper and a ballpoint. She wrote on the paper and handed it to him.

Ben saw that she had put down her name, address, and telephone number. He took his wallet out of his back pocket and carefully tucked the bit of paper away in it. "Thanks. I really appreciate it."

"Sure. Call me anytime." She drained her glass and put it down. "And now, I should be getting on home. Thanks very much for the drink."

140

"My pleasure, Margot." And was that the truth.

Outside the rain had stopped and the late afternoon sun was casting slanted rays across the tall buildings, reflecting brilliantly from myriad panels of glass. The shower had cooled the air and the humidity was down from where it had been earlier. Ben noted that the traffic had also improved. They reached her apartment house in only ten minutes or so. It was like most of its neighbors, he noted, a postwar high rise with plantings out front. A uniformed doorman opened the passenger door of the Ford and tipped his cap as Margot got out.

She turned back. "Thanks again for the ride, Ben. And be sure to call me." She smiled, and to him it was if she had switched on all the lights. "Even if it's not to talk about the business."

Then she was gone and he pulled away, feeling a little foolish again but elated at the same time. She had seen right through his clumsy line of bullshit, but she'd also let him know it didn't matter. And he certainly would see her again—he was already delighted by the prospect. So what if they were from totally different worlds? Sometimes it wasn't smart to think about what didn't make sense or what couldn't happen. Better to just be thankful for something that came your way. And having Margot Dennis come his way was really something to be thankful for.

Besides, what he had told her wasn't just a pitch. Not altogether, anyway. She probably could help him, and maybe a lot.

23

ALAN Stein leaned forward and turned off the TV set. He took the cassette out of the VCR and returned it to Ben. "Sure you don't want a drink?"

"No, thanks. I've got too much work to do." He held up the cassette. "So what do you think?"

The psychiatrist sat back in his chair. He scratched his jaw, apparently ruminating on the tape of the newscast. Ben had sent it over to him just after it had aired, but this was the first time they had reviewed it together. They were in Stein's study, the small room as cloying and stuffy as ever.

"I think it probably did some damage," Stein said finally.

"Damage how—you mean it made him angry, or had some kind of bad effect on him?"

"I think so, yes." He looked at Ben. "I keep warning you, all I'm doing is conjecturing, giving you opinions based on what's gone on. But the net of it is, I think the impact on him was very likely negative."

"Okay, how?"

"Well, let's look at a few things that've happened here. I told you I see a fairly distinct pattern of paranoia. The ritualistic nature of the killings, and so on. If anything, the photograph was a confirmation of that. It answered the need to have a record of what he's been doing, a device he can use to recall the thrill of the murders, and put it on a grand scale."

"I understand that," Ben said. "It fit right into what you told me to expect."

"His actions also fit another pattern. Which is the compulsion the killer has to take center stage. Oftentimes a personality like this has felt downtrodden or unappreciated all his life. That's a holdover from his childhood, and the abuses he suffered. Now suddenly, for the first time, what he's done is making the world take notice. Look at me, he's saying. I told all you stupid bastards I was somebody special, and now I'm proving it to you. Even communicating with the news media fits in perfectly."

"Son of Sam," Ben said.

"Exactly. Or Jack the Ripper. He wrote to the London *Times*, telling them how smart he was."

"So you really pegged him."

Stein smiled. "To tell you the truth, Lieutenant, I wasn't so sure. People like Krafft-Ebing wrote books on patients like the guy you're looking for. But I doubt they saw many who operated on this level. The intelligence, the artistic side of his personality, the need for acclaim—it's all here. A classic."

"Terrific, Doc. When we catch the son of a bitch you can write a book of your own. But first I have to get him."

"Right. And the questions we're dealing with now are one, how did he react to the newscast, and to what this reporter said about him. And two, what's he likely to do next?"

"That's it."

"Let's take part one. This time, Weston wasn't so complimentary. That is, instead of describing him as a creative genius, which is more or less what she did the first time, she put the idea in the form of a question. Said maybe it would be more accurate to call him a monster. Her description of the photograph itself wasn't quite so laudatory, either."

"Which would be likely to piss him off."

"All of that would."

"And part two?"

"Let me ask you, Ben. What do you think he'll do?"

"Show her she was wrong. Try to top himself, to prove he really is a genius."

"I hate to say it, but I think that's right on the money."

24

Maria's Restaurant was on Waverly Place, near Washington Square. As he drove toward it, Peter reflected that this was the best part of the day. Twilight was gathering, creating shadows that softened the harsh lines of the buildings and deepened the green of the foliage on the trees. The air was milder now as well, with the sun gone and a gentle evening breeze ruffling the leaves. He drove past the restaurant and then swung down the ramp of a parking garage a few doors farther along the street.

The restaurant was well occupied but not crowded, its interior pleasant and homey with red-and-white-checkered tablecloths and a lighted candle in a tiny lantern on each table. Sue Connery was already waiting for him when he arrived. She flashed a big smile, and he took her hand when he sat down and gave it a friendly squeeze.

"How are you, Sue—hope I haven't kept you waiting too long?"

"Oh no, I just got here. But it took some juggling. I had to change plans for tonight."

A warning light went on in his head. "I'm sure he understood."

"Oh, I didn't tell him what it was about."

He relaxed and returned her smile. She looked wonderful—every bit as good as he had remembered, and her manner was easy, as if they were old friends. She was wearing a blue-and-white-striped frock, just right for a weeknight dinner date in the Village. They ordered drinks: white wine for her, Chivas for him.

When the waiter had left she said, "To be perfectly frank, I was a little surprised when you called."

"Really? Why?"

"I don't know. I guess I wasn't sure you meant it."

"Hey, don't be silly. I'm glad to be able to help you. So now tell me." He lowered his head in mock seriousness. "What kind of a day did you have?"

"The truth? I had the dumbest, most boring day you could imagine."

"Tell me about it."

"I worked from nine until five-thirty calculating what changes in the prime rate would do to the bank's business."

"What bank?"

"Oh, I didn't tell you, did I? I work for a bank. First Metropolitan Savings. On Fifty-seventh Street."

"Sounds fascinating."

"I'll bet. The thing is, we're in trouble. Not just us, but all savings banks. We've got these long-term mortgage loans at low interest rates that go back years. We're losing money on all of them, and it's really a problem. So now our management is running around trying to figure out what we should be doing when the rates fluctuate in the future, whether we'd be better off making all loans on an adjustable-rate basis, or what."

"Adjustable-rate means it goes up and down as the prime changes, right?"

"Right."

"That ought to be a good solution."

"Good for the future, maybe. But it doesn't have any effect on all the business we did in the past. I'm afraid we were operating with our heads in the sand for a long time." There was an undercurrent of excitement in her conversation that he knew had nothing to do with banking. She was looking forward to the photography session, although she hadn't mentioned it.

When the waiter returned with their drinks, they touched glasses and she went on with her rundown of the bank's problems. Peter gave her his full attention, as if he were deeply interested in what she was telling him. She had washed her hair, he noted, and the dark strands looked thick and shiny and he imagined how they would smell if he were to bury his face in them. Sweet and fresh, no doubt, and her cheek would be warm when it touched his. She wore almost no makeup, a little eyeshadow and a dab of pale lipstick, and that was it. Good, he liked that. Beauty that was young and natural was not only lovely but also very photogenic.

He sipped his drink. "But that doesn't have anything to do with you, does it? You weren't running the bank back then."

"No, I wasn't. And I'm not running it now."

"So what's a nice girl like you doing in a place like that?"

She smiled at the old gag and gave him the punch line. "Just lucky, I guess."

"No, really. What are you doing there?"

"Really? I studied economics at Cornell and the bank had what I thought was a good training program. Now in a couple more years I might make assistant vice president. If we're still in business."

"Or if you don't get married and settle down with a bunch of kids."

"Not a chance. There are too many things I want to do before anything like that happens."

"No special guy in your life?"

"Well, one. But I'm not going to get married for some time. Hey, tell me about your day. I'm sure it was a lot more interesting than mine."

"Okay, but why don't we order first? We've got work to do tonight."

She smiled at that, her eagerness showing. "Right, we have. What's good here?"

"Everything. How about letting me handle it?"

"Great."

He ordered clams *origanata* for them, and veal *piccata* and a tossed salad and a bottle of Barolo. When the waiter moved away, Peter went into a description of a fashion shoot, because that was what seemed to fascinate girls the most.

She leaned forward. "Who was it for?"

"Bloomingdale's. I do a lot of work for them."

"For their ads?"

"Yeah, and catalogs and stuffers."

"Stuffers?"

"You know, those slicks they send you with your monthly bill. Might show dresses or sometimes perfume or whatever. They're called envelope stuffers."

"Oh, sure. And was this for clothing, today?"

"Yeah. Skiwear."

Her eyes widened. "Skiwear, now? Ah, I get it. They have to work far in advance, right?"

"Right. I'm always shooting bikinis in the middle of winter, furs in the summer. I'll tell you, it's enough to make me want to go into banking."

She laughed. "Who were the models, anybody I'd recognize?"

"Just one today, and no, you wouldn't know her. A new girl, from Rome." He was amused that she was no different from any of the rest of them, hanging on each of his words, so eager to hear about every aspect of his work, trying to imagine herself in the business.

"What would she get, for pay?"

"Oh, I think her rate's a hundred twenty-five an hour. And we worked for six hours, so what's that?"

"Seven-fifty."

"Not bad, for the day. And she's booked most of the time." He knew that would lead her to compare the figure to her own salary from the bank. She'd be thinking about the money and the glamour and where it could all lead.

"Is that average?"

"No, actually it's low, for somebody good. But that's because she just got here. In a few weeks her agency will bump it to three hundred an hour or better." He watched her absorb this, knowing she was making further calculations in her head.

Their clams arrived, hot and spicy, and the waiter was back a moment later with the bottle of wine. He opened it, and after Peter had tasted it and the waiter had filled their glasses, she said, "I guess everybody wants her because she's new."

"Not just new, but different. She's got that distinctive something going for her. All the good ones have that. *You've* got it, Sue. I saw it the minute I first looked at you. And that's what everybody wants most. If a girl has that, she'll have so much work she can't keep up with it. You'll see."

She was silent, a thoughtful look on her face as she chewed her food. He let it sink in for a few moments, again aware of exactly what was going through her mind.

"Who knows," he said. "Maybe in a couple of months I won't be able to afford you."

"Don't worry, Bill. No matter where this goes, I'll be grateful to you. And if it does lead to something, you can be sure I'd be happy to work for you for nothing."

"Thanks, that's nice of you." He kept his face straight, despite the fact that her thoughts had become so transparent it was as if he were reading her mind. She'd already imagined herself as the next Kelly Emberg, the conceited little cunt. Listening to her talk, watching her, he saw plenty of good things about her features, but there were flaws as well. Her jaw was a touch too wide, for one thing. It would be awkward in head-on shots. And her neck should have been longer. His contempt was rising, turning to anger, and he had to make an effort to control it. Get it together, he told himself. Don't let her see or sense anything. There's plenty of time.

She noticed nothing, obviously too busy playing around in her fantasy world to pay attention. When their entrees arrived, she ate quickly, pausing only to ask an occasional question about his work. Did he prefer European models, or didn't it make any difference? Was there more of a demand for blondes? Did he have to travel much?

He answered casually, as if he were completely blasé about the interesting work in beautiful places with beautiful girls. Oddly, reality and fantasy sometimes became mixed up in his own head, so that he couldn't quite remember what was true and what he had woven from his imagination.

She drank only a little of the wine, and refused dessert and coffee. What Sue couldn't wait for was to get in front of his camera. He knew the signs, he'd seen them before.

She put her napkin down. "What are we going to do tonight? I mean, what are you going to shoot?"

His answer was offhand. "Oh, a range of things. What you'll need for a good portfolio. Different head shots, with a variety of expressions and changes in lighting. Then some full-figure things." He felt so totally confident, he couldn't resist a probe. "Maybe a few nude shots, too."

Her mouth dropped open. "Oh, gee. Do you think I'm right for that? I'm not exactly a *Playboy* type, you know."

"Don't kid yourself." His gaze moved down to her breasts, and then back up to her eyes. "You've got more than enough. I could light you so you'd be sexy as hell. You *are* sexy, Sue."

She seemed hesitant, and he reminded himself not to push it. "We'll see how it goes when we get to work," he said. "Okay?"

150

"Sure. I think that would be better."

He signalled for the check and paid it, taking care to use cash.

Outside it was night, and the air was chilly as they walked along the sidewalk. He linked his arm with hers, feeling the warmth of her body through her light spring dress.

When they reached the garage and he guided her down the ramp, she seemed surprised. "I thought your place was right here somewhere. On Fourteenth Street, isn't it?"

He handed the parking ticket to the attendant. "I moved," he told her. "Soho. Got a terrific new studio down there."

"That be twelve-fifty," the attendant said.

He paid the man, who then trotted down the circular ramp. A minute later the wagon came roaring up the incline, tires squealing on the concrete. Peter held the door on the passenger side open for her, and shut it behind her. He tipped the attendant a couple of dollars and then got into the driver's seat and pulled the car up the ramp and out onto the street.

It was a beautiful night, and Sue Connery was a beautiful girl, and now it was all about to begin.

25

He drove south at an easy pace, knowing there was no reason to rush; it was going exactly as planned. He turned onto Seventh Avenue, just moving along with the stream of traffic until they were through the Village and into Soho, and then made a left on Houston Street.

She seemed interested in her surroundings. "I don't know much about this part of New York. Soho is kind of the new 'in' place, isn't it?"

"It's supposed to be a lot like what Greenwich Village was years ago," he told her. "Full of art galleries and antique shops." He gestured at the huge, barnlike old buildings on either side of the narrow streets. "A lot of these places were factories at one time. Some of them are actually built of cast iron. They made everything down here from furniture to toys. Now people have discovered they're terrific for conversion to apartments, or studios, like mine. But it's like everything else—once a good idea gets around, the rush is on. Try to find one for sale now, especially at a decent price. Here we are."

He pulled down a steep driveway to a metal door below street level in one of the buildings. He touched a button under the dash and the metal door rattled upward. When they were inside, the door closed behind them.

He helped her out of the car and guided her to a stairway. It led up to another door, and when they reached it he got out a set of keys and opened two locks, then swung the door open.

"Some security," she remarked.

"Great, isn't it? That's another thing I like about this. My own garage, with no parking jocks to bash in the fenders, and I can keep the car right where I live." He followed her inside.

"You live here?"

"Sure. Live here, work here. My studio and my apartment are all in one place." He turned on the lights and double-locked the door, smiling as she gaped at the high, vaulted ceilings with exposed steel beams painted white, at the brick walls, at the wide-planked floors almost black with age.

"It's fabulous," she said. "What was it originally, do you know?"

"It's been a lot of things, over the years. Belonged to a fur-importing company when I bought it. They used it as a warehouse."

She walked slowly through the open areas, taking it in. "I really love the way you've done it. Did you put in all these walls?"

"Uh-huh. All the interior walls, the white ones. The brick ones I left natural, as you can see."

When she reached the living room, she stopped and stared at the huge black-and-white blowups that covered the walls. "What a beautiful woman." She moved closer as realization struck her. "They're all the same one, aren't they? The same model."

"Yes, they're all the same one."

She was walking along them now, pausing before some of the pictures before moving on. Most of the photos were head shots, but there were many other poses as well, in all manner of dress. Some of them showed the model in sporty things, some in evening wear. Some were location shots, with her walking a pair of hounds on a leash, and playing tennis, and wearing a polo coat at what appeared to be a football game. There was one of her at a table in a nightclub, and printed on an ashtray was the inscription STORK

153

CLUB. They covered her from every angle, and from every one she was stunning.

Sue turned to him. "Who is she?"

"Just someone who used to be a model, a long time ago." It was making him uncomfortable, having her stare at the pictures and question him about them. They were private—none of her business.

He took her arm. "Come on, let me show you the kitchen."

When they walked into it, she clasped her hands as she looked at the tables and the countertops with butcher-block surfaces, at the oversized range and refrigerator. "It looks like what you'd see in a restaurant."

"It is. All this stuff is professional. I thought, why not? It's nice to have the room, I might as well take advantage of it. How often do you see this kind of space in an apartment?"

"Never. At least, I never have. You should see my kitchen. You could put the whole thing in your freezer."

"Uh-huh. My bedroom is over this way."

Inside the room her eyebrows lifted. "That's the biggest bed I ever saw. You could sleep a basketball team in it."

"Why would I want to sleep with a basketball team?"

She giggled. "Oh, come on. You know what I mean. Did you have it made? You must have."

"Yeah, I did. Hey—don't you want to see the studio?"

"I thought you'd never ask."

He made it light, with an effort. "Right this way."

When he had unlocked the door and followed her inside, he snapped on the lights and now he really enjoyed her reaction. She was wide-eyed at the array of equipment: strobes, scrims, rolls of no-seam in various colors hanging overhead, metal taborets containing prints and raw stock, white Formica-topped counters, bins full of lenses and filters and odds and ends. And standing on its tripod in the center of the room, as if in command of all this, his Hasselblad.

He pointed casually to a door in the wall to his left. "My darkroom's in there. Enlarger, printer, all that."

She turned to him. "You know, this is a big kick for me. It's the first time I've ever been inside a real studio."

"Would you like something to drink?"

"No, thanks. But I could use a mirror."

He stepped to a drawer, taking out a mirror and handing it to her. While she studied her reflection, he went to a countertop and riffled through a stack of cassettes. The Stones would be perfect. He snapped on the amplifier and put on a tape, feeling a physical jar when the beat came thundering out of the huge floor speakers. Then he placed a stool in the center of the studio and set up lights and reflectors on either side of it, moving easily and surely, appearing absorbed by what he was doing but aware that the girl had put the mirror aside and was watching him. It was exhilarating, going through all this bullshit, his emotions whirling inside him. The Stones were doing "Hang Fire," and the bass notes made the floor vibrate and rattled the boxes of film and the loose equipment on the countertops. He found himself moving in sync with the rhythm.

The rolls of no-seam were attached to the ceiling like so many oversized window shades. He had decided on red when he had first planned this, when he had first conceived what he wanted to shoot. He pulled the wide sheet down from the roll to provide a backdrop, and when it was in place he moved the Hasselblad closer. He stepped back, studying the setup, then turned to the girl and beckoned her to take her position on the stool.

She was obviously self-conscious. "You sure it's all right that I don't have on much makeup? I could put more on if you think I need it."

"No, you're fine. Get up there."

155

"Okay." She climbed onto the stool, looking at him for instructions as to how she should sit.

His hands moved over her back and her shoulders gently, coaxing her into an erect position, with her body at an angle to the camera, her face straight on. He frowned, looking her over with great care, the consummate artist preparing his subject.

But there was nothing phony about his excitement. What he was doing was foreplay, and it was real. He could feel his heart pounding when he bent over the camera. Raising his free hand above his head, he stared at the image in the viewfinder. "Good, Sue. That's it, baby. Chin a little higher. Fine. Hold that, now."

He hit the trigger and the strobes boomed. He fired again, and with each shot she flashed those perfect white teeth and her eyes sparkled in the dazzling light. When he'd made about two dozen exposures, slapping fresh magazines onto the camera back, he knew she was ready. He kept on shooting, calling out to her that she looked fantastic, wonderful. Then he left the camera and went to her, smiling as he deliberately reached behind her and pulled down the zipper of her dress.

She jumped a little, but she didn't resist. He slipped the dress down over her shoulders, pulling her arms out of it, and then she got off the stool and he slid the dress down over her hips. She stepped out of it, and he tossed it over onto the love seat. She was wearing a bra and a pair of bikini panties, both as thin as gauze. He felt himself grow erect as he saw the dark patch of pubic hair showing through, and then he again reached behind her, this time unhooking her bra and removing it.

Damn, she was beautiful. Her breasts were firm and erect, with wide, dusky nipples, and it was all he could do to keep from bending down and taking one into his mouth. He was fully erect now, and although he knew she might notice, he didn't care. He took her elbow and eased her back onto the stool, and when she got into position this time he took longer to get just the right angle of her body, letting his fingertips drift lightly over the smooth skin of her back and her shoulders and her belly, gently brushing those lovely breasts.

The image in the viewfinder was marvelous. He wiped sweat from his eyes, hitting the trigger and filling the studio with bursts of light. He felt as if he were watching all this from outside himself, while the studio was in the center of a roaring storm, the boom of the music and the flashes of the strobes like thunder and lightning. He stepped back to her, reaching for her panties.

This time she recoiled. She got off the stool and pushed his hand away. "No, Bill. That's far enough. No more, really."

He was dimly aware that there was something else in her expression now, a look of uncertainty and confusion that was rapidly turning to fear.

She frowned. "What is it? Why are you looking at me like that? Bill, stop. Give me my dress."

He slapped her alongside the jaw so hard it sent her sprawling to the floor. She opened her mouth to scream, but if she did he couldn't hear it over the music and the roaring inside his head. He reached down and grabbed her hair, dragging her up into a kneeling position before him. She struggled, but it was like the feeble efforts of a child. It was impossible for her to hold him off. He struck her again, even harder this time, the force of the blow snapping her head back.

There was no fight left in her now. Her face was a mask of agony and terror. She was whimpering, "Please don't hurt me. Oh God, please don't."

He drew her close to him, continuing to hold her by the hair with one hand while his other tore open his trousers.

157

Standing before her, he exulted in the wild sense of power he felt, the sense of complete domination. She was his to do with whatever he wanted—to use, to punish, to destroy. Later on he would use her in a different way, but for now there was only his driving, insatiable need.

He forced her mouth open, experiencing an incredible intensity as the hot wetness surrounded him. The roaring sound was louder, pounding at him, battering his skull, and he seemed to be looking at the scene through a red filter. His orgasm burst, and he shuddered as in its wake came a feeling of emptiness, a void that rapidly filled with deep, vicious anger.

She choked, and he looked down at her, his shoulders heaving as he drew air into his lungs. His hands moved. One gripped the back of her head, the other closed on her jaw. His fingers were like steel clamps, the pressure distorting her features, making her eyes pop.

His strength was enormous. He twisted her head completely around on her neck, forcing her face backward, away from him. A single sound rose above the flood of music, a crack as loud and clean as a pistol shot.

She was instantly limp in his hands. He released her and she slumped forward to the floor, her fingers and toes twitching. He stood over her for a few seconds, breathing heavily, his body wet with sweat. Reaching down, he ripped the panties away from her buttocks. An animal cry came boiling out of his mouth, and then he fell upon her, his teeth ripping and tearing at her flesh.

26

BEN sat at his desk, looking at the overflowing pile of DD-5s, the daily reports that detectives hated to write, but not seeing them. His mind was on another subject, one he hadn't been able to stop thinking about for days. Even though this case was driving him crazy, with the cops under his direction turning up reams of information that led them nowhere, one corner of his brain stayed focused on a woman. He got out his wallet and took the scrap of paper from it, debating whether he should call the number she'd jotted down. He was even surprising himself with his indecision, feeling a little sheepish, a grown man acting like some fucking moonstruck kid. But then he thought the hell with it and reached for the phone.

She answered on the second ring, and sounded pleased to hear from him.

"I was wondering," he said, "if we could get together again."

"To talk about the business?"

He knew she was teasing him, but she was being good-humored about it, and he could hear the friendliness in her voice. "Sure. But mostly because I want to see you."

There was a pause, and for an instant he wondered whether she was thinking he was just a smart-ass on the make, but then what she said next made him feel wonderful. "I'd like that, too, Ben. Tell you what. I'm not the world's greatest cook, but I can work up a pretty good spaghetti dinner. How does that sound?"

"It sounds terrific. When?"

"Tomorrow night would be okay, if you can make it."

"I'll make it—nothing could stop me."

"Great. What time can you get here?"

"Around eight, but I might be a little late. It can get hectic, and I never know what to expect."

"Whenever you arrive will be fine."

He hung up and let out a whoop.

The door opened, and Ed Flynn stepped into his office. The sergeant's eyebrows arched. "You look like you're in a good mood, Lou."

"What makes you think so?"

"I—uh, nothing."

Ben pointed at the stack of reports. "You know what this stuff is? Dog shit. We got people running all over the place and there isn't a thing in here, as far as I can see."

"But you know we're talking to everybody we can find who might have seen the girl or might know something about the picture."

"He's a photographer," Ben said. "That's one thing we're sure of."

"Lou, there's just over ten thousand photographers in New York. We're doing the best we can with what we got."

Ben snorted. "Ten thousand? That must include every asshole who owns a Brownie. You should be concentrating on the studio guys, the pros."

"I'm telling you, we are. Most of them are downtown now, from Chelsea down to Soho. We got men combing the area, talking to people. Checking studios, labs, even the joints where they hang out."

"Uh-huh. You know, not one of those girls was a professional model. What about model schools? That might be an angle."

"Yeah, it's an idea."

"So look into it."

The phone rang, and as Ben answered it, Flynn left the office.

"Sixth Precinct, Lieutenant Tolliver."

"Lieutenant, this is Jack Olson, chief of police in Hamilton, New York."

"Afternoon, Chief. What can I do for you?"

"I been seeing a lot about this case of yours—the homicides in Greenwich Village?"

"Okay, what about them?"

"I got the flyer you put out on the last one. And then there was that picture of her on TV."

The guy didn't talk as fast as the people Ben was used to hearing. "Yeah, we got an ID on her. Name was Danvers."

"I saw that. What I wanted to tell you was, we had a case up here some years back that something in your flyer put me in mind of."

"That so?" Where the hell was Hamilton, anyway?

"Our case was never solved. College girl. Student here at Colgate."

Colgate. That was why Ben had heard of Hamilton. It was where Colgate University was, upstate someplace. "All right, Chief. What happened, in your case?"

"The girl disappeared. She went to some house parties on a Saturday night, and that was the last time anybody saw her alive. Deer hunter found her in the woods a month later. Neck was broken, and the body was nude."

"Yeah." This was at least the fiftieth call Ben had had in response to the flyer on Ellen Danvers. All the others had been from police officers trying to make a connection between some open case in their files and the Danvers homicide, usually with no vague resemblance between them. "So what was it you saw that was similar, Chief?"

"Well, first off, they were rape murders. Your case and ours. And both the victims were young girls."

"When was this, your case?"

"Eight years ago."

161

Ben wondered how many girls had been raped and murdered in the state of New York between then and now. "Yeah, I see. What else was there?"

"The one we had, the body wasn't decomposed. Gets cold up here early, you know. We get snow from October on. Also it was under some trees, so it was in fairly good shape. Only reason this fella found it was he was tracking a deer and he saw a foot sticking out of a snowbank."

Ben began to think about how good a drink would taste. It had been a long day. "Uh-huh."

"But then when we dug the body out of the snow, we found bites on it. Didn't think too much of that, right away. Get a lot of small game around here. Fox, weasels, and so on. Anything like that would feed on dead meat."

"Sure."

"But these bites were made by a human."

"Where on the body were they?"

"The back. Most of 'em on her rear end."

Ben sat up in his chair. "You sure, Chief—they were human bites?"

"Oh, yeah. See, the coroner here is an attorney, not a medical man. So the autopsy was done at the County Medical Center. Got a very good facility there. I went myself when it was done, the next day. Doctor there said positively those bites were made by a man and not an animal. They were deep, too, like in your case. You could see places where the teeth came together in her cheeks."

"And the case was never solved?"

"No, never was. We put on a damn good investigation, too. Interviewed over a hundred people, had help from the state crime lab. But we never got one suspect you could call worthwhile."

"Chief, you said the victim was raped?"

"That's right. Actually, it was sodomy."

Ben tensed. "Did the post give you that?"

"Yes, it did. Nothing in her vagina, but there was material in her mouth. That's another way the cold helped us, you know? Preserved it, the doctor said."

"What's the best way for me to get up there, from New York?"

The chief laughed. "Got your attention, did I?"

"I'll say you did."

"Fastest way would be USAir. Flies into Syracuse."

"I could rent a car there."

"Hell, I'd meet you. When would you want to come up?"

"Sooner the better," Ben said. "Tomorrow, if there's a flight."

"Oh, there is. They got a couple every day."

"Okay, let me see what I can do. Call you back."

27

Usair's first flight out left La Guardia at 7:05 in the morning. A businessman's special, from the look of the passengers. The airplane was packed. Ben wore a navy blazer and a pair of gray slacks, which for him was practically going formal. No tie, however. That would be too much of a concession. There were two stewardesses aboard, one moderately ugly, the other cute, with a nice smile and a pert ass. They ran back and forth, barely getting everybody a cup of dishwater coffee and a Danish before the jet landed.

Jack Olson turned out to be younger than Ben had pictured him. Voices could be misleading. He put the chief's age at somewhere near his own, in the late thirties. Olson was as tall as Ben, too. He was skinny, with a hard, narrow face, looking starched and crisp in a light-blue summer uniform. The holster on his right side carried an S&W .357 Magnum. He reminded Ben of the guys you saw in the Marine Corps who became career NCOs. His car was an unmarked blue Plymouth sedan.

The drive took almost as long as the flight from New York, and Ben enjoyed it. It was a clear, sunny morning and the air was nothing like what he'd been breathing in the city all week. This was farm country, with stands of corn and rolling meadows where cows were grazing. You could see neat houses and barns spaced far apart, and tall trees and stone walls. Everything was startlingly green. It would be nice, he thought, to live up here and have a job like Olson's. Run a small-town police force, do a little hunting, fishing. And in about six months go out of your fucking mind.

"How many students at Colgate?" he asked the chief.

"Little over twenty-seven hundred. Fifteen hundred are men."

"Didn't used to be coed, did it?"

"No. Started taking women in seventy or seventy-one."

"College must keep you jumping."

Olson smiled. "Not really. There's a lot of shenanigans on the campus, but the university has its own security force. Kids get drunk and raise hell, but mostly it stays there, and it's almost never anything serious. Might be a fight once in a while we get called in on, but that's rare. Get a robbery now and then too, but those're even rarer. The bad things we see are when kids get liquored up and drive cars. Then we gotta go out and scrape 'em off the road. That happens maybe once a year."

"So that homicide was way out of the ordinary for you."

"Oh, yeah. Only one I've seen involving a student in the twelve years I been on the force. We've had a couple in the village in that time, but they were different. A family fight, a ruckus in a bar. No mystery there. But the girl was something else."

"What was her name?"

"Benoit. Pamela Benoit. Nineteen years old. A junior."

"You said you never had a worthwhile suspect?"

"Not a damn one."

"Any theories?"

"Some. I believe the killer was another student. Not somebody from outside who went on the campus and attacked her."

"Why's that?"

"Condition of the body. Except for the bite marks and the bruises on her neck, there were hardly any other signs of violence. No cuts, no contusions."

"So it didn't look like she'd put up much of a struggle."

165

"Didn't seem like it to me. I think she blew some guy she knew and then he broke her neck."

"Then maybe it wasn't even rape?"

"Maybe. I thought about that, too. Although he could have forced her by threatening her."

"What about the bites?"

"Medical Examiner said he was pretty sure she got bitten after she was dead."

"I see." What he saw was a naked female body with bloody, blue-black wounds in the flesh of the back, many of them in the buttocks. A body like Malik's, and Cunningham's, and Danvers'.

The chief wheeled the Plymouth along at a steady sixty miles an hour, both his big hands on the wheel. "We questioned everybody we could find who'd been anywhere near her that night."

"She have a date?"

"Yeah, but he passed out early. She visited a bunch of fraternity houses after that, going from party to party. We talked to all the people who'd been in those houses."

"And nothing?"

"Nothing. We even had a dentist make casts of the teeth of some of the boys, but none of them matched the bites."

"We've got a bite expert working on our case, too," Ben said. He told Olson about Dr. Brody and his growing reputation as one of the foremost authorities in the country on human bites.

The chief listened with interest. When Ben finished, Olson asked about the homicides in New York, and Ben gave him a summary of what had gone on to date, including the play the photograph had been given by the media. Olson said he'd seen a lot of it on TV.

When they pulled into the village, it reminded Ben of all the small towns he'd ever been in, little more than a main drag with stores and a church and tall trees. The university was just a stone's throw to the south, up on a hill, and he could see stately stone buildings rising above the foliage. The police station was on the main street. It was a small structure that looked as if it had been converted from a house, painted gray and white.

A cop was inside when they walked in, talking into a radio mike. He waved a greeting as Olson led Ben into his office and shut the door. It was a compact, neat room housing a desk, a couple of straight-backed chairs, some filing cabinets. A large map of Hamilton and the surrounding area covered one wall, and on another was a bulletin board with wanted posters tacked onto it, along with a list of cops' names and the shifts they were assigned to.

There was a stack of files on the desk like the ones Ben had been working with himself the past few months. The chief indicated a chair and told him to help himself to the files; they were organized chronologically and contained hundreds of reports. He said he'd get them some coffee.

The quality of the work was a surprise. There were more than three dozen photographs, starting with the crime scene and going all the way through the autopsy. Again Ben felt an eerie sense of precognition as he looked at them. There was a stark, wooded hillside in winter, a small white foot protruding from a mound of snow. There were close-ups of what had once been a pretty face, the eyes glazed in death and coated with ice. There was a fragile throat wearing a collar of blackish bruises. And there were shots of the girl's buttocks, the flesh ripped and torn, clearly by human teeth.

Olson returned with two china mugs of coffee and sat down. He gestured toward the photographs. "Any of that look familiar?"

"Oh, yeah." Ben lifted his mug and sipped some of the steaming contents. Cops were the same anywhere. What they ran on was black coffee. "It sure does. Where was she from?"

"Cincinnati. Father owns a real estate agency there. Two other kids, both grown now. Nice family, never had any real trouble before."

"What about the girl herself?"

Olson took a swallow of his coffee and set the mug down on his desk. "About as ordinary as you could get. She was well liked, an average student majoring in French. Lived in Russell, one of the newer dorms on the campus. Had a roommate named Anderson, from Concord, New Hampshire. We spent hours talking to her."

"And the boyfriend?"

He wasn't really a boyfriend, just a date. And like I said, he got loaded and by nine o'clock he was out of it. The last time anybody remembered seeing her was a little after two A.M. in the bar at the Deke house. Not drunk, either. Just having a good time."

"Where's this place where the body was found?"

The chief got to his feet and stepped over to the map on the wall. He peered at it and poked a finger. "Here's where we are now."

Ben joined him at the map, which detailed the village of Hamilton, the university, and the surrounding countryside.

Olson's finger traced a line south to another point. "This here is the Deke house, last place she was seen." His finger moved again, to a place northeast of the campus, and stopped. "Right here is where she was."

Ben squinted. "How far is that, from the house?"

"Little more than half a mile."

"Could she have been driven there?"

"No. Not even in an off-road vehicle. There's a stone

wall right here." He pointed. "And the terrain is too rugged. Heavy woods."

"I see."

"But for that matter, we don't even know where she was killed. It's possible that it happened in the Deke house, although it's unlikely, with all those people around. And of course, we had no way to fix the exact time of death. Some people said they thought they saw her leaving the bar, but they weren't sure. She could have been killed anywhere in the area."

Ben continued to look at the map. "Okay, but wherever it happened, the killer had to carry her to where she was when you found her."

"That's right. Couldn't have driven her, and nothing on the body indicated she was dragged."

"How big was she?"

"Five-one, hundred ten."

"Small girl."

"Yeah, she would've been easy to handle. But still, it must have been a trek. In the woods, at night."

"Any of her clothing ever turn up?"

"Not a stitch."

"Who reported her missing?"

"Roommate. At first she thought Pamela was probably at some party in an apartment here in the village. Some of the students live off-campus. Or that she might've taken off somewhere, maybe with some guy. But then when she didn't hear from her by Sunday night, she got worried and reported it. Pamela's family hadn't heard from her, either. Monday the campus security called us in, and we started combing the area. It'd snowed in the night, and that didn't help us any. Had everybody looking for her, including a lot of student volunteers. I'll bet we passed within a few feet of her while that search was going on."

"I'd like to have a look around," Ben said.

Olson nodded. "Sure. Plan to give you a tour any time you'd care to go."

"Fine. But first I want to go through these files."

"Okay, make yourself comfortable. I got some things to do myself, so I'll just leave you in here. You want anything, holler."

28

For a small-town police department, Olson's force had done a highly professional job of investigation. Ben was aware, however, that a homicide up here was a big deal. Even with limited manpower, the chief and his men had had plenty of time to work on it. Nothing like the Sixth Precinct, where every day could bring you a fresh load of burglaries, muggings, knifings, and Christ only knew what else. He scribbled notes on a pad as he went through the files. The longer he worked at it, the more similarities he found between this case and his own. And the deeper he dug, the more he felt a growing conviction that Jack Olson had put him onto something.

At noon the chief took him across the street for a hamburger. There were a couple of locals in the diner who looked Ben over, obviously curious about the stranger who was having lunch with the chief of police. Olson led him to a booth, and after they gave the waitress their orders, Ben said he thought the investigation had been a good job.

The chief smiled. "Thanks. I thought so, too. But a lot of people didn't."

"Oh? Like who?"

"Newspaper editor, some of the university officials, few of the townspeople. Called us jerkwater cops, said it was outrageous how we couldn't solve the case, stuff like that."

Ben smiled. "You catch some of that too, huh?"

"Guess it goes with the territory."

"Any territory. A cop is a cop."

"You find anything in the files you want to ask me about?"

"Yeah, several things." The waitress brought their cheeseburgers and coffee and Ben waited until she left before he went on. "You turned up a couple of male students this girl had been friendly with. Guys who admitted having sex with her."

Olson dumped ketchup on his cheeseburger. "Yeah, those were some of the ones we concentrated on. But with both of them it was kind of casual. No big romance. And neither one of them was with her that night."

"So your report said. But what I was interested in was whether you got those guys to go into detail about what happened physically. What kind of sex they had with her."

"It was all straight. Nothing you could call kinky or even unusual. But you know what we were going for."

Ben spoke around a mouthful of hamburger. "Sure. You wanted to know if the young lady was in the habit of giving head."

"That's right. And she wasn't. At least not with those two."

"Which might mean something or might not. But the ME told you she hadn't had intercourse before she was killed, didn't he?"

"Yes, he did. The semen he found traces of was all in her mouth and throat."

"Blood type A."

"Correct," Olson said. "And that matches, too, doesn't it? According to your flyer."

"Yeah, it does. Of course, type A is also the most common, as you know. But there's another thing I was curious about. All those people she was with in the bar at that house, nobody had any idea of where she might have gone when she left."

"That didn't surprise us much. Two o'clock in the morning at a college party, everybody drinking, celebrating. Colgate won a football game that afternoon, and when that happens, they get even rowdier."

"I saw that, about the game. Lehigh."

"Right. So the parties were sure to be kind of on the wild side. Anybody could have gone in or out without causing much notice."

Ben swallowed the last of his cheeseburger. "There were some alums there too, that right?"

"Yeah, but only a few. Wasn't homecoming weekend or anything like that. I still think whoever did it was a Colgate student, a friend of hers. I also think he was right there in that bunch at the bar, but all that's nothing but hunches."

"Okay, so what's next?"

"What's next is we go for another ride. On the scenic route." Olson finished his coffee and reached for the check, beating Ben to it. "My treat, Lieutenant. You can get the next one, when I come to New York. We'll go to one of your fancy restaurants."

They got back into the chief's Plymouth and drove south a little over a mile to the Colgate campus, Olson pointing out different things of interest on the way. When he came to the first place that afforded a good view, he pulled over and stopped. Looking ahead and to the left, Ben saw that most of the university buildings were on the side of the hill, which was heavily wooded.

The chief pointed. "Up there's the original buildings where the school got started, around a hundred thirty years ago."

"Any connection with the soap company?"

"Oh, yes. Old Mr. Colgate himself founded the place, and his family was involved with it for years."

"Looks beautiful."

"It is. They got fourteen hundred acres altogether. The newer buildings are the ones down there, the athletic facilities and the new dorms. These big houses you see on

173

Broad Street here, the ones all along on your right, those are the fraternities."

"So that's where she was that night, in one of them?"

"Yep. We'll go right by it." Olson started the car and crept along the street. There was a small lake on the left, between them and the main campus.

As he drove, the chief called out the names of the fraternities whose houses they were passing. He stopped before one of them, a stately building that appeared to be one of the oldest and largest.

"That's DKE," Olson said. "The Deke house."

Ben studied it, imagining what it must have looked like the night of the murder, ablaze with lights, full of people celebrating.

The chief pulled away. They had come to the end of fraternity row, and next he pointed out the football stadium and the gymnasium, the athletic center, and the tennis courts. He turned left, climbing toward the center of the campus.

Students were ambling along the tree-lined walks in twos and threes, carrying books, nobody appearing to be in much of a hurry. All of them were casually dressed, mostly in pants and open-necked shirts, a few wearing shorts. Here and there couples were sitting on the expanses of grass, and Ben noticed one guy lying with his head in a girl's lap. She was a pretty blonde who was leafing through a notebook, paying no attention to the guy. These people probably hate to see the semester coming to an end, Ben thought. He didn't blame them.

Olson waved a hand. "Right over there, that cluster of buildings, that's the Bryan complex. Russell is the building on the left. That's the one she lived in."

Ben looked at the buildings. "Both men and women students live in there?"

"Yes. They're divided by floor. But I don't think they stay divided a whole lot."

They stopped in front of the administration building to pick up the head of the campus security police, an older guy named Art Waterford who'd been one of the town cops before he retired. Olson explained he'd called Waterford to let him know they'd be coming.

Waterford climbed into the backseat of the car and Olson introduced him to Ben.

The security man pushed his cap back on his head. "How's everything in New York?"

"Swell," Ben said.

Waterford grunted. "I'll bet. I get down there maybe once every two years. When I do, I can't wait to get the hell out again."

"Great place to visit," Ben said.

"Friend of mine's a sergeant in the Ninth Precinct. I went to see him there one time."

"East Village," Ben said. "Across town from us. I'm in the Sixth."

"Yeah? Well anyhow, he took me along on a tour with him and his partner. Patrol car on a Saturday night. There was more action than I ever saw up here the whole time I been a cop. About thirty years' worth."

"That so?" Ben said. "In New York we consider the Ninth a quiet area."

Waterford stared at him for a moment, then grinned broadly. "Bullshit, Lieutenant."

Ben laughed. "I think some of our cops would like to trade places with you."

"Hey," Olson said. "It's a nice life, up here."

They drove past the handsome native-stone buildings, and along a road that ran up the side of the hill from the campus. There was an old cemetery back in there, and beyond it, Ben could see where trees had been cleared out, a long slash farther up the steep grade.

"That's the ski slope," Olson told him. "And about a hundred yards over this way is where the body was found. You see what I mean that you couldn't drive in there." He stopped the car.

They got out and trekked up the hill, Olson leading. There were tall trees, mostly oak and maple as well as cedar and hemlock, all of it dense, and the going wasn't easy. About fifty yards up the hill Olson stopped near the base of a gnarled oak. He gestured. "Right there is where she was. Lying on her back." He looked at Ben. "Different now than it was in the pictures."

"Uh-huh." Everything was green, warm and pleasant, a canopy of leaves over their heads, and above that blue sky. Ben recalled how it had looked in the photographs under a blanket of snow, when the weather had been cold and raw.

"You can see how we missed her," Olson said. "No leaves on the trees then, but there was brush over the body, and all of it covered with new snow."

"We had dogs, too," Waterford said. "But they didn't pick up anything."

"That because of the snow?" Ben asked.

"Partly, but also it was because she'd been carried up here, and it was cold. Wasn't much of a scent for them."

Ben looked back down the hill. "I see what you mean, about the guy carrying her up here through these trees in the dark."

"Couldn't have been easy," the chief said. "But you know, wasn't for that hunter, we wouldn't have found her for a lot longer time. She would've been here at least till spring."

They stood around for a few more minutes, Ben studying the site, and then Olson asked if he'd seen enough.

"Yeah, I think so."

"You want to talk to somebody at the university now?"

"I sure do," Ben said.

"I told Dean Trumbull you were coming," Waterford said.

They got into the car and Olson drove them back down to the main campus, parking beside one of the athletic buildings. The dean was a surprise, a youngish guy with close-cropped hair who was jogging on the track. He was wearing a sweat-soaked T-shirt and a pair of faded blue shorts and it occurred to Ben that he looked more like a coach than a dean of students. His manner was relaxed, but Ben knew this wasn't easy for him, having three cops dredging up an eight-year-old murder of a student. He shook hands and led them to a wooden bench beside the track.

"Only chance I get for some exercise," he explained to Ben. "Gets pretty stuffy in the office on a warm afternoon."

"Sure," Ben said. "I'm glad you could give me some time."

Trumbull nodded. "Art here tells me you think there may be a connection between the Benoit case and the one you're working on in New York."

"That's correct," Ben replied. "It might seem like a long shot, but I believe there's a real possibility. Enough for us to want to check it out."

Trumbull was apprehensive, Ben could see. Not that you could blame him. He picked up a towel and wiped his face with it. "Lieutenant, that was probably the most devastating thing that ever happened here. It was terrible. For the poor girl, of course, and for her family and friends. And for the university, too. And it's also terrible that it was never solved. It's been like an open wound, ever since."

Ben glanced at Jack Olson, but the chief's face was impassive. He'd no doubt taken enough shit on this subject to last a lifetime.

"So as long as you're not sure," Trumbull went on, "we'd appreciate it if we could be kept out of any of the media attention you're getting. It's been quite lurid so far, wouldn't you say?"

"Yes it has," Ben admitted. "But you have my word we'll do our best to keep the lid on. We don't want a lot of publicity on this angle, any more than you do."

Trumbull nodded. "All right, then. How can we help you?"

"You must have detailed records of your alumni, don't you, Dean?"

"I was afraid that was the direction you were going in."

"Sorry," Ben said. "But it's possible all these murders were committed by the same man, and that maybe he was a student here when he killed Pamela Benoit."

"I understand that, Lieutenant. But at the same time, it might be reaching pretty far, don't you think?"

Olson spoke up. "There's a lot of similarities, Dean. Between the Benoit murder and the ones in New York."

"The way the girls were killed," Ben explained. "Condition of the bodies, the killer's methods, a number of other things."

"I see."

"I was asking about your records," Ben said. "Use them for fund-raising, probably?"

"Among other things, yes."

"How many of your alumni live in the New York area?"

"It depends on how you define the area. If you include the city and the surrounding towns, in Long Island, New Jersey, Westchester, and Connecticut, the total is about six thousand."

"So it would be possible for us to get a good rundown on somebody if we wanted it, right? Everything from the guy's academic record to where he is now, what he does for a living, and so on."

178

Trumble's expression was grim. "Lieutenant, I would hate to think of your upsetting Colgate alumni when you have nothing more than a theory to go on."

"Look, Dean," Ben said. "I know how you feel. And I don't blame you. But I promise you we're not going to turn this into some kind of a witch-hunt. We'll keep it very low-key, and as I told you, we'll do our best not to let the news media in on any of it."

"Very well. We'll do all we can to cooperate."

"Good. Would you have pictures of your graduates in your files?"

Trumbull pursed his lips. "No, not in most cases. We have some, but it would be spotty. Only of people who were noteworthy for their careers, or their accomplishments. Things like that."

"How about undergraduate photos?" Olson asked. "Like in old yearbooks. That might help."

"Good idea," Ben said. "Somebody wouldn't change all that much in eight or ten years."

"The library has the yearbooks," Trumbull said. "If you want to borrow some of them."

"Sure," Ben said. "Could be very useful."

"What else can we do for you?" Trumbull asked.

"I think that'll be it for now," Ben replied. "I'll send a couple of my men up to go through your records and get the yearbooks. If there's anything else I think of, I'll let you know."

Trumbull stood up. "All right, Lieutenant. And thank you for your understanding."

"Thank you, Dean. I really appreciate your help."

Olson drove Ben back to his office, where Ben sorted through the Benoit files once again, picking out material he wanted to take with him. Then they got into the Plymouth and headed for Syracuse and the airport.

On the way Ben felt a growing excitement as he thought

about what he'd seen and learned. At the same time, he reminded himself, the dean was right: it could be a hell of a reach. But somehow he was convinced it wasn't. Too much of this fit too well. Oddly, what came into his mind was the experience of developing a photograph. The paper was swirling in the tray of fluid, and an image was slowly becoming distinct. It wasn't quite there yet, but Ben could see the figure of a man in shadowy outline.

I know you're out there, you miserable son of a bitch. You're out there, and you're laughing at us, just like Weston said. But I'm going to find you, if it's the last fucking thing I ever do. And when I get you, you're going to wish you'd cut your rotten throat before any of this ever started.

They got to the airport in plenty of time for USAir's early evening flight to La Guardia. As he got out of the car, Ben thanked Olson again for all his help.

"Glad to do anything I can," the chief said. "In a lot of ways, I want to see this cleared up as much as you do."

"Yeah," Ben said. *An open wound*, Dean Trumbull had called it. "I'm sure you do."

It wasn't until the flight had been airborne for twenty minutes or so that Ben began to relax. He had plenty of problems to contend with, including the need for still more men, especially with this new development, but all that could wait until tomorrow. Tonight he had an invitation for dinner. He'd told her he might be a little late, and he would be. But the thought of seeing her again was making his pulse race.

29

WHEN he touched the buzzer Margot opened the door
with a big smile on her face, and Ben thought she was even
more beautiful than he remembered. She had on a frilly
apron over a green dress with puffy sleeves, and her hair
was just a touch disheveled, he supposed from working in
the kitchen. He'd bought a bottle of Chianti on the way to
her place and he held it up to her; she thanked him and
took it from him.

Then she moved her face closer, as if to offer it for a
friendly greeting kind of kiss, but their eyes locked on each
other, and as they did her smile faded, and Ben didn't care
whether he might be making a fool of himself or not. He
didn't even bother to think about it. He pulled her into his
arms and mashed his lips against hers and he felt her body
seem to melt into him, and then her mouth opened and
his head was reeling. It was as if all the fantasies of the last
few days were suddenly and unbelievably coming true, and
he could dare to think maybe she'd had fantasies of her
own, because for all the heat and hunger he felt now, she
was returning it with a fervor that was every bit equal to
his own.

They stood that way for several minutes, devouring each
other. Then he took the bottle back from her and put it
down on a table. She pulled away a little, the expression
on her face very serious now, and still half-clinging to him
led him through the apartment to her bedroom. They fumbled with each other's clothing, pulling and hauling at but-
tons and zippers and then seeing the humor in it and
laughing delightedly. Ben unbuckled the ankle holster with

the short-barreled Smith from his left leg and tossed it aside.

Finally they stood naked before each other and he looked down at her, thinking nobody could be that lovely, it just wasn't possible. Her body was firm and lush and her breasts were tipped with broad, puckery nipples and she had that look on her face again. Her eyes were wide and her lips were parted a little, and this time when he drew her to him her bare flesh was hot to his touch.

They fell over onto the bed and Ben felt he was drowning in her, driving as deep into her passion as he could take himself, finding her, knowing her, exploring all the mysteries of her body with his.

Afterward they lay in each other's arms, their limbs tangled, their skin cooling under tiny rivulets of sweat. Not moving, just breathing together.

She looked at the ceiling. "You must think I'm crazy."

"Tell you the truth, the same thing was going through my mind, about what you'd think of me."

"I guess I was just going on instinct," she said. "That's about all I had."

He turned and raised himself on one elbow, looking down into her eyes. They were a deep violet, almost black in the dim light. His emotions welled up, and he kissed her gently this time, then more passionately as again desire flooded into him. They made love easily now, almost lazily, able to control it and make it last for a long time. Later he must have dozed, for when he looked at his watch, it was nearly midnight and he was alone on the bed.

He sat up rubbing his face, not quite sure that any of this had happened, and then he became aware of delicious cooking smells drifting into the room. He got up and went into the bathroom, and then he pulled on his shirt and pants, not bothering with shoes.

She was in the kitchen when he went in there, wearing

a white cotton robe, her back to him as she busied herself at the stove. He put his arms around her from behind and she nuzzled against him.

He squeezed her. "Smells terrific."

"I was afraid I'd burned the sauce."

"But you didn't."

"No."

"It would have been worth it, anyway."

She turned and put her arms around his neck and he kissed her very tenderly.

"I'm so glad I'm here," he said.

"Me too."

They had dinner the way women liked it best, the only illumination in the small dining area coming from a pair of tall candles, and with soft music from the stereo that Ben thought was Mozart, but he wasn't sure. Through the window beside the table the city seemed much less harsh than in the daytime, its glittering lights stretching away to infinity.

Margot had cooked the pasta Sicilian-style, smothered in spicy tomato sauce with bits of peppers and thin slices of hot sausage. She served it with a salad and warm chunks of Italian bread and Ben ate ravenously. In contrast, she took only a bite or two of the pasta, and a few sips of Chianti, no doubt keeping an eye on her figure.

Ben didn't notice. He never thought about his weight, because it never seemed to change. Which was probably due to his erratic eating habits. Tonight he stuffed himself, thinking that he couldn't remember anything ever tasting better. While they ate they talked about life in the city, and about the modeling business, and some of the things she told him he tucked away.

She'd worked with dozens of photographers and several agents, and she'd known scores of models and people in agencies and sometimes their clients. In some ways it was like a lot of other businesses Ben was familiar with, ranging from good to sleazy. The way it treated women was no surprise; there was room at the top for a handful of superstars, and from there down the levels broadened until they included hangers-on and hopefuls who didn't make enough to live on. What went on in the garment district was the pits, with women often used as currency, the garmentos dropping them on buyers as favors. It was an area Ben hadn't thought much about, and he made a mental note to check it out.

When they finished he helped her clean up the kitchen, and he had to laugh at himself, sliding into this domestic groove as if he belonged in it. He felt happier and more at ease than he had in months. He called the Sixth and left her telephone number and then they went back to bed. He was full of food and wine and he'd been operating for a long time on short sleep; he was sure he'd simply drop into oblivion. But when she curled her warm body close to his, he astonished himself by responding once more.

30

Brennan stuck out his jaw. "Are you out of your fucking mind?"

Ben reminded himself to be patient. He had pretty much expected this reaction, but now that he was getting it, he was having a hard time keeping his anger under wraps. It was nine o'clock in the morning and they were in Ben's office and this time they were drinking coffee. Despite the hour, Ben wished it was vodka.

The zone commander shook his head. "So some college broad got knocked off eight years ago, and just because they found bites on her ass, you think it was the same guy?"

"I told you, there were a lot of other things, too. She was sodomized, and she died of a broken neck."

Brennan sighed. "Jesus Christ, Lieutenant. All that is common in rape murders. A blowjob, and then the guy chokes her or busts her neck. And bites are common, too. You know that, as well as I do."

Ben shifted in his chair. "It just seemed to fit. A lot of what I saw up there was like what we're dealing with here."

"Yeah, and I just told you why."

"Okay, but a bright guy, maybe college educated, all that could—" He caught himself, realizing he had been about to refer to what Stein had been telling him. Any mention of the shrink would really send Brennan through the roof.

The captain leaned forward. "Get back to the basics, you hear me? There's enough heat on this fucking case without your running down some goddamn blind alley just because you got a hunch."

"Okay," Ben said. "You're probably right. I won't waste

time on it. But I will do a routine check, maybe just see if anything of interest turns up on a rundown of their alums, all right?"

Brennan's mouth twisted in distaste, and for an instant Ben thought he might put an end to the whole thing. But then he said, "Just don't use up a lot of man-hours on it, understand?"

"Sure, I understand." I understand very well, he thought. You antique Irish fuck. Your ideas are all locked in cement, and the cement is in your head. You haven't had a new idea in twenty years, if you ever had one.

"So what have you got on photographers?" Brennan asked.

Ben reached for a stack of DD-5s. "Nothing much so far. But we're running every angle on them."

Brennan nodded. "Good. That's got to be where we'll find this son of a bitch."

"Sure, Cap." You ought to get a medal for keeping your face shut, he told himself.

186

31

OF all the overburdened facilities of the NYPD, the lab probably was the worst. Part of the problem was due to a shortage of adequately trained personnel, part of it due to a lack of modern equipment. Although New York had the largest police department in the country, many other cities were far ahead in such areas as computerized information files, forensic medicine, and ballistics, to name a few. When Ben walked in, the place impressed him as disorganized and confused, as usual.

It was only recently that the lab had installed a full-time department of dentistry. It took him about ten minutes to find the crowded area that housed Dr. Brody's operation. When he did, Brody was all apologies, explaining that he was shorthanded and swamped with work. So what else was new? Ben followed the dentist into a room where a technician was working at a bench on plaster casts of teeth.

One wall of the room contained light boxes, and Brody had affixed a string of photographs to them. They were blowups of bites in the flesh of the young women whose bodies had been found in Greenwich Village, and alongside them were some of the pictures Ben had brought back from his trip to Hamilton.

Brody adjusted his gold-rimmed glasses and indicated. "If you'll look here, Lieutenant, you'll see that what I've selected are the cleanest examples on each body."

Ben stepped close to the photographs. They were color shots, and the predominant hues were those of purple and black impressions made deep into white flesh. Even to his untrained eye, the similarities of the patterns the teeth had made were unmistakable. Looking at them, he was again reminded of a dental chart. "I have to tell you, Doc. They sure look alike to me."

"They are alike," Brody said. "As I think I've explained, odontology is not an exact science for forensic purposes. Not nearly as accurate as fingerprints or DNA, for instance, as a means of identification. But sometimes you find evidence like this and there's little room for doubt."

"Then the man who bit the Benoit girl is the same guy who did the biting on these others?"

"In my opinion, yes."

"How sure are you, Doc—I mean, your own deep-down gut feeling?"

Brody smiled. "As sure as I can be. I'd bet on it."

So he'd been right. Just as Chief Olson had been right. It was another step—a big one—and it was going in the direction he'd hoped it would. Ben moved along the row of photos to the ones on the end, the ones of the bites on the Benoit girl's body. "These were made eight years ago. So I gather his teeth haven't changed much, in that time?"

"No, they haven't. At least not the ones that made these bites." Brody pointed to one of the photographs. "These impressions in the center of the bite were made by the incisors. And these by the canines, or cuspids. You'll notice that the uppers were larger and stronger than the teeth in the lower jaw, which is normal. What's unusual is the extreme regularity. Very strong, very healthy, very even. I'd say the man you're looking for has a beautiful smile."

"Yeah," Ben said. "So we figured. Tell me, would it help to get out a flyer on this? Maybe another dentist would recognize the teeth."

Brody shook his head. "I doubt it very much. You see, the problem here is that the teeth that made these impressions were too good. For our purposes, anyway. What a dentist would be able to spot would be work that could be identified. Inlays, or a bridge, or whatever. If we were very lucky, that is. But with these teeth, it would take a miracle."

"Okay," Ben said, "just an idea."

"Nevertheless, I'd be glad to make one up."

"Sure, it couldn't hurt. Anything's worth a try." He spent a few more minutes studying the photographs, and then he thanked Brody and left.

When he climbed into his car, he started the engine and just sat there for a few moments. *One thing I got out of this, my asshole friend. I know now you're the same creep who killed that girl at Colgate. So inch by inch, I'm learning more about you. And I'm going to go right on learning, until I know your name and where you live and the color of your eyes and everything else there is to know. And then I'm going to bust those big beautiful teeth of yours right out of your miserable fucking head.*

He slapped the wheel exultantly and pulled the Ford out into the traffic.

32

SARAH Weston returned to the studio at a little before noon. She'd been covering a fire in Brooklyn, a tenement blaze that had killed two children. The mother was a twenty-two-year-old unmarried black woman hooked on crack who had gone out the previous evening leaving the kids, one three, the other eighteen months, alone. Apparently they had tipped over a kerosene heater sometime this morning. The cops were looking for the mother now.

It wasn't much of a story, for several reasons. For one thing, the only footage Weston's cameraman had been able to get was a shot of a scorched window in the building, looking up from the street. The fire department had been there within minutes and had extinguished the flames quickly, although not in time to save the children, who had been asphyxiated. When the WPIC-TV van rolled up, an ambulance crew had already removed the bodies. So the visual interest was next to nothing. She had a few seconds of an interview with a cop and that was about it. And underlying all this was her conviction that black junkie mothers who went off and left kids to die in fires had about as much news value in New York as the weather.

So now the problem was the same one Weston faced every day: how to build what she had into a worthwhile story for the station's evening news. It wouldn't be easy. Shit.

Another thing that was eating at her was the lack of new developments in the Greenwich Village murders. After a great start, one in which she herself had played a major role that had brought her coverage in the newspapers and even grudging recognition from the other TV stations and the networks, the story had more or less dried up. She had kept it alive as long as she could, showing and reshowing the mysterious photograph of the blonde and conducting interviews with everybody in the NYPD willing to talk about it, but after a while it had paled. She had tried other angles as well, talking to photographers and models, but her producer, Jerry Baum, had finally told her to put it aside until she had hard news.

She sat down at her desk and stared at the screen of her word processor, wondering how she could get something halfway decent out of the fire in Brooklyn. Maybe she could build up the crack angle, imply that the mother had been in trouble with the hoodlums in Brownsville who ran the business. It wasn't much, but it was worth a try. She dug a package of Kents out of her bag and lit one.

And saw the envelope.

It was sitting on the pile of papers that littered her desk, just as the first one had been. It was the same size, 8½-by-11, and it was the same shade of gray paper. But what really caught her eye was the lettering. Her name was on the face of it in block capital letters, printed in black marker. No return address, just her name and the name of the station, and it was marked PERSONAL. She stubbed out the cigarette in an ashtray, and picked up the envelope. When she tore it open, she noticed that her fingers were trembling.

Inside was a photograph, as she'd known instinctively there would be. It was in color with a matte finish, and when she slid it out she was almost afraid to look at it, yet at the same time barely able to contain her excitement.

Once again, the subject was a young woman. But the photo was nothing like that of the blonde, with one exception: this girl was also naked. She had dark hair, and she seemed to be suspended in air, her arms extended, as if she were flying across a bloodred sky. There was a reddish haze over her flesh as well. The red tone partially obscured details of her face, making it impossible to tell what color her eyes were, or exactly what expression her features wore. The picture made Weston think of one of those strange medieval paintings, with humans made to look like animals, or birds. In this, the woman was soaring over you, as if you were looking up at her from some hellish place.

Weston stared at the photograph, and shuddered. Questions flooded her mind. Was this for real? Had the same man sent it? Who was this girl? When the photo was taken, was she alive or dead? She turned the photograph over and placed it face down on her desk, looking around to see if anyone had noticed. But it was business as usual, the room full of people talking, typing, moving about, no one paying any attention to her.

Weston picked up the envelope and went over it again carefully. It certainly looked like the first one, the one that had contained the shot of the blonde, but she couldn't be sure. She had no copy of that one to compare this to. But wait a minute—it had to be from the same source. No one else would have known what the first one looked like. So this couldn't be a fake, an effort by some wacko to con her. And anyway, who else would take a photograph as weird as this new one? Even though the concept was totally different from the first, it certainly was as strange. And it had also been produced with considerable skill.

She flipped the photo over and examined it again. As far as she could see, it would have been much more difficult to create than the one of the blonde. And God knew it had as much impact, probably more. She opened a drawer in her desk and placed the photograph and the envelope inside and then shut the drawer and locked it.

So now what? Her mind raced through the possibilities. To begin with, there were the cops to consider. She'd agreed to contact Ben Tolliver at once if anything new turned up. But there was no telling what he might do when he heard about this new picture. There was a good chance he might try to put a muzzle on her, tell her she couldn't show it on the air. More bullshit about material evidence, or some such. Well, screw him. She wasn't about to miss an opportunity like this to suit the whims of some cop. And besides, she had an obligation to the public, didn't she?

But the important thing—the *main* thing—was to handle this in the way that would do the most good for Sarah Weston. And that had to start with doing a story on the photo. The lieutenant would blow his cork, but so what? She could blame it on WPIC's management. In fact, that was exactly what she'd do. Let *them* take the heat; after all, she was the one who'd made this the biggest story the station had ever had. And as far as the police were concerned, she'd be doing them a favor, when it came right down to it. Just by showing the picture of the blonde she'd made more progress than they had in months. That's what had led to the Danvers girl's quick identification. And it was also the reason the NYPD had finally gotten off its ass and assigned all those cops to the case.

First off, she'd have to let Dave Pirenza, the news editor, know about this new photo. And then the producer, Jerry Baum. Just as she had with the Danvers picture. They lived and died by the numbers, and WPIC's ratings had kicked up eight whole share points as a result of her coverage of the murders. And the ratings had also fallen off again when the story grew stale. Pirenza and Baum were as hungry as she was. Well, almost.

She flicked on the processor and began to set up her lead. She wanted to be well organized before she went in to see Pirenza. A smile curled the corners of her mouth. This would sure as hell beat a piece on some Brooklyn crackhead.

She'd been at it about a half hour when her phone rang. She picked it up, a little annoyed at having her concentration broken. "Sarah Weston."

The voice was that of a young man. His tone was pleasant. "Hello, Sarah."

"Who's this?"

"You don't know my name, but you know a lot about me."

This was no time for games. She was about to hang up when an eerie thought crawled into her mind. "Who are you?"

"As I told you, I'm someone you know a lot about. In fact, awhile back you said I was highly intelligent, and that I was probably laughing at the police."

She was suddenly finding it hard to breathe. "How do I know you're that person?"

"I can prove it to you."

"How?"

"Do you like the new photograph?"

"I—"

"Well, do you?"

Christ, it *was* real. The man on the other end of the line was the killer. What do you say to someone like him—how do you keep him talking? How do you avoid angering him? She was into the most exciting thing that had ever happened to her—the break of her life—and she couldn't even speak.

"Still there, Sarah?"

She managed to force the words out. "Yes. I'm here." Instinct told her what to say next. "And I like the new photograph very much. I think it's beautiful."

"Ah. I'm glad you do. It's different, isn't it?"

"Yes. Very different." She was warming up to it now, encouraged by having pleased him. Maybe she could gain his confidence, if she played it right. "It has an almost mystical quality."

"Yes. You saw that, did you?"

"Of course I did. It's very powerful. You couldn't help being moved by it."

"Did you know who had sent it?"

"I—wasn't sure." She decided to push it a little further. "But it was so well done, I thought it must have come from you."

"You're very perceptive, Sarah. And very intelligent yourself."

"Who was the model?"

His tone abruptly turned harsh. "What difference does that make?"

"It doesn't," she fumbled. "It's just that I was, you know, curious."

"The only thing that counts is the quality of the work itself. I could have used anybody as the model. If you look at it again, you'll see she wasn't that important."

"No, I'm sure she wasn't." Don't flip him out, she told herself. Don't lose him.

"The concept, and the way it was carried out, those are the things that give it power."

"Of course. I understand that."

He sounded mollified. "Do you know why I sent it to you?"

"I—no, I don't."

"Because I knew you'd be able to appreciate it."

"I see."

"You'll show it, won't you—on the air?"

"I might. But only if you promise to call me again."

"I'll call you, Sarah. But if you tell the police we've spoken, or if you try to record my call, you'll be very sorry. Do you understand?"

"Yes. You have my word I won't do anything like that."

"Good. I'll be watching, Sarah. Good night."

She heard a click, and the hum of the dial tone. Her shoulders slumped, and she felt a trickle of sweat between her breasts. Then the full realization of what she had and what it could mean to her struck her like a belt of cognac. She sat bolt upright in her chair and unlocked the desk drawer, taking one more quick look at the photograph before getting down to work on the processor. She couldn't wait to show the picture to Pirenza and Baum.

But then she stopped and thought for a moment. There was one thing she wouldn't tell either one of them about, and that was the phone call. That was something that belonged to her alone. It was her secret, her ace in the hole. She wasn't quite sure how she'd play it, but she'd know when the time came.

She leaned forward again, and her fingers flew over the keyboard.

33

W HEN Ben stepped into the bunkroom, it reminded him of a flophouse. Every one of the double-deckers had a detective on it, dressed except for shoes, most of the guys not even covered by a blanket. The snoring was a low-level roar, accented by snorts and whistles and an occasional fart. None of these characters would be in here for more than a couple of hours, and as soon as a bunk was freed up, another cop would roll onto it. There were no windows, and the air was ripe with the smell of sweat and bad breath and unwashed socks and other choice odors. The room had been like this for weeks, and would go right on as it was until they broke the case. The only reason Ben went into it now was because the coffee urn was on a table at the far end of the room, near the lockers. He had trained himself years ago to catnap at his desk for fifteen minutes or so at a time, and was able to go for days on no more than those occasional snatches when he had to. Last night he had worked straight through, and he was feeling it. He stretched, and then filled a Styrofoam cup with the steaming black liquid, thinking about the day's activities and frustrations.

Running down the Colgate people was turning into a monumental pain in the ass, just as he'd known it would. He had Flynn on it, and four teams of detectives, and it wasn't nearly enough. The university records his men had brought down from Hamilton were in fairly good shape, well kept and apparently up to date, and that was a big help. But there were endless interviews to go through, and

197

miles of tracking. At this point they hadn't even finished sorting out what they had.

Meantime, the photography angle was as dry as ever. He had more guys on that now, but it hadn't given them so much as a good lead, let alone a suspect. Only the borrowed vice cops were finding it productive, because they kept turning up porn operators. But as far as this murder case was concerned, it was a zero. Everybody who looked at that goddamn picture of the blonde had a hunch, or a theory, or an opinion, none of them worth a shit. So what the cops were doing was grinding it out, knocking on doors, asking questions, talking to people, running down everything that might take them somewhere, however slim the chance. It was what Captain Brennan referred to with relish as old-fashioned police work, and to Ben it was like counting grains of sand in a desert. The only problem was, he didn't know a better way. He went back to his office carrying his coffee and sat down at his desk.

He looked at his watch, feeling guilty because he knew what he was going to do, even though he hadn't yet admitted it to himself. It was a few minutes before eight, still early evening. Finally he said the hell with it and picked up the phone.

When she answered, he said hello, and she said, "I was hoping it was you," and that made him feel wonderful. He asked if she'd had dinner, and she said she hadn't and suggested he pick up something on the way.

"Sounds fine," Ben said. "What would you like?"

"You."

"For dinner."

"You."

He laughed then, but the message was making him feel even better. "Am I the main course, or dessert?"

"Both. Anything you bring is just to snack on, in between."

He said he'd see her soon and hung up. After he'd put the phone down he went on thinking about her, a smile lingering as he saw her in his mind. There were no pretenses with her, no playing games. She didn't try to mislead him or keep him off balance. And there was sure as hell no reason for her to be interested in him other than himself. Which was a puzzle of another kind. What did he have to offer her? A cop who lived the Job, and whose worldly possessions consisted of a beat-up car and a few pieces of crappy furniture in a rented one-room apartment, plus some scraps of clothing. And that was it. Not exactly everywoman's dream, the rich and powerful stud who could whisk her away from earthly concerns to a life of ease, forever free from worry.

But he was smart enough to figure that out, too. The truth was that whatever he might be, he answered a need in her as well. Maybe his own straight-ahead, no-bullshit approach to life was a welcome change for her, after what she'd been dealing with. And beyond all that, beyond anything you could call rational, there was the sheer animal attraction, the chemistry that made him feel as if he owned the world, just by thinking about her. She also had to be feeling something like that, about him.

He left his office and told Flynn the telephone number, then bounded down the stairs. On the way uptown he stopped at a Chinese restaurant off Union Square and bought several cartons of food, sort of a mystery medley. When he got to her building he parked the Ford, and as he went into the lobby he again experienced a twinge of guilt, but then he figured fuck it. He'd been working long stretches, seven days a week, and if he was lucky enough to be able to spend a night in a real bed with a beautiful woman he was crazy about, then he would damn well spend it.

She greeted him at the door with one of those kisses that

staggered him, and he was glad Chinese food was easy to keep hot. Margot put the stuff into a warm oven and from there they went straight into her bedroom. They made love for an hour or so, passionately and hungrily at first, and then once again just tenderly sharing each other. It was amazing to him what it was like, being with her. All the knotted-up emotions, all the frustrations, just seemed to melt away, leaving him relaxed and supremely happy.

Afterward she served the food—which turned out to be moo goo gai pan and sweet-and-sour pork and a few other things he wasn't sure of—with cold beer, and as usual he was ravenous. They were sitting at the small dining table, and when she asked him how his day had been, he looked at her for a moment, startled, and then threw his head back and laughed.

"What's funny?"

"We are," he said. "Just like an old married couple."

She smiled. "As far as I know, old married couples do not usually greet each other the way we just did."

"They should. Divorce rate would go way down."

"You could be right. But your day—was it okay?"

He spoke around a mouthful of pork. "Not bad, but not good, either. A lot of hard work, with nothing much to show for it."

"How are you doing with photographers?"

"Lousy, so far. Everybody's got ideas about that picture, but nobody's given us a decent lead."

"Uh-huh. Have you been talking to the reps?"

"Some. Why?"

"I think they know more about what's going on generally than the photographers themselves do. You know, who's doing what kind of work, who might be somebody you should look at."

"Yeah, maybe you're right."

She watched him eat for a couple of minutes. "Are you tired?"

He grinned. "Think you wore me out? No such luck."

"That's not what I meant, Lieutenant. In that respect, I think you're indestructible."

"At least you tried."

"You mean I'm trying. I haven't given up yet. But are you? You must be. I mean, you have to sleep sometime."

He shrugged. "Yeah, I guess I am, a little. But the case keeps me pumped up, keeps me going."

"Is that how it usually is? On all cases?"

He looked at her. "No. But what you're really asking me is whether this case is something special, right?"

"It is, isn't it?"

"I guess it is."

"A personal thing, to you?"

He thought briefly of Stein asking more or less the same question. It must have been pretty obvious to anybody taking a close look at him. But then he surprised himself. Instead of keeping it all inside, the way he had for years, he decided to open up to her, realizing that for once he really wanted to talk about it, wanted to tell it to someone he could trust. "Yeah. It's a personal thing."

He drank some of his beer. "When I was a kid, I had a girlfriend. I was just out of high school, working as a shipping clerk in a department store. She was a salesgirl in the same place. Lived with her folks in Brooklyn. I was over there seeing her one night, and we went for a walk in Prospect Park. We were sitting under a tree, all wrapped up in each other, and four black guys came along the walk."

He took another swallow of beer, seeing the scene again in his mind, the spades wearing black T-shirts and jeans and with chains around their necks, Afros sprouting from their heads. He hadn't been aware of their presence until they'd been within a stride of where he'd been sitting with the girl. "They beat the hell out of me, and when I was out of it they raped her, and then they smashed her head with a rock. When I came to she was still alive, but not by much. The cops took her to a hospital, and then they arrested me on a charge of attempted murder, said we'd had a fight. But after two days she became conscious long enough to say what had happened."

He finished his beer. "And then she died."

Margot's voice was very small. "Oh, God."

"Yeah. A month later I joined the Marine Corps."

She was quiet for a time. "So now I understand."

"Uh-huh. Truth is, I'm glad I told you. I feel better, somehow."

"Yes." She was looking at him with a direct, open expression. "It helps, doesn't it?"

"I guess it does." He returned her gaze. "I know it does. Thanks for listening."

"Still hungry?"

He shook his head, and looked at his watch. "Hey—ten o'clock. Let's catch the news."

They went into the living room and turned on WPIC-TV.

34

Sᴀʀᴀʜ Weston had that breathless look, the one that said she had something monumental to tell you about. Ben had to hand it to her, she could make you think you were hearing the news story of the century—Chicago Fire, San Francisco Earthquake, all rolled into one. And the honey-colored hair and the green eyes and the swell of her breasts above the V of her blouse didn't hurt any. She had a hell of a presence.

When she opened her mouth, however, what she said caught him off guard. "Tonight we have an exclusive for you, on what may be another astonishing development in the grisly and unsolved Greenwich Village murder case."

Ben leaned forward on the sofa. What the hell was this about?

Weston: "You'll recall the uproar that was caused a few weeks back, when someone sent a photograph to this re-porter. That someone was believed to be the killer, and the picture was of his latest victim."

Cut to the photo, Weston's voice-over: "Here is that pho-tograph, of Ellen Danvers. Some authorities believe it was taken after Miss Danvers was raped and killed. Thus far the police have been unable to develop any leads on who the killer was, or whether it was the killer who took the photograph."

Cut to Weston: "Today, I was stunned to receive—" she paused, and her delivery slowed "—a second photograph. Once again, it was a highly unusual full-figure portrait of a young woman."

"Goddamn it," Ben said. "God *damn* it."

Weston: "This new photo is perhaps even more powerful than the one of Ellen Danvers. I'm going to show it to you, and I want to warn you that its subject is also nude."

Cut to the photograph, Weston's voice-over: "Who is this beautiful girl? And who staged this strange and emotionally evocative photograph? Anyone seeing it would agree that once more we have a work of genius. However odd it may seem—even otherworldly—you cannot help feeling its tremendous impact. The questions are, Who is she? Who took this picture? And finally, is this girl also . . . dead?"

Ben jumped to his feet. He wanted to kick the fucking tube out of the set.

Cut back to Weston: "Anyone who has any information as to the identity of the young woman you have just seen, or any knowledge of the photograph and who might have taken it, is urged to call me, Sarah Weston, here at WPIC-TV. All calls will be kept in strict confidence."

"That bitch," Ben said. "That dizzy bitch." The program was onto another news story. He snapped the set off.

Margot got up and put her hand on his shoulder. "What's going on? Shouldn't she have called the police?"

"You're damn right she should have. I told her that if she got anything else, she should call me right away."

"That picture—God, it gave me the creeps. Do you think it was the same guy?"

"I have no idea, but I'm sure going to find out." He headed for the door.

"Ben?"

"Yeah?"

"Was she dead?"

"I don't know that, either." He shut the door hard on his way out.

35

THE guy was fat and balding, in shirtsleeves and with his tie pulled down. The expression on his round face was the same one he might have worn if he'd been accosted by a bum. "You're Lieutenant Tolliver?"

"That's right," Ben said. He took the case out of his back pocket and flipped it open, displaying his shield.

The fat guy glanced at it. "I'm Jerry Baum. I produce the news. You want to talk, come into my office."

Ben followed him out of the WPIC-TV newsroom and through a door. The minute he was inside, Ben knew he'd been set up. Sitting in the office were Sarah Weston and two men he didn't recognize.

Baum said, "This is Dave Pirenza, the news editor. And George Robertson, our attorney. I think you know Miss Weston."

Pirenza was also in shirtsleeves. He had buck teeth and a red mustache. Robertson was dark-haired, wearing a navy pin-striped suit. The men were side by side on a sofa, Weston was in an armchair. None of them spoke, but only stared at Ben.

Baum went over to his desk and sat down. He waved a hand toward a chair. "Have a seat, Lieutenant."

Ben folded his arms. "No thanks—I'll stand."

A small smile flickered across Baum's features. The smile said, okay, asshole—have it your way.

Ben looked at the reporter. She was perfectly posed, her legs crossed and her skirt hiked to about three inches above her knee. He spoke directly to her. "Miss Weston, you showed another photograph on the news tonight. One you said was sent to you today."

Her gaze met his. "That's correct."

"That photograph could be a piece of evidence in the murder investigation I'm conducting."

She made no reply.

"The last time something like this happened," Ben went on, "I told you it was important to call me first, if you got anything that could have a bearing on the case."

Pirenza spoke up. The mustache looked like a caterpillar crawling on his upper lip. "Sarah didn't make the decision on this, Lieutenant. We did. And we cleared it with counsel before we put it on the air."

Before Ben could answer, George Robertson said, "I saw no reason the photograph shouldn't be shown."

"The decision was not yours to make," Ben said. "Not any of you. I should have been contacted as soon as you got it."

There was a slight drawl in Robertson's voice. Ben had heard that inflection in people's speech before; it usually came out of a mouth whose owner thought he had the world by the balls, and to get anything he wanted, all he had to do was squeeze. "Sorry, Lieutenant," Robertson said, "but I'm afraid I can't agree with you. The photograph was sent to Miss Weston, and the management of the station felt it was newsworthy. Whether it had anything to do with your case was purely conjectural."

Would you listen to this haughty fuckhead? Ben took a deep breath. "She herself said it had to do with the case, on the air."

"I said it *may* have," Weston said.

The lawyer raised his hands, palms up. "You see? All just conjecture."

Ben's voice was hard and flat. "I don't give a shit whether it was conjecture or not. If there was even a chance it was connected, I should have been notified. First. Now where is the picture, and how did it arrive?"

Robertson picked up a cardboard file jacket from a table beside the sofa. "We think it came by messenger, but no one is quite sure. Apparently it was left at the door of the mailroom. I have the envelope and the photo right here, if you'd care to examine them."

Ben took the jacket from him. He opened it and peered inside, at the gray envelope and the photo. Then he closed the jacket and tucked it under his arm. He looked up at them. "I want you to know you're asking for a lot of trouble, if you're going to insist on interfering with our investigation."

Robertson's drawl grew more pronounced. "What investigation, Lieutenant? Are you telling us there's been another murder? Do you know whether this girl is another victim?"

Ben was beginning to feel like a gold-plated idiot. "You have a choice. Either you agree to let me know if anything is sent here that might have to do with the case, or I go to the district attorney."

Robertson's mouth curled into a supercilious smile. "Really? I'm not so sure you'd want to get involved in anything like that. You don't actually want to test an important news medium's First Amendment rights, do you?"

They had him, Ben knew, by the gonads. The last thing in the world the city government would want to mess with would be a contest with the media over their right to report on the progress—or the lack of progress—the NYPD was making in a sensational murder case. So all Ben was doing was backing himself into a corner it might be hard to get out of. Hard? Hell, it would be impossible. The police commissioner was in enough trouble over this goddamned case without giving the gentlemen of the press more reason to roast his ass in public.

Nevertheless Ben tried to tough it out. "I'll let the DA decide that." He looked at the producer. "A restrictive order would give you a lot of problems, Mr. Baum. Seems to me that's not something anybody in your business would want."

It wasn't much of a shot, but it went home. Baum blinked, and looked away.

Robertson said, "Is that a threat?"

"Wait a minute," Baum said. "I don't see anything wrong with contacting the police." He looked at Ben. "So long as you don't try to interfere with our right to run a news story."

"That's fair enough," Ben said. "But anything that comes up ought to be considered on its merits. One thing at a time."

"Impossible," Pirenza said. He turned to Baum. "Listen, Jerry, who do you want running this news department—the cops? You want people like this deciding what we can put on the air and what we can't? Jesus, Big Brother isn't just watching, he wants to come right in here and take over."

"Keep something in mind," Robertson said. "Nothing is more important than the public's right to know."

God almighty, Ben thought. The broadcasters have got to the point where they don't just use the air, they think they *own* it. But he wasn't deceived. All this holy horseshit was just a screen for their real purpose, which was to get anything onto the tube that might help them beat the competition. And if that meant fucking up a murder investigation, so be it.

But Baum wasn't looking for a fight. He had too much going for him and his nickel-shit news program now to take a chance on getting the DA's office into this. "Look, Lieutenant. Anything else comes along, we agree to let you know. And you agree not to try to put restraints on us."

"Okay, I'll buy that," Ben said.

Pirenza shook his head in disgust.

Ben gestured toward the file jacket under his arm. "I'll want to take these with me."

"You have our permission to do that," Robertson said.

Great, Ben thought. The fucking pope has given me his blessing. He left them then, closing the door behind him.

As he walked through the studio offices on his way out, he heard someone call his name. He turned to see Sarah Weston hurrying toward him.

When she caught up with him she linked her arm with his. "Ben, I'm sorry. I really am. But there was nothing I could do. They've been watching me like hawks. The minute that envelope arrived they were all over me. You saw how important this story is to them."

He looked down at her. The green eyes were very wide and he was conscious of the warmth of her body pressing against him. "So? You should have called me anyway. We had an agreement, right?"

"I was afraid to, Ben. It could have meant my job."

"I doubt that."

"You don't know those guys. But look—I'll do anything to make it up to you. Anything you want."

"You can tell me what else has been going on that I don't know about."

"That's all, I swear it. The picture arrived and they insisted I build a story on it. And it's true that nobody even knows for sure whether it's legitimate."

"Okay, Sarah." He disengaged himself from her.

"Ben?"

"Yeah?"

"If anything else happens, I'll call you no matter what."

"You do that." He turned and walked out.

36

THE reaction to the latest photograph was mostly media hype. The newspapers—especially the *Daily News* and the *Post*—gave it a big play, and the TV stations covered it in newscasts for a couple of days, but Ben couldn't help but wonder if the whole thing wasn't phony. Maybe some crank had sent it, if it had been sent at all. He wouldn't put anything past Weston and her friends at WPIC. The bottom line was that it was a photograph, and that was all it was. No body, no evidence of another murder, just the goddamn picture.

Brennan had stormed around, wanting to know what it was about, and Ben told him of his visit to WPIC. When nothing more came of it, the police brass took the position that this was just another example of TV putting out crap that served no purpose and would only get gullible citizens worked up.

Ben had copies of the shot made and gave them out to the detectives he had working on the case, instructing the men to show them around while they were questioning people, to see if they might turn up something on it. He also asked Ed Feldman and Alan Stein for their opinions.

The ME's reaction was that the photo was too indistinct for him to know what condition the girl might have been in when it was made. He also was unable to tell whether there were bruises on her body; the reddish hue of the lighting and the vague shadows across her form made it impossible to tell.

Stein said there were a number of interpretations that could be made. The one that seemed likeliest to him was that, if the photo was genuine, and he thought it could be, what the killer was saying was that the woman was a devil. Or perhaps that all women were evil creatures from the netherworld.

The shrink's theories sounded like bullshit to Ben, but he was willing to listen. Stein did come up with one good suggestion, however. He asked Ben if it might be possible to look into the university medical records of the alumni who had been at Colgate at the time of the Benoit murder. Ben said he'd try to get them.

37

For the first few days after WPIC-TV aired the new photograph, Peter Barrows was euphoric. Whenever he thought back to what Sarah Weston had said about it, and about him, the rush of pleasure made his head swim. Her description had been the truth: it was indeed the work of genius. And it was also the finest thing he'd ever done, by far. As good as the shot of the blonde had been, this one was better. And this time there were no dirty little loose ends, no gang of stupid cops stumbling around a body, no idiotic comments from some fartbrain who thought he was a detective.

The actual reliving of the whole experience, through the wonder of videotape, was even more satisfying. All he had to do was turn on the machine, and he'd get *all* of it. There was the marvelous photograph itself, somehow even more exciting when he saw it on the tube than when he held a print of it in his hands. There was the re-creation of the thrill of the session in his studio with Sue Connery. And then there was Sarah Weston describing the photograph's emotional impact, its power. It was glorious, and it would be his forever.

Or would it?

Oddly, the highs evaporated almost as suddenly as they had appeared. One night he went into his bedroom and looked at the cassette, and it was like going through an old, worn book he'd once enjoyed, but had long since tired of. Or like the few times he'd tried cocaine, when he'd been sailing over the moon for an hour or so, then afterward had been hideously depressed. Re-creating the night with

Sue had been lovely, but abruptly and inexplicably, the memory had crumbled. After that, even the pleasure of recalling his talk with Sarah Weston on the telephone had paled.

This afternoon he was feeling nervous and edgy. He made a half-assed attempt to do some work, but in fact he was merely shuffling papers around on his desk. A meeting was scheduled for 4:00 P.M., in the agency's offices on Madison Avenue at Forty-ninth Street, and Peter killed time until he was ready to leave for it.

He walked up there, in order to avoid sharing a cab with Farnsworth. She was already in the conference room when he arrived, along with the key people in the Tynex account group, McLean, Phillips, and Krakaur. Also present were Josh Epstein, one of the agency's commercial producers, and his assistant, a good-looking girl named Judy something. Epstein was a young guy with longish hair, wearing a stopwatch on a lanyard around his neck, which Peter supposed he thought made him look like a film director.

They went through the usual handshakes and coffee orders, then McLean started the meeting by reminding them they were assembled to see videotapes of candidates for the role of Tynex spokesperson in the new campaign. Epstein took over at that point, explaining how they'd screened dozens of women, finally narrowing the field down to the six they had on tape. He said they were all fine actresses, all highly qualified, and frankly one of the best groups he'd ever seen. He was obviously building this up, so that the client and the agency people would know how hard he worked and how professional he was. He asked that everyone take notes so they could discuss their choices afterward, and then he told Judy to roll the tape on the oversized TV monitor at the head of the room.

As far as Peter was concerned, the entire procedure was a crock of shit. He thought the new concept was stupid, but he also knew why they were running with it. This was an unvarnished effort by the agency to kiss Farnsworth's ass. He sneaked a glance at her, sitting midway down the table.

For just a moment he was a child again, and she was Freda, he felt a wave of fear and disgust. He thought about how satisfying it would be to rearrange those smug features with a claw hammer. But his anger came up too fast, and he could feel his pulse throbbing in his forehead, his nails digging into the palms of his hands. He had to look away, telling himself to calm down, to relax. He took out a handkerchief and wiped sweat from his forehead, and then concentrated on the monitor.

Each of the women had been shot in a medium close-up, holding a Tynex bottle in one hand and speaking to the camera, stating her name first and then reading the copy from a TelePrompTer. Epstein had been right; they were all attractive and they were all competent. And they were all boring as hell. It was hard for Peter even to pay attention, let alone take notes. But he went through the motions, nevertheless.

Until the fourth woman on the tape appeared.

When he looked at her he thought his heart would stop. He blinked his eyes rapidly, to be sure his vision was clear, and that he was actually seeing what was on the screen. But there was nothing wrong with his eyesight. The face was unmistakable. There was the soft plume of auburn hair, flowing down one side of her forehead in a gentle sweep. There were the violet eyes, large and wide-set, their depth revealing so much sensitivity. There were the matchless cheekbones and the small, perfect nose, and the generous mouth with just a hint of a smile at the corners.

She said her name was Margot Dennis.

Peter could hardly breathe. He stared at the monitor, one part of his brain wanting desperately to believe while

214

another part screamed out that it wasn't true, that it couldn't be true.

But it was. She was alive and breathing, and even speaking, in the low-timbered voice that was so familiar. Peter couldn't understand the words, even though he could easily have recited the commercial copy from memory. It was as if his mind simply was unable to accept all this incredible information at one time. And then suddenly it was over, and she was gone.

He looked around the table quickly, to see the reaction of the others. Not one of them seemed to have noticed there was anything amiss, or even the slightest bit unusual. Krakaur was doodling on a pad, Farnsworth was making notes. Epstein was riffling through some head sheets, and McLean and Phillips were pretending to be interested. But why should they think anything out of the ordinary had occurred? They didn't know; they couldn't.

Another woman was on camera now, just finishing up her speech. Then came a few seconds of blank tape, to give them all time to make notes. And then the last of the six was on, reading the copy.

Maybe I imagined it, Peter thought. Maybe it was just one of those quirky things that happen to me sometimes, that have always happened, for as long as I can remember. One of those little tricks my mind plays. Like when I think about something taking place, and then later I'm not sure whether it really did or not.

"That's it," Epstein said. "Want to see them again, or would you rather discuss them first?"

"I think we ought to run through the tape again, Josh," McLean said.

Judy rewound the cassette and hit the play button.

It took a total of only a few minutes to get through the first three candidates, but it seemed like an hour. Peter sat staring at the monitor, half seeing the images on it, his heart thudding in his chest. He clasped his hands under the table, where they would be out of sight, and tightened his grip until he felt real pain.

And then she was on the screen once more. Achingly beautiful, and astonishingly, impossibly, alive. There was no mistake—no one else in the world could ever look like that. Did he believe in reincarnation? What difference did it make what he believed in—or what he didn't? She was there; she was a fact. This was no trick of his mind. It might be a trick of fate, in fact had to be, somehow. But that was not only beyond his ability to reason, it was a mystery he didn't want to unravel, as if in finding the answer he might destroy what was happening here, and it would all turn out to be nothing but an illusion, a cruel dream. No. She was here, and it was a miracle. And that was enough.

When the tape ended this time, the group went into an inane discussion of the women they'd seen. Farnsworth thought this, and Krakaur thought that, and McLean thought some other idiot thing. Peter paid no attention. His mind was already whirling, focusing intensely on what he would do next. This was an opportunity of the kind that might occur only once in his life—and he had to be absolutely sure of what to do with it.

"So what do you think, Peter?" It was McLean.

He cleared his throat, pretending to consider his answer carefully. "I think that first of all, we owe Josh a vote of thanks for doing a first-rate job. These people are all every bit as good as he told us they were."

Epstein beamed. The horse's ass.

"As far as a choice is concerned," Peter went on, "I personally thought number one and number three were excellent."

"We all pretty much agree with that," Krakaur said.

Peter reminded himself to handle this carefully. He would have to be very adroit to bring it off. At the same time, he was aware of his ability to respond quickly and coolly under pressure. "But I also remember something Marilyn pointed out to us, which was that any new Tynex advertising has to be nothing less than outstanding. So with that in mind, I find myself leaning toward number four. What was her name—Dennis? I thought she had some highly unusual qualities."

There was a moment of silence, and then Krakaur said, "Too gorgeous. Not believable."

Peter screwed up his lips, as if he was considering this bit of wisdom. "That might be. But you'd certainly remember her."

Farnsworth took the bait. "I think there's a lot to what Peter's saying. Whoever we come up with, she has to be special. Somebody who'd get high awareness."

"Why don't we sleep on it?" Mclean suggested. "It's too important to make a snap judgment on, anyway."

"Sure," Peter said. "I'll want to have a copy of that tape. On VHS, so I can see it at home."

"I'll get one over to you right away," Epstein said.

The meeting broke up shortly after that. Peter left the agency feeling dazed by excitement.

38

Bᴇɴ squeezed the Ford into a narrow space between two patrol cars. He went into the precinct house and up the stairs to the detective squad room, feeling as if a tractor had run over his head. The latest photograph remained as much a mystery as it was when he'd first seen it on the air, and once again the media coverage had slowed to a trickle. Missing Persons had been deluged with people who claimed to recognize her, including a young guy who thought she might be his girlfriend. The girl, he said, worked for a midtown bank and had disappeared some days back. But he wasn't sure. Meantime, Brennan had kept the pressure on, visiting the Sixth daily.

When he walked into the squad room, the first thing Ben saw was Ed Flynn bent over his desk. The sergeant didn't look as dapper as he usually did. His collar was open, his tie askew. There were fatigue lines at the corners of his eyes and dark circles under them. He was drinking black coffee from a Styrofoam cup, and smoking a cigarette. An ashtray at his elbow held a mound of butts.

Ben stopped at the desk. "Hey, Ed. How's it going?"

Flynn was working on the Colgate alumni. He'd been spending a lot of time on it, despite Brennan's admonition, directing the activities of four teams of detectives. He looked up. "It's fucking wonderful. We ever get this case wrapped, I'm gonna get a broad and go off to a beach someplace and stay there. I might even retire."

Ben grinned. "Balls. You getting anywhere?"

Flynn shrugged. "I don't know. At least we got rid of

the impossibles. We're down now to a bunch of maybes. There's a pile of stuff on your desk."

Ben looked around the room. No other regular members of his squad were there at the moment, only a few of the loaners Brennan had sent in from other precincts. They were doing grunt work at Flynn's direction, talking on the telephones, typing reports. Kurwitz, Rodriguez, O'Brien, Petrusky, and the others were all out on the street, most of them running down people in the photography business. Ben turned and went into his office. The reports he and Flynn and the others had put together on the Colgate investigation were in manila folders. He sat down at his desk and opened the one on top of the pile, reviewing what they had so far.

There had been just over twelve hundred male students enrolled at Colgate at the time of the Benoit homicide. Of those, fourteen were now dead. Most of the living were scattered around the United States, and some were in other parts of the world. One hundred forty-seven were in the greater New York area. Most of these were honest, upstanding citizens who were working hard at good jobs and who had no police records. Many were married and raising families. A few were extremely successful, among them a guy who had founded a chain of computer stores and another who was packaging shows for the television networks. There were several professional athletes. A handful were doctors. There were bankers and stockbrokers and insurance salesmen and lawyers and architects. But mostly they were young men who were at the middle-management levels of large corporations. Not one was in a business connected with photography.

Some of them had been ruled out because they hadn't been in New York at the time the murders were committed. One of these traveled around the world most of the year for one of the major oil companies. And one had been hospitalized with osteomyelitis.

There were also a few bad guys. One had been indicted recently by a Manhattan grand jury for bank embezzlement. Another was awaiting sentencing after conviction for mail fraud, having run a scam offering bogus municipal bonds. It would be some time before that one would again contribute to a Colgate fund-raising drive.

Ben spent an hour going through the reports. He was familiar with most of what they contained, but going over them helped him to focus on the mass of information. He was still reading when Flynn walked into the office. Ben glanced at him. "How soon do you figure we could show that old lady some of the yearbook pictures?"

Flynn dropped into a chair. "Bessie Koppel? I think we could probably do it now. But I'm not so sure what we'd get out of it. Over a hundred photos, and the shots are all at least four years old. If you take the last yearbook, when the last of these guys graduated."

"Yeah, but still it's something. She's the only one who actually saw the guy."

"Uh-huh. If you could call that seeing him. An old lady, half blind, looking out her window across the street at night. And not only that, how much can we depend on the pictures? A lot of things could've changed. You take weight alone, a guy loses twenty, thirty pounds, he looks a lot different."

Ben grunted. "When guys get out of college, they don't lose weight, Ed. They put it on."

"Okay, but either way, the guy's not gonna look the same."

"Maybe. Maybe not. She said she saw a slim guy. It's a pretty good bet he was like that in college, too."

"All right, we'll give it a shot. I've had blow-ups made of

the ones who are possiblities so far. You want to see them now?"

"Yeah, I do."

Flynn stepped out of the office, returning a moment later with a stack of eight-by-ten black-and-whites. Along with the pictures was the drawing the police artist had made with Bessie Koppel's guidance. Ben looked at it. The sketch showed a thin face topped with dark hair. He began comparing the yearbook pictures to it, one at a time. When he was about halfway through the stack, he began to realize that the approach wasn't turning out to be as helpful as he had hoped. But he plodded through the photos nevertheless, studying each one carefully before going on to the next. When he finished, he sat back in his chair.

Flynn lit a fresh cigarette. "Not so easy, huh? We got a drawing we don't know how accurate it is, and then we're trying to match it up with pictures that are all old."

Ben decided Flynn was right. After the first few they'd all started to look alike. "Maybe Bessie'll spot something."

The sergeant looked skeptical. "I hope so."

"What happened to the dead ends—you run those down, too?"

"Oh, sure. Hang on a minute, I'll show you." He went out again and came back with photocopies of more yearbook pictures. The first was of a swarthy young man with jet black hair parted in the middle. Notes scribbled on the sheet said his name was Radi Nair and that he was from New Delhi, India. He was thought to have returned there after his graduation from the university. Attempts by the alumni association to contact him had been unsuccessful. The man in the next photo was blond and bland-faced, and the word *junk* was scrawled across the picture.

Ben looked up, questioningly.

"Guy's an addict," Flynn explained. "He's at a rehab center in Brooklyn. Right now he's in a methadone program. We ran him down good. He's not our boy."

The man in the third picture was strikingly handsome, with soft dark eyes and his hair combed down over his forehead in bangs. "Gay," Flynn said. "Lives with an actor as the guy's wife."

"So?"

"We checked anyhow, Lou. He's clean."

The following shot was of a slim youth with curly hair and a pleasant smile. His name was Peter Hewitt and the notes said he was living in Europe.

Ben tossed the photos back down onto his desk. "Look, Ed. I know this is frustrating as hell for you, but I'm convinced we're onto something. The guy we're looking for could be right here someplace in this pile."

Flynn exhaled, the stream of smoke going out of him like air from a balloon. "Okay, Lou, he could be. But then again, maybe he's not here at all. I keep thinking, what if the guy wasn't a student? What if maybe he wasn't connected to the college? Maybe he was one of the visitors who was there for the football game, or maybe he was some guy who graduated and just came back for the weekend. Or maybe he was one of the people who lived in the town. Any of that's possible, too."

Ben hated to admit it, but Flynn could be right. "Yeah, well. Anything's possible. But the odds are, he was a student, and he's here someplace, right in front of our noses."

Flynn ground out his cigarette in an ashtray. "The thing is, we only got so much manpower. All these goddamn photographers and the labs and the model agencies—it's gonna take us months to cover what we got."

"Yeah. But unfortunately, our friend doesn't give a shit about our problems. He's out there, and he's been quiet for a while. We may not know what he's up to, but he does."

39

PETER got on the IRT local at Grand Central. He sat down on a cracked plastic bench and placed his attaché case on his lap. The bench was hard and uncomfortable, but at least he had a seat, which would have been out of the question during rush hour. The car was supposed to be air-conditioned, but that was a joke; its interior was like a steam bath. A black wino swathed in rags was flopped out on one of the other benches, and the rest of the passengers looked like zombies, staring dully at the littered floor as the train lurched along.

But he didn't care whether the car was uncomfortable or not, or whether it was dirty or clean. Excitement was pumping through his system, making his nerves hop like live wires. He couldn't wait to get home and put the cassette into his VCR. Seeing it this afternoon had been staggering to him, so unexpected and at the same time so wonderful, it was hard to grasp that it had actually happened. Now what he had to do—couldn't wait to do—was to look at it again in private, where he could determine once and for all if he had been right.

He became so deeply immersed in thinking about it he almost missed his stop. He saw the sign saying Spring Street and hurried off the train. The worn concrete steps leading up out of the subway stank of urine, and it occurred to him that the bums were the only people who put the subway to its proper use. Up on the street the evening air was fresh and cool, in sharp contrast to the rank hole he had emerged from.

As he hurried toward his building, he was conscious that

Soho was a fascinating place. Its narrow streets and side-walks were thronged with people and vehicles at all hours. In some ways he preferred the area the way it had been before the present boom, before it had become New York's new Bohemia, picking up where the Village had left off. But in other ways this was good, too. Some of the art galleries were truly amazing. You could find paintings and sculpture of any kind in them, but you especially saw so much great modern stuff. And most of the galleries were open at night, the way they were on the Left Bank in Paris.

His eyes roved back and forth, taking in the vast assortment of people. They were young, old, black, white, Hispanic, male, and female. There was a hot dog vendor on one corner, and on another a man was selling ice cream from a refrigerated cart. Just beyond was a flower stand that offered irises and anemones and roses and peonies. A blend of odors struck his nose: the pungency of meat roasting, the sweet scent of flowers, the acrid bite of marijuana smoke. As always, his gaze sought women, especially young, attractive women.

He stepped off a curb, waiting for a break in the traffic, and caught sight of a man parking a car on the other side of the street. The car was a nondescript blue sedan, a Buick maybe, or an Oldsmobile. Its driver was wearing an open-necked yellow sport shirt with the tails hanging out over his polyester pants. He was thick around the middle, and his sparse black hair had been combed from the back and one side in an unsuccessful attempt to cover a bald spot. He was carrying a large manila envelope.

There was nothing remarkable about him, and yet something struck Peter as familiar. For a moment he thought the man was someone he knew—the owner of one of the galleries, or someone who ran a restaurant in the area. He watched, curious, as the man stepped onto the sidewalk and looked down the street in one direction and then the other. When his head swung back Peter got a good look at his face, and realization made his nerves buzz.

The man was a detective.

He was that oaf who'd been in the TV newscast, the one who mumbled about the police identifying Ellen Danvers as the latest victim in the Greenwich Village murders. Looking at him, Peter was positive. He stood as if rooted, one foot on the curb, the other on the street, his brain racing.

What was the cop doing here? How in God's name had he traced Barrows to Soho? Did he actually know who Peter was? Had Peter made some stupid mistake he wasn't aware of? What had led the man to this street? Were there other cops with him?

Wait a minute, he told himself. For Christ's sake, calm down. The only thing for sure was that this dull-looking jerk was a detective, and he was in this neighborhood. So what? According to the stories on TV and in the newspapers, there were droves of cops swarming all over New York, searching for any clue, any speck of information on the murders. And what had they come up with so far? Absolutely nothing.

And yet the man was here. He was only yards away from Peter's apartment. Was that a coincidence? The hell it was. Peter had to have stumbled someplace, had to have made some goddamn dumb error. As he watched, the detective walked a short distance down the sidewalk and stepped into Kerrigan's Bar & Grill. Peter felt panic wash over him in waves, making him dizzy, chilling him with fear, drowning him in it. All he could think of was to get away from here, to run. He turned and sprinted for his building.

Once inside, he put his case down and tore off his jacket and tie, flinging them aside. Christ—how had this happened? What had he done wrong? Any minute he could expect to hear a knock on the door. So what was he going to do—sit here and wait for it? And when it came, then what? He didn't even have a gun.

Again he forced himself to choke back his fear, to think rationally. If the cop had known who he was looking for, and where to look, he would have come straight here. But he hadn't. So what was he doing? Searching Peter out, of course. And what was Peter to do about it? *Think*, he told himself. *Goddamn it, think.*

Did the cop know what Peter looked like? Maybe. Maybe not. An idea took shape, and he hurried into his bedroom, where he studied his appearance in the mirror. It was simply that of a healthy, rather good-looking young man. None of his features was all that distinctive.

Except his hair.

Damn it, his hair really was something out of the ordinary, a thick mass of brown curls. He'd been meaning to buy a wig, so that he could make a radical change in his appearance when he wanted to, but he hadn't gotten around to it. He certainly could use a wig now, but that couldn't be helped. Ah, but he could do the next best thing. He stepped to the closet and rummaged around on the shelves.

There—found it! Triumphantly, he held up the New York Yankees baseball cap, giving it a little flip and then pulling it down on his head. Returning to the mirror, he was delighted by what he saw. The cap not only obscured his hair, but its peak cast a shadow over his face. Wearing it, his appearance was considerably altered. He headed for the front door. In the hallway he opened the box containing the circuit breakers and snapped a switch. Then he ran down the stairs.

40

Returning to Kerrigan's. Peter slowed down as he approached the entrance. When he stepped inside he saw the place was crowded as usual, many of its customers people who lived and worked in the neighborhood. He made his way slowly down the length of the place, studying each of the male patrons.

And there was his man. The detective was standing at the bar, a glass of whiskey in front of him. As unobtrusively as possible, Peter squeezed in alongside, taking care not to look directly at him, but watching his reflection in the back-bar mirror. The cop looked like a total slimeball, with his doughy face and his pathetic hair, sweating in his cheap yellow sport shirt.

He was talking to the bartender, showing him some pictures. Peter heard him tell the guy to take a good look, asking if he'd ever seen the man in the bar. The bartender shook his head, and then the cop held up copies of the photographs of Danvers and Connery. Again the response was negative, and Peter could see that the bartender was irritated at having to put up with this. People were waiting for drinks, and he was the only one tending bar. The cop persisted: "You sure? The guy's a photographer. Maybe he's got a studio around here someplace."

Bang. That was another jolt. Maybe Slimeball wasn't as dumb as he looked.

But the bartender was saying no—he'd never seen the man in here. He went back to mixing drinks and Peter waited his turn, finally ordering a beer. When it was set in front of him, he paid for it and sipped a little from the glass, watching. The detective was working on his drink, the set of prints lying on the bar.

Deliberately, Peter looked at the pictures. The one of the man was on top. It was the drawing that had been on TV, depicting a young man with a thin face and a thick mop of curls. Peter looked at his own image in the back-bar mirror. With the Yankee cap pulled down on his head he was somebody else entirely.

And yet, goddamn it, the cop was *here*. He was in this bar with the drawing. He was looking for Peter Barrows. Somehow, they could be *onto him*. Peter couldn't just wait for this idiot to stumble across him. He had to *act*.

He waited for a moment, swallowing more of his beer. *Now.*

"Hey, mister?"

The cop turned to him, his eyes a little bleary. "Yeah?"

"Excuse me, but I think I may know that guy." Peter pointed to the sketch.

The eyes narrowed. "That so? Who is he?"

Peter's tone was apologetic. "I could be wrong. I mean, I'm not really sure."

The cop shoved the print closer. "Here, look at it."

Peter picked up the print and squinted. He shook his head regretfully. "No, I guess I made a mistake. This doesn't look like the guy I meant. It's just a drawing, isn't it?"

The cop was watching him closely. "That's right. But who did you think it was?"

Peter's reply was casual. "There's a photographer who's got a studio a couple of blocks away from here. Looks a little like this. But I could be wrong."

The detective moved his face closer. His breath was all bourbon fumes. "You say he's a photographer?"

"Right."

"What's his name?"

"I'm not sure. Hey, you're not a bill collector or anything, are you? I wouldn't want to cause the guy any trouble."

The cop smiled, exposing stained, overlapping teeth. "No, nothing like that. I'm a police officer, but relax. I just want to ask him a couple questions. Say, lemme ask you. Where's this studio, exactly?"

"Like I said, it's a couple of blocks away. Take your first left, and it's in the middle of the block. You can't miss it." Peter finished his beer and set the empty glass on the bar. "Well, I gotta go. So long, Officer."

41

JOE Kurwitz saw that the building was one of those old factories or warehouses typical of Soho. For years many of them had been little more than rat warrens, vandalized until they were burned-out shells. Derelicts slept in them and junkies used them as shooting galleries. But it was obvious that this one had been renovated. The stone and yellow brick facing was clean and the metal door had been freshly painted in tan enamel. The windows were well above street level and protected by black steel bars.

When he reached the door, he hesitated. It was taking a chance to go nosing around without a backup. He remembered his days as a rookie in Harlem, his partner a veteran black cop. They had chased a street pusher who had cut a junkie's throat. The suspect had run up five flights of stairs in a tenement to his girlfriend's apartment and bolted the door, the cops puffing after him. When they kicked the door in he was standing in the darkened apartment, begging them not to hurt him. Joe's partner went in first and the guy gave him a load of 12-gauge double-0 buckshot in the chest. Kurwitz dropped to the floor just as the pusher let go with the second barrel, the charge missing his head by an inch. Joe emptied his service revolver, three of his shots going wild but three others punching holes in the guy's torso and slamming him over backward. He flopped around for a few seconds and then was still, blood pumping out of the holes, his eyes glazing. The only sounds after that came from people whimpering in fear and a baby crying. Joe was so scared he stayed right were he was, flat on the floor and with his pants soaked in piss, the empty

.38 still gripped in his white-knuckled fists, until help arrived.

Yeah. Going in alone was asking for trouble. And as he
knew from experience, even *with* somebody it could be bad
enough.

But fuck it. He could handle himself. And if he could
bring this off on his own, it would be the biggest score of
his life. He'd be taking a chance, but it would be worth it.

There was no street number on the building, and no
name beside the door. Only a buzzer. Kurwitz pressed it
and cocked his head, listening. If the device made a sound
inside, he couldn't hear it from out here. He pushed the
button again, longer this time, and waited. No response.

So what the hell. The guy had probably gone home for
the night. The character he'd met in the bar hadn't been
all that sure. That one had seemed a little goofy anyhow,
maybe the kind who watched detective shows on TV and
then got a hard-on when he rubbed up against a cop. So
maybe all this was just bullshit.

He tried the door.

It was unlocked, for Christ's sake. Whoever this photographer was, if there was a photographer, he was one careless son of a bitch. Out of habit, Kurwitz flattened himself
against the wall. Then he pushed the door open. It swung
back silently and he peered into the opening. It was dark
inside, but he could make out a narrow hallway leading to
a flight of stairs straight ahead.

His right hand went to the small of his back and pulled
the .38 Colt Detective Special from its holster. The gun
had a two-inch barrel, but it was still twice as heavy as an
S&W Airweight, which most of the guys carried. Which
was fine with him. The heft of the steel frame made the
piece seem more solid to him than the alloy of the Smith.
He felt more secure, more powerful, with the Colt in his
fist.

He stepped through the door and stayed close to the wall as he inched toward the stairs, holding the .38 out front, his ears alert to the slightest sound that might come from the darkness ahead of him. Tucking the envelope under his arm, he felt around for a light switch and finally found one. He flicked it but nothing happened. He stood still for a moment, listening. Still nothing. Taking a deep breath, he put one foot on the first step.

The way to go up stairs without making them creak was to avoid the center of the treads and step only on one side, as close to the wall as possible. He took them slowly and carefully, holding his mouth open to keep his breathing quiet. His heart was banging against his ribcage. He wished he could see, but the stairway was black as hell.

There were ten steps. When he got to the top he found himself on a landing with another door leading off it. He waited, reminding himself to take all the time he wanted. If there was anything dumber than going into a joint like this alone and in the dark, it was doing it in a hurry. He gripped the knob and turned it. This door was open, too. Another deep breath, and then he slipped inside.

Now he seemed to be in a large, open area, with some light in it. There were windows in one wall, and that was where the light was coming from. It was little more than a dim glow, probably from the streetlights below. He blinked, impatient for his eyes to adjust to the semidarkness. The space he was standing in might be a living room. There were some bulky shapes just below eye level. Probably pieces of furniture. The walls were an eerie white. Looking up, he thought he could make out that the ceiling was vaulted.

He took two tentative steps into the area, and then he heard a sound. He jumped, and instantly went into a crouch. The noise had been like a muffled click, but he couldn't tell the direction it had come from.

"Who's there?" His voice sounded startlingly loud. His heart was really going now. Christ—it felt as if it could batter its way out of his chest.

He straightened up slowly, swinging his gaze from side to side.

Then his head exploded.

42

PETER Barrows stood beside the door as the detective entered the room. He could hear the rasp of the man's breathing, could see him outlined clearly against the dim light from the windows. Stepping close behind him, Peter gripped the haft of the fire ax in both hands and set himself. A floorboard creaked, the sound a faint click.

The detective instantly dropped into a crouch. "Who's there?"

Peter heard the harshness in his voice, heard the telltale tremor. He was so near he could smell the son of a bitch, the odor rank with sweat and booze and fear. The detective held his position for a moment, and then Peter saw him slowly straighten up.

Do it.

With all his strength, he swung the ax in a tremendous overhead arc. The heavy, razor-sharp blade struck the detective's skull with a mighty whack, as if he had driven it into soft pine. The shock traveled through Barrows' hands and arms and shoulders, jarring him all the way down to the soles of his feet. The detective's body hit the floor like a sack of cement, the ax pulling free.

Peter ran down the stairs and reset the circuit breaker, holding the ax in one hand. Then he went back up to the living room and touched a button on the wall beside the windows. An electric motor silently closed the heavy draperies. He flipped a switch, turning on the lights.

What remained of the cop was a revolting mess. He lay sprawled on his face, the top of his head split wide open. Blood streamed from the gaping hole, forming a thick, dark red pool on the highly polished planks of the floor. Peter could see splintered bone and oozing, putty-colored tissue. He'd have to hurry—there was work to do.

First he'd haul Detective Asshole out of here before he ruined the floor. Peter ran into the bathroom and dropped the ax into the tub, returning to the living room with a towel. He wrapped it around the man's shattered head, then grabbed the body under the armpits and dragged it into the darkroom. There it could stay until he got a few other things taken care of. He went into the kitchen and put on a pair of rubber gloves. Then he filled a plastic bucket with hot water and liquid detergent, taking the bucket and some rags back into the living room, where he swabbed the gore off the floor. He had to make two trips before the planks were clean enough to satisfy him, but when he finished, the surface was spotless.

The detective's gun and the envelope containing the photographs were lying a few feet from where he had fallen. Peter picked them up and took them into the darkroom, placing them on a counter. Next he bent over the body and went through the pockets. They contained a leather billfold with a detective's shield clipped inside it, a couple of crumpled bills and some change, cigarettes and a disposable lighter, some sheets of folded notepaper, a ballpoint pen, a comb, and a set of keys. He took all this stuff into the darkroom, as well. Shoving the keys into his pocket, he turned off the lights and ran down the stairs and out into the street, slamming and double-locking the door behind him.

The car was a piece of shit. There were dings and scratches all over it, and from the look of the moldy blue paint, it had never been washed. The seats were stained and torn, and an empty beer can lay on the floor. It took him several minutes to start it, tromping on the accelerator and grinding the starter motor. The thing finally caught and he raced the engine, sending clouds of blue smoke into the air before he dropped it into gear and eased away from the curb.

He was nervous at first, but then as he moved along in the flow of vehicles, the tension eased. It was late enough now so that the traffic was no problem. He headed for the nearest bridge, the Williamsburg, and crossed into Brooklyn. From there he drove to the Long Island Expressway, following it in an eastbound direction until it let him into the Van Wyck.

It was laughable, now that he could relax and think back about it. A dumb, half-bombed detective who couldn't find his own cock if his life depended on it. Barrows was probably the first guy with any real intelligence he'd ever come up against. He certainly would be the last. The fire ax had cleaved the cop's head like a rotten melon.

Even his car was a joke. It sputtered and coughed and steered like a truck. Barrows stayed well over in the right-hand lane, driving at a slow, steady pace, ignoring the faster traffic that whizzed by on his left. He took the Van Wyck south until the green-and-white overhead signs told him he was approaching Kennedy, and then he drove even slower. It would be foolish to screw up now by getting careless.

Once inside the airport, he drove the car to the long-term parking lot and left it there. Then he stripped off the rubber gloves and stuffed them into a pocket. He took an airport bus to one of the terminals, where he caught a taxi for Manhattan. When he got back to his apartment he checked his watch. Just after midnight. Now the real work would get under way.

In the darkroom the detective's body lay as he had left it, except that the white towel had a stain soaked into it that was almost black in the harsh glare of the ceiling light. Looking at it, Peter realized the body was much too big and heavy to dispose of as he had the remains of the Connery girl. He put the rubber gloves back on, then went down into his garage and got a hacksaw from his tool bench, carrying it with him back into the kitchen. There he collected several knives and a stack of white plastic bags before returning to the darkroom.

He was right; the corpse was heavy as hell, and extremely awkward to move. Rigor mortis had already stiffened the limbs. He heaved it up onto the drainboard, face down, the bloody head resting on the stainless steel floor of the sink, the arms and legs sticking out at odd angles. He reached for a knife and began cutting away the man's clothing.

When he finished, a pile of bloody, sweat-sodden rags lay on the floor at his feet. That stuff he could throw out later. He went into the studio and got a can of Coors out of the refrigerator, popping the top and gulping down half the cold beer. Then he took a cassette from the rack and shoved it into the machine.

As he returned to the darkroom, the booming sound of music filled the area. The cassette was *The Singles*. It was by The Police, and the song they were doing was "Every Breath You Take." He looked over at the cop's naked white ass and laughed out loud at the joke. He drank the rest of the beer and put the can aside before stepping back to the sink.

He studied the body for a moment and decided that the first thing he had to do was drain the remaining blood. He picked up a knife and slit open the jugular. A thick crimson stream oozed from the incision. Without the heart pumping, gravity would have to do the job. He grabbed the body by the legs and heaved the feet upward to hasten the flow of blood.

Two hours later, all that was left of Detective Joseph Kurwitz was a neat pile of plastic-wrapped packages that rested on the counter beside the sink. Even the man's possessions—his wallet, his pistol, the pictures, and the rest—had been enclosed in a white vinyl bag and taped shut.

Barrows scrubbed down the sink with Ajax and a brush, taking care that not one shred of flesh or drop of blood remained anywhere. The rags that had been the detective's clothing he stuffed into a large garbage bag, along with the man's shoes, setting the bag inside the front door to be dumped in the morning. Then he carried the smaller packages into the kitchen and stacked them in the upright freezer. It took three trips to transport the bundles, and when he finished he noted that there was still plenty of room in the cavernous white compartment.

From here on, getting rid of the remains would be easy. He would take his time, dropping a package here, a package there, all at distant points around the city. The best places to put them would be in the garbage cans set out on the sidewalks by restaurants. It would be extremely unlikely that any of them would come to the attention of the police, and if they did, it would drive the cops apeshit. He laughed again, thinking about it.

The bundle containing the detective's personal effects was another story. Peter wasn't exactly sure how he'd dispose of it, but there was no reason to rush that, either. For the moment he'd just tuck it away, out of sight. He took the bundle into his studio and put it into one of the cabinets. He pulled off the gloves and went into the bathroom, removing his clothes and dropping them into the laundry hamper. His back and shoulders were a little stiff from all the hacking and cutting he'd done on the cop, but a good hot shower would take care of that. He stepped into the tile-and-glass enclosure and turned on the water full blast, luxuriating in the hot, needle spray, soaping and resoaping his body.

After he toweled himself dry he put on his favorite robe, a red silk, and took the cassette out of his attaché case. He slid the cassette into the VCR and turned on the machine. Then he sat down in a comfortable chair close to the set, his heart beating fast, his fingers trembling. When Margot Dennis' image came onto the screen, he was already close to orgasm.

43

THE *Lucy B* was a sport fisherman out of City Island. She slid through the oily waters of New York Harbor at a little after six o'clock on a Friday morning, heading south for Sandy Hook, where the blues were running. There was a party of five on board, middle-aged guys from Westchester who were having Budweiser for breakfast. In the distance to starboard they could see the Statue of Liberty, the lady's newly renovated copper coat corroded green and streaked with gullshit. Only a few ships were anchored in the harbor.

The captain was steering from the *Lucy B*'s flying bridge with his throttles backed off. He wanted to get out to where the fish were, but you had to be careful in here. Along with the floating garbage and the used condoms there were pieces of debris that could stove a hole in your hull. The visibility wasn't great either. Later on it would be a nice day, but right now gray clouds of morning fog were rolling off the water, and you had to be alert. The skipper was keeping a sharp eye, which was why he saw the black object just breaking the surface.

At first he thought it might be a log. But then as the *Lucy B* came within a few feet, he realized it was a bundle of some kind, about five or six feet long. He would have paid no more attention after that, if it hadn't been for what he saw next.

Sticking out of the bundle was a hand.

The captain stood up, staring down at the thing as it bobbed past, rolling in the greasy swells. There wasn't any doubt now. He pulled the drive handles into reverse and yelled to the mate to get out a boat hook.

44

THIS time Ben couldn't tell whether the girl had been pretty or not. With her belly swollen to grotesque proportions and most of her features eaten away by the fish or the crabs or whatever lived on the bottom of the harbor, she was just a mound of rotting flesh. All he could be sure of was that she had been a brunette.

But he also saw that her neck had been broken, and that her buttocks were a mass of wounds made by human teeth. A piece of electrical cord was tied around one ankle. The other end of that cord had probably been fastened to a weight, he reasoned, and it had come loose. Anything more he might get would have to come from the postmortem, which was an event he'd just as soon skip. He knew what to expect when the ME opened the abdomen and released that awful cloud of fetid gas. He thanked the attendant and walked out of the morgue and up the steps to Bellevue's front entrance, glad to be getting back outside into the fresh air. He climbed into his car and drove back down to the precinct house.

When he got there, the scene was near pandemonium. Reporters crowded around the entrance, arguing with cops who were preventing them from going into the building, and Ben had to push and shove his way through the pack. Shouts went up when they recognized him, but he ignored their questions and pleas for an interview.

It didn't get much better inside. Brennan was waiting for him in the squad room, talking with Ed Flynn as Ben walked in. Detectives were crawling all over each other and the noise level made the place sound like bedlam. He followed the captain into his office and shut the door. Brennan refused a drink, and after they sat down, Ben noticed that for once the old Irishman was looking bleary-eyed himself. Ben told him about his visit to Bellevue, adding that they had a number of reports from Missing Persons that could match, and that he thought they might get an ID in less time with this one.

Brennan was quiet for a moment. He seemed to be studying Ben. When he finally spoke, his voice sounded the way his eyes looked. Ben suddenly realized he'd never seen the zone commander in this shape.

"Listen to me, Lieutenant," Brennan said. "We are in a shitload of trouble. The mayor is screaming for a shake-up, and the PC don't have any more excuses to give him. Waiting for an ID ain't going to do much to help the situation."

Ben was surprised that he didn't feel anger. Instead, he was numb with fatigue and all but overcome by a sense of hopeless frustration. "What do you want me to do, Cap?"

"I want to see a suspect."

"You know we don't have one."

"Yeah. But I want to see one anyhow."

"Where am I—"

"I don't give a fuck where. Or who. Round up a known sex offender. We need an arrest."

This time his anger did come up, but he choked it off, waiting a few beats before he replied. "How do we hold him?"

"You pick a guy with a long sheet. Somebody who's been in and out of the joint. That way we got a better chance of keeping him for a while."

Ben sat back in his chair.

Brennan looked at him. "You better face reality, Lieutenant. We have got to produce a perpetrator. It don't matter whether it sticks, we just can't stand around here

242

with our thumb up our ass while the media goes nuts. If we got somebody, a guy who could be a legitimate suspect, it takes the heat off a little bit. And then if the court orders a release, that shifts more of it off of us. At least we get some breathing room. And by the way, I just changed my mind about that drink."

Ben got the Popov bottle and a pair of paper cups out of his desk drawer, filling both cups and extending one to Brennan. The captain never glanced at it as he knocked back its contents and held it out for a refill. Ben poured him another and then drank off his own.

The vodka tasted hot and raw. He shuddered as it burned its way down. "What happens then?"

Brennan shrugged. "Maybe we get another one. Maybe we get a real break by then. Who knows? The only thing I'm sure of is, we show some action or it don't make a shit what happens down the road. You and I could both find ourselves reassigned to less strenuous work. Do I make myself clear?"

"Yeah. You do, Captain. Entirely clear."

"Good. It's a sad fucking day when the TV shitheads are calling the tune in this town, but that's the way it is. Now what's this about one of your men is missing? What's his name—Kurwitz?"

"Right. Joseph Kurwitz. He was on the street, checking photographers. Been gone a couple of days. But it's not the first time."

"What's his problem?"

"He gets on the sauce, now and then."

Brennan could have pushed it, but he didn't. Instead he merely drained his cup and said, "Let me know."

"I will, Cap."

The zone commander put his empty cup down on the desk and got to his feet. "And I want that arrest by tomorrow."

"All right."

Brennan left the office, and Ben shook his head. The order was pure bullshit, as blind dumb a reaction to pressure as you could find, but there was no better solution at hand. Not that collaring some bum was a solution. It was a Band-Aid that would disappear the minute a smart reporter picked at it. But Ben also knew that Brennan spoke the truth. If the cops didn't do something fast—anything that could look like progress—then somebody else would be handling it. He got up and went to a cabinet, opening a drawer and taking out a thick file on men with records of sex offenses, returning with it to his desk.

He'd been at it for a half hour when Frank Petrusky stuck his head in the door. "Call for you, Lou. On two. It's that Weston, from WPIC."

The phone had been ringing constantly, but Ben had ignored it. He was about to tell Petrusky he was out, but then he thought better of it. He picked up the phone, and Petrusky withdrew, shutting the door. "Lieutenant Tolliver."

"Hello, Lieutenant. Sarah Weston." She sounded friendly. But then, she wanted something.

"What can I do for you?"

"It's about the body that was found in the harbor."

"I can't tell you much about it. We don't have an ID yet. But there's a new angle we're working on." He felt like a whore, saying it.

"Good. Can we talk about it?"

He was about to refuse, but that would be stupid, in light of the situation, and his discussion with Brennan. "Sure. But we don't have much, at this point."

"You know what the key question is. Does this look like the same girl who was in the second photograph?"

"I honestly don't know. The body is in pretty bad shape, from being in the water."

244

"I understand her neck was broken."

Ben silently cursed Weston's skill as a reporter. She'd undoubtedly found some big-mouthed cop to latch onto. Or maybe she was trying to trick him into giving her information. "We'll have to wait for the medical examiner's report."

"Uh-huh. I'll be doing a story on this tonight, of course."

"Yes?"

"And if you remember, Lieutenant, you agreed to give me an interview."

His immediate reaction was to tell her to fuck off, but again he kept his cool. Brennan was right about one thing: the TV people could cut you to pieces, and the last thing Ben needed now was even more pressure from them. "That's right, I did, didn't I?"

"Tell you what. I understand your problem better than you think I do. So instead of my coming there or you coming back here to the studio, why don't we meet someplace? We could have a private talk, and anything you tell me is off the record won't go any further. What's more, I've got a new angle, too. One I think you're going to find interesting. In fact, I think it could be a lot of help to you."

"Okay," Ben said. "Where and when?"

"How about my place, tonight after my show? That way nobody will see us together."

Ben was wary, but he was also curious. "Fine." He took down the address, noting that it was only a few blocks from Margot's apartment.

"Let's say twelve o'clock?"

"See you then." He hung up.

What the hell was this about? She had a new angle? He trusted Weston about as much as he would a junkie or a gambler, maybe less. But he couldn't afford to miss any bets.

45

PETER pulled a comfortable chair close to the TV in his bedroom. He turned on the set and sat down, sipping a fresh Scotch and waiting patiently for the titles and the commercials and the rest of the crap to get over with. He was amused by the realization that he'd developed an almost proprietary attitude toward Sarah Weston, especially now that he'd made contact with her by telephone. She'd become his own private newscaster.

He'd figured her out, of course. The silly twitch actually thought she was using him, thought she was manipulating him so that she'd be able to play an even bigger role in the story than she already had, and it delighted him to see through her tawdry little schemes. Women were all alike, every stupid one of them. And with her pisspot job as a TV reporter blowing her opinion of herself even more out of proportion, she had to be worse than most.

But he also knew she was in awe of him. He could tell from her tone when they spoke that she was bowled over by his talent and his power. How many women actually encountered anybody in all their lives who had one or the other, let alone the combination of the two he possessed?

Of course, the biggest joke of all was that it was he who was in fact doing the manipulating. The plan he'd developed was marvelous. Margot Dennis had been sent to him, he was sure of it. He didn't know how or why, but certainly it was part of a grand mosaic. She would become the centerpiece in the finest work he'd ever created. What Weston was too involved in her own self-importance to grasp was that she had become the means for him to bring his masterworks to the world.

Weston's image appeared on the screen now. Peter sat back and drank more of his Scotch. She looked quite attractive, as usual. The top she was wearing appeared to be silk, with blue and cream stripes. He liked the way it clung to her breasts, especially when she moved. But when she began talking about the Greenwich Village murders, he snapped to full alert.

Weston: "Today another piece in this terrible puzzle fell into place, when the body of a young woman was discovered floating in the harbor."

Cut to a shot of a wharf with a fishing boat tied up alongside. Weston's voice over: "This is the *Lucy B*, a sport fisherman that was on her way out to sea when her skipper noticed a large bundle in the water. Once again, it was a black plastic garbage bag, and once again the bag contained a dead body."

The camera panned to reveal police cars on the wharf, and an ambulance. Cops milled about as attendants rolled a gurney with a trussed-up form on it into the back of the ambulance. Weston over: "The corpse has not yet been identified, but all the signs are pointing in the same grim direction."

Cut to Weston: "A police source, who asked that his name not be used, said that, like the other victims, this girl's neck had been broken, and she appeared to have been sexually attacked. But perhaps the most chilling thing of all is that, even though the body was in poor condition, it bore a striking resemblance to the girl in the bizarre photograph that was sent to this reporter a short time back."

Cut to the photo, Weston over: "Like the mysterious young woman in this picture, the girl in the harbor had dark hair, and had been a real beauty. There is little doubt that they were one and the same person."

247

Cut back to Weston: "So what many people thought might have been a genuine work of art has been revealed instead as the work of a madman. If the killer took the photograph, and there certainly is reason to believe he did, he has shown himself to be a hideously low form of animal—a murderer who rapes and destroys young women and then poses their bodies for his horrible pictures. Tonight concerned citizens everywhere are once again praying that the police capture this depraved creature before he kills again. The message they're sending to the mayor and the police commissioner is a very clear one: Do your duty and protect our young women. Stop the killing by apprehending the killer and bringing him to justice. This is Sarah Weston, reporting to you from the WPIC-TV newsroom in New York."

Peter sat still for a moment, staring at the TV set in stunned silence. Then he threw his glass at the screen. It bounced off the tube and landed on the rug, throwing a spray of Scotch and ice cubes in all directions. He got to his feet and kicked the control button until the picture disappeared from the screen.

In no more than a few minutes, all his plans, all his carefully devised intentions, had been totally destroyed. Before millions of people, he had been reviled and debased. Sarah Weston had torn him to pieces. He threw his head back and let out a long, mournful howl.

46

WHEN she came off the set, both Jerry Baum and Dave Pirenza had big grins on their faces. They fell all over themselves, congratulating her on a great story. Pirenza said she ought to win a pile of awards, and Baum topped that by saying she deserved a Pulitzer. Sarah smiled, basking in the flood of kind words, but at the same time aware that both these guys would be doing their level best to take as much of the credit as possible for her work on the murders. So let them. It wouldn't matter in the end, because if she played this right, and so far she had played it brilliantly, she'd go from here straight into a network job. Her agent had already had feelers from CBS and ABC, and by the time the case was wrapped up, she'd have ridden the Greenwich Village murders to national prominence.

They wanted to take her out for drinks, but Sarah begged off, saying she was tired and had a lot to do in the morning. What she didn't tell them was that she'd be meeting Lieutenant Tolliver an hour from now, and she wanted to be at her best when he arrived at her apartment. She went into the ladies' room and used cream to remove the light coat of Pan-Cake from her face, conscious as she did that WPIC didn't even have proper makeup facilities for its newscasters. Anything you put on or took off you handled yourself. Talk about bush league. But all this would be behind her soon.

She took a cab home as usual, arriving in only a few minutes. In the lobby the inside doorman gave her a wave and said he'd watched her newscast and thought she was terrific. He kept a little set at his desk and never missed her on the news. He wanted to know if she thought they'd get the murderer soon and she told him she certainly hoped so. That was a kick, the way people had begun to treat her not only as a celebrity, but as an authority on the case as well. She told the doorman she was expecting a visitor, a detective from the NYPD, and she could see that he was impressed by that, too.

Once inside the apartment, she stripped off her clothes and went into the shower. The spray massaged her back and her shoulders and her breasts, and by the time she got out and toweled herself dry she was feeling great. The excitement of anticipating Tolliver's visit was pumping her up, and she thought about how she'd handle him.

The lieutenant struck her as a standard-issue cop. Bull-headed, arrogant, sure that the best way to handle any problem was to hit it over the head with a hammer. And yet it was interesting, the way they'd forced him to back down when he'd come huffing and puffing into the station after she'd shown the second photograph on the air. Either he was smarter than she'd thought or he wasn't really as ballsy as he pretended. She decided the former was more likely.

But he was also a man. And as a matter of fact, a good-looking one, in a macho, big stud kind of way. She wouldn't be out to seduce him exactly, but having this talk alone with him in her place added a certain spice she found highly enjoyable. It would be interesting to see how he reacted. She brushed her hair out so that it tumbled to her shoulders in loose, honey-colored waves, and then she applied just a dab of lipstick. After that came a few touches of Joy, behind her ears and between her breasts, and lastly she put on the pale green negligee that looked so smashing with her coloring.

As far as what she had to tell him was concerned, that was a sure bet to knock him over. When he learned the killer had been in contact with her, there would be only one way for him to react. He'd want to set a trap, with her as the bait. Which meant she'd not only go on playing a role in the story, she'd become its heroine. Jesus, what a fabulous opportunity.

She'd taken a chance, of course, by going as far as she had on the air tonight. What she'd said almost certainly would have angered the killer, but that had been carefully calculated, too. She hadn't heard from him in some time now, and she wanted to jar him, to needle him hard enough to make him respond. She couldn't be sure, but from the impressions she'd taken away from their telephone conversations, he'd get in touch with her again soon, in all likelihood whining over what she'd said about him. How she'd play it at that point would depend on a number of things, one of them how her ploy with Tolliver worked out.

The lieutenant would be here soon. Anticipating his arrival was making her flesh tingle. She checked the living room to see that everything looked neat and orderly, and then turned the lights down so that the room was in semidarkness. She opened the drapes, and the effect was beautiful, with Manhattan's lights ablaze as far as she could see.

The bell rang, and even though she was expecting it, she jumped. She took one last quick look at her image in the foyer wall mirror, and then she opened the door.

And froze.

The man who stood in the doorway was not the lieutenant. He was tall and had regular features and even white teeth and a cap of brown curls. He was wearing a windbreaker.

Sarah opened her mouth, and then closed it, as fear rose in her like a black tide. Her knees suddenly felt weak, and for an instant she thought her legs might go out from under her. The man was a total stranger, someone she was sure she'd never seen before. And yet she knew, beyond all doubt, beyond even thinking she could be wrong, who he was.

Again she opened her mouth, to scream this time, but he raised his hand as if in warning, and the sound died in her throat. He stepped into the apartment and she gave way, backing up as he came toward her. He pushed the door shut behind him and kept coming, moving her backward through the foyer and into the living room.

He stopped, and she looked up at him, her mind engulfed by terror but at the same time trying desperately to find a way to deal with this.

"Hello, Sarah."

Her voice was a hoarse whisper. "Hello."

"You know who I am, don't you?"

She could barely get it out. "Yes."

"The things you said on the air about me tonight. They were terrible."

"I—I really only wanted to get you to talk to me again."

One corner of his mouth curled in a faint smile. "Is that so?"

A tiny current went through her, the merest hint of a return of her confidence. She looked at him, as if trying to see a way out by gauging his appearance. He was younger, somehow, than she had thought he'd be. And actually quite nice looking. Even handsome. Christ—what a crazy thought that was.

She nodded. "Yes. I was hoping you'd realize that."

But instead of pacifying him, her words seemed to kindle his anger. The smile disappeared, and in its place a grimace formed. "You're lying, Sarah. You're trying to deceive me. You meant those things. You're nothing but a nasty, devious little cunt."

"No—please. I swear to you—"

His hands shot out and gripped her shoulders. The fingers dug into her flesh, forcing her to her knees. One of the hands continued to hold her, while the other went to his belt, opening the buckle, and then unzipping his fly.

God, was this really happening to her? Was he really going to force her to do this? But wait—if it was what he wanted, why not? Maybe this would be the way she could take the rage out of him, get him to calm down. She'd do anything to soothe him, *anything*. Then she'd be able to handle him, to reason with him.

Wouldn't she?

47

BEN watched the newscast with Margot, sitting with her on the sofa in her living room. She had made hamburgers for them, and he wolfed his, washing it down with a couple of cans of beer. It was obvious right from the first shot that Weston intended to make the discovery of the body in the harbor even more sensational than it already was—if that was possible—and that grated on him. But Brennan was right. The case was a circus, not only made to order for the scavengers who ran the TV news, but at the point now that the newscasters could give the impression to the viewing public that they were running the investigation. Or at least speaking as a kind of authority for the city when they called for action by the police.

And what was he supposed to do tomorrow? Come up with some whacked-out sex freak to dangle in front of the media as evidence that the cops were right on top of this? Jesus. And yet it wouldn't be the first time the NYPD had run a shuffle to cover its own ass. What a fucking mess.

But as Weston went on, Ben began to see that this time she might be going too far. Recalling his talks with Stein, he realized there was no telling how the killer might react to what she was saying about him tonight. Certainly there was no question Weston's words would enrage him. As Ben listened, he felt an increasing sense of foreboding; she could be goading the guy until she was putting herself in danger.

For an instant he thought about calling the studio, but the damage was done now. One thing was for sure: when he saw her later tonight he'd read the riot act to her. She apparently had no idea how much of a chance she was taking. When Weston's piece ended, he leaned forward and turned off the set.

Margot said, "Have you found out who that girl in the harbor was?"

"No, we don't have anything on her yet."

"Is that right, what was on the news—she's the same girl who was in that last photograph?"

"We don't know that, either. Maybe. We just don't know." He didn't want to cut her off, but at the same time he didn't much want to talk about the case and this latest development, either. Discussing it would be like revealing to her that he was a helpless fool who was unable to handle the situation. Which in his opinion was not far from the truth.

It was a little after twelve when he left her apartment. Weston's address wasn't far, only a few blocks, and he reached it in the Ford in a couple of minutes. The building was another of those glitzy postwar efforts at opulence that had risen all over the East Side, a yellow tower with a circular drive and a fountain out front. He showed the doorman his shield and went into the lobby. There was another uniformed guy inside, and he waved the shield at this one as well. The carpeting in the area was chocolate-colored and inches deep, and the walls were all travertine marble. He took an elevator to the twenty-second floor.

The hallway was long and straight and absolutely silent, the floor covered in the same dark brown carpet as the lobby. When he walked down the length of it to her apartment, his feet made no sound. He stopped at her door, surprised to see it ajar. Whether she was expecting him or not, and no matter how secure the building, leaving a door like that was something nobody in their right mind should ever do. He pressed the button and heard soft chimes sound inside.

But there was no response.

He hit the button again, and again heard the soft musical sound from within. And that was all. He waited a few more seconds and then pushed the door open.

"Sarah?"

Nothing. He stepped inside, finding himself in a dimly lighted foyer. Beyond this space he could see a living room. He went on into it.

She was sitting in a chair, facing him. In the faint light, most of it coming from a small lamp at one end of the room, he made out that she was wearing a negligee. The top of it was open, revealing her breasts. Oddly, her hair had been pulled forward over her face. And she was completely still.

He knew something was wrong, very wrong. He'd been a cop too long not to know it in his bones, not to be almost able to smell it. He crouched, snaking the Smith out of the ankle holster on the inside of his left leg, his gaze sweeping back and forth in the room. But except for Weston, there appeared to be no one else in here. Cautiously, his eyes still moving from side to side, he went to her.

And saw why her hair had seemed to be pulled down over her face.

It was because her head had been twisted completely around and was facing away from him. What he had been looking at was the back of her head.

Her flesh was still warm.

48

THE press conference was held outdoors in front of the NYPD headquarters at Police Plaza, and was covered by all three television networks as well as CNN and the New York stations. Reporters for the wire services were there, and people from *Time, Newsweek*, and a dozen newspapers.

The first speaker was the police commissioner, who said that the murder of Sarah Weston was a great tragedy for the city of New York, and that no police officer would rest until the killer was apprehended. He said an attack on a person who brought the news to the people of the city was an attack on society. He said there was no evidence that Miss Weston's death was connected to the Greenwich Village murders, although it was a possibility that was being investigated, along with many other possibilities. He then turned the floor over to Chief of Detectives Anthony Galupo.

Galupo announced that over a hundred detectives had been assigned to the case, and that he was personally directing the investigation. He said it was possible Miss Weston may have known her assailant, inasmuch as the door to her apartment had been open when the police had arrived. Her personal friends and her acquaintances were all being checked out, and dozens of interviews had already been conducted. He said he hoped anyone with any information that might bear on the case would contact the police at once.

As bad as the situation was, the mayor wasn't about to let a press opportunity like this go by. He liked to present himself as a conciliator, a man of compassion who could draw conflicting factions together. Unfortunately, one of those factions saw him as a leader whose mission was to use his power to stomp whitey, and another considered him an idiot tool of drug dealers and black militants. He recognized today's issue, however, as one on which New Yorkers were already united: they were scared shitless.

When it was his turn to speak, the mayor looked out with his sad eyes at the reporters and the cameras and the spectators, his dark face contrasting with his gray hair, and spoke eloquently. He said that everyone had to support each other in this time of crisis.

He said that this latest terrible loss should remind women everywhere to use utmost caution at all times, which was His Honor's way of putting a little distance between himself and the police department's failure to apprehend the Greenwich Village murderer. He said he was personally committed to seeing that those in charge did their duty in bringing this horrible case to a successful conclusion, with those responsible punished to the full extent of the law.

After that reporters were permitted to ask questions, which turned out to be thinly disguised attacks on the cops and their procedures. How come the police had made so little progress? Why were there no leads? How could the police speculate that there may have been no connection between Weston's death and the Greenwich Village victims when all of them had died of broken necks? And when Weston had been so personally involved in the case? How could a TV personality who had received photographs from the killer been given so little protection? Would the FBI be called in?

Ben Tolliver was standing with the public officials and the two dozen or so police officers throughout the conference. It was a hot, muggy day, and the cops and the reporters were mopping their faces and squinting in the bright sunlight. For Ben it was like having a spotlight shining on him, while the world heard all about what a failure he was. The feeling grew even worse when a guy from the *News* asked Galupo what a police lieutenant had been doing in Weston's apartment at that time of night. The chief handled it well enough, replying that the police had been keeping a close eye on Miss Weston. But then the reporter wanted to know why the detective hadn't protected her, and hearing it, Ben wanted to crawl into a hole. When the conference finally ended he was soaking wet.

And it didn't end there, by a long shot. He and Brennan were called into Galupo's office, and when the door was closed and they were seated before the chief's desk, he fully expected to learn he had been busted down in rank, or worse.

But Galupo surprised him.

The man's black olive eyes fixed him with an icy stare. "You can consider yourself very fucking lucky, Lieutenant."

That was unlikely, but he made no reply.

"What you deserve," Galupo went on, "is to have your ass thrown right the hell off the force. But to do that would give those shitbrains out there just that much more to chew on. It would be admitting to them what they already know. That this investigation is a fucking disaster. Months of work, thousands of man-hours, and what have we got? Five dead women, and not one goddamn arrest."

Brennan shifted in his chair. "Chief, I told you we were ready to—"

"Shut up, Brennan." Galupo's skin was swarthy even when he was calm, but when he was pissed it took on the color of cordovan leather. "When I want to hear what you got to say, I'll ask you."

Ben was aware from the exchange where the order to collar a known sex offender had come from, and he was conscious of some other undercurrents as well. For almost a hundred years, the upper echelons of the NYPD had been the exclusive province of the Irish. Until a few years back, an Italian chief of detectives would have been not merely unheard of, but impossible. Not only was Galupo not about to take any shit from Brennan, but Ben sensed that he didn't entirely trust the grizzled zone commander, either. But Ben had plenty of problems of his own, and this wasn't one of them.

"What you are going to do now, Lieutenant," Galupo continued, "is keep a low profile. You are no longer in charge of this investigation. Is that clear?"

"Yes sir," Ben said.

"You will keep working, but only because if you didn't, it would tell those fucking vultures you were even more of a screwup than you obviously are. From now on," he swung his gaze to Brennan, "You will be operating out of the Sixth Precinct. I will be there myself a lot of the time. As far as the world is concerned, I am personally in charge of the case until it's broken. Any questions?"

The expression on Brennan's face told you more about what he was thinking than his words did. What he said was, "No, Chief."

"Then get the fuck out. And Tolliver?"

"Yes sir?"

"Take a couple days off. You look like shit."

49

BEN's vacation lasted less than twenty-four hours. He took Margot to dinner at a small Hungarian restaurant on East Nineteenth Street, where they talked well into the night over veal paprika and two bottles of wine, the words running out of him as if a floodgate had opened. He knew that was largely due to a sense of relief, even though nothing had been settled and the case was in a deeper mire than ever, but somehow he felt he'd been given a reprieve, even if it was only a small one. At least he'd be able to go on working on it, and maybe even more effectively. Let Brennan keep track of all the administrative shit—that was no longer Ben's concern. What he was going to do now was get a good night's sleep for once, and then go after a number of new theories, some of them involving Sarah Weston.

"Why don't you really take some time?" Margot asked.

"What do you mean?"

"I mean there's no sense killing yourself. You've done everything anybody could do, you've worked yourself to the point that you're ready to drop, and all the thanks you get is to be shoved aside and told to take some time off. So why the hell don't you take it?"

He grinned. "I do believe the lady cares."

She shook her head in a show of exasperation. "Of course I care. That couldn't be more obvious if I were wearing a sign. But you have to think of yourself, Ben. Nobody can just go on forever—you need to keep your strength up."

"I thought I was pretty good at keeping it up."

"Will you be serious? I'm worried about you, if you want to know the truth."

"Hey, I'm okay. But if you like, how about taking a couple days and we'll drive up into the country someplace?"

"I'd love to, but I can't. Not right now, anyway. I'm up for a job, and believe me, I need the work."

"All right, then—here's the deal. You finish your job and I'll finish mine. Then we'll take some time together."

She smiled. "That sounds wonderful."

They went to her place after that. She'd never been to Ben's rathole on Bank Street, and if he could help it, she never would. They made love for a long time, Ben calling on reserves even he didn't know he had, and then they fell into a deep sleep, nestled in each other's arms.

50

THE telephone's ring was like a pneumatic drill boring into his ear. He fumbled around on the bedside table until he found the instrument and picked it up. "Tolliver."

"Ben, Ed Flynn. We got an ID on the girl from her boyfriend."

"Who was she?"

"Name was Sue Connery. Worked in a bank—the First Metropolitan. She was living with this guy. He's a computer salesman."

"What about him?"

"Looks clean, so far. He's here now. We'll stay on him, but there's nothing to put him in it. He's one of the people contacted Missing Persons earlier. We'll get everything we can out of him."

"Okay. Brennan around?"

"Yeah. And raising hell. This morning he said the college angle was total bullshit. He pulled the guys we had working on it off that and put 'em on Weston. We got people running all over WPIC."

"Uh-huh. What else?"

"You got a call from Jack Olson—the chief in Hamilton?"

"What did he want?"

"I don't know. I told him you'd call him. I figured it'd be better that way, you know?"

"Right. I'll check back with you later. And Ed?"

"Yeah?"

"Thanks." He hung up and hauled himself out of bed. He headed for the bathroom, wanting to take a leak and splash water on his face. He was surprised to see that his watch read 12:30; he hadn't had this much sleep in weeks.

Ben usually didn't bother with breakfast, but it was now lunchtime. And anyhow, he was starved. He went into the kitchen and scrambled a couple of eggs. There was a pot of stale coffee on the stove, which he heated and drank when he ate the eggs. While he finished the coffee he decided that when he finally hung it up he ought to donate his stomach to an organ bank. Other people could leave eyes and kidneys, but he probably had the only gut in the world that could go on forever.

When he finished he put the dishes into the sink and went back into the bathroom, where he showered and then shaved with Margot's razor. He also used her toothbrush, hoping as he did she wouldn't mind. What the hell, he'd had his mouth on hers often enough, as well as on every other part of her. Although women could be funny about certain things. He decided he wouldn't mention using the toothbrush.

When he returned to the bedroom he got dressed and dug Olson's phone number out of his wallet. He called the number. Olson came onto the line and said, "Looks like you got more trouble, Lieutenant."

"A lot more." He didn't want to get into a discussion of the Weston homicide, although he knew the police chief would have seen the TV news coverage and would be full of curiosity.

Olson must have sensed Ben's reluctance to talk about Weston; he didn't push it. "Got some information for you from the university's infirmary records."

"Good, let's have it."

"Okay, but keep in mind, they wouldn't have to release this stuff without a court order. We got it as a favor through Art Waterford. You remember Art?"

Waterford was the old campus security cop. "Sure I do."

"Just so you're careful not to let on how you got it. I went through all this myself, and there wasn't much of anything could be of interest. Except maybe for one situation that caught my eye. There was a student enrolled here at the time of the Benoit murder who was out from time to time for medical reasons. Name was Peter Hewitt. Went to a private hospital in White Plains, New York."

"What was wrong with him?"

"The file gives the reason as severe depression, other emotional disturbances."

"Mental problems."

"That's what it sounds like."

"Was he questioned at the time of your investigation?"

"No. Y'see, he wasn't here when the murder was committed. He was in the hospital. That had to be why we never talked to him."

"Uh-huh." It sounded pretty thin. The guy had been away when the girl was killed. And yet . . . a young man with a mental condition so severe he had to be hospitalized? And not once, but several times? Thin or not, it wasn't something he could let go by.

"You want the name of the hospital?"

"Yeah, I do."

"Place called Pembroke. Address is Laurel Road, White Plains."

"All right, Chief. Maybe I'll run it down. And thank Art for me, will you?" He hung up, turning the information over in his mind. The more he thought about it, the more there was he wanted to know.

An idea occurred to him, and he dug back into his wallet for another number, this time calling Alan Stein. A nurse answered, and said that the doctor was with a patient. Ben told her to interrupt him.

When Stein picked up the call Ben said, "Sorry, Doc. But I'm in kind of a hurry."

"That's okay, Lieutenant—what can I do for you?"

"You ever heard of a private mental hospital in White Plains called Pembroke?"

"Yes, I think so. If it's the place I'm thinking of. Wait a minute—I've got a directory right here."

Ben hung on, continuing to work out possibilities.

Stein came back on a few moments later. "Here it is. And it's the place I thought it was. Small private hospital, run by a Dr. Martin Herlitzer."

"What kind of patients would go there?"

"Rich."

"What?"

"The place charges twelve hundred dollars a day."

"Jesus, that their package rate?"

Stein laughed. "Let me put it in perspective for you. This hospital doesn't deal with alcohol or drug problems. It only takes people with emotional difficulties. And obviously, only those who can afford it."

"So it's kind of a country club?"

"In a way, yes. It attracts prominent individuals who want privacy. Highly placed business executives, actors, politicians, people who wouldn't want the world to know they needed treatment."

"How good is it?"

"Oh, I imagine the staff is competent enough. But don't kid yourself—a place like that is not only privately run, it's privately owned. It has one objective above all others."

"To make money."

"Exactly. Now tell me why you're interested."

Ben gave the psychiatrist a recap of what Chief Olson had told him.

"Interesting," Stein said.

"I think so too. Worth checking out, anyway."

"You going up there?"

"Yes."

"Don't expect a lot of cooperation. About the last thing in the world a place like that wants to see is a cop sniffing around."

"Don't worry," Ben said. "I'm used to being unwelcome."

"You want their phone number?"

Ben took it, thanked Stein, and hung up. He made one more call, this one to Pembroke Hospital. He told the woman he spoke to who he was and said he'd be paying them a visit that afternoon. He said to tell Dr. Herlitzer to be sure to be there when he arrived. He said to tell the doctor he wanted information on a former patient named Peter Hewitt. The woman said she'd have to check all this with Dr. Herlitzer, but Ben ignored her and put the phone down.

On his way out of the bedroom he saw a note on the dresser he hadn't noticed earlier. The note had his name on it. It read: *Eggs in the fridge. Make fresh coffee. Hope you slept well. Important to keep your strength up. I think I love you. M.*

He grinned and stuffed the note into his pocket as he left the apartment.

51

As Ben drove past Yankee Stadium he thought about the times he'd sat in the bleachers as a kid. That was years before the city had renovated the place at a cost of over a hundred times what it had taken to build it. Mickey Mantle had still been playing then, and Roger Maris, and Ben had believed that if there was one thing he wanted to be when he grew up, it was a big-league ballplayer.

He turned off the Major Deegan and onto the Cross County and then the Hutch, following the signs for White Plains. What had been farms and country homes along here not so long ago were all corporate headquarters buildings now, huge modern complexes of stone and glass that looked like giant blockhouses on either side of the highway. When he reached the city he stopped and asked directions for Laurel Road.

Pembroke Hospital occupied what appeared to have been an estate at one time. It was set among acres of grass and trees and surrounded by a high, ivy-covered wall. A guard met him at the gate and Ben waited while the guy telephoned for an okay to let him in. Then he drove on up to the main building, a towering granite structure, Victorian in design with wings and gables and cupolas, obviously well cared for. He parked the Ford and got out.

People were strolling around the grounds, and a croquet game was in progress under the shade of lofty oak trees. All of it seemed peaceful and quiet. If you were going to have emotional problems and you could afford it, this was the place to have them. From what he could see, most of the patients were men and women middle-aged and older. Only a few of them appeared to be young.

Dr. Herlitzer was in his fifties, Ben judged, a tall, slender man with a mustache and a neatly trimmed gray Vandyke that gave him a scholarly look. Which was probably why he wore it. He greeted Ben courteously enough, his manner of speaking faintly British, and Ben wondered if the accent had the same purpose as the goatee. Herlitzer led the way into his study, a large, book-lined room with windows overlooking the lawns and gardens. Ben sat down in a comfortable chair and the doctor took his seat behind his desk.

Herlitzer came directly to the point. "I'll be glad to help you in any way I can, Lieutenant. But you must realize we keep our patients' records strictly confidential. Just as any other medical institution does."

"I understand your position, Doctor," Ben said. "But you have to understand mine. We're conducting a homicide investigation. If I have to, I'll get a court order that'll force you to release those records to us."

Herlitzer was unruffled. "That won't be necessary, I assure you. But you see, Pembroke is a hospital that treats many well-known people, some of them quite famous. Obviously it would be injurious not only to them, but to the hospital as well, if there were a lot of publicity concerning the institution."

"So what are you saying, Doctor? I need to know about one of your former patients."

"Peter Hewitt."

"Yes. I want to know why he was here, and what kind of treatment he received. Among other things."

The doctor rested his elbows on the arms of his chair and placed his fingertips together. "And I'm most willing to tell you anything I can about him. All I ask in return is that you do everything in your power to keep Pembroke's good name out of the press."

Ben thought of Alan Stein's comments about Pembroke operating as a business. With the rates the hospital charged, it had to be grossing more than fifteen million bucks a year. No wonder Herlitzer didn't want anybody tipping over the pie. "I'll do the best I can, Doctor. You have my word we'll make no mention of our interest to the news media."

Herlitzer nodded. "Very well. But let me ask you, Lieutenant, what is this case you're working on?"

Ben had a feeling this guy knew goddamn well what case it was, but he remained polite. "Recently a number of young women have been murdered in New York."

If Herlitzer was an actor, he was a good one. "My word. So that's it. Of course I'm aware of the case—it's been given a great deal of rather, uh, sensational coverage. Wouldn't you say?"

"Yes, it has." About as much as any fucking case he'd ever heard of. You'd have to be living in a cave someplace not to get that coverage dumped all over you every day.

"Surely you don't think Mr. Hewitt was involved in anything like that?"

"We're investigating hundreds of possibilities, Doctor. Not necessarily focusing on any one direction at this time."

"I see. Well." Herlitzer gestured toward a sheaf of papers on his desk. "I've gone back through Mr. Hewitt's case file, anticipating our discussion. The young man was here on four occasions, all of them while he was a student at Colgate University."

"What was the problem?"

"According to our analysis, he was suffering from severe depression. Actually, a cyclothymic disorder."

"Which is?"

"The essential feature is a chronic mood disturbance. Typically, the patient will have periods of depression, followed by periods of hypomania. In Hewitt's case, the affective syndrome was brought about by his intense desire to prove himself worthy of his mother's love. For that reason, he drove himself to perform extremely well academically. In fact, to achieve goals beyond his capabilities."

"You say he did this because of his mother?"

"Yes. It was to her, you see, that Hewitt was constantly attempting to demonstrate his value as a person. He would exhaust himself through his efforts to attain high grades, sometimes to the point that he became deeply depressed. It was during those periods we treated him here. At least on the first three occasions."

"And the fourth?"

Herlitzer emitted a small sigh. "The fourth was when his mother died, after his graduation. He was devastated, as you can imagine."

"Yes, I can."

"On that occasion he was here a total of five weeks. But he responded to treatment very well."

"During all those times he was here, you must have gotten to know quite a lot about him."

"Yes, of course."

"Where was he from?"

"Greenwich, Connecticut."

"Were there others in his family?"

"No. He was an only child."

"What about his father?"

"Parents were divorced."

"Then who handled his financial affairs after his mother's death?"

"Uh, a lawyer, I believe."

"Who was he?"

Herlitzer hesitated for a fraction of a second. But then he glanced at the papers on his desk. "His name was Brian Holt."

"From Greenwich also?"

"Yes."

"Let's get back to Hewitt's personality. What can you tell me about his sex life? What was that like?"

Herlitzer looked away for a moment, tapping his fingertips together, then returned his gaze to meet Ben's. "Rather limited, I would say, for an otherwise healthy young man. He had affairs, but sex for him was little more than an occasional relief of tension."

"Any special girlfriends?"

"No, not as far as the records show. At least, there seem to have been no important relationships, nothing beyond infrequent, casual encounters."

"Uh-huh. And what contact did you have with him, after that last stay here?"

"None, actually. He seemed to have made an excellent recovery."

"I see." Ben looked through the window at the scene on the lawn outside the doctor's office. It looked like the kind of thing you might see at some genteel resort, ladies and gentlemen walking together, sitting on benches or on the grass. Farther off there were tennis courts, and people were playing on them.

"Is there anything else I can tell you?" Herlitzer asked.

"Looks as if you have pretty good security here," Ben remarked.

"Oh, yes. Very good." It was apparent from the wary expression on his face that the doctor didn't know quite what direction this was taking.

"What happens if somebody wants to leave?"

"To leave? Why, there are no restrictions. No one is committed here, you know. A patient may leave anytime he wishes."

"Are you aware, Doctor, that while Hewitt was a student at Colgate, a rape murder was committed on the campus, and that it was similar in some ways to the ones we're investigating in New York?"

Herlitzer stopped tapping his fingertips and leaned forward in his chair. "I certainly was not aware of it. So that's why you're so interested in him. You think there may be a connection."

"We're looking at the possibility."

"Let me assure you, Lieutenant, I would stake my professional reputation on my belief that Peter Hewitt would have been incapable of committing such an act."

"Incapable?"

"Absolutely. He was a shy, gentle boy who tended to overreach, to strive to accomplish more than he was able, as a rather pathetic offering to his mother. When his parents were divorced, he dropped his father's name and took his mother's. That's how devoted he was to her. But the last thing he would do would be to exhibit criminal psychotic behavior."

"Uh-huh. You say he took his mother's name?"

"Her maiden name, yes."

"Which was?"

"Barrows."

"So he became Peter Barrows?"

"Yes."

"When was that?"

"I believe it was shortly before her death."

"I see. Anything else you can think of that might be helpful to us?"

"Mmm. Nothing offhand. There really wasn't anything so extraordinary about Peter. I'm only glad we were able to help him through a very difficult period of his life."

"What was your prognosis, when he left here that last time?"

"Rather good, actually. But you see, the kind of disorder he was suffering from is usually not long-lived. It occurs most frequently among young people, and then as time goes on, the symptoms appear less often. When they do, they're not as severe. In my judgment, Peter is probably living a well-adjusted, useful life, wherever he is."

Ben stood up. "Okay, Doctor. Thanks for your help."

Herlitzer rose from behind his desk and escorted Ben to the door. "Not a bit, Lieutenant. I appreciate your understanding of our need for discretion in matters affecting our patients."

"Sure." Ben noticed that Herlitzer moved slowly, as if he were deliberately showing restraint, not hurrying. But it was also apparent that the doctor was delighted to be getting rid of him.

On the way out, Ben saw one of the nurses leading an elderly man by the arm. It was a warm, sunny day, but the guy was wearing a sweater and a tweed jacket. The nurse was a well-built brunette, and she was smiling and jollying the old codger as they walked by. Timing, Ben reflected, is everything.

As he drove through the gates, he thought about his discussion with Herlitzer. As soon as he could get an order from the DA's office and find a judge to sign it, he'd send a cop up here for those records. If there was one thing he knew when he saw it, it was a bullshit artist.

52

MARGOT had worked for Jarvis & Cullen several times, on still photography assignments for magazine ads. She had never done a television commercial for the agency. When she got out of the cab on Madison Avenue at Forty-ninth Street, she felt like a kid on one of her first auditions. The agency occupied the entire building, with its name in bronze letters over the glass doors. She squared her shoulders and marched into the lobby, determined to make a strong impression.

She was to see Hal Klein, a television producer, on the twenty-ninth floor. When she stepped off the elevator she found the reception area occupied by male and female models, most of them young and sloppily attired. Margot had been in countless waiting rooms exactly like it. She gave the receptionist her name and found an empty chair.

As usual she was better dressed than the others, but for this audition she had deliberately underplayed it, wearing a white cotton sweater and a lightweight beige skirt. Looking around, she noted that not all the other talent was so young, at that. Seeing them was reassuring. It confirmed what Matt Farrelli had been telling her.

There were trade publications on a coffee table near her chair. She picked up a copy of *Advertising Age* and skimmed through it, until her name was called. A young woman wearing jeans was standing at the reception desk, waiting to show her in. Margot recognized her as Klein's assistant. She had been at the audition taping. Margot said hello, and the young woman led the way down a hallway to a conference room.

When she walked into the room, Klein greeted her. He was wearing his wire-rimmed spectacles as usual, along with his customary denim shirt. He introduced her to a group of people seated around the table. All the others were wearing business clothes. Some were with the agency, she gathered, and some with the client organization. She wasn't quite sure who was what.

There was a guy named Jock McLean who was the account supervisor—she got that much—and a woman who seemed important. At least the others deferred to her. That one's name was Marilyn Farnsworth, and she looked to Margot as if she might be a dyke. The others were a young guy named Peter something, good-looking and with a nice smile and curly brown hair, and another young man whose name she didn't catch at all. There was also a guy who reminded her of Gene Shalit. His name was Krakaur, and Margot thought he was the creative director.

Klein sat her at the far end of the table and said he appreciated her coming in.

She smiled graciously.

"What we want," he explained, "is to get a little better feel for your personality. You looked fine on the audition tape, and the way you handled your lines was terrific. But before any decisions are made, we thought it would be good if we could get to know you better. Maybe just ask you a few questions, if you don't mind."

Margot made it seem that she was among friends. "That's fine," she said pleasantly. "Ask away."

McLean leaned forward. "How much acting experience have you had, Margot?"

She played it straight. "Only a few commercials, and none of them had lines. Mostly I've been a print model."

"What were the commercials?" McLean asked.

"Let's see. One was for Revlon, another for Fabergé. Also a Kodak and a Hallmark."

"How about the print?"

"A lot of it—all kinds. Everything from fashion to travel to more cosmetics."

The Farnsworth woman asked if she'd ever used Tynex.

Margot had been expecting that. Right after she learned she'd be doing this audition she'd bought some of the stuff. "Yes, I have. I get headaches once in a while, especially after I've had a tough day shooting, and I've always taken aspirin. But lately I've been using Tynex."

Farnsworth was watching her closely. "How do you like it?"

Careful, Margot thought. Don't overdo it. "Well, it seems to work fine, but what I really like is that it doesn't upset my stomach. I take one or two and the headache's gone and I feel okay. Seems to work faster, too." She smiled disarmingly, and reaching into her bag, came up with a small red plastic bottle. "I even carry it with me now."

Farnsworth looked as if Margot had just let her in on the secret of curing cancer. Score one. Margot dropped the bottle back into her bag.

"How would you feel about changing your image?" Klein asked.

She looked at him innocently. "Changing it how?"

The producer tapped his pencil on the table in front of him. "Everything you've done up to now has been glamour, wouldn't you say?"

"Yes, I suppose so."

"And these commercials are going to be realistic. No makeup, or hardly any. The concept involves showing the audience somebody they can really identify with. You'd have to come across as friendly, but no high-style model."

"I see," Margot said. Of course she saw. She'd been told all that at the casting office. And the copy she'd read for the audition tape was hardly a bunch of laughs. Where did they get these assholes, anyway?

"Naturally, the fact that you're very attractive, have a lot of poise, that's important, too. Don't misunderstand me," Klein said. "But the key word here is believability. The commercials would depend on how much the audience believes you."

"I see," Margot said again. "So you'd want me to come across a little on the plain side, but very convincing about what I'm saying."

Klein nodded enthusiastically. "That's it exactly. Would that be any problem for you, projecting a less flattering image?"

Jesus Christ. If they asked her to do this with an eye patch, she'd agree. But she hesitated for a moment, as if giving the question careful consideration. "No. I'd have no objection to that. In fact, it's kind of exciting to me. A challenge, sort of. Doing something different."

The room was quiet for a moment. Then the one Margot thought was the creative director spoke to McLean. "It could be a good thing, Jock. Nobody would recognize her. They wouldn't know she's been around a long time as a model. She'd be just that much more real, you know?"

It was fascinating. This guy was talking about her as if she weren't there. As if she were a piece of meat and he was going over the good points and the flaws. Slaves had probably felt like this, standing on an auction block while men talked about whether they were skinny or fat or how their tits rated. But at least what Krakaur was saying was positive, more or less.

"I don't know," McLean replied. "Seems to me the lack of acting experience could be trouble. She was okay on the tape and all, but this is going to involve a whole series of commercials. I'm not sure whether she could carry it."

Margot wondered how he'd like a good kick in the nuts.

"Margot?" It was the one called Peter, sitting at the opposite end of the table. He'd been quiet, up to now. "How

278

did you get started in this business, if you don't mind my asking?"

The question surprised her a little, but she smiled as if she were glad he'd inquired. "A friend of mine knew a photographer. He took some shots of me and sent them to a model agency."

The young man glanced at some notes lying on the table in front of him. "And you're with the Farrelli agency now?"

There was something odd about this guy, now that she noticed. He'd been so quiet she hadn't paid much attention to him, but now that he was questioning her she sensed a strange intensity about him. He really was quite good-looking, in a clean-cut, athletic way, and the brown curls made him seem almost boyish. But all of that was somehow in conflict with his manner.

"What kind of work would you say you were best at? That is, what kind of photography?" he asked.

"Why, I guess I've always done pretty well with romantic stuff."

His voice softened. "Ah. Tight close-ups, head shots. Right?"

She wasn't sure why, but he was making her uncomfortable. "Yes, exactly."

He placed his elbows on the conference table, continuing to stare at her. "Would you mind showing me your profile, please? Left side first."

It was his eyes, Margot decided. When it came down to it, the eyes were what was weird. It was the look in them, when he studied her. But she kept her composure, giving him the left profile and then the right, holding each for a few seconds before returning her gaze to meet his. When she looked back into those eyes she felt as if she were sitting naked in front of him. It was crazy, but she got the distinct impression he was about to have an orgasm.

"Thank you," he said.

She looked away.

The rest of them chimed in then, asking a few more inane questions. Finally Klein thanked her for coming in and said they'd let her know.

Margot said good-bye and left, suddenly aware as she walked back to the reception room that she had a slight headache. To hell with Tynex. What she needed now was a stiff drink.

She took an elevator down to the lobby, and when she got there she debated for a few moments what she would do next. Walk a few blocks to clear her head? Go to Farelli's office and tell him about the interview? Return to her apartment and have that drink? As she stood thinking about it she heard someone call her name. She looked around and was surprised to see the strange young guy who'd been in the conference room—Peter something—approach her.

"Excuse me," he said. He smiled engagingly. "We really didn't get a chance to talk much in there. I know how tough those auditions can be."

She made light of it. "Oh, it wasn't so bad. All part of the business."

"Sure. My name is Peter Barrows, by the way, if you didn't catch it. I run the Tynex brand for the Whitechapel company."

So he was the client. "I see. Well, it was nice to have this chance. I'd love to get the assignment."

"Frankly, I think you'd be great for it. I'll have to convince the others, but I'm pretty sure I can handle it okay."

Her antenna went up. What was this all about?

He smiled again, his white, even teeth seeming to light up his face. "I was wondering, maybe we could get to know each other a little better."

So that was it. He was going to make a move on her. It certainly wouldn't be the first time somebody had tried it;

over the years she'd had her share of propositions from casting directors and producers and photographers and admen, and clients as well. You do this, baby, and I'll do that.

But the hell with it. As much as she wanted this assignment—as desperately as she *needed* it—she'd be damned if she'd let this character hustle her. Or anybody else, for that matter. Somehow the relationship she'd entered into with Ben Tolliver had changed the way she felt about a lot of things. And she wasn't going to overturn those feelings for a lousy job, no matter how important it was.

He moved closer. "Why don't we have a drink?"

Margot thought of Jean Sandoval and her string of opportunities. What was the difference? "No, I'm sorry." She turned to leave, but before she could move away, he grasped her arm.

"Hey, look," he said. "Don't get the wrong idea. I was just thinking it could be—"

"Will you please let go?" She struggled to free herself, as his grip tightened. "Damn it, let go of me!"

His face darkened; he was suddenly angry. "Stop being a fool!"

He made a grab for her other arm, but before he could get hold of her she swung her bag as hard as she could against the side of his head.

His teeth were clenched. "Stupid bitch!"

Margot twisted, trying to knee him in the balls. She was frightened now—this guy was acting like a real wacko. People had stopped to look, but not a damn one of them lifted a finger to help her.

He seized a handful of her hair and she stomped his foot with her heel. He yelled in pain.

"Peter!"

She saw it was the Farnsworth woman, coming toward them from the lobby doors. Farnsworth was wearing an expression of disbelief, which turned quickly into outrage.

Margot didn't wait to see what happened next. She pulled herself free and ran across the sidewalk to a taxi.

53

Ben stopped at a gas station, and while the attendant was filling the Ford's tank he got on the phone. Information gave him Attorney Holt's number in Greenwich, and when he called it he learned that Holt was a partner in a firm there. The lawyer's secretary told him Holt was out for the remainder of the day. He asked for directions anyway, figuring as long as he was that close he might as well take a run up to the guy's office; there was always a chance he could learn something just from nosing around. He paid for the gas and drove north on the Hutch and on up the Merritt Parkway into Greenwich, the first town over the Connecticut line.

The law firm of Chichester, Megow and Holt was on Mason Street, in a building that appeared to have been converted from one of the old houses typical of the downtown area. Unlike Stamford, its next-door neighbor on the coast, Greenwich had turned up its well-bred nose at all efforts to rebuild it into an urban center complete with high-rise office towers, high-rise taxes, and high-rise crime rates. Tolliver didn't know much about the town, beyond its reputation as the wealthiest per capita community in the northeastern part of the United States. It might share its name with Greenwich Village, but in character the two seemed as far apart as the earth and the moon. Maybe farther.

Holt's secretary was prim and starchy. She was sorry, she said, but Mr. Holt couldn't be reached. If Ben would care to make an appointment for another day, she'd be glad to arrange it. He showed her his shield and explained that he was there on New York police business, adding he knew Holt would be disappointed to have missed his visit. That threw her off stride, but she was adamant. So he waited until she'd gone back to her office and then asked the receptionist, a cute young thing who giggled and told him Mr. Holt was playing golf at his club. The Stanwich, she said. He got directions, and left.

The club was about eight miles up into the country, on North Street. There were polo fields on one side of the road, and the entrance to the Stanwich was on the other. A long drive wound through the woods and led up to the clubhouse, a huge white colonial that straddled a hilltop, with the golf course laid out around it. Ben nosed the Ford in among the Mercedes and the Porsches and the Jaguars in the parking lot and walked up to the wide front steps.

He asked for the manager, telling the guy who he was and explaining that he had important police business with Holt. The manager wasn't about to give a New York detective an argument, especially when he had to know Holt was a lawyer. He told Ben Mr. Holt was probably on the course, and then showed him to a table on the terrace where he could wait. Ben asked a waiter to point out Holt when he showed up.

For a weekday, the place seemed very busy. From where he sat, Ben could see a number of people playing golf, some of them walking with caddies and others riding in carts. It was a beautiful day for it, the afternoon shadows lengthening now, and a light breeze turning the leaves of the maples and the oaks and the willows. The terrace was also busy, men and women wearing bright-colored sports clothes drinking and chattering at the tables. The view from here was spectacular—you could see all the way across the sound to Long Island. About forty minutes went by before the waiter called his attention to a foursome coming off the eighteenth green.

Brian Holt was about sixty, Ben guessed. His hair was silver, but it was still thick, and he looked out at you from piercing blue eyes set deep in his ruddy face, with an expression that told you they didn't miss a whole lot. He was wearing a green shirt and a silly pair of orange pants, but his physical presence still came off as hard, taut, and spare. Ben doubted he had much patience for bullshit.

Holt seemed mildly surprised to learn that a cop had tracked him down. Nevertheless if he was annoyed at this cheeky interruption of his afternoon leisure, he didn't show it. He excused himself from his friends and told Ben to come on into the locker room; they could talk in there.

They sat down on a bench, and as Holt took off his spikes, the blue eyes fixed on his visitor. "You say you have an interest in a client of mine, Lieutenant?"

"At least he was a client a few years back," Ben said. "His name is Peter Hewitt. Or Barrows, now."

"Mmm. What about him?"

"I'm trying to locate him. I want to ask him some questions in connection with a homicide investigation I'm working on in New York."

Holt's gaze never flickered. "The Greenwich Village murders. That right?"

It was Ben's turn to be surprised. "How did you know that?"

"Been hearing a lot about it on TV and in the newspapers. Saw your name in a couple of the stories. When that reporter was murdered it really turned the lights up, didn't it?"

He'd been right—this guy didn't miss a thing. "Can you tell me where Barrows is now?"

Holt took off his shirt and hung it in a locker. "No, I can't."

Ben wondered if the lawyer was putting up a stone wall. But that wasn't it. "The last I heard, he was living in Europe."

So at least Herlitzer had been telling the truth about Hewitt's whereabouts. "He is your client, isn't he?"

Holt continued to undress, taking off his pants and putting them on a hanger before depositing them in the locker. "His mother was. Before she died. I drew her will, and I was its executor. Under its terms, I set up a testamentary trust for Peter, who was her only child."

"Are you a trustee?"

"No. The trustees are the Chase Manhattan Bank. The funds are very conservatively invested, mostly in bonds."

"And the bank distributes proceeds to Barrows?"

"On a monthly basis." Holt took off his shorts and wrapped a towel around his middle.

"Have you had any further contact with him, or done any more legal work involving him?"

"Not for years. Now if you'll excuse me, Lieutenant, it's been nice talking to you, and I wish you luck with your investigation. I'm going to take my shower." He turned and marched off, his back straight as a ramrod.

Ben sat back on the bench, leaning against the wall. Instead of satisfying his curiosity, the discussion with Holt had only intensified it. He wasn't about to just walk out of here now.

He looked around at the other men in the locker room. In a way, the sight was comical. Every one of these guys had the same odd markings: faces, necks, forearms and hands sunburned to shades ranging from red to deep tan, while the rest of them was a pasty white. They also seemed to share another physical characteristic: huge bellies hanging off the front of them like pouches. But they acted like kids, guffawing at each other's dumb jokes, kidding and teasing. One guy snapped a wet towel at another's ass and then roared with laughter when the other chased him. Boys will be boys, Ben thought. Some of these clowns reminded him of the detectives in the Sixth Precinct squad.

When Holt returned to his locker and found Ben still sitting on the bench, he shook his head. "I'll give you one thing, Lieutenant. You're persistent."

"Look," Ben said, "I'm sorry if I'm being a nuisance. But I really would appreciate any further information you can give me."

Holt cocked his head, contemplating his visitor as if he was trying to make up his mind. "I've already told you more about any client of mine than I ordinarily would. Or any former client, for that matter. But I'll grant you that these circumstances are unusual. This case you're working on isn't only sensational, it's also dreadful. And I gather you think Peter might have been involved somehow. Even though he's been out of the country for years. Is that correct?"

Ben said it was. He then told Holt about the murder at Colgate and the similarities between that case and the ones in New York. He explained that they were checking out all the men they could find who had been at the university at the time Pamela Benoit was killed.

Holt listened intently until Ben finished. Then he asked questions that said a lot about the kind of lawyer he was. "Can you prove a link between the murder at Colgate and the ones you're working on now?"

"No."

"Was Peter questioned during the investigation at Colgate?"

"No. He'd left the campus a week or two before the murder. He was in a private hospital in White Plains."

"Pembroke."

"Yes. You know about that?"

"I was aware of Peter's emotional problems. But if he

was in a hospital when the girl was killed, how could he have been involved?"

"I don't know how. Not exactly, anyway."

Holt reached into his locker for a fresh sport shirt, a blue one this time, and put it on. "Pretty much of a reach, isn't it? You're trying to make a connection on the basis of—what? The young man was a student at the university when a murder was committed. But he wasn't on the campus at the time. He was in a place where his presence would be on record. Years later, a series of homicides were committed in New York which bore a superficial resemblance to the earlier murder at the university. But there is no proof they were in fact related. And as far as the possibility of linking the young man to these new crimes is concerned, he hasn't even resided in the United States for years."

Ben felt like a prize asshole. It occurred to him that he wouldn't want to be cross-examined by Holt on a witness stand. But he still wasn't ready to give up. "Mind if I ask a few more questions about his background?"

Holt went on dressing, pulling on a pair of gray slacks. "No, I suppose not. I'll tell you what I can."

"Does he have any other family living here in the States?"

"Not as far as I know. His father was living in Florida, but he died a few years ago."

"Was he the mother's only husband?"

"No. He was her third."

"Who were the others?"

"I'm not sure. One she married when she was quite young. I have no idea who he was."

"Who was number two?"

"An Italian, I believe. Didn't last very long. But she was married to Peter's father for many years."

"Why did Peter drop his father's name?"

Holt turned a steady gaze on Ben. "Apparently he didn't

288

get along with his father very well. After his parents were divorced, Peter had his name legally changed."

"Can you think of any reason he'd come back to the U.S. from time to time?"

There might have been a faint flicker of amusement across the ruddy features. Or there might not have been. "I can think of lots of reasons why he might. But I have no knowledge that he has."

Ben stood up. "Thanks for your help."

Holt held out his hand. "You're welcome, Lieutenant. If I can be of further assistance, let me know."

Ben shook the hand. "There is one thing."

"Which is?"

"Where in Greenwich did they live?"

"On Round Hill."

"House still there?"

"Oh, yes. It's turned over a couple of times since then."

"Can you tell me how to get there? I'd like to drive by."

Holt gave him directions, and Ben left the locker room. Back upstairs in the clubhouse he went into a telephone booth and called Ed Flynn. He told Flynn what he'd learned, and instructed him to get in touch with the Chase Manhattan Bank and find out everything he could about a young man named Peter Barrows. Then he walked back to the parking lot, got into the Ford and drove back out to North Street, following Holt's directions to Round Hill.

54

THERE was a bar in the Roosevelt Hotel near the Forty-sixth Street entrance. Peter went inside and climbed onto a stool, grateful for the cool darkness after the glare of the afternoon sun. He ordered a Scotch on the rocks and when the bartender put it in front of him he sat there for a time, waiting for his hands to stop shaking and his breathing to return to normal.

It was hard to believe what he'd done. Losing control that way, making a spectacle of himself. No matter how thrilling it was just to be in the same room with her, no matter how staggered he was by her presence, it was impossible to justify his actions. He had simply erupted—gone crazy—when she brushed him off. Brushed him off? Christ—she'd rejected him. Flat-out *rejected* him. No wonder he'd lost his head.

What would she think of him now? How could he ever repair the damage? He had to find a way to restore her confidence in him, make her see he wasn't some harebrain.

Because he had to have her if he was to carry out his plan.

And Farnsworth. Goddamn that meddling, officious bitch. She must have followed them into the reception room and then down into the lobby of the J&C building. Jesus, the look on her ugly face. And then he'd blown up at her—another piece of stupidity. It was a wonder he hadn't gone completely berserk at that point. God knew it would have been understandable if he had.

So now he had some mending to do. Handling Farnsworth after that outburst would be a problem. He'd have to give her some bullshit story, if he could come up with one that made sense. Maybe he could get away with telling her he'd been exhausted from overwork. Or maybe turn it around, tell her Margot Dennis had caused the problem. The trouble was, he wasn't sure just what Farnsworth had seen. Christ, what a mess. But he'd think of something.

He nursed the Scotch for close to an hour, and it helped. There weren't many people in the place, and the bartender didn't try to hurry him, or get him into a conversation. Between the alcohol and the cool, quiet atmosphere he felt much better, even soothed. He dropped some bills on the bar and left.

When he got back to his office he knew there was trouble from the funny look on Evelyn's face. She was getting ready to leave for the day, and she said Mr. Torrey wanted to see him. Peter wanted to pump her as to what it might be about, but she avoided his gaze, saying she was in a hurry and had to go. For an instant he thought about ducking out, putting off seeing Torrey until the next morning, when he'd be in better shape all the way around.

But that would mean he'd have to spend the evening worrying, not knowing what it was he'd have to contend with. Better to know now. If Farnsworth had cut him up behind his back he'd deal with it, nip it early. He adjusted his tie and walked down to the vice president's office at an easy pace.

Torrey was not his usual jovial self. When Peter walked in and offered a pleasant hello, the VP looked up with a dour expression on his jowly face. He told Peter to shut the door and sit down.

Despite his outward calm, Barrows' pulse was hammering, and he'd developed a brutal headache. It felt like a steel band tightening around his skull. He leaned forward in the chair, waiting to find out where he stood, telling himself to stay cool, to think and talk his way out of this.

But Torrey never gave him a chance. He folded his arms,

and in a quiet voice he said, "Afraid I have some bad news for you."

Peter tried to be casual. "Really? Such as?"

There was no change in Torrey's expression, nor in his tone. "We think it would be best for everyone concerned, Peter, if you were to leave the company."

Leave the company?

Could this be for real? Could he be getting *fired* over the one misstep he'd ever made here? After posting an absolutely brilliant record? He opened his mouth, but nothing came out of it. The headache had suddenly gotten much worse. It felt now as if the steel band would continue to crush his skull until his brains burst from the top of his head.

Somehow he made himself say, "I don't think a silly argument calls for anything that harsh."

"I'm not talking about a silly argument, Peter. What happened this afternoon was disgraceful. We don't expect our people to conduct themselves in such a fashion, ever."

Peter tried to interrupt, but Torrey raised a hand to silence him.

"For that matter," Torrey went on, "this afternoon isn't the major issue. As bad as it was, all it did was bring the situation to a head. Marilyn has been very dissatisfied with your performance, right from the moment she took over the business."

Again he was stunned. "But that can't be. She certainly hasn't said anything about it to me."

"Come on now, of course she has. She's kept me closely informed of all the discussions between you."

"Look, I'll admit we've had our disagreements from time to time. But that's all part of doing business. The fact is, it's been my thinking that's built the Tynex brand. Everybody knows that."

"Do they? There's quite another point of view held by

management. We think the brand would have grown at a much faster rate, except for certain mistakes that were made with it. We felt you were doing a reasonably good job, under the circumstances. But it was clear that a steady hand was needed over you. That's why Marilyn was appointed group product manager. And I must say, she's done a fine job of straightening out the problems, getting the brand back on track."

Peter heard himself speaking, but the sounds issuing from him were unintelligible, even to him. It was as if suddenly he was outside himself, watching this scene from a distance.

Once more Torrey raised a hand to shut him off. "That's enough, Peter. The decision has been made. You're to clean out your desk before you leave. Tomorrow you can contact the personnel department about severance."

It was over; there was nothing more to say. He stared, his head throbbing, as Torrey stood up and extended his hand.

"No hard feelings, Peter," Torrey said. "I'll be glad to give you the best recommendation I can."

Peter got to his feet and shook the proffered hand. He left the room and went back to his own office, barely conscious of his whereabouts.

Sitting down at his desk, he realized he was sweating heavily. His shirt felt wet and clammy next to his skin, and his jacket was damp. He took out a handkerchief and mopped his face.

So she'd succeeded. She'd done this to him, deliberately. All in accordance with a carefully worked-out plan. Dissatisfied with his performance from the time she took over? How true that must have been. And all the while she'd been cutting him to the bone with Torrey behind his back. She'd discredited him, shamed him. But in fact she'd done much more than that—she'd *ruined* him.

And yet, was this such a surprise, after all? Could he have expected anything else? Wasn't this how Freda had always treated him? *Always?*

He picked up the antique dagger from his desk. Its ornate handle felt hard and cold in his fist, and light from the fluorescent bars overhead reflected in glittering pinpoints from its blade. He carefully placed the dagger in his inside jacket pocket, stood up, and left his office.

55

THERE was a stone wall around the place, and it was set in a grove of trees, but Ben could see enough from the road to get an impression. What had once been the Hewitt residence was a rambling old three-story gray house, with a columned entrance and tall windows, and dormers in a slate roof. But he wasn't so much interested in this house as he was in the ones on either side of it.

Not that it was the kind of neighborhood where you'd go next door to borrow a cup of sugar. He guessed that every one of the homes along this road was sitting on at least ten acres of land, and some of them probably had a lot more than that. If you were looking to buy a house around here and you had a million dollars to spend, a broker would laugh at you. But Ben knew what every cop knows: people are people, and most of them love to talk about their neighbors.

The first two tries were strikeouts. In one the owners were away, and in the other the occupants had bought the house only five years ago. But in the third, maybe a half mile farther up the road, he got a hit.

The main dwelling was at the end of a long driveway that curved around through formal gardens. The house was even bigger than the others, a sprawl of fieldstone that looked to Ben like a hotel. He parked the Ford and went up the steps to the front entrance. At first a maid tried to shoo him away, but he kept his patience, and after a minute or two of earnest discussion an old lady came to the door and asked what he wanted. Ben showed her his shield, explaining that he was a New York police officer and that he wanted to ask questions about the Hewitts. The old lady seemed pleased. She told him to come right in.

Her name was Ethel Wharton, she said, and she had lived in this house most of her adult life. Her parents had had it built back in the thirties as a wedding present for her and her husband. That was just about the first thing she told him, and Ben supposed it was so he wouldn't get the idea she was one of those nouveaux riches stockbrokers or something. She led him out to a terrace and told the maid to bring them iced tea.

The terrace was about forty feet long, built of bluestone, overlooking a pool and a pool house. There were tall shade trees and flower gardens beyond that, and neatly clipped green lawns that seemed to go on forever. Ben and the old lady sat on patio furniture covered in chintz with yellow flowers printed on it.

Wharton must have been a beauty in her time. Now her hair was white with a touch of blue, and her skin was almost transparent, but the wide mouth and the cheekbones and the nose gave you a good idea of what she'd once looked like. Her body was still trim, too. She was wearing a black-and-white-checked blouse and a gray skirt. She said her husband had died a few years ago, and her children, a boy and a girl, were married and living with their own families. One in Chicago, the other in San Francisco. She'd known the Hewitts well, and had been to parties at their house. And they'd belonged to the same club, the Round Hill.

"What was she like?"

"Brenda? Spectacularly beautiful, but on the wild side. Drank too much, flirted too much, did whatever she pleased. Not that her husband was any prize. George Hewitt had a whole string of mistresses in New York and everyone knew it. But Brenda didn't care. She knew she could just crook her little finger and get any man she wanted."

Ben wondered if that had included Wharton's husband, but he decided not to pursue it. Instead he asked if she'd known the men Brenda had married before Hewitt.

"No. That was all before she came here. From what she told me, neither of them was anything but trouble. The first one ruined himself with alcohol and drugs and died quite young. Came from a wealthy family, but there was some sort of scandal he was mixed up in while he and Brenda were living in New York. I think it involved little boys, if you follow me."

Ben did.

"And the second one was an Italian count she met in Rome. He went mad over her the minute he met her. He'd seen her picture in magazines and was just dazzled by her."

"Picture in magazines?"

"Yes. She was a famous model, you know. Number one, in her day."

A famous model. Ben felt the hairs come up on the back of his neck.

"You'd see her face on covers all over the place," Wharton said. "I was aware of that, even before I ever knew her. But that marriage didn't last long. Brenda became bored with Italy, just as she became bored with everything else, sooner or later. And also the count was having financial difficulties. So she left him, and then she met George."

"They were together quite a while, weren't they?"

"Yes, but if you ask me, the only reason she stayed married to him was because it was convenient. He also came from a rich family, you see. They owned an investment banking firm. He and Brenda had the house here, and an apartment in New York, and a place in Palm Beach. She had plenty of money and total freedom. For somebody like her, it was ideal."

"What about her son?"

"Ah, Peter. That was sad. He had some terrible emotional problems. Worshipped his mother, but she had no time for him at all. Treated him like some pet dog she might pat on the head, if she happened to notice him. Which wasn't often. Frankly, I think she considered him a nuisance."

"You said he had emotional problems?"

Wharton sipped iced tea. "That's a euphemism, Lieutenant. He was sent away several times. Brenda called them boarding schools, but I knew better. He had mental troubles from the time he was a small child. Always seeing psychiatrists."

"What was wrong, do you know?"

"Well, I don't know what the psychiatrists said, but I could give you some theories. One would have to do with his father. I just have to believe there were some weak genes there. And the relationship with his mother was certainly not normal. When I say he worshipped her, that's an understatement. But she paid as little attention to him as possible. Right after he was born, she just turned him over to a governess. That was the one who actually raised him."

"What was she like?"

"Freda? She was domineering, strict, and cold as ice. I never had a nanny for my children, and I never would. But if I had, I assure you I never would have let someone like her anywhere near them."

"What about the boy's relationship with his father?"

"There wasn't any. Peter couldn't stand him, and I'm sure the feeling was mutual."

"I understand Peter went to Colgate?"

"Yes. I'll give him one thing, he was bright. And when he got older, when he was a teenager, he seemed to straighten out. They sent him to Deerfield, and he did well. So he had no trouble getting into college."

"And did okay there too, didn't he?"

"Oh yes. But then his mother died, and apparently that just shattered him."

"How did she die?"

"Suicide. You see, after they were divorced, George retired. Went to live in the house in Palm Beach. Then Brenda's drinking got worse. She began to lose her looks. Put on weight. The more she drank, the heavier she got. And the heavier she got, the more she drank. And then one day I guess she looked at what had happened to her, and she shot herself. Unfortunately, Peter was home at the time. He found her."

"And after that?"

"After that the house was sold, and the last I knew Peter went to Europe. I haven't heard anything of him since."

They talked awhile longer, but most of what Wharton had to say from that point on was just elaboration on what she'd already told him. Ben finished his iced tea and said he appreciated her help. She seemed sorry to see him go.

On the way out he asked if he could use a phone, and she showed him to one in the library. While he waited for the call to go through, Ben looked at the floor-to-ceiling bookcases and wondered if anybody had ever read all this stuff. He'd never been in a house as elaborate as this, and he couldn't imagine living in it, no matter how much dough he had. Not that he'd ever have the problem.

When Ed Flynn came on the line, he sounded as if he'd just run up a flight of stairs. "Lou! This guy Barrows? He's right here in New York. Works for a company called Whitechapel. He was with them in France, but then they transferred him back here two years ago."

"Where are they located?"

"Park at Fortieth Street."

Ben looked at his watch. "Go there, Ed. Wait for me in front of the building. I'll be there in less than forty-five minutes." He put the phone down and ran through the house for the front door, jumping down the steps and into the Ford.

56

PETER walked into Farnsworth's office and shut the door. She looked up, her thin lips compressing in a familiar expression of distaste. Her gaze was cold and steady. "Have you spoken with Rick Torrey?"

"Yes, I've spoken with him."

She folded her arms. "I'm sorry it had to end this way, Peter. It's too bad we couldn't work together. And now I have nothing more to say about it than that. So good-bye, and good luck."

He smiled. All his life he'd lived with this burden, feeling her foot on the back of his neck, suffering the pain and the humiliation. Now that he knew how to end it, he was suddenly elated, realizing he'd finally be free.

She frowned. "I think you'd better just leave."

"Do you? Is that what you think? You think I should just do as I'm told and leave now?"

"Yes, exactly. Haven't you created enough scenes for one day? Now please go, without causing any more trouble. Do you understand me?"

"I understand." But instead of leaving, he moved slowly around the desk until he was standing over her, continuing to stare at her with the smile carefully in place.

For the first time, a suggestion of doubt crept into her expression. And then it was replaced by one of fear. "What is it? What are you doing? Why are you looking at me like that?"

"You know why, you bitch. You know exactly why."

"How dare you—"

"Did you think I was so stupid I'd just take it, just go on swallowing your shit? Did you really think that?"

"Get out, damn it. Before I call security."

"It's too late, Freda. Too late for you to call anybody now. It's all over."

"What—what did you call me?"

"I called you by your *name*, Freda. Did you think I wouldn't figure that out?" He reached into his jacket and withdrew the dagger.

He held the blade inches from her face. "You know what this is, too. Don't you?"

Her eyes were wide with terror. She stared at the knife, and then she made a desperate lunge for the telephone, at the same time opening her mouth to scream.

But he was much too quick for her. His free hand shot out and gripped her by the hair, forcing her head back. Her eyes bulged, and her lips contorted with pain. The scream became a small shrill cry that died in her throat. She pawed at him, but he ignored her efforts and raised the knife.

He stood over her, his voice hoarse with rage. "You want it, don't you, Freda? Look at it. See? It's big and hard, just the way you like it. Well here it is, goddamn you. Now SUCK IT!"

He rammed the blade down into her open mouth, twisting it back and forth, the razor-sharp steel cutting through tissue and arteries. Blood erupted in brilliant red spurts, splattering him and filling the air with a pink spray.

She writhed and bucked, but her strength was no match for his. She might as well have been a rag doll, fluttering and kicking in his powerful grip. He pulled the dagger free and then slammed it into her mouth again.

And again.

And again.

And again.

Then he stood back, looking at her, and was happier than he'd ever been in his life.

57

As soon as he hit the parkway, Ben put his foot on the floor. He had the flasher on and the siren going, but he didn't want to contact the Connecticut State Police on his radio even though regulations required it, because the whole procedure would have been a much bigger pain in the ass than it was worth. It was better just to take a chance on running into a bear; if he had to, he could always let the guy know he was on business. He went down the Merritt like a rocket, weaving in and out of traffic, scaring the shit out of people who were doing 80 and thought they were going fast.

As much as he tried to concentrate on his driving, his brain refused to cooperate. Instead his senses were focused elsewhere, in a swirling mixture of rage and excitement:

I knew, you son of a bitch. I knew from the minute I saw what you did to the Benoit girl at Colgate. I knew every step of the fucking way, no matter what Brennan said. And no matter what kind of bullshit story that phony bastard of a doctor tried to hand me. No matter that your lawyer and the old lady all tried to tell me you weren't even in the country. I knew. So you've had a tough life? So your mommy didn't give a shit about you—turned you over to a nanny? So what? You grew up in a big house in a nice town and you had doctors wiping your nose from the time you were born. Your folks had a pile of money and they belonged to a country club. They sent you to a private school and then to college. And then mommy left you a big fat trust fund. So you've got emotional problems? So who the fuck doesn't? I'm close now, asshole. Very close. I can almost smell you.

When he reached the Hutch the stream of vehicles was

thicker, but he kept right on burning it. The Ford wasn't the best machine in the world for a rapid run, or even for picking his way through quick openers. Its old-fashioned suspension featured a stiff axle and leaf springs, and the slightest bump sent the car chattering and shuddering, so that half the time he felt he wasn't so much maneuvering as he was hanging on. But at least it had a big V-8 engine, and once you got it rolling you could haul ass. He flew down the Deegan and blew his way around the tolls on the Triborough. After that he had the FDR Drive to contend with, its surface more rutted than those of the parkways, every pothole a trap that could snap a wheel off the car.

He turned off on the Fifty-third Street exit, and then the real struggle began, as he fought his way through the tangle of cars and trucks and taxis that choked the midtown streets. When he skidded to a stop in front of the Whitechapel building, his watch told him he'd made the trip from the old lady's house in Greenwich in thirty-two minutes.

Ed Flynn was waiting for him on the sidewalk. It was after business hours now, and when they asked the security man in the lobby where Peter Barrows' office was, the guy had to put on reading glasses and fiddle through a directory, the two cops hopping up and down as if they had to take a leak. Finally he said Barrows was on the forty-third floor, and they ran for an elevator.

There were still a number of people up there, secretaries typing and executives working in shirtsleeves, and when Ben inquired, one of the girls pointed out Barrows' office. He hurried over to it and opened the door, but the room was unoccupied. Another secretary was busy at a desk nearby. Ben asked this one if Barrows had left for the day.

The girl gave him a blank look. "Who are you?"

He pulled out his shield and held it up in front of her.

The expression didn't change, except that her eyes grew a little wider. "I think he did, if he's not in his office. I haven't seen him."

He looked around for someone else to ask, but then the girl said, "I think his group head might still be here."

"Who's that?"

"Her name's Marilyn Farnsworth." She indicated. "Down that way, turn right, third door on your left."

They ran to the office, which had a piece of yellow paper taped to the door. Scribbled on the paper were the words WORKING DO NOT DISTURB. Ben knocked once and opened the door.

Holy sweet screaming Jesus.

A woman's body was sprawled in the chair behind the desk, her head thrown back and the handle of a dagger sticking out of her open mouth.

There was blood everywhere. The woman's face was covered with it, and streams of gore had run from her mouth down her neck, drenching her blouse and her jacket and her skirt. There were half-dried pools of blood on her desk and on the carpet and there were red splatters on the wall and on the venetian blinds over the window. Everywhere he looked, Ben saw blood. It was like walking into a slaughterhouse.

He stepped over to the woman and grabbed her wrist; it was cold but flaccid. She probably had been dead less than an hour.

"Goddamn it." Flynn was behind him, staring at the carnage.

"Get on the phone," Ben barked. "Get some cops in here." He ran back down the corridor to Barrows' office, thinking there might be something there that would help locate him.

The stuff on the surface of the desk appeared to be all business—reports, memos, invoices, trade papers. He opened the top drawer and found it full of junk: paper clips, scissors, a stapler, Scotch tape, odds and ends. The only thing that looked as if it could be personal was an envelope addressed to Barrows, but it was empty. He stuffed it into a pants pocket and went through the other drawers, but they also appeared to contain only business papers.

He started to turn to the filing cabinet when a folder on the desk caught his eye. He opened it.

What he saw knocked the wind out of him. It was a brochure of the kind he'd seen dozens of in the past few weeks, four pages in black and white showing pictures of a model in various poses and outfits.

The model in this one was Margot Dennis.

For once Ben couldn't move. He stood staring at the thing, his chest feeling as if it had suddenly been caught between a pair of enormous pincers.

Then he forced himself to snap out of it and riffled through the folder, thinking maybe this was just one of a bunch of brochures the guy had been looking at. There were a dozen others, all right, but they were identical. The subject in them was Margot.

He snatched up the phone and punched her number, sweat popping out on his forehead.

It rang. And rang. And rang.

He cut off the call and hit 411, asking information for the number of the lobby in her building.

When he got the number he called it and the doorman answered. Ben told the guy who he was and asked him if he'd seen Miss Dennis.

"Sure, Lieutenant. One of your men is here with her now."

"One of my *what*?"

"One of your detectives. Wait a minute, I made a note of his name. Got it right here. It's Kurwitz. Detective Joseph Kurwitz."

58

WHEN Margot arrived home, the first thing she did was take a bath. She felt dirty physically and emotionally, and when she eased her body into the hot, sweet-smelling suds, it was like purging herself.

What an absolute misery of a day. She'd done exactly what she'd hoped to do in the audition at J&C, and she was sure she'd made a very positive impression. They *liked* her. She knew it from their questions, and from the expressions on their faces when they heard her answers. And they liked what they saw, too. She'd looked just right, coming off as very sincere and believable. She'd had it nailed.

And then that unspeakable creep had destroyed it all. What could have been a triumph had turned straight into disaster. He'd ruined everything with his crazy, clumsy effort at a pass. A pass? Hell, that was an assault. Or as close to one as she'd ever want to come. Compared to him, the guys who'd tried to hustle her from time to time over the years had been noble gentlemen.

How in hell could a big company like that have such a freak in an important position? It wasn't just that he'd tried a move—that wouldn't have been a surprise at all. What was amazing was his reaction when she brushed him off. He not only wouldn't take no for an answer, he'd gone flat-out nuts. Jesus—the look in his eyes. What would have happened if she hadn't been in a public place, where she could belt him and take off?

And what would happen to the Tynex job now?

Oh hell, Margot, she told herself, face it. That's gone. It's out the window. You could grovel to him now and you'd never repair the damage. And even if you could, would you want to? Would you ever want to have him near you again? What if there was another time and you couldn't cut and run? What would you do then?

So forget it. Farrelli would just have to come up with something else. But God—it hurt to lose this one. She hadn't been counting the money, exactly, but she certainly had been thinking about how much it would help.

She stayed in the bath for quite a while, replenishing the hot water occasionally, until she felt better. Then she got out and dried herself, trying not to think further about the incident at the agency. That was something she'd cope with tomorrow. If there was any coping left to do. She got dressed, putting on a blue-and-white-print cotton dress and hoping its bright pattern would help lift her spirits. She was also hoping Ben would be coming back early, now that he was off for a few days, or semi-off, or whatever he was.

The relationship with him was like nothing she'd experienced. He was probably the strongest guy she'd known, and at the same time one of the gentlest. An odd combination of traits for a cop. Not that she had anybody to compare him to, but he didn't fit her conception of what a detective would be like at all. She was also aware of how much she'd begun to care about him. Which was another thing that didn't make too much sense. At least from a practical standpoint it didn't.

She made the bed next, stripping it and putting on fresh sheets, and that kept Ben in the front of her mind as well. There certainly wasn't any doubt about how good *that* part of the relationship was.

When she finished she checked her answering machine. One call from Jean Sandoval, and one from Matthew Farrelli. Matt would be wanting to hear how the audition had gone, but she wasn't up to telling him. Not yet, anyway. And Jean? Probably another proposition, another big spender on the line. Shit. She decided to push all that out of her mind and concentrate instead on what she'd have for dinner if Ben showed up. Steaks, maybe. She had a couple of good ones in the freezer. Say with baked potatoes and Italian bread and a salad. And a bottle of wine. He'd like that. Which was something pleasant to think about, anyway.

She wandered around for a time, tidying up the apartment, and then she was suddenly aware of being tired. This really had been a hell of a day. She sat down in one of the deep chairs in the living room to relax for a moment or two. When she opened her eyes she was surprised to see that the room was nearly dark. She must have dozed off; outside the streetlights were coming on. Evening was falling.

And a bell was ringing. As the fog cleared she realized the sound was coming from the telephone. She got up and crossed the room to answer it.

It was the doorman, calling from the lobby. He said there was a police detective down there who wanted to see her.

"Sure, Pat, send him up." She put the phone down.

It must be one of Ben's men, she thought. But why was he here? Had Ben sent him? Or was there something wrong—had something happened to Ben? Stop being silly, she said to herself. You'll know soon enough.

A minute later her doorbell sounded. She stepped into the foyer and opened the door.

And was astounded.

He was looking at her with that same expression on his face, and with the same peculiar look in his eyes. His right hand was holding a pistol. He was pointing it at her face.

He smiled. "Hello, Margot."

59

Ben slammed the phone down and sprinted from Barrows' office to the elevators. He had to wait for what seemed like hours, while he debated whether to forget it and take the stairs. But then an elevator finally arrived and he jumped into it. He was running again when he hit the lobby, racing out of the building, across the sidewalk and into the Ford. He pulled the car away from the curb and into a shrieking U-turn, barely missing a cab. The taxi skidded past, its driver shaking his fist and shouting curses, and Ben accelerated hard as he roared up the Grand Central Viaduct, heading north.

He had the flasher on and the siren going, but he still had a tough time threading his way through the early-evening traffic. He whipped the wheel back and forth and yelled at other drivers, thinking about how New York had to be the worst town in the world to try to drive anywhere in a police vehicle. In other cities drivers would pull over when they heard a siren, but here it was Fuck you, buddy, I'm in a hurry too.

At Fiftieth Street a long black limousine was drawing away from in front of the Waldorf, its driver arrogantly ignoring Ben's siren and lights. Ben veered, but it was too late. He slammed into the limo, the Ford lurching sideways and bouncing off the larger car. A chauffeur struggled to get out of it, but Ben paid no attention to him. Served the son of a bitch right. The front end of the Ford was shoved in, but the car would still drive. He continued north on Park, the Ford crabbing a little and its roadholding now worse than ever.

The traffic became a touch better up here, the three-lane river of cars and taxis thinning out some, and he darted into the holes when he could find them, slipping from one side of the broad street to the other until he was able to turn east toward Margot's building. He leaned on his horn to add its noise to that of the siren, but he could do no better than crawl along the clogged streets. He was still a half block away when he spotted them.

With her auburn hair, Margot was unmistakable. The guy with her had his arm around her and he was holding her close. He was just far enough away so that Ben couldn't make out his features clearly, but he could see the guy was taller than average, with curly brown hair and wearing a tan suit. There was no doubt whatever in Ben's mind who he was.

They saw Ben, too; both of them looked back at the Ford, its siren whooping and the red light flashing from its roof, and then they hurried across the sidewalk. Ben jammed the transmission into park and leaped out of the car, but before he could take a step he saw Margot and the man get into a brown station wagon that was parked at the curb in front of the building.

Goddamn it. If he ran like hell he might catch them, might not. If he missed, he'd have no chance. He decided to stick with the Ford and jumped back in behind the wheel. He hit the horn again and deliberately banged his bumper into the ass end of the car in front of him, at the same time shouting at the driver to get the fuck out of the way. Farther up he could see the station wagon moving. He tried his radio, but it was dead. The collision with the limo must have taken it out.

The traffic was impossible. Every time he managed to pass another car and pick up a little speed, the wagon seemed to match him, snaking in between and around other vehicles until it reached the southbound entrance to the FDR Drive. Ben saw him pull onto the highway, but by the time he made it himself he could no longer spot the other car.

That left him with only one choice, and he took it. He wound the Ford up to all the speed there was in it and blasted down the rutted road, weaving his way in and out of the lanes of cars. It felt as if he were hurtling through a tunnel, with the elevated highway over his head, the buildings on his right and the roiling waters of the East River on his left. He was in luck: a mile or so down he again caught sight of the brown station wagon, and he seemed to be gaining on it.

The trouble was, he could draw no closer. Barrows must have spotted him; he was pushing the wagon harder than before. They streaked past the UN building and the medical center, and then Ben saw him turn off the drive onto Fifteenth Street.

Ben took the exit on two wheels, the Ford shuddering and chattering, a piece of its mangled right front sticking up in the air like a pennant. Dodging a truck, he threaded his way between two taxis and just got through the intersection at First Avenue before the light changed.

At Second Avenue he had no chance. The stream of vehicles came to a halt at the light, and Ben could see the wagon fast disappearing farther along on Fourteenth Street. He decided he'd be damned if he was going to just sit there and give up. He pulled out and around the cars and into the oncoming lane, mashing the accelerator to the floor in an effort to get across before the traffic coming down Second Avenue blocked his way.

He almost made it.

A bus crashed broadside into the Ford, flipping it over onto its roof. Ben wasn't wearing his seatbelt, and he wound up on his head, arms and legs tangled and the wind knocked out of him from colliding with the steering wheel. He lay there gasping, not sure if he was badly hurt or not.

The window on his side was open, and he crawled through it onto the pavement. There was pain in his chest and in one ankle, and when he got to his feet he felt dizzy momentarily, but outside of that he seemed to be all right. He looked around, thinking like a civilian that there was never a cop in sight when you needed one.

Within seconds the traffic jam was horrendous. Cars, trucks and taxis were backed up in every direction, the drivers all blowing horns and cursing, while the wrecked Ford lay upside down in the middle of the intersection like a stricken turtle with its feet in the air. The siren was still wailing, and steam was coming out of the radiator. From all sides rubberneckers were gathering.

The wagon, Ben thought—where was the goddamn wagon? Where had Barrows been heading—and where was he taking Margot?

"You dumb son of a bitch!"

He turned to see a man advancing toward him with a wild expression on his face. There was blood streaming from the guy's nose, and he was wearing some kind of uniform. Ben realized he was the bus driver.

"Stupid shit!" the driver screamed. "You coulda killed us all!"

That was true enough.

Ben turned and ran to the sidewalk, the ankle a little sore but bearable as he made for a phone booth on the corner. When he reached it he hesitated. Maybe calling for police help at this point wasn't such a good idea. It was clear from what he'd seen of the butchered female in the Whitechapel building that Barrows had gone berserk. The last thing to do now would be to set him off again when he had Margot in his hands.

But where the hell was he?

Wait a minute, Ben thought. There was the envelope he'd taken from Barrows' desk. He pulled it out of his pocket and looked at the address. It was in Soho—not all that far from here.

Damn it, he couldn't afford *not* to get help. He dropped a quarter into the slot and called the Sixth. He got Petrusky on the line and told him to take a couple of patrol cars full of cops to the address, warning the detective not to sound sirens, and not to make a move on the place until Ben gave the word.

"You hear, Frank? I'll be there waiting for you. Whatever you do, use extreme caution."

"Yeah, Lou. Got it."

Ben hung up, and stuffing the envelope back into his pocket ran down Second Avenue until he spotted a cab parked at the curb.

The driver was drinking coffee from a cardboard cup. Ben waved his shield and yelled the address as he opened the rear door and jumped in.

"Hey, Officer," the cabby said. "I'm takin' a break."

Ben leaned forward. "A *break*? Drive, shitbrain—or I'll break your fucking head!"

The cab pulled away from the curb, the driver still holding his coffee in one hand.

60

MARGOT wasn't sure exactly where they lost Ben, but it was somewhere on Fourteenth Street, soon after they turned off the FDR Drive. The sound of his siren faded and then was gone, and she felt her hope go right along with it. Barrows slowed down after that, and she thought about jumping out of the wagon—even steeling herself for an attempt a couple of times—but she knew it would be foolish to try it. He was still pointing the pistol at her, its muzzle inches from her side.

It was dark now and they were driving through a part of the city she didn't know very well. She kept telling herself to pay attention, to try to keep track of where they were and where he was taking her, but the route was confusing and she had difficulty seeing street signs. She thought she saw one that said Delancey, but she wasn't sure.

Then they were on narrower streets in among huge old buildings that looked like warehouses, and she thought this was probably Soho. Barrows was silent the entire time, driving with a kind of cold determination that was almost as frightening as the pistol. He turned a corner and they went down a short, steep driveway, the headlights shining on a metal door in one of the buildings. The door rattled upward and he drove inside, the door closing behind them.

He got out of the wagon, dragging her with him, and forced her up a flight of stairs. At the top he opened another door, pushing her in ahead of him. She found herself in what appeared to be a large apartment. There were brick walls and a high, vaulted ceiling painted white. The apartment was handsomely decorated with modern furniture.

Barrows seemed to relax a little then. He opened a drawer in a table and put the pistol into it. He beckoned to her. "Come on, I want to show you something."

She followed him into a living room, not knowing what to expect but not trusting him for an instant, no matter how rational he might seem at the moment. He snapped on the lights, and she saw that the walls were covered almost entirely with huge, black and white photographs of a woman. There were dozens of poses, the kind you'd see in fashion magazines, some of them close-ups, some full figure. The woman was wearing a wide variety of outfits, ranging from formal to casual. All the clothes seemed to be very old-fashioned, from the forties or fifties maybe; it was hard to tell.

There was something familiar about the woman's face. Margot took a good look, and her jaw dropped.

The resemblance was uncanny.

It was like looking at herself across a great span of time. As if she'd lived a long time ago and had posed for all these pictures. The nose, the cheekbones, even the way the woman wore her hair, in a smooth sweep down off her forehead, made Margot feel as if she were seeing images of herself.

"Wonderful, aren't they?" His voice was soft and he was looking at the photographs reverentially, lovingly. He moved along the walls, studying the photos as if he had never seen them before.

She stood where she was, afraid to move, stunned by what she was seeing. Who was this woman, and where had the pictures come from? It was obvious there was a connection of some kind between the woman and Barrows, but what was it? The model was a professional—that was one thing she felt sure of.

But the most chilling thing was the way the woman looked so much like Margot herself. That had to be why

Barrows had abducted her, why he'd brought her here. She was in a madhouse, and instead of a keeper, an inmate was in charge. She looked around, trying desperately to come up with a plan for escape, an opportunity to run out of here, and seeing none. She told herself to be calm, to wait for a chance to present itself. And above all, to be careful. If she did anything now to anger him, there was no telling how he might react.

He turned to her. "As beautiful as they are, I don't think a single one of them does justice to you. They don't really capture you. They don't have your life, your spark. It's your *personality* that's lacking. Do you see what I'm saying?"

She nodded dumbly, wondering what the hell he was talking about. Did he really believe she was the model in these old pictures? Could that be?

He waved a hand at the collection on the walls. "It's the photographers, of course. None of the people who shot these were very good. Most of them were nothing but hacks. I don't believe any of them understood you, or realized what it would be possible to do with you. You deserved so much better."

He looked around the room again, and then back at her. "But I know what could be done. I know what's possible. And I know exactly how to do it. What I'm going to create will be marvelous. Do you hear? Marvelous."

She didn't dare answer. The look on his face was like that of a mystic, or one of those loonies who went around dressed in rags, convinced he was God's right-hand man.

Barrows took her arm. "Come on, we have work to do." He led her out of the living room and down a hallway to a door. He opened it and guided her inside, turning on the lights.

Again she was astonished. The room was a completely equipped photography studio. There were light tracks on the high ceiling, along with bright-colored rolls of no-seam, and cabinets along the walls. More lights were mounted on stands, and there were stanchions for rigging flats and props. At one end of the studio was a set featuring a huge white fan-backed wicker chair on a raised platform. There were also potted plants, their thick green leaves framing the chair. On the wall beyond was a photographic drop, showing gardens and lawns and trees. The scene was what you'd see from the terrace of a large country house. A tripod-mounted Hasselblad stood nearby.

Margot gaped at the set, unable to accept what her eyes were showing her, what her mind was shrieking.

He's a photographer? With a studio hidden away in this strange house? And a photographer who's obviously crazy, obsessed with taking pictures of women? Oh, my God. Now I know who he is. I know exactly who he is. Oh, my God.

He reached over to a counter and hit the switch on a stereo tape deck. Heavy rock rhythms boomed from floor speakers. When he turned back to her he said, "Take off your dress."

"What?"

"Go on—take it off."

She opened her mouth to protest, and then she looked at his face. The expression in his eyes had intensified, so that his gaze seemed to burn into her. She pulled the cotton dress up over her head, and as soon as it came free he took it from her and tossed it aside.

Now she was wearing only a pair of bikini pants and her shoes. She was conscious of his eyes again, as the intense stare moved slowly down her body. His mouth was partly open, and his lips were wet. He looked like an animal in heat.

"Sit in the chair."

She did as directed, stepping up onto the platform and lowering herself onto the chair, facing him.

He stood looking at her face for a full minute, his head

cocked to one side. Then he followed her onto the platform. He put one hand on the small of her back, exerting just enough pressure to coax her into sitting as straight as possible. The other had drifted slowly over her breasts.

His touch was as light as warm air, and in spite of herself Margot felt her nipples become erect. She could hear him breathing over the pulsing beat of the music, the sound coarse and rasping. He was looking into her eyes, and it seemed to her the strange light was burning even brighter.

He stared at her for a moment longer, and then he stepped back to where he had positioned the Hasselblad. He bent over the viewfinder, and she was aware of the tension in his voice. "Hold that," he commanded.

The strobes flashed, and flashed again.

The sensation was bizarre. It was as if the camera was a sexual instrument, and he was raping her with it. He crouched there, firing it, looking up at her from time to time, his features contorted with lust and excitement. She had no idea how long the shooting went on; the effect was draining her, exhausting her physically and emotionally.

He stopped. And then slowly approached her once more. But the look on his face was suddenly different. The sexual hunger was still there, but now there was anger, as well.

As she watched, fear gripped her and froze her in position in the chair. The muscles of his face twitched, and she was aware that his emotions were rising to a boil, that anger was rapidly becoming rage. His eyes were bulging, the whites showing all the way around the pupils. He opened his mouth and his lips drew back, revealing the teeth in his upper and lower jaws. Again she thought of an animal, but this time she saw a wild beast about to attack, its fangs ready to rip and tear its victim. His breath was coming in short gasps as he moved closer, and he was pulling at his belt buckle.

She knew what that meant. She'd heard enough about

this murderous bastard to know what he intended to do to her; she'd heard it from Ben and seen it on TV and read it in the newspapers until it had been like a recurrent nightmare, the same hideous dream that had terrified women throughout the city.

But this was not a dream. She was alone and defenseless and facing a psychotic killer and he was coming for her. One of his hands was fumbling to open his pants and the other was reaching for her head. She felt a wave of terror wash over her.

Suddenly his eyes snapped up, his gaze fixing on something above and behind her. His voice was a snarl. *"Goddamn it."*

He jumped down from the platform, his chest heaving. "Stay quiet. I'll be right back." He stepped quickly to the door, and left the studio. She heard a key turn in the lock.

Margot stood up, her legs trembling. Swinging her head around, she saw what had startled him. Mounted high on the wall was a silent alarm box. A red light in the device was blinking.

61

THE building was like a fortress. Ben made a quick tour, and then stood in the shadows across the way, studying it. There was a glimmer of light showing at the edges of several of the windows in one end, on a floor above street level. The rest of the structure was dark, a gloomy, foreboding shape that extended some distance down the narrow street. The only entrances he'd been able to locate were one at the front, and a garage door down a steeply inclined driveway. Both doors were metal, and both were locked. There were heavy bars over all the windows.

How in Christ's name was he going to get into this thing without blowing off one of the doors? He'd seen banks that weren't as sturdy. The trouble was, any noise could tip off Barrows. If this was in fact where he'd taken Margot. But it had to be. The station wagon had been streaking toward this building from the time Ben had begun chasing it.

And where the hell was Petrusky? He should have been here by now. But standing around waiting for him was out of the question.

So now what? Ben moved slowly down the street, thinking hard. If there were no other doors except the two he'd spotted, and all the windows were barred, the only other possibility might be the roof. But getting up there would be some trick. That human-fly shit looked great in the movies, but crawling up the side of a brick building in the dark was nothing he was about to try.

There was a neighboring building at the far end. Ben stepped down to it, looking it over. This one was completely dark. It appeared to be another old factory or loft building, at first glance as impregnable as Barrows'. But then he saw it had one feature the other didn't: a fire escape. If he could get up that to the roof, maybe he could cross from one building to the other. The problem was that the swing-down stairs on the fire escape were maybe ten feet above the sidewalk.

Several garbage pails stood against the wall. He moved one of them into place under the stairs and then climbed onto it. His footing was shaky, and the ankle he'd banged up when the Ford was wrecked was aching again. Nevertheless he'd have to take his chances.

He crouched, and then he sprang upward with everything he could put into it. His hands caught the bottom step, and the stairs slowly creaked downward. When they came down far enough for him to crawl onto them he scrambled up to the landing. From there he made his way to the top of the fire escape, and then he climbed up the framework to the roof, hauling himself over the parapet. He walked to the end closest to Barrows' building and looked across.

Goddamn. The space between the two buildings might have been six feet, might have been eight. Barrows' roof was also flat, and a little lower. He'd have to make the jump from the parapet on this one, which was about three feet high. There was no parapet on Barrows' roof. So he'd have a slight advantage in taking off from a point higher than where he hoped to end up, but he'd be unable to get a running start. What a trade. If he missed they'd be scraping his ass off the cement in the alley.

For an instant he thought screw it. And then Margot's face came into his mind and he knew he'd have to try. He set himself, realizing the idea was crazy as hell, and then he jumped.

And missed.

His feet scraped the edge of Barrows' roof and slid down

the wall and he made a desperate grab for anything to hang on to. One hand caught a piece of the tile coaming on the edge of the roof and he clung to it. He kicked and scrambled, clawing for a grip with the other hand, and when he got one he pulled himself up onto the surface and lay there gasping for air. He got to his feet unsteadily, amazed that he'd made it. He waited until his breathing slowed down before he moved again.

There was a wooden enclosure in the center of the roof with a door in it. He made his way over to it, doing his best to step softly. When he got there he found what he'd expected—the door was locked. He tugged at it but it was metal, like all the other doors in this goddamn place, and there was no way he was going to budge it.

He looked around and saw a duct of some kind with an aluminum cover over it. He went to it and hauled on the cover until he got it off. In the opening was a narrow chute leading down from it, probably an intake for a ventilating system.

This might be a way in, but he hesitated. Crawling into that hole would be taking a hell of a chance. The shaft appeared barely wide enough to fit his body into, and if he got stuck he could rot there.

He again looked around the roof, and saw no other possibility. It was the duct or nothing. He slipped his legs into the narrow opening and wriggled his way downward, his arms extended over his head.

It didn't work. A few feet below the surface he found himself wedged tight, barely able to breathe, let alone move. You dumb shit, he thought. You really blew it. He squirmed and twisted, but the effort produced no progress. He was unable to get himself any lower, and moving upward was out of the question.

Now what? *Think, damn it. Think.* The only way he might be able to get some purchase would be with his hands. He

324

pressed his palms flat against the smooth metal walls of the chute and pushed.

Nothing.

He waited a few seconds, gathering himself. Then he pushed again, this time straining, straining, refusing to quit until he effected some movement. He got himself perhaps an inch further down. And was aware that what he actually could be doing was wedging himself in tighter. But what choice did he have? He waited, struggling for breath, and then tried again.

It was torture, but he managed to worm his way lower by a few more inches. And then a few more. It was pitch black in the shaft, and the muscles in his arms and shoulders and chest burned like fire. He forced himself to keep going, refusing to acknowledge the pain.

And got a break. His feet touched a surface below him, and he realized he had come to a bend in the shaft, where it turned from vertical to horizontal. It was logical that there would be a joint in this angle piece. He kicked at it and found he was right; the piece came loose. Cautioning himself to be as quiet as possible, he shoved the piece away from the upright part of the chute with his feet and continued to push and squirm, until most of his body was dangling out of the open end.

His position was plenty shaky, and whatever this space was he was hanging in, it also was black as hell. As he hung there, trying to think of something sensible to do, he heard the rustle of tiny feet below him. This end of the building had to be unused, except by the rats he'd apparently disturbed. He could smell the dust and the stale air and the ratshit. He pushed free, praying the floor wouldn't be too far below.

It wasn't; he landed in a crouch and rolled, the only problem the thump he made when he hit the floor. That and the stab of pain in his ankle. He got to his feet and groped his way until he reached a wall. He followed it, touching the surface and taking one tentative step at a time, unable to see a damn thing. Then he found a flight of steps and went down them, all the while moving slowly and carefully. At the bottom he found another wall. This one had a door in it, and the door was unlocked. He opened it and slipped through.

There was a glimmer of light in here, but it was so dim Ben was unable to make out his surroundings. He extended a hand, which didn't help; his groping fingers found nothing ahead of him or to either side. He might be in a storage area of some kind, but that was only a guess. And yet this space was obviously different, somehow, from the one he'd just come from. He blinked, hoping his eyes would adjust to these light conditions, that he'd get his bearings, figure out where he was.

But he couldn't. No matter how hard he tried, he still couldn't see worth a damn. He stood there for a moment, and remembered a trick he'd once heard of from another cop. He closed his eyes, and shifted the burden to other senses.

The first thing he became aware of was a faint sound. He tilted his head, his ears straining to catch it. To his surprise, he realized that what he was hearing was music. Its volume was so low he was barely able to recognize what it was, except that it had a rhythm he could feel rather than hear.

The second message his synapses delivered was that the smell wasn't the same. His nose was no longer picking up the faintly acrid odors of ancient dirt and rodent turds; wherever he was, the air in here was actually clean. Or cleaner, anyway.

He realized then that he'd stumbled into the occupied part of the building—the part Barrows used. What he used it for, Ben didn't want to think about. But Margot was in here somewhere, he was sure of it. She was here, and so was Barrows. Reacting instinctively, he crouched down and opened his eyes, slipping the Smith out of its holster. He couldn't see enough to hit anything, even if he had a target. But the feel of the snub-nosed revolver was reassuring, nevertheless.

He crept toward the sound he thought was music, holding the Smith out front, moving crab-like in the gloom, taking one careful step at a time. After he'd covered what he estimated to be ten feet or so, he found another wall dead ahead. He touched it with his fingers, and followed it until he reached a break in its surface.

This was a passageway. He stopped to listen, thinking that the sound was a little louder now. He thumbed back the hammer of the pistol, the click startlingly loud to his ears, and stepped into the opening, hugging the wall as much as possible. He was aware that his heart was pounding and that it was hard to breathe.

You silly shit, he admonished himself. Why not wait for the backup? You're stumbling around in the dark in this old barn, just begging for that crazy fucker to blow you away without you even knowing what happened. So why not use what little brains you've got and wait for help?

Because he's a madman, that's why. And what he wants is Margot. Just the way he wanted all the others. Why not wait? Because there is one thing I'm running out of, and that's time. By now the son of a bitch could be doing anything to her. Keep moving.

When he got to the end, the passageway jogged at an angle. The music was a little more discernible; it sounded like a Stones recording, but he wasn't sure. His nerves were taut wires, and he was careful not to put too much pressure on the trigger of the pistol. An accidental shot here could blow the whole fucking ballgame. But he felt in his gut that something was waiting for him around this corner. He took a deep breath, steeled himself, and made the turn.

The hallway he was in now had just a bit more light. He looked down it and was startled to see a man at the far end, facing him.

Ben dropped into a combat stance, spraddle-legged with the .38 out front in a two-handed grip. The man was motionless, standing as still as a statue, staring at him.

Jesus Christ. It was Joe Kurwitz.

What the hell was going on? What was Kurwitz doing here? Ben instinctively opened his mouth to call out to him, and then he shut it. There was something odd about the way Kurwitz's eyes were fixed on Ben with that steady gaze. As if he were strung out on drugs. In the dim light Ben could make out that he was dressed strangely, too. He had on what looked like a long cloak.

Ben moved closer, extending one hand toward him. He whispered hoarsely, "Joe—it's me, Tolliver. You all right?"

Kurwitz did not answer. Nor did he move. His eyes continued to hold Ben in that same unblinking stare. Maybe he was out of it, Ben thought. Dead drunk, or in a trance. Hypnotized? What was it? He took another step closer and then his fingers touched the other man's cheek. It was hard and cold and clammy, like a piece of frozen meat.

Ben jabbed with his forefinger and Joe Kurwitz's head rolled off his shoulders, falling to the floor with a sickening thud. It bounced once and turned over, face upright, the eyes still wide open.

Ben jumped, letting out an involuntary gasp. At the same instant he heard an unholy shriek to one side of him, the piercing sound startling him as much as the fall of Kurwitz's head. He turned toward it, and out of the shadows stepped a man with an ax raised high, his eyes wild and his gaping mouth emitting a scream.

In the fraction of a second Ben had to take in what was happening, he saw that the man was big, and he was moving fast. The sound boiling from his mouth was more animal than human, accompanied by a spray of spittle. He swung the ax in an overhead arc, its steel blade glinting in the dim light.

Ben twisted sideways and fired two shots, the pistol reports as loud as cannon fire in the confined space. As he turned his body the ax head glanced off his left shoulder, the force of the blow stunning him. In the muzzle flash he saw one of his shots go wide and the other slam into the man's chest, knocking him back against the wall. The ax fell from his hands and he slowly slid down the wall, blood staining his shirtfront.

Ben staggered and went to his knees. The shoulder was numb, and excruciating pain lanced his neck and his arm. The pain nauseated him, leeching his strength. He had to fight to keep from vomiting. He stayed there, unable to move, lights flashing in front of his eyes, his head reeling.

Barrows was only a couple of feet away. Ben could see him struggling to get up, and losing the battle. His mouth was working, but no sound came out of it. A crimson bubble appeared at one corner. It burst, and blood trickled down his chin. As Ben watched, the man's efforts grew feebler, and then they stopped. His eyes took on the terrible fixed dullness Ben had seen too often, the pupils dilating and then clouding over.

As soon as he could manage it, Ben pulled himself upright. When he did he felt faint, and for a moment he thought he would pass out. But then he got himself under control, a prickly sensation going through his head as blood returned to it, and looked at his attacker.

Peter Barrows was dead. The .38 slug had done its work, and he lay slumped against the wall, his eyes as sightless now as Kurwitz's.

Ben studied Barrows' face. Instead of triumph or elation,

he felt only the same cold rage he'd felt all along. Only this time he was at last seeing the man who had never been out of his mind, awake or asleep, for all these months.

The features were not what he had envisioned, somehow. They were even and regular, not at all threatening, or even much out of the ordinary. Except that they were what women would probably find attractive. Barrows looked quite peaceful in death, and it was hard to imagine him committing the string of murders that had terrorized the city.

His mouth had sagged open, revealing his teeth. They were large and white, and the sight of them reminded Ben he had promised himself to smash those teeth out of the guy's head when he got the chance.

But now he felt his anger drain away, leaving behind it only emptiness and disgust.

You rotten bastard. I wish you'd had more time to suffer.

62

Ben turned his attention to Joe Kurwitz's head. The glassy stare was still fixed on him, like one of those trick pictures where the subject's eyes follow you around a room. He looked up, and saw that what he had thought was Joe's body was a stepladder with a blanket wrapped around it. Ben wondered where the rest of him was. But the hell with it—right now he had to find Margot. He stepped past the ladder and made his way down the hallway toward the source of the music, his left side throbbing with pain.

There was another jog in the passage, and then he came out of it and into an open area in what appeared to be a large, well-furnished apartment. He kept going until he reached another door. Whatever this room was, the music was coming from inside it. There was a key in the lock. Ben turned the key and opened the door, calling Margot's name. She threw her arms around him, sobbing.

He held her close, still feeling light-headed, but now as much from relief as from pain. He pushed her back a little, looking anxiously into her face and at her near-naked body. "You all right? Did he hurt you?"

She shook her head, terror still showing in her eyes. "Where is he? I heard shots."

"Dead," Ben said. "I killed him."

Again she clung to him, tears running down her cheeks. Her fingers touched his left arm and she stared at the blood on them. "Ben—your shoulder. Oh, my God."

"Hey, it's okay. Not as bad as it looks." He didn't really know how bad it was; the shoulder was still numb. And the pain in his left arm was getting worse. He was aware of a sensation like having his fingers jabbed with needles, although he couldn't move them. And on top of that the pounding music was threatening to cave his head in.

Margot found her dress and put it on, and as she did Ben shoved his pistol back into its holster and looked around the room. Christ—it was a photography studio. And from what he'd learned from having visited a bunch of them over the past few weeks, this one was very well equipped. Seeing it answered a lot of questions. He reached over to the stereo and turned it off.

Margot again touched his shoulder lightly. "Ben, you've got to get help. That looks awful."

"Yeah, I will." He continued to take in his surroundings. At one end of the studio was a set. The scene appeared to be an outdoor terrace. As he looked at it, he realized it reminded him of his visit to Ethel Wharton's house in Greenwich earlier in the day. With the view of the lawns and the gardens and the trees in the background, it was eerily similar. Not the same, exactly, and yet—

There were two other doors in the studio. He went to one and opened it, seeing that it led into a darkroom. He glanced inside briefly, and then went to the other door and opened that one. The room appeared to be some sort of gallery. He stepped inside and snapped on the light switch, and what he saw both stunned and amazed him.

Tiny spotlights in the ceiling sent beams down onto framed photographs that lined the walls. There was the shot of the blonde, Ellen Danvers. And beside it was one he had never seen before, but with whose subject he was very familiar. It was a nude shot of Helen Malik, the first of the girls whose bodies had been found in this series of murders. And alongside that was one of Donna Cunningham, who had been number two.

He stared at the photographs, open-mouthed. He recognized one of Pamela Benoit, whose frozen body had been found in the woods at Colgate. And over there was the shot of Sue Connery. There were others in here, too, of girls he couldn't identify. Each of the faces wore the same empty expression he'd come to know well. It was the one that had often appeared in his dreams—the sightless eyes staring, the tongue protruding lewdly between half-parted lips. All of the girls were nude. And all of them were dead.

There were other photographs also, in a grouping on the far wall. Ben moved down to them, curious. He knew at a glance they were all many years old. And it was obvious none of them had been posed—they had the unmistakable look of candid shots, taken when their subjects hadn't suspected someone had been pointing a camera.

In each picture a woman appeared—a woman who looked so much like Margot it was startling. Ben gaped at the images. In one she was sitting in a lawn chair, wearing a summer dress and drinking from a champagne glass. In another her head was thrown back and she was laughing. There were several other people in the photograph; apparently they were sharing a joke. She had a glass in her hand in this one, too. In still another she'd been caught sunbathing, lying naked on a chaise longue, her eyes closed. He glanced over the photos, noting that she was in every one of them. It wasn't hard to figure out who she was, or who had taken the photographs. He was about to turn away when a man in one of the pictures caught his eye.

The guy was good-looking, in a rugged, athletic way. He had his arm around the woman and he was nuzzling her. Ben wondered what there was about him that seemed familiar. Alongside this shot was another one with the guy in it that must have been taken on the same occasion. In this one he was kissing her passionately, and she seemed to be giving it right back to him. Her arms were around his neck, and his hands were cupping her buttocks. His face was in profile, and Ben could see it clearly.

The man in the picture was Brian Holt.

The lawyer had been years younger, of course. His face was leaner and his hair was dark, with only a touch of gray at the temples. But there was no mistaking his identity.

Ben went back into the studio and again held Margot. He'd just as soon she didn't see the collection of photographs in the gallery. She was still trembling; he had to get her out of this madhouse. And she was right about his shoulder needing medical attention, although he wasn't about to admit it to her. The pain had grown steadily worse. But at least his head was clearer than it had been. After a moment she quieted down.

And then a muffled noise reached Ben's ears. It came from the far end of the house, and it was unmistakable. It was the sound of a door closing.

63

MARGOT heard the sound as well. She looked up. "What was that?"

"I'm not sure. Sounded like a door, but—"

Her eyes widened.

He patted her shoulder with his good hand. "Hey, take it easy. I told you, he's dead. Could have been the wind or something. I'll check it out. You stay here."

He wanted to seem as if he wasn't worried, and he deliberately moved almost casually as he left the studio. He closed the door behind him and again bent down and pulled the Smith from its holster. He'd nailed Barrows, he was sure of it. Hit him square in the chest with a soft-nosed .38. Shit, that would stop a bear. Holding the pistol ahead of him, he walked through the hallway he'd come down earlier.

The door to the hallway was closed. Had he shut it himself? He couldn't remember. Or was it what he'd heard close from inside the studio? Using the same hand that was holding the Smith, he cautiously opened the door.

The hallway was empty. He moved down it, his ears tuned to pick up the slightest sound. But there was nothing. The old building was as silent as a tomb. He had nearly reached the bend in the passage. As he approached it he moved more slowly. When he got there he stood stock-still for a moment, then made the turn.

There was the ladder with the blanket draped over it. And there was Joe Kurwitz's head, the eyes staring at Ben as if accusing him. It lay on the floor, just as it had after he'd knocked it off its perch.

But there was no Barrows.

Ben cursed under his breath. How the fuck had the guy taken that slug and got up again? Was Ben kidding himself? Had he missed after all? No, that was impossible. He'd looked into Barrows' face and seen death. And now blood was visible on the wall, and a splintered hole. The shot had gone clear through him. So how was it possible he could still be moving?

Ben turned and ran back down the hallway. When he got to the studio he pulled open the door and called Margot's name.

And was relieved to hear her answer. "Yes—I'm here."

He stepped inside.

She was there, all right. But so was Peter Barrows. His eyes were wild, and there were streaks of blood on his face. His shirt was stained dark red. He held her in a tight grip, his left arm locked around her neck. In his right hand was a Colt Detective Special, its muzzle pressed against her temple.

Barrows bared his teeth as he stared at Ben. "Give it up, asshole. Throw your gun over here, or I'll blow her brains out. *Now.*"

Ben looked at him. The range was maybe ten feet, and about two-thirds of Barrows' head was in the clear. The Smith was no great shakes for accuracy, but maybe a snap shot, placed just right—

Barrows' voice grated. "I said give it up, Goddamn you."

Ben saw the finger tighten on the Colt's trigger, saw the terror in Margot's eyes. He tossed his pistol toward Barrows, and it bounced and clattered on the floor.

Barrows' face twisted into a grin. "So, stupid. You lose."

"So do you," Ben said. "You're not going anywhere."

Barrows laughed, the sound tailing off into a bubbling wheeze. Ben knew what that meant; his lungs were filling with blood. But somehow he was still in control of himself.

"You're wrong again," Barrows said. "I *am* going somewhere. And so are you." He grinned once more, a terrible grimace that made Ben think of a death's-head. Continuing to hold the Colt against Margot's temple, Barrows took his left arm away from her neck and groped at the cabinet behind him. He opened it and reached inside, never taking his eyes off Ben. When he straightened up he lifted a gallon jug of clear liquid and set it on the counter. Ben could read the label: XYLENE. CAUTION—FLAMMABLE!

Barrows twisted the cap off the neck of the jug and tossed it aside. Then he reached over to a tray of junk on the countertop and picked up a pack of matches.

Ben's mouth went dry. "Wait. You've still got a chance, if you want it."

Barrows looked at him as he would at a cockroach. "A chance? What kind of a chance?"

"Lock us up in here and then take off."

This time Barrows didn't get past a smile before the wheezing started. He bent over, his bloody chest racked by a fit of coughing. But his gaze stayed fixed on Ben, and the pistol never wavered. When he could speak again he said, "Who are you kidding, asshole? I've got a plan of my own. You want to know what it is?"

Ben knew from experience the only way to deal with a maniac was to try to keep him talking. "Sure, tell me."

Barrows once again put his arm around Margot's neck, keeping the Colt trained on Ben. "The plan is that we're taking off, while *you* stay here." He gestured with the pistol. "Now get over there to the darkroom and go inside."

Ben got it then. What Barrows meant to do was to leave him locked in here while the place burned. Jesus. If Ben tried to jump him he'd catch a bullet in the head. If he did what Barrows was ordering him to do, he'd fry.

His only hope was Margot. His gaze flicked to hers for a fraction of a second and then it went back to Barrows.

"Move," Barrows grated.

Ben took a step toward the darkroom, and as he did he again shot a glance at Margot.

She understood. With one hand she hit Barrows' wrist, sending the Colt flying. It landed on the countertop and skittered along the surface. With the other hand she punched him in the face with all her strength. He staggered against the cabinet and the jug of xylene went over. It fell to the floor and shattered, filling the room with a biting chemical stench. Then she ran to Ben.

Peter Barrows howled in rage. "You bastards!" He was still clutching the pack of matches in his left hand. He tore a match out, and as he did Ben darted to the countertop and grabbed the Colt. He raised it just as Barrows struck the match.

There was a mighty *whump* as the place where Barrows stood erupted in flame. His clothing had been drenched when the jug broke, and now his entire body was afire. He writhed and twisted, covered in brilliant, leaping flames.

Ben held the pistol in both hands and fired again and again, the Colt bucking in his fists. He was sure the heavy slugs were going home; at this range he couldn't miss.

But the thing in front of him would not die. Ben could see Barrows' body recoiling from the shock of the bullets, as the skin on his face bubbled and cracked and his hands turned to blackened claws. Yet somehow he remained upright, a blazing torch. A scream issued from his mouth and he stumbled away, wreathed in flames and black smoke.

The fire was spreading rapidly, catching on the cabinets and the walls and the rolls of no-seam overhead. In seconds the place had become an inferno. Ben threw the empty pistol down, and grabbing Margot's arm ran out the door of the studio.

From somewhere he could hear the sound of battering. That would be the cops, breaking in. He bent over, half-dragging her along, both of them choking and coughing, their eyes streaming from the smoke. As they moved toward the pounding he realized they had to be going in the direction of the front entrance of the building.

A few more steps, and they came to a stairway. They stumbled down it, and when they reached the foot of the stairs a door burst open, and men in blue pulled them out into the street.

The fresh air was the sweetest thing Ben had ever smelled. He held Margot close to him, telling himself he'd never let go. They were surrounded by cops, and as he rubbed his eyes he saw Petrusky and Carlos and O'Brien among them.

Then they were being hurried toward a police emergency truck and Frank was saying something to him about his shoulder. There was a lot of shouting, and Ben saw that the cops were struggling to hold back the gathering crowd of rubberneckers. He could hear sirens in the distance, which meant more cops or fire engines or both.

He looked back at the building and saw orange tongues flickering in the windows. As he watched, the glass in one of the windows burst, and a column of smoke and flame billowed into the night sky.

Inside Peter Barrows' apartment, fire leaped through the rooms. It roared and crackled as it danced on the furniture and charred the huge photographs that lined the living room walls.

The face of the woman in the pictures became gnarled and misshapen. Her mouth and her eyes twisted into a grotesque leer.

And then she was gone.